D1239160

Divine Punishment

Also by Sergio Ramírez in English

FICTION

A Thousand Deaths Plus One
Margarita, How Beautiful the Sea
To Bury Our Fathers
Stories

NON-FICTION

Hatful of Tigers: Reflections on Art, Culture and Politics

Adiós, Muchachos: A Memoir of the Sandinista Revolution

Divine Punishment

a novel by

Sergio Ramírez

Translated from the Spanish
by Nick Caistor, with Hebe Powell

With an afterword by the author
and a note by the translator

McPherson & Company
Kingston, New York
2015

DIVINE PUNISHMENT

Published by McPherson & Company
Box 1126, Kingston, NY 12402.
Book and jacket design by Bruce R. McPherson.
Typeset in Monotype Fournier.
Printed on pH neutral paper.
Manufactured in the United States of America.
First edition.
1 3 5 7 9 10 8 6 4 2 2015 2016 2017

LIBRARY OF CONGRESS CATALOGING-IN-PUBLICATION DATA

Ramírez, Sergio, 1942-
[Castigo divino. English]
Divine punishment : a novel / by Sergio Ramírez ; translated from the Spanish by Nick Caistor, with Hebe Powell ; with an afterword by the author and a note by the translator.
pages cm
ISBN 978-1-62054-014-5 (alk. paper)
1. León (Nicaragua)--History--Fiction. 2. Trials (Murder)--Nicaragua--Fiction. I. Caistor, Nick, translator. II. Title.
PQ7519.2.R25C3713 2015
863'.64--dc23
2015005034

To the combatants,
On all the war fronts,
Who have made this book possible.

To Gertrudis, who invented
the hours to write it.

Divine Punishment

Of human flesh
This smells to me,
You give me none,
So I'll eat thee.

Federico Garcia Lorca
(*The Billyclub Puppets*)

A printing error caused the following credit to
from the jacket of the first printing of *Divine Pu*
Cover: René Magritte, "The Menaced Assassin," 1927. ©
vici / Artists Rights Society (ARS), New York.
Digital image © The Museum of Modern Art/Licensed b
Resource, NY.

Dramatis Personae

Oliverio Castañeda: *Guatemalan expatriate, murder suspect*
Marta Jerez: *wife of Oliverio Castañeda*
Octavio Oviedo y Reyes: *friend and colleague of Castañeda*
Doctor Juan de Dios Darbishire: *prominent physician*
Doctor Atanasio Salmerón: *physician, protegé of Darbishire*
Don Carmen Contreras: *businessman*
Dona Flora de Contreras: *wife of Don Carmen Contreras*
Maria del Pilar Contreras: *daughter*
Matilde Contreras: *daughter*
Rosalío Usulutlán: *journalist*
Cosimo Manzo: *merchant*
Augustín Prío: *proprietor of Casa Prío bar*
Mariano Fiallos Gil: *presiding judge*
Captain Anastasio Ortiz: *police chief of León, commander of National Guard garrison*

PART ONE

Presenting the Evidence

Forget the one who forgets you,
Love not the one who loves you not;
Whoever fails to remember this
Places his life in danger.
From this mortal peril
Heart, you cannot be cured,
And are sure to die.

Song
Juan de Tapia
(*Stúñiga Songbook*)

CHAPTER ONE

A Howling of Dogs in the Night

AT APPROXIMATELY nine o'clock on the evening of 18 July 1932, Rosalío Usulutlán, aged forty-two, divorced, journalist by profession and employed in said capacity as editor-in-chief of the *El Cronista* newspaper, quit his seat at the end of the first screening of the MGM film *Payment Deferred*, starring Charles Laughton and Maureen O'Sullivan.

He made his way through the audience to the foyer. As he pushed through the red plush curtain weighed down by the accumulation of years of dust, he felt a playful tap on the shoulder. Turning round, he discovered it was his friend Cosme Manzo, aged fifty, bachelor, owner of a hardware store, whose broad grin revealed a glint of gold beneath his handlebar moustache.

Putting his arm around him, Manzo used his hat with its broad red band to steer a path through the crowd, and invited the journalist to the Casa Prío, which faced onto the Plaza Jerez only a block away from the Teatro González, to share a Xolotlán beer (the first beer brewed in Nicaragua, only recently put on sale and distributed in the city of León by the aforementioned Manzo, also the sole distributor of Scott Emulsion cod-liver oil). Replacing his own hat, Rosalío Usulutlán willingly accepted the invitation.

Once inside this establishment, which at that time of night was busy with its usual post-movie customers, the two men walked over to a corner table near the bar, where they were personally served by the owner, Agustín Prío, twenty-nine years of age, affectionately known to his regulars as 'The Captain'. Most of the city's gossip originated here, making it feared and earning it the nickname of 'the accursed table'. It was at this table that the circle of friends to which the two newcomers belonged held its sessions, presided over by Doctor Anastasio Salmerón, surgeon and general medical practitioner. Although the doctor was absent on this occasion, we shall in due course become well acquainted with him.

All kinds of scurrilous stories were raised and assessed at this 'accursed table': tales of adultery, broken marriage promises, forced abortions, pregnancies resolved at gunpoint, clandestine cohabiting. A close scrutiny was kept on children born in dubious circumstances; widows who opened their doors on the stroke of midnight; acts performed in the vestry by lustful priests. A strict record was kept of other scandals involving the city's leading families: the fleecing of heirs, swindles, unpaid debts, forgeries, real estate fraud, fake bankruptcies.

Captain Prío took the Xolotlán beers from his Kelvinator refrigerator (which ran on kerosene burners) and, screwing up his eyes at the smoke from the cigarette dangling from his lips, snapped them open with the bottle-opener he always carried on his key ring. Then, as if to compensate for his small stature, he walked on tiptoe to take the beers to their table.

He sat down, hooking his feet comfortably round the chair strut, and congratulated Rosalío Usulutlán on the articles he had written in that evening's edition of *El Cronista*, all of them dealing with matters of great urgency.

The first of these was the main story on the front page of the four that made up the newspaper. It dealt with the city council's debate on the signing of a new contract with the Metropolitan Water Company, the suppliers of drinking water to the city of León. The company owners were pressing for a renewal of the contract solely in order to raise their rates, which would make them prohibitively expensive for many families, and so deprive the poorest households of this precious liquid. Rosalío had been fervent in his support for the group of councillors headed by the mayor, Doctor Onesifero Rizo, who condemned the increase as not only arbitrary and inappropriate, but grossly unjust, and had castigated the other members of the council, whose inexplicable lack of firmness in this matter he had condemned as incompatible with the interests of the community.

His two other articles also appeared on the front page. One referred to the proliferation of malaria-bearing mosquitoes following an exceptionally wet winter, and went on to denounce the negligence of the public health authorities, who were surely to blame for the massive increase in the number of these noxious insects. They multiplied, he argued, in the fetid puddles and streams of filthy water that poured out of kitchens and laundries into even the busiest streets, in such numbers that if the insects had been hens, there would be a glut of eggs, and if they had been cows, the city would be overflowing with milk. Such an anomaly constituted a grave danger for the citizens of León, since mosquito bites had caused an outbreak of blackwater fever, an acute strain of malaria that had already claimed the lives of several people, especially children and adolescents.

The last of the three articles focused on the alarming number of stray dogs roaming freely on public highways and in other busy sites such as the city's markets, arcades, and squares. They pestered customers in the doorways to pharmacies and drapers' stores, wandered onto the platforms and disturbed passengers at the Pacific Railway station, and were a particular nuisance for both horse-carriage drivers and motorists. The yellow Bayer powders imported by the Argüello drugstore had proved ineffectual, in spite of which local residents persisted in sprinkling them round their front doors and on the sidewalks in the vain hope of scaring away the troublesome creatures, but succeeding only in making the city streets seem even more untidy.

As though this were not enough, the aforementioned canines had already caused several cases of rabies. In his article, Rosalío Usulután therefore called on the police chief, Captain Edward Wayne of the United States Marine Corps, to authorize (as his superiors had so commendably done in the past) the purchase of poison by citizens of good character to rid the city of this threat. In his view, strychnine was the most effective of the lethal alkaloids employed for this purpose.

By the time the two friends said good night, the Sagrario church clock was showing ten. Rosalío Usulután walked along the Calle Real on his way home to Calle la Españolita in the Laborio neighbourhood. In shirtsleeves because he considered a jacket was more trouble than it was worth, his collar done up with a copper stud, he whistled to himself as he strolled along the deserted sidewalk, thinking about *Payment Deferred*. He definitely preferred the Spanish title: *Castigo Divino*, or *Divine Punishment*.

'Clearly Unsuitable Film Ought To Be Banned' was the title of the article he was planning to write the next morning. He intended to warn his readers of the dangers inherent in the film's plot: merely by attending the cinema, unscrupulous persons would be able to learn how to prepare lethal poisons. In the film, the young aristocrat so memorably portrayed by Charles Laughton employed cunning and deceit to poison the most beautiful young women among Boston's high society one after the other, all the while keeping a list of his innocent victims in a pocketbook that later fell into the hands of the police. Too late, for the cyanide had already done its deadly work, and the method was clearly shown on the screen. Rosalío further planned to express his strong distaste for the final scene: the murderer, before meeting his death in the electric chair, refused the prison chaplain's offer of the comfort of religion, laughing a sinister laugh in his face.

Distant flashes of lightning lit up a sky heavy with dark clouds. The streetlights strung the length of the Calle Real were burning beneath their tin hoods, but their wan glow failed to penetrate the deep shadows engulfing the doorways, porches and closed-in balconies of the houses stretching from the Casa Prío to the San Francisco church: 'inadequate public lighting, incapable of protecting honest citizens from assailants even on the city's main thoroughfares. Tell me, councillors, precisely what use is made of the taxpayers' money?'

His thoughts were interrupted by the howling of dogs. The loudest noise came from out in the street, but there was also loud barking from behind doors and walls, as if all the dogs in the darkened houses had been roused simultaneously in a sudden panic. A few steps further on, Rosalío came across a dog writhing on the pavement, retching. Further down the street he saw another one dragging itself into a doorway, its hind legs stiff and useless.

As he reached the corner by the San Francisco church, he spotted two shadowy figures struggling outside Doctor Juan de Dios Darbishire's surgery. He flattened himself against the wall. He recognized one of the men as none other than Doctor Darbishire, whom he had seen leaving the cinema an hour earlier. His crimson-lined cape whirled as he lambasted a portly individual with his cane, heaping breathless curses on the unfortunate man. Rosalío Usulutlán was astounded to hear the elderly man of science, always so affable and courteous, cursing in this manner.

The fat man playfully tried to snatch the cane from the doctor, but slipped and fell to the ground. As he struggled to his knees, Doctor Darbishire seized the opportunity to rain blows on his back, which brought cries of real pain from his victim. At this point, as the journalist was later to testify, he heard a mocking laugh from the shadows, and on turning round caught a glimpse of a figure, dressed in strict mourning, beside one of the tall cypresses in front of the church. Both hands resting on the top of his own cane, the stranger was observing the beating with obvious pleasure.

Doctor Darbishire stopped flailing for a moment to point his cane with disgust at a dog trying to haul itself up the surgery steps. The fat man took advantage to escape by crawling away with amazing agility for someone of his girth. Snatching his straw boater from the ground, he stood up and ran after a horse-drawn carriage that was slowly moving down the streets, reins dangling. He succeeded in catching it up, checked the horses, and clambered quickly on board. Safely installed in the driver's seat, he signalled to the man in mourning, who quit his observation post in leisurely fashion, and sauntered over to the waiting carriage. As he passed by Doctor Darbishire, he greeted him nonchalantly with a wave of his cane.

On 19 October 1933, the aforementioned Doctor Juan de Dios Darbishire, sixty-three years of age, twice a widower, by profession a medical doctor, declared to the court that he had been unaware of anyone going past him or greeting him because at that moment he was bending over one of his dogs, by name Esculapius, in order to wrap him in his cloak and carry him into the surgery, where he subsequently administered emergency treatment in the hope of counteracting the effects of the poison his pet had swallowed. Unfortunately, his efforts were to no avail, as Esculapius passed away soon afterwards.

In his testimony under oath of 17 October 1933, the witness Rosalío Usulutlán, whose age, profession and other characteristics are already known to us, gave a detailed description of that night's events. In response to the judge's questions, he affirmed that to the best of his knowledge and ability, the portly individual being beaten by a cane in the street was Octavio Oviedo y Reyes, a native of the city of León, at that date an articled law clerk and now an attorney and public notary, someone he knew personally and met socially. He further declared that the person observing the incident from in front of the church was Oliverio Castañeda, a native of Guatemala, who at that time was an articled clerk in the legal profession and was now also an attorney and public notary, and was known to him personally.

To lend further weight to his testimony, the witness stated that he had had the opportunity to relate the entire incident to Alí Vanegas that same night, as he sat studying in the doorway of his room a block further down Calle Real, next to the house where Rubén Dario had once lived, and where the mad poet Alfonso Cortes was kept locked up. The court had only to ask Vanegas if it were true that he, Rosalío Usulutlán, had informed him, as he now averred, that the dog poisoners were none other than Oviedo and Castañeda.

Vanegas, present in court in his capacity as clerk, made no comment at this point since it was forbidden for him to intervene in the proceedings. He limited himself to copying the statement into the official record of the case, but when on 18 October 1933 it was his turn to take the stand, he corroborated Rosalío Usulutlán's statement in all particulars.

Pressed by the judge to elaborate on the identity of the man in mourning watching the scene from the church, the witness Rosalío Usulutlán asserted that he was convinced it was Oliverio Castañeda, because although it was true that the night was dark and the street lamps gave off inadequate light, he had been able to make out the man's features thanks to one of the constant flashes of lightning. He further stated that the man's gait and general appearance were equally unmistakable when he saw him walk off down the Calle Real, greeting Doctor Darbishire as he passed by with a wave of the mother-of-pearl topped cane he always carried with him.

CHAPTER TWO

The Search for the Deadly Poison

ESCULAPIUS, Doctor Juan de Dios Darbishire's dog, was the final victim of a lethal campaign started on the afternoon of 18 June 1932 by the two legal clerks, Oliverio Castañeda and Octavio Oviedo y Reyes, who used chunks of cooked meat laced with strychnine for this deadly purpose. This is borne out by the testimonies to the judge appointed by the León Regional Criminal Court.

The first affidavit was from Señor Alejandro Pereyra, sixty-two years of age, married, a former member of the Nicaraguan armed forces, at that time a secretary in the city police headquarters under the command of Captain Morris Wayne, USMC. Confined to bed due to his disability, the witness declared that:

> At approximately ten a.m. on a day he believes must have been in June 1932, the legal clerks Oliverio Castañeda Palacios and Octavio Oviedo y Reyes made their appearance in Captain Wayne's office. The witness knew them to be a pair of pranksters, inclined to practical jokes and rowdy behaviour, but who nevertheless followed the correct procedures in all the legal business that frequently brought them to the police headquarters. While waiting for Captain Wayne to arrive, the visitors struck up a conversation with the witness. Among other topics, their talk concerned the steep rise in the price of domestic drinking water, which was causing quite a stir among the residents of the city, and the proliferation of stray dogs. The witness declared himself to be in favour of the call by *El Cronista* newspaper for trustworthy members of the pub-

> lic to be permitted to administer poison to rid the town of these animals. It was at this point that the two young men took the opportunity to disclose the reason for their visit. This was to request Captain Wayne's written permission for the purchase of a bottle of strychnine from one of the city's pharmacies so that they could personally start to dispose of the dogs.
>
> Since the pair were known to be honest and reliable, the witness considered that it was within his authority to grant their request without waiting for Captain Wayne. Accordingly, he proceeded to give them an almost full bottle of the poison, identical in size and appearance to those dispensed in the city pharmacies, kept in a drawer in the office by his commanding officer. As a result, there was no need to issue them with any authorization.

For his part, Señor David Argüello, by profession a pharmacist, married, fifty-two years of age, owner and manager of the Argüello Pharmacy on the Calle de Comercio, León, domiciled at the same address, declared in his written testimony of 19 October 1933 that on receipt of a signed document from the Chief of Police, said document being kept in his files and being available for inspection, he supplied Oviedo and Castañeda with a full, unopened one ounce bottle containing 30 grams of strychnine. This was sufficient for the preparation of twenty chunks of meat each containing one-and-a-half grams of the poison, enough to cause the death of an equivalent number of canines. Señor Argüello described the bottle as being identical to those used for Doctor Ross's pink laxative pills.

Puzzled by the discrepancy between these two accounts, and determined to discover whether the dog poisoners had in fact been supplied with strychnine on two separate occasions, the judge proceeded to question Octavio Oviedo y Reyes (a married man, twenty-seven years of age, by profession a lawyer, domiciled in the San Juan district of the city of León).

The witness, commonly known as 'Oviedo the Balloon', informed the judge in a lengthy deposition dated 17 October 1933 that it had only been on 18 June 1932, when Señor Pereyra issued them with the permit signed by Captain Wayne that they had obtained strychnine. There had been no other occasion when they were given a bottle of poison directly from a desk drawer. He therefore attributed Señor Pereyra's statement, when it was read out to him, to a lapse of memory.

The signed permit, subsequently handed over to the court by the pharmacist Argüello and added to the case files, did as stated bear the date 18 June 1932.

On the evening of 26 September 1933, prior to the opening of the legal proceedings in which he was to figure as a witness, Oviedo the Balloon was summoned by Cosme Manzo to appear before the 'accursed table'. This he did almost immediately after the end of the performance at the Teatro González, which he attended whenever he could, whatever the movie.

In his role as chairman of the table, Doctor Atanasio Salmerón wished to question Oviedo about what exactly had happened the day when he and his friend had set about poisoning the stray dogs in the streets. For reasons which will later become clear, he carefully wrote all this information down in his notebook (supplied courtesy of the Casa Squibb). After imbibing several glasses of Campeón Rum (mixed with Kola Shaler—the perfect pick-me-up for convalescents) Oviedo the Balloon regaled them by recapping all the details of the adventure, oblivious to the motive behind the questioning.

On the morning of 18 June 1932, clad only in nightshirt and socks, Oviedo the Balloon lay sprawled over the bare kitchen table littered with the remains of his abundant breakfast, reading the previous afternoon's edition of *El Cronista*. As every morning, his wife Yelba was shouting at him for being a pig while she watered the plants on their patio.

Also, just like every other morning, Oviedo drank a glass of Picot grape juice to help relieve his chronic heartburn. He put the glass down and returned to the article about the stray dogs. He could not get the thought of the pack of Alsatians kept by Doctor Darbishire out of his head. Since the death of his second wife, these animals had been the elderly Sorbonne graduate's only companions in his Calle Real surgery. The desire to poison them stuck like a burr in the Balloon's mind.

At nine o'clock he left home. He was wearing his tan linen suit, a green polka dot bow tie, and wore a straw boater perched jauntily over his thick curls, smoothed down with brilliantine. He headed for the Metropolitan Hotel, where he was to meet Oliverio Castañeda so that the pair could begin revising for their final law exam. The hotel stood several blocks away from his house, but that morning the Balloon was in the mood for a walk. Although surprised not to come across as many stray dogs as the alarmist article in *El Cronista* had led him to expect, he was still toying with the idea of wreaking havoc among Doctor Darbishire's canine companions.

Dressed in strict mourning and with cane in hand, Oliverio Castañeda was already waiting for him at the door to the room that he and his wife had occupied ever since their arrival in León. The two men set off across the road and up a block to the University Library, where they counted on finding the volumes of the penal code and other reference books they needed for their studies. Their walk took them past the Contreras family home.

At that very moment, Don Carmen Contreras appeared at the corner door leading directly into his living room, carrying a copy of *El Cronista*. The two students greeted him, without intending to stop, but he called them over with a wave of the newspaper.

They crossed the street and waited for him to join them on the sidewalk outside La Fama store. The three of them struck up a conversation beneath the huge wooden sign of a bottle of Vichy-Celestins medicinal water hanging on two chains from the store roof.

'Are these powders,' asked Oliverio Castañeda, pointing to the yellow dust on the sole of his shoe, 'any use at all?'

'None, I'm afraid,' said Don Carmen, shaking his head ruefully.

'Like it says there, poison's the only answer,' Oviedo the Balloon insisted, pursing his lips at the newspaper Don Carmen was holding.

'In this rag? It publishes nothing but lies,' sighed Don Carmen. 'Now it's me they're attacking. Do they want the Water Company to go bust, and have us all die of thirst? I can't make a living with the rates as low as they are now.'

'Don't worry, I'll help you out there.' Switching his cane to his other hand, Oliverio Castañeda put his arm round Don Carmen's shoulder. 'I'll have a word with Rosalío like I promised. He's a good sort.'

Not having read the article criticizing the rise in water rates, Oviedo had nothing to add. His mind was still on the stray dogs and the best way of getting rid of them, 'considering the constant nuisance they are to defenceless citizens, who are not only pestered by unruly packs of mongrels roaming the public highways, but also run the risk of an unfortunate bite.'

'Instead of these powders, Don Carmen,' said Oviedo, scraping his boot clean on the curb, 'why don't you, as a law-abiding citizen, ask for permission to put down poison? That way, the dogs wouldn't upset your customers anymore.'

'You're right, my friends,' sighed Don Carmen. 'And you should see what a pest they are when the engineer and I go to inspect the pumps at the water tanks.'

'Much more of a nuisance than Chalio Usulutlán in *El Cronista*,' laughed Castañeda, clapping his hands in delight.

Don Carmen gave a hollow laugh. The newspaper looked strangely out of place in his hand.

'We could take care of the dogs at the water tank,' said Oviedo, fanning himself with his straw boater. 'If we got hold of some poison, that is.'

Don Carmen looked at him with renewed interest. Oviedo later remembered the ironic gleam in Don Carmen's beady eyes beneath the bushy eyebrows, the quick flare of his aquiline nostrils as though he were about to make a sarcastic riposte, his thin lips apparently on the point of making some cutting remark, but which eventually parted only to utter a few hasty words. A mouse of a man despite all his money, Oviedo the Balloon told the members of the accursed table, his face grimacing contemptuously as if rolling a mouthful of Campeón rum round his tongue.

'If you get the poison, I'll supply the meat,' muttered Don Carmen, staring down at the ground. 'And we could cook the portions at my house.'

'They don't need to be cooked,' said Oliverio Castañeda. He was so offhand about it, taking out his pocket watch as he spoke, that Oviedo was worried the idea no longer interested him. 'In Guatemala we call bits of poisoned meat for dogs "snacks". But we give them to them raw.'

'Here in Nicaragua we usually cook the meat,' stammered Don

Carmen, obviously distressed at not being able to explain this huge difference in national customs.

'Meat is meat, raw or cooked,' Castañeda said in a whisper, inviting the other two to draw closer to share his joke. 'How do you like your "meat", Don Carmen? The "heavenly meat" as Rubén Dario used to call it.'

'Go and get permission from the Yank for the poison. Here's the money for the meat,' said Don Carmen, pretending not to have heard Castañeda's last remark, and fumbling for his wallet. Flustered, he took out a five-cordoba note. 'Tell Wayne I sent you.'

Oviedo didn't hesitate for a second, almost snatching the money out of his hand. His double chin quivered with mirth as he recalled the expression of disgust on Oliverio's face as he took the note.

'Once you've got the strychnine, I'd like to go with you to deal with the dogs at the water tank,' said Don Carmen, putting away the wallet.

Oliverio Castañeda bowed ceremoniously and touched his hat brim in farewell. He didn't say a word to Oviedo as they walked along, but when they reached the street corner he pointed to the police headquarters in Plaza Jerez. They made their way there.

As we have already seen, Oviedo the Balloon was called to appear before the examining judge on 17 October 1933. His statement ranged over many different matters. These will be outlined in due course; at present we are concerned only with the dog poisoning of 18 June 1932. The crowd completely filling the courtroom pressed against him in his chair in front of the judge's dais. They passed on the details of his testimony to all those forced to stand in the corridors outside the room. Oviedo was sweating as profusely as if he had just had a bath with all his clothes on, and was so nervous he had lost all the breezy swagger he had shown when relating these events to his friends at the accursed table some weeks earlier.

Taking constant sips from a glass of water that members of the public keep refilled for him, Oviedo replied as follows to the judge's questions:

> The witness declares that once they had obtained the bottle of poison at the Argüello drugstore, he and Oliverio Castañeda did not as planned spend their time revising for

the law exam, but instead returned to his house in the San Juan neighbourhood to prepare the poisoned bait, Castañeda absenting himself just long enough to go to the Contreras family home and fetch the meat Don Carmen had promised them.

After emptying the contents of the bottle onto a piece of glass removed from a portrait frame in his living room, the witness states that he cut the poison up into twenty doses with his pocket knife. He then spread these on to the chunks of meat at the bottom end of the yard, as far away from the kitchen as possible to avoid any risk of contaminating food. The two men then tied a piece of thread round each portion so that they could handle them without touching the poison (the thread having been obtained from a bobbin in his wife's sewing machine drawer). Once the twenty chunks of poisoned meat were ready, the witness can state with absolute certainty that no strychnine remained in the bottle, and that he personally threw the empty container down the toilet in order to be sure that his children, who were always up to some mischief or other, would not get hold of it.

He had wanted to embark on their hunt immediately, but Castañeda persuaded him to wait, arguing that if people in the city saw them poisoning dogs in broad daylight they would take them for suspicious characters, even if *El Cronista* had said that only responsible citizens should undertake the task. His wife, who was joking with him all the time as they prepared the meat, agreed with Castañeda, and refused to have anything to do with the affair.

Castañeda had returned with the news that Don Carmen insisted on accompanying them. This surprised and annoyed Oviedo, because he had not taken seriously what the latter had said that morning, and the fact that he would be going with them meant his plans might be upset.

Castañeda reassured him, stressing that Don Carmen would only go to help them kill the animals near the water tank, as he had indicated that morning. He also jokingly added that as *El Cronista* recommended that the poison only be administered by people of good repute, what better than to have Don Carmen accompany them at the start of their mission? This elicited a further remark from Oviedo's wife, to the effect that it was not Don Carmen who would fail his exams if they were caught skulking around the streets when they should have been studying.

Don Carmen arrived in his black Packard at about six in the evening. The three men set off to lay poison around the water tank. Don Carmen drove, and on this occasion seemed especially light-hearted and talkative: whenever he saw a dog taking the poisoned bait they had thrown, he let go of the wheel, rubbed his hands together gleefully, and chuckled to himself.

After they had finished at the water tank, and before he dropped them back at Oviedo's door, Don Carmen asked the two men not to forget to save one portion of the meat for Don Macario Carrillo's dog. Don Macario was a music-lover who lived four doors from Don Carmen, and whose pet had the unfortunate habit of shitting on the sidewalk outside La Fama store, with the result that Don Carmen was constantly having to spread sawdust over the offending droppings. That dog was in fact the first to be poisoned, at approximately a quarter past eight that evening, after they had enticed it into the doorway to Don Macario's property.

Oviedo further stated that it was about eight o'clock when they hitched up the horses to the carriage for their final trip. They took with them the fifteen or so remaining portions of meat, in a small pinewood box of the kind used to contain La Estrella soap. They trotted around the streets as if out for an evening ride, while surreptitiously throwing the bait to any dogs they came across along the way. Most of the dogs were killed in the Calle Real, towards the end of their expedition.

They left Doctor Darbishire's surgery to last, calculating they would arrive at San Francisco church around ten, when the doctor would already be in bed. By then they had only one portion left, which they gave to the only Alsatian they saw outside the surgery, although usually several of the said Doctor Darbishire's many dogs stood guard there all night.

> Oviedo stated that he climbed down from the carriage holding the piece of poisoned meat by its thread. Knowing Alsatians to be a very fierce breed, he took every precaution to avoid the dog biting him. Eventually, using all manner of coaxing and cajolery, he managed to lure the animal towards him, and it took the fatal meat and gobbled it up.
>
> He was preparing to go back to the carriage when Doctor Darbishire, whom they had thought was safely in bed, suddenly appeared in the middle of the street. No sooner had the doctor spotted Oviedo acting suspiciously outside his house, and seen his dog eating the meat, than he immediately realized what was going on, and reacted with unaccustomed violence.

'I stumbled, and that old sonofabitch started beating the living daylights out of me with his stick,' Oviedo told the members of the accursed table. He flailed around as though he were wielding a cane, then threw himself to the floor, clutching his head theatrically.

'And did Oliverio Castañeda defend you?' Doctor Salmerón wanted to know, loudly cracking the knuckles of each hand.

'The coward jumped down from the carriage and ran to hide behind a cypress in front of the church,' moaned Oviedo, still curled up on the floor, warding off the blows.

'And you say you poisoned twenty dogs?' Doctor Salmerón licked his finger and leafed through the pages of his Casa Squibb notebook.

'Yes, twenty, I've already given you the list,' Oviedo the Balloon nodded, panting as if still recovering from the run he made to the carriage in order to escape more blows. 'We used up all but one of the pieces before we got to Doctor Darbishire's. But there was only one dog there anyway. It ate the last bit.'

'So there was no poison left at all.' Doctor Salmerón put down his pencil and unscrewed the top of a fountain pen. He began to write hastily, as if making out a prescription.

'Not a spoonful. Twenty doses, twenty dogs out K.O.,' yelped Oviedo the Balloon, rattling his chair and howling like a poisoned canine.

CHAPTER THREE

'I am Innocent,' the Cry from the Dungeons

Exclusive interview granted by Doctor Oliverio Castañeda to our Reporter, Rosalío Usulutlán

THE DOORS OF THE XXI PRECINCT JAIL OPEN WIDE FOR EL CRONISTA — A DESCRIPTION AND SHORT BIOGRAPHY OF THE PRISONER — WHAT HE THINKS OF HIS PREDICAMENT — EVENTS SURROUNDING THE SUDDEN DEATH OF RAFAEL UBICO IN COSTA RICA — SWEARS HIS WIFE SUFFERED FROM CHRONIC ILLNESS — HIS RELATIONS WITH THE CONTRERAS FAMILY — 'I NEVER GAVE FOOD OR MEDICINE TO DON CARMEN OR MATILDE' — NOT CONVINCED BY THE UNIVERSITY LABORATORY TESTS — HIS THOUGHTS ON THE POSSIBLE EXHUMATION OF THE BODIES — HIS REASONS FOR RETURNING TO NICARAGUA — SPEAKS OF JEALOUSY AND POLITICAL PERSECUTION — WILL CONDUCT HIS OWN DEFENSE —

DAY draws to a close. It is six o'clock in the evening of 15 October 1933; filled with compassion, the noble city kneels at its Angelus prayers. To the distant sound of bells on the basilica tower, I mount the steps to the jail. Captain Anastasio Ortiz politely leads the way inside. When we reach the far end of the dark, dank corridor he tells me: 'This is the cell.' The silence here is overwhelming, comparable only to that found in deserted temples or lonely cemeteries. I pause to take in the sight of a single window through which filters the dim, checkered twilight; a tidy cot, a thoughtful-looking prisoner sitting, arms folded, at a small unscrubbed pine table that serves as desk and dining-table; a few books and magazines, a china mug and a bottle of water. Nothing else.

All at once, he looks up. Pale-skinned, of medium height, beard and moustache shaven, oval face with a pronounced lower jaw; black, straight hair, eyes tranquil but vague behind his spectacle lenses. Small mouth and thin lips, sunken frontal sinuses, average forehead, base of the nostrils also sunken, straight nose. A physiognomy revealing a mixture of determination, cunning, and shrewdness that could serve as a test case for those criminologists to prove their much talked-of theories concerning inherited traits leading to crime. Yet beyond any such scientific considerations, we are obliged to admit we find ourselves in the presence of an attractive male specimen, whom the fair sex in León's high society came almost without exception to regard as irresistible. Irresistible, and cruel? Does the one necessarily mask the other?

He is wearing a fine black cashmere suit with a black tie. Even in the isolation of his cell he adheres strictly to the mourning attire that has always been his trademark, something which for friends and strangers alike adds a touch of mystery to the young foreigner's personality. Apparently, he always wears black in honor of his mother, who died when he was still a child. It is said that this tragic event—the boy witnessed his mother pass away in fits of indescribable agony—not only prompted him to adopt mourning clothes ever after, but over the years came to have a profound effect on his behavior.

Seeing me standing at the cell door, he raises his eyebrows quizzically, then invites me in. I greet him. He returns my greeting, visibly affected. Can this sad, lonely prisoner be the same gentleman who so dazzled the salons of León's smartest set, the beau of all its young ladies? Can this be the smooth talker always ready with a quip, so witty and intelligent, so seductive in all his gestures? Yes, it is the very same, though cast down by the bitter blows of fortune.

Our interview begins.

Doctor Castañeda, the national and international press is full of speculation about the tragedy that has shaken the whole of León; you yourself are the subject of lively debates and the center of a web of conjecture. Would you be willing to answer a few questions for the benefit of the avid readers of El Cronista*?*

He considers my request, moves his head in thought, then replies: 'With pleasure, Mr. Usulutlán.' (A short pause).

He clasps his head in his hands, leaning on the table with obvious distress as he peers up at me. His gaze betrays weariness and despair. He removes his glasses.

How old are you? What is your family background?

'I was born in Zacapa, in the Republic of Guatemala, on 18 January 1908 (a slight frown creases his forehead). My father's name is Ricardo Castañeda Paz. He's a retired army officer, who has been suffering terribly from rheumatism these past six months. My younger brother Gustavo is seventeen, and is about to take his third year exams at the Faculty of Medicine in Guatemala. My other brother, Ricardo Castañeda, is currently finishing his studies as a surgeon at Munich University in Germany.'

And what studies did you pursue?

'I attended primary school at the Colegio de Infantes in Guatemala. I finished high school at the Eastern National Institute in Chiquimula, then went on to study Law at the University of San Carlos Borromeo, and subsequently here at the University of León, from where I graduated on February twenty-first of this year.'

What official posts have you occupied?

'In 1926 I worked in the Department of Education in Guatemala, and in that same year became the under-secretary for education.'

Are you saying that, at the age of eighteen, you were a member of the government of Guatemala?

He looks at me in surprise, as if this were a foolish question, but quickly smiles indulgently, and replies:

'Yes, that is so. And a few years later I entered the diplomatic corps. In 1929 I was appointed as an attaché to the Guatemalan legation in Costa Rica, and at the end of that year I was appointed first secretary to the Guatemalan legation in Nicaragua. That was the start of the great affection I have for this country.'

In Costa Rica, did you know someone by the name of Rafael Ubico?

His face clouds over with keen mistrust. His fingers begin to drum on the rough table-top.

'Of course. He died on 22 November 1929 in San José. He was the secretary in the legation there, when I was an attaché. We became close friends.'

What was the cause of his death?

Castañeda looks even more disturbed. His gestures become irritated and impatient.

'The unanimous opinion of the doctors who attended him was renal failure brought on by alcoholic intoxication. My friend Ubico lived in the Alemana boarding-house, close to the Central Post Office on Plaza de la Artillería. I lived in another boarding-house, the Niza, on the far side of the Edificio Metálico, near Parque Morazán.

'On the evening before Ubico's death, the wedding of Miss Lilly Rohrmoser (Castañeda politely helps me spell her last name in my notebook) to Don Guillermo Vargas Facio was celebrated in San José. The splendour of this event was unprecedented in the Costa Rican capital.'

Did you personally attend the wedding reception?

'No, but Rafael did, and drank copiously, as was his custom. At about three in the morning, after having rested for an hour or so in one of the drawing-rooms of the bride's house, where the celebrations were taking place, several of his friends carried him back to his room in the Pensión Alemana. He was given medication there and then to try to reduce the effects of his drunkenness.'

Did you come to his aid?

A dark shadow flits across his face. He tries to brush it away as if it were a troublesome fly.

'I went to help him about nine the next morning. I got a phone call from a chambermaid at the Pensión Alemana asking me to go to his bedside. When I saw how ill he was, I first telephoned to the Guatemalan doctor Pedro Hurtado Peña, and then went in search of our ambassador, Alfredo Skinner Klee. He came to the boarding-house, and in his presence the doctor diagnosed Ubico's state as critical. Another doctor, Mariano Figueres, who had been summoned by his landlady, concurred in this opinion.'

Forgive my question, but did you administer any kind of medicine to Ubico?

'Whenever he was suffering from the effects of alcohol, my friend used to take a patented medicine known as Licor Zeller, a salt preparation. When this brought no relief, and since Doctor Peña had not yet arrived, Ubico asked me to go to the pharmacy to fetch him some sodium bicarbonate. At the pharmacist's suggestion, I took him some Bromo-Seltzer. That also proved ineffective. The doctors gave him injections and enemas. But to no avail.'

And following Señor Ubico's death?

'Ambassador Skinner Klee called for an autopsy. He also ordered tests on all the medicines given to the deceased.'

Why did he take all these measures? Was there a suspicion that Ubico had not died of natural causes?

The young lawyer slips his spectacles back on, and looks at me pityingly.

'Because that was the procedure stipulated in the Guatemalan Diplomatic Code in cases of this kind.'

And what were the results of the tests?

'Señor Gastón Michaud, head of the Costa Rican national laboratory, drew up an official report, which is on file. Following the most careful analysis, no trace of any toxic substance was found in his bowels or liquids. The same was true of the medicines examined.'

The shadows of night have fallen. In the cell roof, a single bulb shines on the end of its cord. A few moments earlier, the prisoner had risen to switch it on.

Is this the first interview you have given the Press?

'Yes. It is only now, after a week of being held incommunicado, that I am able to talk. Meanwhile, however, the newspapers have been free to say whatever they like about me, without the slightest proof. I am extremely grateful to you, Señor Usulutlán, for giving me the opportunity to present my version of events. I trust this will bring some comfort to my friends, who must know that my conscience is crystal clear.'

Are you aware of the reasons for your arrest?

The prisoner strides indignantly up and down the tiny room.

'I was arrested on the orders of the director of the National Guard, General Anastasio Somoza. But it was only today that the relevant judicial authorities informed me of the arrest warrant, a fact which only serves to underline the illegality of this whole procedure.'

This is not a direct answer to my question. I have no wish to force him, but my duty as a journalist obliges me to press him further.

Have you heard anything of the rumours circulating about the death of your wife, Marta?

He stops pacing, and collapses onto his chair, overwhelmed with grief.

'Yes I have, the more's the pity. My wife's health was always fragile. She often suffered from menstrual haemorrhaging, and was unfortunate enough to have contracted acute malaria here in Nicaragua. I asked the judge to order the exhumation of my wife's body, however painful that might be for me, with the aim of proving once and for all that she did not die of poison but, as the doctors who attended her confirmed at the time, of an attack of blackwater fever. The rumours surrounding her death have wounded me in a way you cannot imagine; the same could be said of the cruel, spiteful gossip being bandied about concerning the death of Señorita Matilde Contreras, whom I shall mourn forever. Her body should also be exhumed.'

The prisoner folds his arms across his chest and raises his chin in a gesture of defiance towards not only me, but the whole of León society: that society which until recently feted him, only to turn against him so harshly now.

You yourself have brought up the question of Matilde Contreras' death. Given the violent circumstances of her demise, the judicial authorities are also seeking to establish whether she died of poison. Do you have anything to say on the matter?

Tears gather in his eyes. For want of a handkerchief, he wipes them away with a finger.

'Rest assured that, had I been a free man, I would have known how to defend myself against such vile calumnies. To me, Matilde was always a fount of virtue, a source of goodness and delight. As with my wife, it was her misfortune to pass away in her prime, both of them laid low by the terrible blackwater fever. Given the affection and esteem in which she held me, she must be suffering up in Heaven to see the desperate situation to which malicious gossip has led me.'

A fresh silence. The prisoner seems unsettled by his memories, as if the shadow of his former life were prowling round the gloomy cell, watching over his solitude. He can sense my next question, and peers at me dejectedly.

You are being held as a consequence of the violent death of Don Carmen Contreras, under whose roof you lived as a guest of the now grief-stricken family. Is there anything you wish to say about that to our readers?

'Don Carmen's sudden death filled me a deep, genuine grief. He was a great friend of mine, and I am honoured to consider myself as one of those who called themselves his friend, as he was always very exacting in his choice of companion.'

On the day of his death, did you give Don Carmen any food or medicine?

'Not at any time. Let the members of his family speak out if they have the slightest suspicion about the probity of my conduct. I call on Doña Flora, his inconsolable widow, to confirm what I say. It was his own family or their servants who served him food that day. And Don Carmen administered his own medicines, as well as locking them away. Why would I be the one to give him medicine? Nor, as my unwarranted accusers are so eager to insinuate, did I ever feed Matilde. Just imagine: they say I offered her a chicken leg dipped in strychnine! I challenge them to bring their vipers' tongues close to a leg of chicken coated in a poison like that, they will soon see how mistaken they are in their accusations!'

But the tests carried out on Don Carmen's internal organs in the León University pharmaceutical laboratory indicate that he died of poison. And animals injected with the substances extracted from his vital organs and juices all died following violent convulsions. Do you not consider those tests valid?

A faint smile tinged with sarcasm plays around the prisoner's bloodless lips.

'There are many objections to procedures of this kind, and although I am no expert, the weaknesses are self-evident. The professors use that laboratory to demonstrate to their students how to make cough syrups and perfumed hair creams. That is how scientific they are! How can you expect me to accept as judicial proof, even if it were not being used against me, this cruel murder of some mongrel dog, stray cat, or luckless frog, which is all they have succeeded in achieving in that lab?'

You have spoken of exhuming the bodies of your wife and Señorita Matilde Contreras, and declare yourself to be in favour of such a move. Once the bodies have been dug up and the autopsies performed, do you think that the scientific examinations should be carried out in León? Or are you perhaps suggesting the viscera should be taken to Managua?

'It is not for me to suggest anything of the kind. That is for the judge to decide. But please note it as an idea worth considering.

It is obvious that there are better facilities in the capital; and at least that would save the lives of any more unfortunate animals, which are bound to die if injected with substances from a putrefied corpse.'

However caustic these remarks, the prisoner Castañeda appears exhausted, drained. And yet I need to pursue other topics, and when I suggest we do so, he readily agrees.

As I understand it, following your wife's death you left Nicaragua for good. Why then, if there was nothing to keep you here, did you decide to return?

He smiles a melancholy smile.

'I came back to gather material for a book: *Nicaragua 1934*. I was preparing this together with Miguel Barnet, a Cuban publishing expert. It was to be a yearbook providing social and economic information on the country, including statistics and photographs. Our idea was to visit the different towns and cities of Nicaragua collecting the data. The contract for the book and all the correspondence with the publishers were among my belongings confiscated by the police.'

Why did you consider it necessary to take up lodging again in the Contreras' family home?

'As a response to the family's extraordinary generosity. Doña Flora begged me to stay with them when I had the good fortune to find myself on the same boat as her and her daughter María del Pilar when they were returning from Costa Rica at the end of September.'

What took you to Costa Rica? Was there any special reason for your stay there?

The young man reacts to my question as if startled by it. But he knows how to control his emotions.

'To make things completely clear, I wish to state that I was in Costa Rica because I was expelled from Guatemala for political reasons, and given a passport for only that country. My meeting with Doña Flora and her daughter in San José was pure coincidence. A very pleasant one. I trust that this clarification will serve to dispel any gossip about our meeting. Absurd tittle-tattle.'

Once you had arrived in León, what prevented you from visiting the rest of the country, as you say you planned to do?

'It was Don Carmen himself who kept me in León. He was anxious to resolve the problem of the new contract for the Metropolitan Water Company, which had been causing him headaches for such a long time. In the presence of his family, he asked me not to leave León, and to see to the contract personally, since I was on good terms with the city councillors who would have to approve it.

'The León city council and the inhabitants can all attest to how loyally I fulfilled my promise as friend and attorney to Señor Contreras. I succeeded in getting the new contract signed, in spite of the reservations of many of those involved. Even then I was unable to leave León. With the sudden, regrettable death of his daughter Matilde, Don Carmen again insisted I stay. He was so distraught that he was even less capable of seeing through the Water Company business, and wanted me to handle the whole thing.'

Time waits for no man, and your faithful servant finds it necessary to consider bringing the interview to a close.

How do you explain the dreadful situation in which you now find yourself? You were always held in such high esteem in this city.

'I put it down to the clever ruses of those determined to bring dishonor to my name, and who in doing so are only furthering the evil machinations of the evil tyrant who holds my native country in his sway. He has a long reach, and I am his sworn enemy. He offers rich rewards to anyone prepared to help him achieve his ignoble aims. These people are envious because I, a foreigner, was able to outshine them here in Nicaragua. They cannot accept that I, who was not born here, won so much recognition and affection in its highest circles. So they willingly sharpened the tyrant's dagger for him.'

The question I must raise now is a difficult, thorny one. I put it to him point-blank:

Do you realize your life is at stake over this?

The prisoner gazes at me defiantly, and proudly straightens his spectacles.

'It is not merely my life which is at stake. Justice itself is threatened by this scandalous procedure. To begin with, I have been committed to prison without charge: the arrest warrant was only produced some time later. Secondly, I have been denied my inalienable right to self-defence, as legal proceedings have been carried out in my absence, when it is my right to be present. And last but not least, I have not yet been formally charged with any of the alleged crimes of which I am accused.

'However, you should know that I am not in the least afraid that this vile conspiracy could lead me to the scaffold. I shall climb the steps with a clear conscience, blessing Doña Flora and her family as I do so. For her and her family, I feel only gratitude. She and María del Pilar have done all they can to lighten my burden here in this cell, and it is only because they have been expressly forbidden to do so by the prison authorities that they no longer send me food and other necessities. What most grieves me is to find myself slandered in this way, and above all that this should come from persons I considered my friends, and others who were my fellow students.'

Do you consider the judge in charge of the case as one of those former friends who have now turned against you?

'Judge Mariano Fiallos did indeed study with me at the Faculty of Law. But you must excuse me if I do not respond to your question regarding him. It is his own conscience that must provide the answer.'

How do you propose to go about conducting your defence?

'As I have already said, until now I have been denied all right to defend myself. But I am waiting to be formally charged before I insist on being given the possibility to conduct my own defence. If I am finally granted my rights, I will represent myself in court, although many leading attorneys, including several from the capital, have already declared themselves ready to undertake my defence.'

Captain Ortíz signals to me from the gloomy prison corridor. I have already taken up far more than my allotted time, and so must bring my interview to a close. I inform my hapless interlocutor of this, and prepare to take my leave of him.

Is there anything you would like to add, Señor Castañeda?

'Through you, Señor Usulutlan, I should like to call on the press in Nicaragua to deal with this matter as calmly and as responsibly as they can. And let them never forget that as a prisoner I am innocent until proven guilty.'

Rest assured I will convey your message to them. Until we meet again, Señor Castañeda.

Shrouded in the shadows of night, the forbidding XXI precinct jail is behind me now. God forbid that you or I, dear reader, should ever find ourselves imprisoned within its walls.

CHAPTER FOUR

True Love is a Once-in-a-Lifetime Thing

At eleven in the morning of 11 October 1933, in pursuance of a court order issued by the judge for the León District Criminal Court, Oliverio Castañeda's belongings were seized from Don Carmen Contreras' house. The inventory, undertaken before Castañeda's effects were transferred to the court building for safe keeping, details the contents of his various items of luggage:

> a) One large metal trunk, found to contain: a number of magazines from Guatemala, Costa Rica and Nicaragua; legal textbooks; bundles of private correspondence, invoices, receipts, cancelled IOUs and assorted bills; typewritten poems on a variety of topics, all bearing the accused's signature; an unfinished typewritten manuscript entitled 'Central America's Economic Ills and their Remedies', also the work of the accused; more typewritten documents ready for the printer in a file on the front of which was written in Gothic lettering: A Funeral Garland for Señorita Matilde Contreras—A Tribute From Those Who Mourn Her.
>
> b) One large pressed-cardboard suitcase, containing items of clothing: trousers, jackets and waistcoats of English wool, all of them black in colour; also, one black tuxedo with its accompanying silk cummerbund.
>
> c) One medium-sized fiber suitcase, containing underclothes, shirts, and Bakelite detachable collars and cuffs; bow ties and rubber suspenders.
>
> d) One portable Remington typewriter, in a case with a damaged lock.
>
> e) One wind-up Victor Victrola, also with case.

f) One wooden chest, with a hand-painted lid depicting scenes of volcanoes and a lake. Contains several black felt hats, various canes and pairs of shoes. In addition, toiletries such as pots of talcum powder, hair cream, and bottles of eau de cologne.

Also discovered in this chest were a tin cylinder, found to contain the defendant's legal diplomas; a copy of the volume *A Manual of Etiquette and Diplomatic Ceremony*, printed in Madrid in 1912; a *Criminal Investigation Manual* bearing the stamp of the central library of the University of León. After inspection, this was duly returned to said library.

In addition, the chest was found to contain two Peerless gramophone records, one with the following musical numbers: 'True Love Is a Once-in-a-Lifetime Thing' (Waltz), and 'Ridge Moon' (Blues); the other containing: 'Sweet Jenny Lee' (Blues), and 'Sing you Sinners' (Foxtrot).

A letter was also found between the pages of the law manual. This consisted of two pages written in pencil on brown wrapping paper. The top half of the first of these sheets had been destroyed by moths. On examination of this, the judge ordered that the letter be added to the case files. It reads as follows:

> ...depths someone once so proud can sink to. I must confess that two months ago I thought it was M.P. who interested you. Something in her manner towards you made me fear (I use that word "fear" because I already knew that I loved you) there must have been something between you, because she is so proud and haughty with everyone except you. Don't be angry, my love, but tell me what I want to know. Was it M.P. whom you liked, and if so, why did you change your mind? Tell me! You can't imagine the doubts that torment me, my darling. I have to tell you all this because sometimes I feel so lonely and want just to hold you tight and feel you close to me. How long have you loved me? And why? I'm terrified it is something you haven't thought enough about, and will soon be sorry for. This thought frightens me so much, my wildest dream is for us to live together always. I feel I hardly know you, darling,

but that's because you will not let yourself be known. I am worried that now I have given you all I have to give you won't be interested in me any more. I'm sorry, but I can't keep anything from you, all the fears and love I feel for you. Am I the one you love? I know that men like you can love lots of women. If one day you find you love me less than another, I prefer you to tell me: I would rather suffer than to live a lie. I love you, my darling; I only wish you could feel all the love I have for you. I'm frightened, my love [here are four unintelligible words]...I'm worried by so many things, I want you to tell me the truth, sometimes the ideas I get in my head make me feel so bad. I love you so much, more than anybody else, I have never felt anything like this before. Why did you come to me? Why did you appear here? And yet you won't trust me. I never know what you are feeling, what's going on inside you. I can never comfort you or [another unintelligible word]...Am I really so silly and ugly that I don't deserve you? Why, even [five unintelligible words]...I've learnt to play that record of yours I like so much on the piano: "True Love is a Once-in-a-Lifetime Thing". Is that truly me? Or is M.P. your one true love? I can hardly bear the pain, my darling.

Formally charged with parricide and premeditated murder, as stated in the arrest warrant dated 28 November 1933, Oliverio Castañeda appeared before the judge on December first to reply to the charges under oath. During a hearing which lasted almost the entire day, the following exchange took place between the judge and the defendant:

JUDGE: You have before you a letter written in pencil on poor quality paper of the kind used as wrapping paper, with no signature or address of any sort. The letter was discovered inside a chest that was among your belongings, and for this reason I presume you were the recipient. In it, a woman writes of her jealousy towards a third person, identified by the initials M.P.

Given that the letter in question makes mention of the

waltz "True Love is a Once-in-a-Lifetime Thing" in its final paragraph; given that this piece of music features on one of the phonograph records found among your confiscated possessions; and given finally that Señorita Matilde Contreras herself played the piano, I must presume that it was she who wrote this anonymous missive. You evidently received it at a recent date, posterior to the death of your wife Marta Jerez de Castañeda, as no mention is made of her in the letter.

It further appears from statements taken in the course of this murder investigation that you paid court to both the Contreras sisters. In her statement of 12 November 1933, Señorita María del Pilar Contreras declares that you showed "especial kindness" in your dealings with her. In addition, in his declaration of 17 October 1933, Señor Octavio Oviedo y Reyes, a close friend of yours, and whom as such I take to be in your confidence, reveals that somewhere around the month of January 1933, shortly before the death of your wife, you showed him another letter from María del Pilar Contreras addressed to you, couched in terms only to be found between two people who are romantically attached.

From all this I am led to the conclusion, which you must also acknowledge, that the letter I am producing now for you to examine and confirm my assertions, was addressed to you by Matilde Contreras. Furthermore, that the person to whom she refers by the initials M.P. is none other than her sister María del Pilar, of whom she is jealous. Both sisters wrote you love letters, and you fomented this rivalry to suit your own purposes.

DEFENDANT: As you yourself point out, this is a letter with no address or signature, and its contents are extremely vague. The initials M.P. have little or no significance, because they could refer to any number of people. Why should they necessarily refer to Señorita María del Pilar Contreras? What grounds do you have for maintaining that the author of this letter, written on wrapping paper and with no indication either of sender or recipient, and as such entirely worthless as evidence, was the charming Señorita Matilde Contreras, of fond memory?

It is true that among the many gifts with which she was endowed was the ability to play the piano exquisitely, but I have come across many women, both in León and other cities, with similar talents. And if anyone has heard her play that waltz "True Love is a Once-in-a-Lifetime Thing"—here I am anticipating, your Honour, the inevitable innuendos that always pursue me—it must be because she learned it from the radio, where it is frequently played on the radio station Le Franc.

As for the declaration made by my friend and faithful student companion Señor Octavio Oviedo y Reyes, I can only assume that on this occasion his memory is at fault, since I refuse to believe that he would wish to harm me or damage María del Pilar's reputation in any way.

JUDGE: All the evidence so far gathered points to the fact that you had conceived a plan with the ultimate aim of leaving the youngest member of the Contreras family, María del Pilar, at your mercy, so that you could then marry her without hindrance. In this way, you hoped to appropriate Don Carmen's fortune, which had been your goal all along. To this end, you first poisoned your wife, Marta Jerez, on 13 February 1933, so that you would be free to remarry. Secondly, on 2 October 1933, you also disposed of Matilde Contreras, whose deep affection for you hampered your criminal intent. It was only your arrest following the death of Don Carmen on 9 October 1933 that prevented you continuing with your diabolical scheme. You had to eliminate Don Carmen because, as you yourself have stated, he was not the kind of man to entrust his business affairs to anybody else. His death therefore meant you would have access to his inheritance. Your next intended victim was undoubtedly his widow, Doña Flora, since you had already removed from the scene the only male member of the family, Carmen Contreras Guardia, by arranging for him to be sent to Costa Rica.

DEFENDANT: This supposed plan does not stand up to any unbiased analysis. If you see economic gain as my motive, I should like to state publicly that the inheritance I received from my wife, with whom I was unable to have any children due to her untimely death, is some five times greater than that of the entire Contreras family put together, including Don Carmen's father, his brothers, and other close relatives. My wife's mother, Doña Cristina, is the owner of the following coffee plantations in Guatemala. The list is far from complete, as I am speaking from memory: Chojojá, Salajeche, La Trinidad, and La Argentina. All of these are situated in the region of Mazatenango, and produce over six thousand bags of coffee annually. She also owns four of the finest properties in the centre of Mazatenango, as well as the mansion on Tercera Avenida Sur in Guatemala City. In addition, she has several substantial bank accounts, plus stocks and shares. Therefore, if it was financial gain I was seeking, and I was married to someone who was not only extremely wealthy, but saintly and self-sacrificing, as well as beautiful, why on earth would I want to take her life?

Moreover, if I really were the kind of criminal I am so artfully being portrayed as, without consideration of my social standing, my family background, my feelings as a proven man of honour or my educational achievements...if, as I say, I were indeed such a criminal, capable of trafficking in human life in this despicable way, then the very least the judicial authorities might concede me is the modicum of intelligence necessary to ensure I ran no risks, for example by taking out a remunerative life insurance policy in US dollars on my wife, and after committing such a heinous crime, to have hidden myself away in some forgotten corner of Central America, where only God would act a witness to my despicable act.

JUDGE: In the sworn statement already referred to, Señor Octavio Oviedo y Reyes declares that as far as he can recall, one of the passages in the letter signed by María del Pilar Contreras which you showed him read as follows:

"My darling, true love is a once in a lifetime thing. Think of me when you're alone and play our record on the Victrola. Or think of me even when you're with her, and she, unlike me, can play it on the piano for you."

Despite the fact that at the time you showed this note to your close friend Señor Oviedo your wife Marta Jerez was still alive, I take it that the 'she' who could play the piano was Matilde Contreras. Or was María del Pilar referring to your wife?

DEFENDANT: I will overcome the distaste I feel at having to refer in these circumstances to two pure souls such as my wife and Señorita Matilde Contreras, may they rest in peace, and categorically deny these insinuations.

I repeat that the note from which you have just quoted never in fact existed, but must be a slip of memory on the part of Señor Oviedo y Reyes, since I refuse to believe he would deliberately betray our friendship in this manner.

As regards the two Contreras sisters, I must confess I saw them as equally radiant, and held them both equally sacred in my esteem. It is only because I find myself so unjustly accused that I must ask you to bear in mind the following distasteful consideration: if I am considered capable of such extraordinary scheming, would it not be only logical to see me as being practically-minded as well? If I were indeed the criminal you and the others accusing me imagine me to be; if I had paid court to both Contreras sisters at the same time, and in my sick mind had decided to keep one of them for myself, would it not have made much more sense for me to have got rid of the fifteen year-old María del Pilar, and spared Matilde, one of the most cultured and enlightened young ladies in Nicaragua, who not only spoke perfect English as a result of being educated in the United States, but was a truly accomplished pianist? In that way I should have guaranteed my becoming not only rich thanks to my crimes, but would also have enjoyed the benefits of a marriage to a remarkable young lady of almost the same age as me, rather than being with a slip of a girl, however attractive she might be.

Only a few days after this confrontation, on 6 December 1933, Oliverio Castañeda sent the court a sensational document. In it, among other things, he flatly contradicted his repeated denials of any romantic attachment to the Contreras sisters. In this new statement, which was to prove decisive to the course of the trial and his eventual fate, Castañeda accepted that the unsigned and undated letter had been sent him by Matilde Contreras. He further called for the handwriting to be verified by experts.

On instruction from the judge, this was carried out by Pedro Alvarado and Rafael Icaza. On December twelfth, after careful comparison of the letter in question to other items known to have been penned by Matilde Contreras, they concluded that she was indeed the person who had written those lines.

In this same new document, the defendant accepted the existence of the note which Oviedo the Balloon alleged had been sent by María del Pilar Contreras. We shall have occasion to return to this and many other love letters and missives in the course of this account.

To finalize this chapter, we can report that on 25 October 1933 the bodies of Marta Castañeda and Matilde Contreras were exhumed from the Guadalupe cemetery. We shall also return to this episode, but suffice it to say for now that Doctor Juan de Dios Darbishire, who as family doctor was present at the autopsy on the body of Matilde Contreras, carried out his own examination of the deceased's genital organs. He asked for his findings that they were intact on her death to be added to the autopsy report. This was duly carried out.

CHAPTER FIVE

The Young Man in Mourning Who Dances the Foxtrot

AT DUSK on 27 March 1931, the Contreras sisters have, as usual, brought their cane rocking chairs to the corner door of their house. As usual, they have spent a long while dressing and applying make-up in front of their mirror, even though all they do is sit on the sidewalk until night falls and it is time for dinner. As usual, lots of other young women are also sitting outside their front doors, rocking lazily as they watch the world go by. The heat of the summer day is still stifling. Gusts of hot wind raise clouds of dust on street corners, while flocks of grackles descend and settle on the tree branches in gardens behind the houses.

But on this particular day, their evening ceremony is interrupted by an unusual event. With their heads close together as they pretend to read the copy of the illustrated *El Ideal Parisien* their mother has just brought them from the capital, they are in fact keeping a curious eye on what is happening on the far side of the street.

A new couple is moving into one of the rooms at the Metropolitan Hotel.

Porters are busy unloading their luggage from a cart in front of the hotel: trunks, suitcases, cardboard boxes, a Victor gramophone in its portable case. A young man with an elegant, relaxed air despite his mourning attire takes this case from one of the porters and sets it carefully down on a corner table.

The two girls watch from their rocking chairs as the man lifts the lid, winds up the phonograph and then, already dancing to the steps of a tune that is not yet audible, he puts on the record 'Sing You Sinners', which they already know. Still dancing, he sashays over to the back of the room, where his partner, a small, plump woman, is busy sorting out clothes from the trunks.

Without knowing why, the sisters find themselves blushing as the young man, one arm high in the air and the other thrust out straight like a sword, urges the woman to dance with him. At first the stranger, still dressed in her travelling outfit—a close-fitted toque, calf-length calico dress and low-heeled pumps—pushes him playfully away. Finally though, she gives in to his insistent invitation, lays the armful of clothes down, and with a tinkling laugh that carries across the street, joins him in the foxtrot.

This is the afternoon that Oliverio Castañeda and his wife Marta Jerez arrive in León. It is only a few days prior to the March thirty-first earthquake that destroys much of the capital, Managua, and is at the height of the occupation of Nicaragua by U.S. Marines. The couple's names appear on the list of passengers who arrived at Xolotlán airport the day before on the Panaire flight from Guatemala, as published in *La Noticia* newspaper in its 'Travellers Come, Travellers Go' section.

They had been married at eight o'clock on the evening of 5 March 1930, in the church of La Merced in Guatemala City. Born in Mazatenango on 1 December 1913, Marta was not yet seventeen.

According to Oliverio Castañeda's ststement on oath to the judge on 11 October 1933, he had decided to return to Nicaragua to continue his legal studies largely due to the memory of the many friends he had made during his first stay in the country from December 1929 to February 1930. However, as Doctor Atanasio Salmerón pointed out at the 'accursed' table, this was an unconvincing argument. He must have made all those friends in Managua rather than León, where he had never previously set foot.

The real reason behind his leaving Guatemala appears to have been that his life was in danger there. During the 1930 Christmas Ball held at the Mazatenango Social Club, he shot and wounded Alfonso Ricci, a coffee plantation owner from San Francisco Zapotitlán. Ricci had been so drunk that he began to urinate on the dance floor while the marimba orchestra was playing 'Your Flashing Eyes'.

Marta had uttered a piercing shriek, but when Castañeda had protested to Ricci, he had simply aimed the jet of urine at the outraged husband's trousers. When Castañeda shot him, Ricci collapsed in a heap, his trousers still gaping open. Oliverio made no attempt to run away. He stood his ground calmly, weapon in hand, until he could give himself up to the Mazatenango Chief of Police, who was also attending the ball. He did not have to spend long in prison: General Lázaro Chacón, the president of Guatemala at the time and a relative of his from Zacapa, interceded on his behalf. But Ricci was a dangerous man to have as an enemy.

The two sisters, blushing as they watch the couple dance in the midst of half-opened boxes and trunks, have no idea who the newcomers are, or of what brings them to León. They only know that the couple travelled in the first class carriage of the four o'clock train with their mother, because she has told them as much. Drawn by the sound on the record, she had come to their door for a few moments, and smiled when she recognized the pair across the street.

From the interview given in his cell to the journalist Rosario Usulutlán on 15 October 1933, we already know that Oliverio Castañeda was born in Zacapa, Guatemala, on 21 January 1908, the eldest of three sons. However, in the interview he neglected to mention that he was an illegitimate child, and Rosalío did not venture to ask him anything about his mother, Luz Palacios, whom he lost when he was only fourteen. Her terrible drawn-out death haunted his dreams from that moment on.

Following his mother's death, Oliverio and his brothers went to live with their maternal grandmother, Doña Luz Urzúa, after their father, who had remarried, refused to look after them. Castañeda once confided to Oviedo the Balloon that he used to visit his father after school, when the old man would be having lunch behind closed shutters while the noonday sun blazed outside. Although Oliverio would deliberately drag his feet to announce his arrival, the former army officer never once deigned to raise his eyes from his soup plate. The boy would stand stiffly to attention beside the table, without ever daring to sit down.

According to him, his father would ladle himself a second helping of soup from the steaming porcelain tureen, carry on his conversation with his wife, and occasionally stick his finger between his teeth to pick out any shreds of meat stuck there, holding them up for inspection. At last, without ever acknowledging his son's presence, he would drop a coin onto the tablecloth. Castañeda would scoop it up and leave.

However, in his statement of 11 October 1933, Castañeda declares that while he was studying law in León, he maintained himself and his wife in a modest way thanks to the hundred dollars a month his father sent him from Guatemala (a sum reduced to thirty dollars when his wife died). Also relevant is a letter asking for financial help which he sent from jail on October twenty-first to his father's home at Tercera Calle Este, Guatemala City:

> Dear Father,
>
> It is only now, after thirteen days held incommunicado, accused of having poisoned Marta (how disgusting of them!) as well as Don Carmen Contreras and his daughter Matilde (I had been staying in their house here), deaths for which the prosecutor is calling for the death penalty! and after an endless stream of unfounded slanders, all of them politically motivated, that I am finally able to send this letter to you, thanks to the kindness of a Cuban friend with whom I had planned to do some work here. He will post it to you from Costa Rica, since he is leaving Nicaragua for good (and who can blame him?)
>
> Yes father, politically motivated. I was so angry at being expelled from Guatemala that I wrote an article for the émigrés in Costa Rica attacking President Ubico. It was entitled "An Operetta Napoleon" and was published in *La República.* I wish I had never allowed them to persuade me to write it. Then, no sooner had I arrived in León than General Correa appeared, with an offer to build a home for the poor old folk here in return for it being called after their Guatemalan "benefactor". Again, I published an article critical of the idea, called "Charity or Blackmail?", which came out in *El Cronista.* And now, as a direct consequence, General Ubico has gotten his revenge thanks to this trumped-up charge of poisoning. So I am dragged through the mud, while he is a saint. Even I must admit that his agents, who swarm throughout Central America in pursuit of his political enemies, are nothing if not astute.

Father, my life is in danger. To think that they are accusing me of killing Marta, my guardian angel! Her personal doctor, who treated her for frequent menstrual hemorrhaging, was present at her death-bed. He diagnosed her death as a sudden attack of blackwater fever (a dangerous tropical fever, "laverania malariae" caused by eggs deposited in the victim's bloodstream by the malaria mosquito. Señorita Contreras died of the same disease—it is very common in low-lying areas such as this, where the heavy rains provide a perfect breeding ground for the insects. The cause of her death was also confirmed by the doctor who signed the death certificate. I wish I could send you a copy of this, but I have access to nothing. Simply getting paper to write to you was a major triumph.

The prosecution alleges that I gave Señorita Contreras a chicken leg poisoned with strychnine at 8 p.m., as a result of which she died at one o'clock the following morning. How ridiculous! How could anyone not only retain strychnine in their stomach for so many hours, but converse calmly all that time with another person, in this case, me? Even more absurd is the idea that anyone could take a bite of a chicken leg sprinkled with strychnine and then chew and swallow it. Wouldn't they have spat it out at once because of its characteristic taste of bitter almonds?

Don Carmen (he was the one who used to change your dollar cheques into the local currency for me), also died of blackwater fever. I saw him die—he died in my arms—and he had none of the symptoms of strychnine poisoning: palpitations, irregular breathing, muscular spasms, feelings of distress, hypersensitivity to light, or acute awareness of sounds and any bodily contact. He had the misfortune of being attended not by a competent doctor but by a charlatan by the name of Salmerón. He had already decided his patient had been poisoned, and consequently did nothing more than extract his stomach juices. But if Salmerón truly believed this, why did he not have the decency to try to save Don Carmen's life by using such well-tried medical methods as emetics (hot water, ipecacuanha, apomorphine) or charcoal tablets, ether,

> chloroform, or injections of oil of camphor? This man is now among my fiercest accusers, so you can see how clumsy the plot is, and how I must be innocent of all the charges.
>
> All their vile accusations are based on coincidence: the fact that they both cause convulsions. And anyway, uremic intoxication also causes them, although they make no mention of that fact. Father, look what all this has done to me: now I've even become an expert in toxicology.
>
> You must make a sacrifice for me, father. You, Uncle Chema, grandma Luz, Doctor Delgadillo and Pancho must be able to raise a thousand dollars between you. That would be enough to pay for the eminent attorney Ramón Romero to act in my defence. My brother Gustavo will have to bring the money in person: if you send it to me, it will be confiscated. The judge, with whom I never got on even when we were students together, has all my letters intercepted. Please cable Señor Romero in Managua asking him to take my case, and promising that his fee will follow. If you fail me, I shall have to defend myself, and then God knows what will happen. You cannot let me die so far from home! You must save me, father—please do all I ask as speedily as you can. Farewell.

Doctor Atanasio Salmerón, whose tenacity as a detective will become abundantly clear in these pages, undertook a thorough investigation of Oliverio Castañeda's past. He was greatly aided in this by an assiduous correspondent from Guatemala City: Carlos Enrique Larrave, the editor of *El Liberal Progresista*, the official organ of General Jorge Ubico's party.

These letters, carefully classified in Doctor Salmerón's dossier on Castañeda, confirm that he did indeed attend the Instituto Nacional de Oriente in Chiquimula, as he told Rosalío Usulutlán. But they add a fresh element: he was expelled from the institute in 1925.

It would appear that Castañeda joined some other students to organize a secret 'Ubico Club' in support of the coup d'état then being hatched to bring General Ubico to power as president. But shortly afterwards, according to Larrave, Castañeda betrayed the group by naming his companions to the authorities. Larrave, at that time a trigonometry teacher at the institute, was the moving spirit behind the formation of the club. His damning letters years later, when Castañeda was facing the poisoning charges in Nicaragua, give some idea of the reasons why he was so scathing about him. The following are a few paragraphs taken from just one of them:

> Even as an adolescent, Castañeda seemed naturally inclined to mock and betray others. He spent all his time and energy devising cruel practical jokes for his own amusement. I can recall one such instance: the staff-room at the Chiquimala Institute, and all teachers were supposed to meet there before school and during break-times, before proceeding to the classrooms.
>
> These rooms were on the first floor, and to reach them we had to go down a staircase with a black, varnished handrail. Our geometry teacher, Señorita Margarita Carrera, always rested her hand on the rail all the way down the stairs. Castañeda must have noticed this, and was heartless enough to repeatedly daub the handrail with excrement, so skillfully that it was almost invisible.
>
> Thanks to this low trick, Margarita's hand always smelled foully, although she could not think why. She took to scrubbing her hand obsessively, but to no avail. In her class, she would constantly raise it to her nose, with a look of despair on her face. In the end, she had a nervous breakdown, and was forced to leave the institute.
>
> Do not be at all surprised therefore that this same individual is now responsible for treacherous crimes that require the use of poison. A poisoner combines the spirit of a traitor—something this man has been since his early days—with that of a torturer—someone who takes pleasure in seeing others suffer. In addition, Castañeda is an incorrigible fantasist. Having never achieved anything in politics in Guatemala, he likes to portray himself as being persecuted by the new regime of peace and order under the wise and prudent guidance of General Jorge Ubico. Castañeda claims to have been the founder of a political "party" here, pompously styled the "Democratic Salvation" party. Its constitution claims it enjoys the "active

> support of peasants, workers, young people, and women..." Yes, and of children and babies as well, I have no doubt...The fact is, there were only ever two members of this so-called party: Castañeda the poisoner, and another agitator of the same ilk, the "journalist" Clemente Marroquín Rojas. Who was it their "salvation" was destined for? Their party had only victims. The first of these was Don Rafael Ubico Zebadua, who was murdered by Castañeda in Costa Rica in 1929, also with strychnine.

There can be little doubt that Castañeda turned against General Ubico in a way that made Larrave his sworn enemy. As he himself stated in response to questions on 28 October 1933, when he returned to Guatemala six months earlier following the death of his wife, he took part in underground plotting against the Ubico regime, and was even involved in arms trafficking to that end. He admitted as much to Don Fernando Guardia Oreamuno during a train journey to the port of Puntarenas, swearing him to secrecy. We shall return to this event subsequently.

This was the reason why, as he claimed to *El Cronista*, he was expelled from Guatemala. In June 1933 he was ordered to leave the country within ten days, this period subsequently being reduced to a mere forty-eight hours. Although there appears to be no evidence that he was in fact plotting against President Ubico, it is true that Castañeda founded an anti-Ubico party, called the Democratic Salvation party, and that the other founder was Clemente Marroquín Rojas, editor of *La Hora* newspaper.

The final paragraph of Larrave's letter may also help explain his change of heart with regard to his former pupil and fellow conspirator. This concerns the sudden death of Rafael Ubico Zebedúa on 22 November, 1929. He was a nephew of the general who a few years later was to seize power in Guatemala. The background to this is as follows:

If Castañeda really was expelled from the Chiquimula Institute, he was somehow reinstated, since he passed his end of school exams there in December 1926. That same month he moved to Guatemala City, where a short while later he was appointed to a position in the Ministry of Education. At that time, Don José María

Orellana was still president of the country. A staunch opponent of General Ubico's, it was he who, according to Larrave, had personally ordered the closure of the 'Ubico Club' at the institute.

In 1927, Hugo Cerezo Dardón was under-secretary for public education. It was as a result of his sudden death that Castañeda, only eighteen years old, took up the position. In another of his letters to Doctor Salmerón, Larrave assured him that his appointment to the Ministry of Education and his rapid promotion to under-secretary were a reward from President Orellana for having betrayed his colleagues in the 'Ubico Club'.

According to one of the witnesses at Castañeda's trial, he often liked to make sly jokes about the mysterious death of his predecessor, under-secretary Cerezo Dardón. During a stay at the Poneloya beach resort organized by the Contreras family in 1932, Castañeda shared a bedroom with Don Carmen Contreras' brother, Luis Gonzaga Contreras, from the city of Granada. In his statement on oath before the Granada District Criminal Court on 21 October 1933, Gonzaga Contreras relates what he claims he was told by Castañeda one night in Poneloya about the circumstances surrounding Cerezo's death:

> The witness declares that during the afore-mentioned holiday, Oliverio Castañeda let him into a secret about the death years earlier in Guatemala of someone by the name of Cerezo, who had been his superior at the Ministry of Education. According to Castañeda, Cerezo was a methodical, hard-working man who breakfasted at first light each morning, and then went to his office, arriving by six a.m. Since neither the doorman nor any of the other employees arrived at such an early hour, he would let himself in with his own key and then shut himself in his office to work alone at his desk for an hour. He would then appear in the doorway to hand out the day's schedule for his staff.
>
> On the day in question, when Cerezo did not appear at the usual time, and knowing that he was in his office since his hat and cane were in the coat-stand, his assistants forced their way into his office. Cerezo lay dead at

his desk, face down among his papers. Ink from the inkwell by his forehead had spilled over files and documents like a bloodstain. However, there was no sign of foul play, and as far as anyone knew, Cerezo had no illnesses. And he had been all alone in his office… "How could he have died? How would you explain a case like that?" the witness recalls Castañeda asking him insistently, with what he described as a "mocking gleam in his eye". The witness felt no great desire to resolve the mystery, and indeed felt sickened by the whole business, and so said nothing. Castañeda however kept returning to the topic, embellishing his account with a wealth of detail and adding fresh speculation and suspense.

The witness goes on to state that it was only when the party returned to León after their trip to Poneloya that he learned from his brother the circumstances surrounding the death of Castañeda's wife a few weeks earlier. This greatly increased his fears about Castañeda, although his concerns were not apparently shared by any of the others in the family. He himself so mistrusted Castañeda by this time that he refused to travel with him to visit a family friend, Don Enrique Gil, in Chichigalpa, as suggested by Don Carmen Contreras. Don Carmen, far from crediting that the young Guatemalan was a dangerous trickster, always wrote of him to his brother in Granada in the most glowing terms.

It would appear, therefore, that the young man in mourning dancing the foxtrot so provocatively before the admiring gaze of the two blushing sisters is a great one for mystery. Further evidence of this is not hard to find in his case file. When Castañeda had first arrived in Costa Rica, and before the death of his friend Rafael Ubico Zebedúa, the newspapers in San José were full of talk about the 'Ghosts in the Guatemalan Legation' scandal. According to *La República* in reports published between 18 and 27 July 1929, strange noises were heard night after night from the second storey of the Victorian-style wooden detached house situated in the Barrio Amón neighbourhood. (A photograph accompanies the text). Pebbles were thrown onto the roofs of neighbouring houses; faucets started running by themselves; toilets flushed when nobody was in the bathrooms; lights were switched on and off. The panic grew so great that the national police had to be called. In his report to the Minister of the Interior dated 2 August 1929, Colonel Alberto Cañas Escalante, head of the National Investigation Corps, makes it clear he regarded Oliverio Castañeda as responsible for all the trouble:

> In accordance with instructions, I sent several of my men to the house in question. They confirmed that several stones were thrown one night. On hearing this, I went personally to the Legation to take charge of the investigation.
>
> I assembled the entire diplomatic staff and embassy employees on the ground floor. I was able to observe Oliverio Castañeda closely. His somber, eccentric appearance, his piercing but shifty gaze, and his habit of lowering his eyebrows whenever he spoke disturbed me greatly. Neither his educated ways nor his apparently polite manner could compensate for these traits.
>
> I spoke about the "poltergeists" to him and Señor Ubico, trying to convince them they must be the work of some unstable person or persons. I stationed several of my men around the house to keep it under surveillance; shortly afterwards another shower of stones could be heard. When I looked for Castañeda, I found he had disappeared. Soon there was the noise of a struggle coming from upstairs. I was about to go up to the second floor, when Castañeda came panting down the staircase. His hair was disheveled, his shirt torn, and he had scratches all over his torso. He was staring wide-eyed, and had the look of a madman. He claimed to have been attacked by a thickset individual who had run off when he fought back. When I pressed him, he was unable to give more precise answers, and contradicted himself more than once. Despite this, he maintained a surprisingly cool, self-confident manner. I scarcely need add there were no further reports of any noises or stone-throwing from the Legation. I therefore closed the case, since I was personally satisfied that Señor Castañeda was the person responsible for the entire affair.

After the death of Rafael Ubico, Castañeda was transferred to the Guatemalan Legation in Managua for several months. He returned to Guatemala in February 1930. Larrave maintains that Castañeda was assigned to Managua simply to remove him from Costa Rica because of the strong suspicions surrounding his friend's death. However, Castañeda himself claims he had to leave Nicaragua after only a short time because he became engaged to his future wife, Marta Jerez.

When Castañeda arrived in Managua in December 1929, he took lodgings in the 'Petit Trianon' boarding house on Calle Candelaria, owned by Doña Roxana Lacayo. Also staying there at this time were the Honduran ambassador, Roberto Suazo Tomé; the young editor of *La Prensa* newspaper, Luis Armando Rocha Urtecho; and the magician Reginaldo Moncriffe. An extract from the deposition made by Doña Roxana Lacayo reads as follows:

> Castañeda loved playing practical jokes on his fellow lodgers, for example hiding their clothes or shoes. One evening, Ambassador Suazo was unable to attend a gala ball at the Managua Club because his newly-cleaned tuxedo had vanished. Castañeda insisted Moncriffe must have done it, as he was the expert in making things disappear. Several days later, the tuxedo was found by workmen clearing out the attic. A note was pinned to the lapel, which read: "Greetings from the Severed Hand". This was a reference to a severed hand that featured in a popular horror film then playing in Managua cinemas.
>
> I tried to show Castañeda how irresponsible his behaviour was, but he simply replied: "I'm young, señora, and young people have to have a bit of innocent fun. I'll know how to behave when 'the snows of time have turned my locks to silver'." These last words were from the Argentine tango "Going Back".
>
> In addition, Castañeda would frequently hide the ventriloquist dummies and other props that Moncriffe needed for his magician's act. Things went too far the day Señor Suazo's wallet, which contained U.S. dollars, also disappeared. The empty wallet was finally found beneath Moncriffe's bed; at the time he was performing at

> Doña Chepita Toledo's private school. I felt obliged to call in the U.S. Marines. When they arrived, they set off in search of Moncriffe. They arrested the poor man in front of the entire school, but did not find a single dollar on him. Although he was released from custody shortly afterwards, his reputation suffered badly. I felt very sorry indeed for him when I discovered him sitting on his bed with his dummy Don Roque, asking him sadly: "We're not thieves, are we, old friend?" "Not a bit of it, Reginaldo, we are poor but we are honest."
>
> The journalist Rocha Urtecho blamed the theft on Castañeda, and in the days following this unfortunate affair, the two men stopped speaking to one another. I was inclined to agree with him, because I had seen Castañeda spending a fortune on flowers for several young ladies in Managua, an extravagance his salary from the Guatemalan Legation could not possibly permit him. He was also always late in paying me for his board and lodging.

Rocha Urtecho admitted his enmity towards Castañeda in his deposition to the judge dated 8 November 1933. He also took the opportunity to add further unfavourable opinions about the defendant:

> The witness would have preferred not to respond on this matter, but since the law must be obeyed, he wishes to state that he found it necessary to curtail his friendship with Castañeda a few weeks before the latter returned to Guatemala. Although this split was not directly connected to the robbery of which the magician Moncriffe was falsely accused, this incident served to confirm his view of Castañeda. He had no doubt it was Castañeda who had put the wallet under Moncriffe's bed.
>
> Frequently, the witness further stated, Castañeda would make disparaging remarks about persons of the female sex whom they were acquainted with, and who held Castañeda in an esteem bordering on worship. Also, despite their apparent friendship, the witness found himself the butt of one of Castañeda's perverse fantasies. He was

not willing to divulge the names of those concerned, but it involved him and a newly-married young woman.

But he was the victim of a worse deception, Rocha Urtecho stated, which he wished to describe in detail as it was typical of Castañeda's behaviour. One evening, when he and the defendant were dining in the Café Florido, a very fashionable restaurant in Managua in those days, Castañeda suddenly raised his hands to his face. He asked Urtecho to get up from the table, dragged him over to a corner, and begged him to leave the restaurant there and then. Once they were out in the street, Castañeda confessed that a young woman with whom he was having an affair had come into the restaurant on the arm of her husband, who had got wind of their relationship and sent Castañeda a letter vowing to kill him.

The very next day, the witness had been astonished to hear from Ambassador Suazo the very different version of the incident that Castañeda had given him. Castañeda claimed he had been forced to leave the Café Florido not because of a jealous husband, but because he, Rocha Urtecho was a spy for the U.S. Marines whose task was to report back on everything that the Nicaraguan politicians he interviewed as a journalist confided to him. Castañeda told the ambassador he had been ashamed to be seen sitting with Urtecho by a group of people who had come into the restaurant and knew him to be a spy.

The witness saw this as an unwarranted slur on his honour. He therefore went immediately to the Guatemalan Legation, to register a formal protest against Castañeda to Ambassador Doctor José Luis Balcarcel. As he entered the legation premises, Castañeda himself came out to greet him. "Poor Balcarcel isn't in this world, he's in the next," he told him, explaining he was under the influence of large dose of cocaine. If Urtecho insisted on going into his office, he would find the ambassador writhing naked on the floor like a lunatic. If the matter were truly urgent, he should return that evening, by which time the effects of the drug would have worn off.

Horrified at the thought, the witness did not even think

> to reprimand Castañeda for his earlier tissue of lies, but left the building at once. He had scarcely gone fifty yards when he saw Ambassador Balcarcel at the wheel of his motor car—further proof, if any were needed, that no one was safe from the perverse snares of a man whom the witness had no hesitation in describing as utterly depraved.

'Sing You Sinners' comes to an end on the Victrola. The young man in mourning appears at his doorway, fanning himself with his hat. He smiles across the street in the direction of the two sisters. They blush even more intensely, and bury their heads in the pages of the fashion magazine, pretending they have not noticed him. To their astonishment, Castañeda now strolls across the road, still fanning himself, and comes up to introduce himself to them.

María del Pilar, the younger of the two, barely fourteen at the time, commits a serious breach of etiquette by standing up and shaking hands with the visitor. She should have remained in her rocking-chair, her elder sister Matilde reproaches her over dinner, when all the talk is of the newcomers at the hotel.

Matilde tells the rest of the family that the young man was perspiring freely, his face bright red from his exertions with the foxtrot. What she neglects to mention is that while she and her sister were shyly exchanging a few polite words with him, his young wife had come to the door of their hotel room and was gazing across at them with a harsh, unsmiling look.

Harsh, unsmiling, Marta Jerez raises a small medallion of the Christ of Esquipulas to her lips and bites it.

CHAPTER SIX

An Infant Jesus of Prague Disappears

IN THE 1930s, the city of León boasted few decent hotels. More common were family-run boarding-houses offering rooms for out-of-town students and commercial salesmen. There were two or three of these near the Pacific Railway station, handy for passengers forced to wait for connections north to the port of Corinto or south to the capital, Managua, or for the less numerous travellers to El Sauce cattle country. The inauguration of this line in 1932, one of President José María Moncada's last initiatives, was delayed by an attack by Sandinista forces commanded by General Juan Pablo Umanzor.

The Casa Prío, standing opposite the cathedral and looking onto Plaza Jerez, had a few rooms to let on its top floor. These were habitually taken by patients visiting the city for treatment from its many renowned medical practitioners. The Casa Prío had seen better days: the poet Rubén Darío himself had stayed in its best, most airy room during his triumphant 1907 visit to Nicaragua. Night after night, enthusiastic serenaders had gathered beneath his balcony, until the sleep-starved poet had begged them to stop.

When Captain Prío inherited the business from his father, he all but abandoned the top floor and chose instead to develop the ground floor. He opened an ice-cream parlour, a bar, billiard tables, and a restaurant which also delivered meals to customers' homes. One of the chief users of this service was Doctor Juan de Dios Darbishire, the captain's godfather.

We already know that Rosalío Usulutlán and Cosme Manzo went to the Casa Prío after the cinema on 18 June 1932. We also know that the members of the 'accursed table', presided over by Doctor Atanasio Salmerón, met here regularly.

The Metropolitan, situated on the corner of Primera Avenida and Tercera Calle Norte, a block from the university, was in fact the only real hotel in the city. It was a two-storey building dating from the turn of the century, whose two wings spread out north and east from the corner occupied by its bar-restaurant. It was here in that memorable year of 1907 that the León Atheneum offered a banquet in honour of Rubén Darío, thus earning it a place in history, providing one draws a veil over the unfortunate detail that the prince of Spanish literature, more than a little in his cups, never actually turned up.

The rear of the hotel's ground floor, which gave onto the courtyard, held the guests' dining room, enclosed by a lattice screen, and the verandah, with scattered armchairs and rocking chairs. The hotel kitchens, bathrooms and toilets were at the far end of a second yard. To the front, there were a number of spacious rooms facing onto the street. These were divided by wooden partitions into bedrooms and living rooms, and each had their own bathroom. These rooms were let to long-term guests, and as we have seen, it was into one of these that Oliverio Castañeda and his wife Marta Jerez moved in March 1931.

Short-term guests were given rooms on the first floor of the hotel, reachable by a wooden staircase with a fleur-de-lys wrought-iron banister. There were a dozen of these rooms, all of them with a double window onto the street. The mock Gothic arches painted above each window, joined above by one larger arch, were the hotel's distinguishing feature.

The Contreras family home lay diagonally across the street from the Metropolitan Hotel. It was a one-storey abode with a tiled roof. The corner door, outside which we have already met the two Contreras sisters, led directly into the living room. It was from here that Don Carmen emerged on the day the dogs were poisoned.

The living-room furniture included: one Marshall & Wendell grand piano; a set of six Louis XV style chairs, covered in red silk; one full-length mirror in a gilt frame; and one Philco radio shaped like the portico of a Gothic cathedral. We know this from the inventory for an auction announced by Don Carmen's widow Flora in the local newspapers on 3 November 1933.

The family bedrooms lay along the west wall of the house. The upper half of their wooden doors were protected by decorative grilles painted green. The first bedroom was occupied by Don Carmen and his wife; the next was shared by the two sisters; Carmen Junior slept in the last one. However, this arrangement was soon to be disturbed. To the rear, all these bedrooms gave onto a verandah that ran alongside the garden, whose dense foliage offered pleasant shade to the whole house. A set of Viennese chairs and the previously encountered rocking chairs made up the furniture on the verandah. In a niche by the door leading into the living room, a plaster statue of the Infant Jesus of Prague with a tin crown encrusted with imitation jewels was kept under lock and key.

The doors along the southern wing of the house all led into the La Fama store, owned by Don Carmen and run by his wife. The range of fabrics sold there was among the widest to be found in León: for men, fine wools and worsteds, linens, and gabardines; chiffons, calicos, taffetas and silks for women. The store also offered perfumes and toilet requisites at the most competitive prices, as well as china and glassware. Another section sold beverages —muscatel wines, cordials and different aniseed-flavoured drinks. La Fama was also the sole distributor of Vichy Celestins medicinal water.

The internal corridor on this side of the house contained the offices of C. Contreras and Co. The company undertook a wide range of commercial enterprises, including the importing of goods wholesale and the export of salted hides, molasses and nambar sugarcane and mangrove timber. The accounts for the Metropolitan Water Company were also kept here. These offices were separated from the family quarters by a wooden partition. The only people who had permission to use the door in this partition were Don Carmen and, whenever he needed to go to the toilet, his brother Evenor, the chief book-keeper. The other clerks and employees were forbidden to cross into the family area—although, as we shall see, they could occasionally make out something of what was going on behind the screen.

The Contreras house was similar in architecture and layout to others belonging to the well-to-do families of León: most of them also divided the rooms between those reserved for the family and others where business was carried out. In fact, nothing untoward had ever happened in this particular dwelling, until that is, Oliverio Castañeda and his wife moved in on 18 November 1932.

Don Carmen Contreras was the majority shareholder of both C. Contreras and Co., and the Metropolitan Water Company. His brother and his father, Don Carmen Contreras Largaespada, who was the most important printer in the city, were the other partners. As well as this house and the La Fama store, Don Carmen owned a holiday home in the resort of Poneloya, and the Nuestro Amo dairy farm situated on the metalled road between León and Poneloya.

The two-storey farmhouse at Nuestro Amo had in the past been used as a weekend home, but had fallen into disrepair after the death of Don Carmen's elder sister Matilde Contreras Reyes, following a lengthy battle with consumption. This ranch, with a balcony that looked out towards the sea, visible as a narrow, shining strip beyond the fields and hummocks of the farm and the coastal mangrove swamps, was destined to play an important part in our story.

Although considered a wealthy man in León, the gossip around the 'accursed table' had it that his business ventures were in trouble. He owed a large sum of money to his close friend Don Esteban Duquestrada; he was behind in his payments to his foreign suppliers; and the Nuestro Amo ranch had been mortgaged to the Banco Nacional. This was seen as the reason why he was so keen to push through the new and much more favourable contract for the Metropolitan Water Company, and also why there were certain undisclosed items in his firm's accounts, as came to light towards the end of Castañeda's trial.

As has been noted, Oliverio Castañeda and his wife Marta Jerez left their room at the Metropolitan Hotel on 18 November 1932. They crossed their street with their trunks, suitcases and cardboard boxes—not forgetting the precious Victrola gramophone. Why did they quit the hotel? Whose idea was it? In his statement of 11 October 1933, Castañeda maintains that:

> Shortly after moving into their rooms at the Metropolitan Hotel, chance proximity led them quickly to establish

> a cordial friendship with the Contreras family. Not only did they soon fall into the habit of taking Sunday lunch at the Contreras' home, but both he and his wife were regularly asked to take part in family celebrations such as name days and birthdays. They also received invitations to participate in social gatherings held at the homes of the Contreras family's friends and relations.
>
> During one of Doña Flora's visits to the couple at the hotel, she impressed upon them how important it was for them to keep up their contacts more regularly in the city. Since this was hardly possible from their hotel rooms, she offered them a place in her own home: her whole family was in agreement. They would have to pay only half of what they were being charged at the hotel. She insisted so much that in the end, considering how generous and kind the Contreras family had always been towards them, the couple had accepted her offer.

For his part, Don Carmen's brother Evenor Contreras Reyes, aged forty-five, chief book-keeper at C. Contreras and Co., made the following deposition on 16 October 1933:

> The witness declares that he would be lying if he said that the Castañeda couple's move to his brother's home had not been welcomed by the entire family. The new guests were splendidly received and treated with the closeness normally reserved for family members. Despite his withdrawn, often surly nature, his brother had placed an inordinate degree of trust in Castañeda. He had confided delicate business matters to him, allowing him to peruse his account books and even to watch him open the firm's safe, which he would not permit anybody, not even the witness, to see. When on one occasion he pointed out how unwise this was, his brother had rebuked him sharply.
>
> The witness adds that his brother liked to sit and talk with Castañeda in the living room or the verandah after meals. Don Carmen invited him to the Social Club, and in return Castañeda would take him for a drink at the Metropolitan Hotel, the Casa Prío or less wholesome places

> frequented by students. Although his brother did not often enjoy this kind of outing, he willingly accepted Castañeda's invitations. More than once, Doña Flora took her husband to task for these visits, and also made it clear to Castañeda that she did not like him taking Don Carmen to these places. The young man invariably made some witty remark that made Doña Flora laugh and forget her annoyance.

Encouraged by this change of heart in Don Carmen, the witness once asked him to have a lunchtime drink at Micaela Peluda's bar. His brother replied curtly that he had a headache, but this was not true, as the witness could see Castañeda waiting for him at the dining table with cold beer and a snack. The two of them then sat down to eat their lunch, and even though his brother could see he was still in the house, he did not invite him to join them.

However, in his statement of 1 December 1933, Carmen Contreras Guardia, a twenty-year-old student, contradicted his uncle's assertion that the Contreras family unanimously welcomed the Castañedas in their home:

> JUDGE: In your view, was the entire family pleased that Oliverio Castañeda was living at your parents' house?
>
> WITNESS: I was always against Castañeda and his wife moving into our home. More than once I told my parents of my concern at having a stranger in our midst, and even though I got on well with his wife, both myself and the rest of my family felt relieved when the couple decided to move elsewhere.
>
> JUDGE: What were your reasons for taking against Castañeda in this way?
>
> WITNESS: I always considered him to be a dangerous, untrustworthy individual, someone capable of using all his wiles to persuade, seduce and deceive. I now understand for example why he was so keen on me going to study in Costa Rica: separating me from my family was all part of his plan. From the moment he entered our house, he tried to convince my parents to send me to San José, doubtless so that I would not be in the way when the

moment arrived to put his criminal scheme into practice.

JUDGE: What were the circumstances which led to Oliverio Castañeda moving into your family home?

WITNESS: A few days prior to their move, Castañeda and his wife rushed in to tell me and my sisters that Lieutenant Fonseca, a National Guard officer also staying at the Metropolitan Hotel, was threatening to report them to the authorities as suspected Communists and Sandinistas. They begged us to hide some dangerous books and pamphlets on their behalf. We agreed, and said nothing to our parents.

Several days after this, Castañeda implored my mother to take them in. He said he was very worried that the National Guard could harass his wife while he was absent from the hotel. My mother replied that we could not offer them any luxuries, and that they would have to make do like the rest of us. She said we did not have enough rooms for the couple to be able to stay in comfort, but since Castañeda kept on insisting, she finally agreed.

JUDGE: During the couple's stay, did you notice anything unusual about Oliverio Castañeda's behaviour?

WITNESS: Indeed I did. I grew increasingly suspicious of him, for things that seemed insignificant at the time but which I can now appreciate in their true light. For example, I recall how shortly after he moved in, a statue of the Infant Jesus of Prague vanished from its niche in the corridor. This mystified all of us, as my mother was the only person who had a key to its cabinet. On a hunch, I directly accused Castañeda of stealing the statue. To our surprise, the very next day the Infant Jesus reappeared back in its place. There is no doubt in my mind that Castañeda had intended to steal the statue, but returned it when he saw I was suspicious.

JUDGE: If you and your family were so glad to see Castañeda leave the house after this, why did you allow him to stay a second time?

WITNESS: Because on the same day that his wife died, when we all went to pay our respects, he started harping on to my mother about how he felt so bereft at Marta's death that he could not bear to spend another night all alone in the place where they were then living. He carried on so much that my mother felt obliged to take him on once more.

I am convinced that he poisoned his wife because he did not love her, and that he rented a house on his own with Marta so that nobody would be present when he administered the strychnine poison. I am sure his plan was to return to our house immediately afterwards so that he could pursue his evil plans. He was determined to get rid of us one by one until he was left free to marry María del Pilar and lay his hands on our family fortune.

JUDGE: Do you know whether Castañeda and your sister María del Pilar were engaged to be married?

WITNESS: I cannot be certain of it. However, I can say that even when his wife Marta was alive, he behaved towards María del Pilar in ways I found extremely distasteful.

JUDGE: Could you elaborate?

WITNESS: He would sneak glances at María del Pilar during our meals together. He would cut up her meat on his own plate, and keep the best slices for her if she were late in coming to table—that kind of thing.

JUDGE: Were you ever aware that this special attention upset your other sister, Matilde?

WITNESS: Matilde was always inclined to be fussy and rather stand-offish, and so I find it hard to say whether Castañeda's attitude towards María del Pilar upset her or not. But now I know that the scoundrel was trying to win the hearts of both my sisters at a time when his own wife was still alive and present, I should not be in the least surprised if Matilde had suffered on his account.

JUDGE: Can you tell the court whether it is true that your sister Matilde used to accompany Castañeda to visit his wife's grave in the Guadalupe cemetery?

WITNESS: Yes, your honour, she did accompany him, because he asked her to. They used to ride in my father's buggy, and take flowers cut from our garden.

These allegations, part of a much longer testimony to which we will have occasion to return, were made by Don Carmen's son in the presence of Oliverio Castañeda, who was in the courtroom waiting to continue his response to the formal charges being made against him. An altercation broke out between the two men. The poet and journalist Manolo Cuadra, a special correspondent sent by *La Nueva Prensa* newspaper of Managua to cover the trial, described this in the 3 December 1933 edition:

> COURTROOM DRAMA FLARES
>
> The accused was not asked to leave the room when Don Carmen's son began his testimony. This oversight, which we point out here with all due respect for our friend Judge Mariano Fiallos, led to an unseemly argument that was only to be expected given the mutual antipathy between Oliverio Castañeda and the witness. Castañeda began by objecting to references the young man was making about his behaviour. Judge Fiallos simply called him to order with a reminder that under the provisions of the code for criminal trials, no defendant had the right to intervene when another person was giving evidence. However, when the witness declared that on one occasion Castañeda had encouraged him to try cocaine in order to seduce women, the defendant burst out laughing so loudly that the witness leapt from his seat and attempted to come to blows with him.
>
> Eventually, Castañeda was removed from the courtroom and made to wait outside in the corridor until the witness had finished his declaration. As he was being led out, Judge Fiallos could not prevent Castañeda shouting out loud: 'If I am such an evil, corrupting and perverse criminal, why did you send a cable to General Somoza calling for my release from prison?' This sally drew thunderous applause from the gaggle of Castañeda's supporters who congregated daily in the courtroom.
>
> Out in the corridor, these supporters crowded round the defendant and congratulated him on what one of them described as the 'gag' he had shut the Contreras boy up with. As usual, they then offered Castañeda drinks and food as it was almost lunchtime.

The question raised by Oliverio Castañeda as he was being taken from the courtroom was undoubtedly a pertinent one. When he learned of his father's death, Carmen Contreras Guardia, then in the first year of his law studies at the University of Costa Rica, immediately flew back to Nicaragua on 11 October 1933, accompanied by his uncle, Don Fernando Guardia. Before leaving San José he had dispatched a telegram to the commander-in-chief of the Nicaraguan National Guard, General Anastasio Somoza. The telegram read:

> PROTEST UNJUST JAILING FINE YOUNG MAN OLIVERIO CASTAÑEDA. VALUED FAMILY FRIEND. BEG CONSIDER PETITION MOTHER, ORDER HIS IMMEDIATE RELEASE TO REASSURE ENTIRE FAMILY. SINCERELY YOURS
>
> CARMEN CONTRERAS GUARDIA

This cable, also published in *La Nueva Prensa*, had already been dissected by the members of the 'accursed table' on 13 October 1933. This was also the session at which Rosalío Usulutlán received approval from Doctor Salmerón to go ahead with the interview with Oliverio Castañeda in prison. This is how the interview came about:

'Take a look at this example of a brother-in-law's devotion,' said Cosme Manzo, passing a copy of *La Nueva Prensa* to Doctor Salmerón. 'And of smart journalism. Manolo Cuadra could teach Rosalío here a thing or two.'

'It's hypnotism,' said Doctor Salmerón, pushing the stub of the red and blue pencil behind his ear. 'Collective hypnotism of both sexes. First a telegram from the mother, then one from the son.'

'Ali Vanegas passes on tips to Manolo because they're both poets. He has it easy,' Rosalío Usulutlán protested, riled by Manzo's comment. Fiddling with his collar stud, he went on: 'But I'll show him with the interview I do.'

'Hypnotism couldn't explain Doña Flora's telegram begging for the turtledove to be released,' said Cosme Manzo, making a hypnotic pass with his hands in front of Rosalío Usulutláns face. 'Or the bunches of flowers she keeps sending him in jail. Or the colognes. And be careful the poet doesn't sneak in and interview him before you. He used to be in the National Guard, so they could well let him in first.'

'To be fair, María del Pilar also sends him flowers and colognes,' said Rosalío, pretending to close his eyes and swaying as if in a trance. 'One is as bad as the other. And don't worry about the interview—Captain Ortiz has promised me an exclusive.'

'That's why I said it was collective hypnotism,' Doctor Salmerón retorted, amused by the antics of his two friends. 'That Houdini fellow must be full of tricks if they still haven't woken up after he has done in half the family. As for your interview, Rosalío, I think it's a trap. They want something out of it.'

'Hypnotism my eye. All his magic is dangling between his legs,' said Cosme Manzo dismissively. He clapped his hands to bring Rosalío out of his trance. 'And trap or not, this is our star reporter's big opportunity. It's your chance too, doctor, to put any questions you have for Castañeda.'

'To blazes with the lot of you,' complained Captain Prío from his post by the cash register. 'You'll bring me nothing but trouble.'

CHAPTER SEVEN

A Storm of Jealousy in the January Sky

OLIVERIO Castañeda was in such poor shape at breakfast on the morning of 10 January 1933 that all the members of the Contreras family grew alarmed. His hand was shaking so much that he poured the coffee essence outside his cup of milk. They grew even more concerned when he left the table in tears and scurried off to the far end of the verandah. Doña Flora went after him to find out why he was so distraught.

He told Doña Flora it was because of the dreadful menstrual pains his wife suffered from. They had started up again in the small hours, and seemed worse than ever. Doña Flora did her best to soothe him. She sent her son Carmen to fetch the family doctor, Doctor Juan de Dios Darbishire, and told the cook to boil water for an infusion. Then she went into the couple's bedroom to personally take charge of the ailing woman.

While they waited for Doctor Darbishire to arrive, Castañeda, noticeably calmer by now, brought in a tray containing peeled oranges, bread and butter, and the infusion of bitter orange leaves that Doña Flora had recommended. Despite his and Doña Flora's entreaties, however, Marta refused to try anything.

Doctor Darbishire appeared shortly after eight o'clock wrapped in his silk cape. Don Carmen greeted him at the corner door, showed him to the couple's bedroom, then discreetly withdrew. The doctor asked the patient several questions, and listened to her chest. Doña Flora and Castañeda remained in the room, the latter succumbing to another attack of nerves and pestering the medical man with anxious enquiries.

In his deposition of 17 October 1933, Doctor Darbishire described the visit as follows:

> Once I had finished my examination, I called the husband over and assured him there was nothing to worry about. This was a problem common to many women during their period of menstruation. I recommended a few days' complete rest, warm hip baths with boric acid, and a course of Apiolina Chapoteaut pills, for which I wrote a prescription. However, since my thermometer showed that the patient also had a high temperature unusual in a case of this kind, I advised Castañeda to make sure his wife had a blood test, as I suspected his wife might have contracted malaria, which was rife in León. When the laboratory analysis of the blood sample confirmed my suspicions, I prescribed the normal treatment.

Questioned by the judge as to whether anything in his patient's behaviour had attracted his attention, the witness replied that he could not recall anything in particular, apart from one thing. Marta Jerez had taken advantage of both Castañeda and Doña Flora being absent from the room to ask him if he knew of any house available for rent. Concealing his surprise at such a question, as he scarcely knew the patient, he had replied that Doña Ercilia González, another patient of his, owned a house close to the university which had been recently vacated.

As Doctor Darbishire left his new patient that morning, enveloped once more in his silk cape and carrying his heavy leather bag, he could not think of any reason why Marta Jerez should have waited to be alone with him to ask such a question. But he walked on unconcerned, in the firm belief he was dealing with a simple case of menstrual discomfort complicated by the symptoms of another of the city's many cases of malaria. By the time he made his statement to the judge in October, however, he was aware why she had behaved in this way, but for reasons we shall discover subsequently, he chose to remain silent about the matter. Nor did he say anything in response to the judge's questioning about the couple.

The revealing testimony offered by a thirteen-year-old girl, Leticia Osorio, can help clarify this matter. She made her statement on 19 October 1933 to a courtroom full, as usual, of curious members of the public, journalists, and people involved in other cases.

Everyone present was astonished at how excellent the young girl's memory was.

> The witness went into service with the Contreras family in November 1932. She was employed by Señorita Matilde, at the wage of one cordoba per month, to assist the other servants in sweeping, mopping, and emptying chamber pots. An extra pair of hands was needed because some strangers were coming to live in the house.
>
> These strangers turned out to be Don Oliverio and his wife Doña Marta, both originally from Guatemala. They took over the young Don Carmen's room. He was obliged to sleep on a camp-bed in the living room, as no more bedrooms were available.
>
> Don Oliverio was always the first up in the morning. He would appear when the female servants were busy lighting the kitchen stove, take a pair of scissors, and cut jasmine, magnolias and gladioli from the garden. He would offer these to María del Pilar as she came out of the bathroom, head wrapped in a towel.
>
> Don Oliverio was also fond of writing poems to María del Pilar, in a silk-lined album with a clasp lock, the key to which she kept on a ribbon round her neck. In the evening, as soon as dinner was over María del Pilar would hand him the album to write fresh verses in. Afterwards, she would take it to her room to read alone in bed. She refused to show them to anyone, which greatly annoyed her sister Matilde.
>
> On Don Oliverio's birthday, María del Pilar had taken a bottle of cologne out of the La Fama window to give him. That afternoon, during the small party that Doña Flora had arranged, Doña Marta burst into tears when she saw Don Oliverio raising a handkerchief soaked in the scent to his nose. Snatching it from his hand, she ran to her room, sobbing bitterly.

When the judge interrupted to ask if she could recall the events of the day when Marta Jerez awoke haemorrhaging, Leticia Osorio had no hesitation in responding that she remembered it well, because that morning she had to empty out several chamber-pots full of blood. And although Don Oliverio had risen early as usual, he had not cut any flowers for María del Pilar, but instead had paced up and down like a caged animal, a worried frown on his face.

The events described in the servant girl's statement must have taken place between November 1932 and February 1933, since these were the months that the Castañeda couple stayed in the Contreras' house. The last incident, involving the bottle of cologne, must have taken place on 18 January 1933, Castañeda's birthday.

Leticia Osorio further stated that during the nights when Marta Jerez was ordered to stay in bed by Doctor Darbishire, it was Matilde who took her place and read legal codes and text books out loud to Castañeda, since he had been advised not to strain his eyes.

Deep into the night, the two of them would sit out in the jasmine-scented verandah on the very same rocking-chairs the Contreras sisters used to take out to the front door on sultry afternoons. While Matilde read to him, Oliverio would listen intently, gently rocking himself to and fro. Leticia Osorio would take them a pot of coffee with two cups, and then retire to her room in the yard beyond the kitchen, and fall asleep to the sound of Matilde reciting the law books with the breathless intonation of someone reading a romantic novel.

She told the court that she remembered how one night as she was passing Marta's room on her way to bed, she caught sight of her peering avidly through the lattice-work of the screen towards the verandah. Realizing she had been spotted, Marta had fled back to her room, trailing her white cotton nightdress like a lost soul.

On the evening of 20 October 1933, Oviedo the Balloon appeared at the 'accursed table'. He had become a regular there, even though its members had taken the lead in trying to prove his friend Castañeda's guilt. On this occasion, Doctor Salmerón jotted down in his notebook what Oviedo revealed that night. He told the others that it was at some point in January 1933, while the two of them were revising for their final law exam in one of the university corridors, that Castañeda took a love letter from María del Pilar out of a book and showed it to him.

'"Be careful, you're playing with fire," I told him,' explained Oviedo the Balloon, shaking a warning forefinger at the others, as he had done to Castañeda.

'The Devil isn't afraid of fire. The hotter the flames the better,' Cosme Manzo corrected Oviedo, a sly glint in his eye.

'"Fire is meant to burn," is what he told me, licking the letter as if it were a cake-spoon,' said Oviedo, returning Manzo's look. 'What did Oliverio have to fear?'

'What about the letter from Matilde they found among Castañeda's things after his arrest?' Doctor Salmerón is not interested in all this talk of fires and the Devil; what he wants to know about is Castañeda's love life.

'I had no notion of that,' Oviedo the Balloon replied, his jowls quivering as he shook his head violently. 'But seeing that they found it in a law book we were studying for the exam, it must have been written around the same time.'

'So he kept letters from the Contreras women in all his law books,' Cosme Manzo chuckled, glancing over at Doctor Salmerón to make sure he is writing down this new information.

'It's those letters the judge wants to question you about tomorrow,' said Rosalío Usulutlán, jostling Manzo's chair. 'He wants to know everything you told your friend Rodemiro the florist.'

'Manzo already knows he's not to say a word. He has to deny everything,' Doctor Salmerón insisted, rolling his pencil across the table towards Cosme. 'I'm the one who is going to tell the judge all he needs to know.'

'Of course I won't talk,' said Cosme Manzo, throwing up his hands in horror. 'And if I see that blabbermouth Rodemiro Herdocia, I'll shove his flowers up his backside, the louse.'

'Getting back to Matilde's letter,' said Doctor Salmerón, replacing the pencil stub behind his ear: 'Castañeda kept it in a law book, and that book was in the trunk he took with him to Guatemala. Does that mean he had the trunk with him in Costa Rica and then brought it back here?'

'No, he didn't take the trunk with him,' Oviedo corrected him with a broad smile. 'I stored it for him. When he returned, I gave it back to him with the rest of his things—his Victrola and his typewriter. I've already told you that. But what I want to know is, what exactly did Rodemiro tell the judge?'

'Things he'd heard from Manzo here about the letters and other confidential matters,' said Doctor Salmerón, feeling for his pencil and thumbing through his notebook. 'You're the blabbermouth, Manzo my friend, not Rodemiro.'

'Fancy swapping secrets with that pervert at your age,' sniggered Rosalío, jumping up from his chair in anticipation of Manzo's angry reaction.

'So if he left his trunk with you, that means he intended to come back all along,' Doctor Salmerón concluded. 'Anyway, what's all this talk about perverts? That's how these things start.'

He went on: 'According to our esteemed journalist friend here,' he paused, smiling at the trap he had prepared for Rosalío, 'it was around that time too that Don Carmen was endeavouring to find out who was behind a rumour besmirching his daughter Matilde's honour. What was the story exactly, Rosalío?'

'Someone was spreading the rumour that Matilde used to slip out of her house at night, and often didn't sleep there at all,' Rosalío reminded him, fiddling with his collar stud once more. 'It was said she would head for the Guadalupe cemetery, along with Noel Robelo. Ah, if those tombstones could only speak, what a tale they'd have to tell...'

At Doctor Salmerón's insistence, Rosalío repeated for the others round the table what he knew about Don Carmen's reaction to the rumours about Matilde:

One morning in January 1933, Rosalío had been busy in his office correcting some galley proofs when he was surprised to see the figures of Don Carmen and his close friend Don Esteban Duquestrada standing in the doorway. His first thought was that they must have come about the leaflets.

A few days earlier, using the pseudonym Presentación Armas, he had sent some leaflets to be printed by the Hermanos Cristianos. In them, he had launched a stinging attack on the new Water Company contract, accusing its owners of trying to bribe the city councillors to drop their opposition. Rosalío had been forced to print these leaflets after the owner of *El Cronista* had expressly forbidden him from carrying on his campaign in the newspaper.

Rosalío had become even more disturbed when he noticed that Don Carmen was armed. Don Esteban kept watch at the door, and as Don Carmen came over to talk him, Rosalío noticed a revolver poking out below the flap of his jacket. He grew even more alarmed when Don Carmen, his bald head shining and the back of his neck dusted with talcum, asked him straight out to tell him who was responsible for the slur on his daughter's name.

Rosalío had barely exchanged more than the occasional greeting with him before now. He at first strenuously denied any knowledge of the rumours. When the other man insisted, he finally conceded that he had heard something of the sort in the corridors of the courtroom, although he swore he had no idea who had started the lie. At this, Don Carmen left the newspaper office as downhearted as when he had arrived.

Doctor Salmerón had been waiting with amused impatience for Rosalío to finish his account. He then read out the statement Don Esteban Duquestrada (a rancher, married, forty-seven years old) had given to the judge two days previously, that is, on 18 October 1933:

> Around mid-January of the present year, Don Carmen got wind of the terrible rumour making the rounds of university students, legal employees, and even the León Social Club, of which both he and Don Carmen were members. The witness does not consider it appropriate to discuss the nature of this malicious rumour, beyond stating that it was an insult to the honour of Señorita Matilde Contreras (R.I.P.).
>
> Perturbed by the serious nature of the scurrilous gossip, Don Carmen had asked the witness to accompany him to find out who the author of it was. For several days the pair of them had questioned university students and visited the law courts and other public meeting places, but without result. Then somebody told them that Rosalío Usulutlán, editor-in-chief at *El Cronista*, was in the know. They therefore confronted him at his office, determined to make him talk.
>
> At first, the journalist had refused to tell them where the rumour had originated, but when he saw there was no way out, he had revealed to them the name of the person responsible. According to Usulutlán, this was none other than Oliverio Castañeda, who had told the whole story in vivid detail not only to the aforementioned journalist but

also to the clerk of the court Alí Vanegas over lunch at the Metropolitan Hotel at some date in January 1933.

In response to further questioning by the judge, the witness declared that yes, he had been astonished at Don Carmen's reaction upon learning this. Once he had uncovered the source of the gossip, he took no steps against the culprit, even though at the time he was living under his own roof. To the contrary, the very next day Don Carmen had asked the witness to appear before the governors of the law faculty to vouch for the good conduct of the said Castañeda, as a prerequisite for his final examination. Like it or not, the witness had felt compelled to comply.

To drive home his point, Doctor Salmerón then read out the statement by Alí Vanegas (single, twenty-five years old, a legal clerk) on 18 October 1933, shortly before he was replaced at the Castañeda trial:

Having read the statement by Rosalío Usulutlán, the witness concurred that it was indeed true that the said Usulutlán had informed him on the night of 18 June 1932 that he had identified Oliverio Castañeda and Octavio Oviedo y Reyes as the two men responsible for poisoning several dogs on Calle Real, including one belonging to Doctor Darbishire. This had provoked the doctor into setting about Oviedo with his cane, from which Vanegas had concluded it must have been these two men he had seen a short while earlier riding off at full tilt down the street in a horse-drawn buggy.

The judge then turned to another matter. He questioned the witness as to whether he was aware that some time previously a person or persons unknown had been spreading malicious gossip about Señorita Matilde Contreras. The witness answered in the affirmative. Pressed to reveal who that person was, and how and where the gossip had originated, the witness said that he had first heard the rumour from Oliverio Castañeda in the company of the aforementioned Usulutlán, one afternoon when the three of them were having a drink at the Metropolitan

> Hotel bar. Castañeda had made them promise not to repeat any of the details of the story to anyone, as he and his wife were staying in the Contreras' family home, and it might prove dangerous for them.
>
> The witness further declared that since he was being asked under oath to tell the whole truth, he no longer felt bound by his promise of silence. He therefore wished to state that in the month of January 1933, Oliverio Castañeda had assured them that Matilde Contreras often spent the night away from home, sneaking out secretly in the early hours. Under cover of darkness, she would open the street door of her bedroom without a sound and slip out, leaving the door on the latch so that she could return unnoticed before dawn.
>
> Castañeda had gone on to tell them that she would then go a block down the street to the spot where Noel Robelo would be waiting for her in his automobile. The two of them would then drive to the Guadalupe cemetery, where they would turn the tombstones into their nuptial bed.

'Aha! It looks as if you've been caught out,' Doctor Salmerón said in a tone of mock reproach to Rosalío Usulutlán, before bursting out laughing. 'You're a journalist, you should be the first to know what's going on in the courtroom. That's why Manolo Cuadra has the advantage over you.'

'So you were scared by Don Carmen, were you?' guffawed Cosme Manzo. 'Why did you lie to us, you old goat?'

'Yes, you're right, I did lie,' confessed Rosalío, beating his chest in a mea culpa. 'I had no option but to tell Don Carmen the truth. What else was I to do? But it was out of pity, not fear. I was saddened to see such a proud man so distraught.'

'What did he say when you told him?' asked Oviedo the Balloon, screwing up his eyes and measuring his man. He was still not convinced by this malicious gossip story.

'He didn't say anything,' replied Rosalío, his fist still pressed against his chest in contrition. 'He simply bit his lip and looked back at Don Esteban, who was still waiting for him in the doorway. Then the pair of them left without a word.'

'It must have all been one of Oliverio's little jokes: he's very fond of them,' said Oviedo the Balloon with a laugh they could all tell was forced.

'What kind of a joke do you call that?' Cosme Manzo snorted.

'As soon as they had gone, I seized a piece of paper,' Rosalío went on, hoping to escape their ridicule, 'and I wrote Castañeda a warning note. I gave it to one of the typesetters to take to him.'

'And I bet Castañeda wiped his backside with it,' chortled Cosme Manzo.

'He couldn't have given a damn,' Rosalío agreed, standing up as if to leave the table, but in fact only to emphasize what a waste of time his attempt to warn Castañeda had been. 'I came across him in the street a couple of days later. When I reminded him about the affair, all he did was laugh and say, "Listen, Don Chalio, forget all about that cemetery story. It's just one of my jokes—I'm always playing them on the Contreras family. They think they're great fun. Why don't we try to sort out the problem of your leaflet about the Water Company instead?"'

'See?' Oviedo the Balloon surveyed his friends in triumph. 'Didn't I tell you it was a joke?'

'But all your friends' jokes end up in the cemetery,' said Cosme Manzo, theatrically clasping Oviedo as if to comfort him for a death in the family.

'Aha! So Castañeda already knew about the leaflet. That means Don Carmen knew as well.' Doctor Salmerón scribbled this down, while asking Manzo to be quiet.

'Castañeda knew about it for sure,' said Rosalío, thrusting his hands behind his back and circling the table. '"Don't worry about how high the new charges seem, I'll make sure the blow is softened," he told me when I saw him. "I think it's outrageous too, but who can make Don Carmen see reason when there's money involved? So please, don't distribute that leaflet of yours."'

'Of course Don Carmen knew about the leaflets,' Cosme Manzo crowed, watching Rosalío pace round as though measuring the gaps between the bricks on the floor. 'And I bet he also knew about the deal Castañeda was offering you.'

'I agreed to it out of friendship,' said Rosalío, making sure he kept well out of Cosme Manzo's way. '"If you hand them out I'm done for," Castañeda told me. "I'll lose the cut I was going to make on the new contract. Why don't you let me have them instead?" he begged me.'

'Come over here, you old devil,' Manzo beckoned to Rosalío. 'Why don't you admit you took the money Castañeda was offering you?'

'You bet I did. When we went to collect the leaflets, I made sure he paid the printers.' Rosalío made as if to sit down again, then changed his mind. 'I wasn't going to lose my money, was I?'

'No sir. Those leaflets cost you twenty pesos. And he gave you eighty,' snarled Cosme Manzo, baring his fangs as if about to bite the journalist. 'And that wasn't Castañeda's money, it was Don Carmen's: the man you had been attacking in your newspaper.'

'That's enough,' Oviedo the Balloon insisted, raising his arms like a boxing referee counting someone out: 'what's the point going on and on about such a trivial matter?'

'Everything's either a joke or trivial to you,' Manzo complained, but he relaxed, and Rosalío Usulutlán edged his way back to the table.

To conclude this account of the stormy days early in 1933, let us return to the evidence given by the thirteen year-old serving girl Leticia Osorio:

> Early in February 1933, as she entered the Castañedas' bedroom one morning to take out the chamber-pot, she heard Doña Marta imploring her husband to remove her from that dreadful house. Don Oliverio tried to calm her, begging her to be quiet because others might hear her. He even put his hand over her mouth. This only made Marta shriek all the louder: "Let them hear me, let them hear me, I couldn't care less." Eventually Castañeda was forced to give in, and promised they would move if that would make her happy. By the time the witness reached under the bed for the pot, Doña Marta was laughing contentedly, as if she had never been crying.

So it was that on 8 February 1933 the young couple left the Contreras family home. They moved into the small house that Doctor

Darbishire had mentioned to Marta, next to the university. According to the cook, Salvadora Carvajal (single, aged approximately sixty), the Contreras family and all their servants were sorry to see them go. Carvajal provided her statement from the XXI precinct jail, where she was being held after the deaths because she was the one who prepared all the food for the Contreras family. She stated of this incident:

> There was a real sense of loss the day the Castañeda couple left. The atmosphere was like a funeral: nobody spoke, and even the work in the kitchen was carried out quietly. Only Don Carmen appeared at table for lunch. Both Matilde and María del Pilar claimed they were not hungry, and stayed in their rooms. No one in the kitchen had any appetite either.
>
> Even during the morning of their departure, Doña Flora was urging the couple to stay, at least until Don Oliverio had graduated, but Doña Marta appeared determined to leave there and then. She had packed all her things early that morning, and swept the empty room herself, not allowing any of the servants to do it for her.
>
> When she realized she could not get them to change their minds, Doña Flora, with tears in her eyes, filled a suitcase with bed linen and towels from her La Fama store. She added plates, cups, glasses, saucepans and a host of other things for their new house, which they were renting unfurnished. She also arranged for a serving girl, Dolores Lorente, to come from Nuestro Amo farm to help them out.

Five days later, at one in the afternoon of 13 February 1933, following hours of terrible convulsions, Marta Jerez died in the bedroom of the only house of her own that she had known in Nicaragua.

CHAPTER EIGHT

Would That Everyone Shone So Brightly

WHEN questioned in her cell in the XXI precinct jail, Salvadora Carvajal either did not know her age or was unwilling to reveal it to the judge; it was Alí Vanegas who guessed it must be around sixty and wrote this figure in the case dossier. Short and stocky, accustomed to carrying armfuls of wood for the kitchen stove, Salvadora walked several miles each morning from Subtiava, but was still in the Contreras family's kitchen before anyone was awake. There was not a single white hair in her shiny black locks, which she always adorned with a sprig of mignonette whenever she washed it.

By the age of eighteen she had finished with men. Tired of having to put up with drunks and ungrateful brawlers, she decided she wanted nothing more to do with any of them. It was soon after her final betrayal in love, when she was already the mother of four children, that she went into service as a cook for Doña Migdalia Reyes de Contreras, the mother of Don Carmen.

When Doña Flora arrived in León as a newly-wed, Salvadora was waiting for her in the only half-furnished house. She was a loan from Doña Flora's mother-in-law who, unhappy with her son's marriage and determined to show from the outset her doubts about Doña Flora's ability to run his household in a proper fashion, temporarily offered her one of her most valuable possessions. However, when some time later she called on her daughter-in-law to send the cook back, Doña Flora refused. This was the start of a long succession of arguments in the family.

When they came to arrest her on 10 October 1933, Salvadora kept the marines at bay with a lighted brand, and refused to move from the stove until her mistress gave her permission. She was hoping Doña Flora would rush to her side to fight them off, as she had done on two occasions the day before when Oliverio Castañeda had been sent for. This time, the lady of the house did not even deign to come out to the kitchen, simply sending word that the authorities should act as they saw fit. Salvadora dried her tears on her apron, and walked head held high all the way to the police headquarters, rejecting all entreaties to ride in the police wagon. More upset at her mistress' lack of consideration than at the dishonour of being imprisoned like a common criminal, Salvadora left the Contreras' home, never to return.

We have already seen from the statement she gave on 17 October 1933 how the departure of the young couple had saddened everyone in the house. She also spoke at length of her opinion of Oliverio Castañeda:

> The witness stated that in her view, Oliverio Castañeda was the most light-hearted and gay person she had ever known. Whenever he passed by the kitchen on his way to the toilet, even before he opened his mouth to speak, the serving girls would start giggling in anticipation of his titillating jokes, which were always very racy, but at the same time extremely amusing. He would constantly make them laugh, often by mimicking members of the family, pulling funny faces and copying their way of speaking, especially Don Carmen's stammer.
>
> Sometimes at night he would creep up on Salvadora wrapped in a white sheet in order to frighten her. Or he would grab hold of her when she was chopping food and make her dance some steps typical of his own country. Sometimes he would take the knife from her and show her how salads were prepared in Guatemala, in particular one known there as chojín. He would make her sit down and tell her tales of mysterious unsolved crimes committed in his country, laughing at her fears whenever she crossed herself. Still wielding the knife, he would cut tomatoes into the shapes of flowers, or make rabbits out of boiled eggs by sticking peppercorns on them for eyes, and strips of chile for their mouths.
>
> She added however that occasionally Castañeda could

> become very sentimental, above all when he recalled his mother, who had died in agony in a hospital when he was only fourteen. She had been wracked by ghastly convulsions for weeks, and they did not let up even on her death bed. Castañeda would swear that he could still feel them in his own guts whenever she appeared in his dreams, so much so that he would wake up in a cold sweat, writhing in bed from the stabbing pains. On several occasions he had asked the witness, with tears in his eyes: "Would you have let your mother suffer like that, Yoyita?"
>
> According to Salvadora, Castañeda was particularly fond of the young serving girl Leticia Osorio. He would often amuse her with magic tricks that he had learned from conjurer friends of his, among them the Great Moncriffe, the one with the talking dummies. The witness remembered how on one occasion Castañeda had taken it upon himself to explain to Leticia that to earn one cordoba a month was a starvation wage, and that she was being exploited as a child labourer. When she did not seem to understand what he meant, he took her head in his hands and stared at her very sadly.

From Salvadora Carvajal's statement, it comes as no surprise that Castañeda was always served first at table, always had the choicest oranges squeezed for his breakfast juice, and had his white shirts carefully ironed and starched, while Don Carmen was often left to complain that the milk for his coffee was cold.

The judge released Salvadora Carvajal on 18 October 1933, the day Oliverio Castañeda was officially arraigned on charges of murder. Shortly afterwards, Rosalío Usulutlán went out to her modest home in Subtiava to interview her. His article appeared in *El Cronista* on 25 October 1933.

This article caused a tremendous scandal, to which we shall return. At present, we are concerned with the feelings that Oliverio Castañeda aroused in León, feelings which ranged from enthusiastic support by the servants to a more mixed reaction among those of his own social standing. Let us look at some of the views expressed by the cook to Rosalío, as copied by Doctor Salmerón in his notebook:

Carvajal doesn't believe a word of the charges against Oliverio. She says that he is in jail out of jealousy. They were always jealous of him, and now that he's down they all want to kick him some more. The victims all died of blackwater fever; one of her daughters had died of it years earlier, and she suffered from the same convulsions. Thinks it comical she herself was put in jail—the judge asked her a lot of foolish nonsense. They are crazy if they think she added strychnine to the food, either because Castañeda asked her to do so, or on her own initiative. Doctors says strychnine has a bitter taste. How then could they eat poisoned food: even dogs would know better.

C. has been every day since her release to the prison gate, to ask to be given Oliverio's clothes to wash. The guard will not listen to her. When he gets out, will offer to be his cook. Would even follow him to Guatemala. That's why she refuses to work anywhere else, although countless households wanted her.

Will never set foot in the Contreras house again. They betrayed her. Gave them her best years, night after night looking after their babies, this is how they repay here, they didn't lift a finger to help her. Now they are betraying Oliverio as well. Has read that Doña Flora had changed her mind and sent Somoza a second telegram calling for the prisoner not to be set free, but to be tried and sentenced. Her mistress thought he was wonderful before; now she wants to see him dead. That's how the rich always behave with the poor and unfortunate. The Contreras women could not do enough for him, were always fighting for his affection. She saw things she wasn't supposed to—kisses, loving sighs and bouts of jealous tears; she heard of furious cat fights. But she won't say a word. Only if Oliverio asks her to, and then she'll spill the beans. Then they had better watch out.

These notes from Doctor Salmerón's notebook are based on the interview she gave to Rosalío Usulutlán that same day, 20 October 1933. He also took down the cook's version of the theft of the Infant Jesus of Prague, previously referred to in Carmen Contreras' statement of 1 December 1933.

S. gave an example of how kind and considerate Oliverio was. Every year, she celebrated the novena of the Infant Jesus. Had never had a statue for her shrine, only a photograph from the Mejoral calendar, that had not even been blessed. Last December at the start of the religious celebration, when O. heard this he told her: "Don't worry, Yoyita. Get your firecrackers and food and drink ready, we'll have a proper celebration for the end of the festivities, with a real Infant Jesus."

This intrigued S.: what did he mean? The mystery was resolved early on the morning of December twenty-third. O. came into the kitchen and explained his plan to the servants. They were going to kidnap the Contreras' Infant Jesus for a day—the statue in the niche on the verandah. And that's what they did. While one of the girls swept the floor and raised a lot of dust, so that the family would stay well away, the others kept a lookout. Oliverio opened the door to the niche using a magic formula the Great Moncriffe had taught him: he didn't need a key. Then he wrapped the statue in a towel and hid it in the boot of Don Carmen's car to take to Subtiava. That was no problem; he was always driving Don Carmen's old crock to get all round León.

They celebrated the end of the novena for the Infant Jesus like never before. It was the first time that a proper statue, decked out in a brocade cape and with a jewelled crown, had ever been in such a humble dwelling. It had been solemnly enthroned in S.'s shrine, covered in madrona flowers and garlanded with coloured paper. The fireworks were beautiful. Oliverio was there too. The next day, the Infant Jesus was returned to its niche, again with no need for a key. O. knew the magic words to open doors —the Great Moncriffe had taught him.

Oliverio Castañeda's talents shone far beyond the confines of the Contreras' windowless house. A few weeks earlier, a gala ball had been held at the León Social club in honour of Nicaragua's new president, Doctor Juan Bautista Sacasa. He had taken office on 1 January 1933, the day the American forces of occupation had withdrawn from the country.

The lengthy piece on the society pages of *El Centroamericano* newspaper in its edition of 12 January 1933, apparently written by a female hand, reads:

> The young man who shone brightest among all the guests was a member of Guatemala's highest society who has been gracing us with his presence for some time now: the lawyer Oliverio Castañeda. Full of charm and elegance, he displayed all the qualities of a born gentleman. He marked the cards of all the most distinguished young ladies of León, who disputed his favours in a gallant tourney. He succeeded in keeping them all satisfied. The orchestra, led by maestro Filiberto Nuñez, began the first round of dances with the waltz "The Loves of Abraham" from the pen of our unfortunate musical genius José de la Cruz Mena; murmurs of approval greeted Señor Castañeda as he took to the floor on the arm of Señorita María Sacasa, the new president's favourite daughter, one of the sweetest-scented roses in the bouquet of León's prominent young ladies. Would that all the foreigners who flock to our hospitable land could shine so brightly in our salons. The leading lights of the León Social Club sparkled as best they might, and yet found themselves in the shade of this remarkable young man.

No mention is made of Marta Jerez. It may be that she was unable to attend the ball because she was still in bed as Doctor Darbishire had recommended. However, she is never mentioned on the society pages of either of León's two dailies, whereas her husband is constantly referred to as having been present at birthday celebrations, trips to the seaside, and other festivities and dances.

In the statement he gave on 1 December 1933 which gives his version of the disappearance of the Infant Jesus of Prague, Carmen Contreras Guardia also touches on one such seaside adventure. This presents a highly unfavourable view of Oliverio Castañeda. It was this part of his testimony that gave rise to the altercation between him and the defendant, as reported by Manolo Cuadra in *La Nueva Prensa*.

> While Marta Jerez was still alive, my mother Doña Flora organized an excursion to Poneloya, to which the Casta-

> ñedas and other friends of the family were invited. At one moment when we were alone together, Castañeda began to explain how by using stimulants such as morphine or cocaine a man could have his way with a woman, and lead her to satisfy all his desires. He said that all you had to do was to rub a little on her lips or hand, or drop it into her glass of wine or other drink. From his detailed account I gained the impression that he himself had often employed this strategy on many unsuspecting young ladies, during the outings to the countryside or the coast to which he was constantly inviting himself.

Doña Flora's older brother, Fernando Guardia Oreamuno (aged forty-five, married), a wine importer living in San José de Costa Rica, visiting the city of Léon as a result of his brother-in-law's sudden demise, gave his testimony on 20 October 1933. Swearing on oath to tell the truth despite his family links with the injured party, he provided further information about these excursions, information he claimed to have heard from Castañeda himself:

> In September of this year, my sister and her daughter María del Pilar returned to Nicaragua after spending some time with me in San José. Oliverio Castañeda accompanied them on the journey. I went with them as far as Puntarenas, where they were to board the steamship *Acajutla* bound for Corinto in Nicaragua. During our train journey, Castañeda came over to me and struck up a conversation along the following lines: he said I would never believe how lax the morals were in León society; that men and women considered honourable and upright indulged in the most scandalous excesses. He used as examples Octavio Oviedo y Reyes' wife, who it was said frequented the brothels of New York when she lived there as a single woman, and Doña Margarita Debayle de Pallais, for whom Rubén Darío wrote the poem "Margarita, How Beautiful the Sea", who, during the U.S. Marines' occupation of Nicaragua would invite officers to her home at night. They would all drink copiously, and then her husband, Noel Ernesto Pallais, would borrow money from them in dollars, at which point he would withdraw

and leave her on her own with them—from which only one conclusion could be drawn.

As for the youngsters of both sexes, Castañeda told me they went on excursions to the coast or to nearby farms. The respectable matrons chaperoning them would turn a blind eye, and allow them to cavort in meadows and woods, or among the sand dunes after dark, when orgies took place to rival those of the decadence of Rome.

Castañeda further assured me that in the Hotel Lacayo in Poneloya there was a room known as the "deflowering bower" because it was there that the young women from León's most prominent families came to lose their virginity in their thirst for men; and if the judge will pardon the expression, since I have sworn on oath to tell the truth, he said they were hungry for virile members. Any foreigner, he said, could obtain pleasure and satisfaction from them for a mere five dollars. He recalled how one Honduran commercial salesman, a friend of his by the name of Reyna, had on several occasions kept a young woman called Deshon locked in his bedroom at the Metropolitan Hotel; he said he knew this because he himself had been staying at the hotel at the same time.

I was so alarmed by all these accounts that I rushed over to my sister, who was in the same railway carriage with María del Pilar. I felt I ought to warn her not to allow her daughters to go on excursions or to fiestas unless she or her husband accompanied them. She was astonished to hear what Castañeda had been telling me.

When he arrived to give his deposition on 1 December 1933, Carmen Contreras Guardia turned over to the judge a cardboard box originally for Tricifero de Barry jars in which he had stored all the books Castañeda had asked him to keep in November 1932. Among the paperback books and pamphlets were: *Stalin: The Five-year Plan*; *The Report of the Frankfurt Anti-Imperialist Congress*; *Sandino versus the Colossus* by Emigdio Maraboto; *The Basics of Theosophy* by Joaquín Trincado; and a pamphlet by the Mexican Hands-Off-Nicaragua Committee (HANONIC), calling for the withdrawal of U.S. forces from Nicaragua.

Castañeda's name also features among the signatories of a manifesto calling on the people of León to join a protest march against the U.S. intervention on 19 July 1931. According to an article in *El Centroamericano*, the students, wearing black arm bands and with mouths gagged, carried a coffin through the streets of the city, in front of which they unfurled a big sheet with the inscription: 'Here lies Nicaragua, killed by the Yankee bayonet.'

The march ended at the entrance of the main university auditorium. President José María Moncada had just been burned in effigy. The chairman of the law students' association, Mariano Fiallos (who was later to be the judge in the Castañeda case) was about to make a speech when a detachment of U.S. Marines appeared. They used their rifle butts to disperse the protestors, injuring many and making several arrests, among them the poet Alí Vanegas.

National Guard Captain Anastasio J. Ortiz, appointed police chief in León after the withdrawal of the U.S. Marines, the man in charge of Castañeda's arrest at the Contreras family home the day Don Carmen died, stated in his 21 October 1933 deposition:

> Over a year ago, when the students were irresponsibly calling for the withdrawal of U.S. troops from Nicaragua, Castañeda was busy stirring up trouble at the university. He was the author of their violent manifesto; it was his idea to rent a coffin from the Rosales funeral parlour so that it could be paraded around the streets; it was in his room at the Metropolitan Hotel that the dummy of General Moncada burnt in effigy was made. It was his wife who sewed the clown's suit the dummy was dressed in. As she was about to give the figure a wig, Castañeda stopped her, saying: "Don't give the old traitor any hair; he's bald. Put more stuffing in his backside, he's a real fat-ass."
>
> When the decision was taken to break up the demonstration, after much disorder and provocation, it proved impossible to arrest Castañeda, who climbed over La Merced church wall and escaped. When I insisted he should be punished, especially as he was a foreigner, Lieutenant Wallace Stevens, head of the Marine Corps intelligence services in León, confided to me: "Don't worry. Even in a small place like this, people don't know much about

> each other. Castañeda is one of our informers. Take a look at this." He showed me a secret dossier with details on Castañeda, his photograph, and the secret reports he had sent, all filed in chronological order.

On the night of 28 October 1933, the same day on which Doctor Atanasio Salmerón appeared in court to give his statement, Oviedo the Balloon took the risk of sneaking over to the rear of the El Esfuerzo store run by Cosme Manzo. Manzo was hiding inside because he and the other members of the accursed table were threatened with prison following Rosalío Usulutlán's article in *El Cronista*, which had caused a real scandal. That afternoon a solemn procession of the Blessed Sacrament had taken place as a token of sympathy for the Contreras family.

'How does your brother the canon know they're about to arrest us?' asked Cosme Manzo, peering out from behind a heap of rice sacks. He was wearing his hat with its broad red band, ready to flee at any moment. 'Perhaps he just wanted to scare you.'

'He must have heard it from Captain Ortiz himself. My brother doesn't take these things lightly,' Oviedo the Balloon replied, trying to settle the three-legged stool beneath his voluminous backside. 'The warning he gave me last night outside the cinema was serious. That's why I passed it on to all of you.'

'What about all this fuss he's making in the streets with the old biddies from his church? He knows perfectly well that everything in that article was true,' moaned Cosme Manzo, shining his flashlight along the wall until it reached the cardboard cod's tail used to advertise Scott's Emulsion cod liver oil. 'Don't tell me your brother believes Matilde was a virgin, as Doctor Darbishire certified?'

'You try to tell him. He even had the gall to add my name to the list of those offering condolences to the Contreras family,' complained Oviedo, trying to right the stool. 'But you lot did go too far. They'll never forgive you for that article.'

'Didn't you go too far when you told the judge about that letter of María del Pilar's? That's not exactly a letter to a friend,' Cosme Manzo snorted, snapping the flashlight off and ducking back behind the rice sacks. His voice resounded in the darkness as if it was coming through a rusty loudhailer. 'You're supposed to be his best buddy, but it was you who helped to sink Castañeda. He still insists there was nothing between him and the two Contreras sisters.'

'That's because he's an idiot. That letter does exist, he showed it to me,' Oviedo said, as the stool gave way beneath him and rolled away. 'But he thinks that wouldn't be gentlemanly. He'll go on denying it even if they put him in front of a firing squad.'

'What a gallant gentleman! Haven't you read what that Guardia fellow from Costa Rica had to say? Even your wife is dragged in,' said Manzo.

'All those are lies invented to condemn him, to make him look like a filthy liar,' Oviedo the Balloon insisted, picking himself up from the floor. 'He would never say anything like that about Yelbita.'

'Are you trying to tell me it isn't true either that he passed information to the U.S. Marines, as Captain Ortiz maintains?' Manzo wanted to know, dodging back when he heard somebody knocking at a door. But the sound came from further down the street.

'No, I don't believe that for a minute. A man like him would never spy for the Americans. Now all we need is for them to accuse him of being a bandit like Sandino.' Oviedo the Balloon wiped the dust from his hands.

'What does María del Pilar write to him in the letters she keeps sending to the jail? Is she feeling sad?' Cosme Manzo crawled on all fours over to his friend, with the flashlight stuffed into his waistband. 'Leticia Osorio says that María del Pilar sent him letters along with the flowers and colognes.'

'He didn't say anything about that,' Oviedo replied, stooping to dust off his knees. 'When I went to visit him, all we talked about was his defence. He has no money for a lawyer.'

'He left you his trunk with all the other love letters in it. They've all disappeared.' Manzo had reached Oviedo's feet, and tugged at his trouser leg. 'I'll buy them from you to cancel your gambling debts.'

'What letters? You know they could send you to jail, and yet you're still up to your old tricks,' said Oviedo, peering down at him over his prodigious belly. 'Anyway, what if I do have them? I'd never sell them. What kind of a suggestion is that?'

'The offer stands.' Cosme Manzo pulled out the flashlight and rubbed the glass against his cheek. 'And I'll pay double if you throw in Doña Flora's letters as well.'

CHAPTER NINE

Forgotten Portraits

AT THE start of his interview with Oliverio Castañeda, Rosalío Usulutlán offers us a short sketch of the prisoner. However, despite the journalist's admission that Castañeda had attractive male qualities, he was trying above all to make his traits fit into the system of morphological types invented by Lombroso. His friend and mentor, Doctor Salmerón, had made him an enthusiast for the Italian School of Criminology, and consequently for the classification of hereditary criminals into prototypes according to size of skull, depth of forehead, length of jaw bone, and so on.

Although he does not go into any great detail about it, Usulutlán also advances the thesis promoted by Doctor Salmerón and widely discussed in the newspapers of the day, whereby Castañeda's personality was seen as being dominated by an enigmatic duality assumed to be typical of sociopathic criminals. Many of the witnesses in the case expressed the belief that behind the defendant's seductive airs (accentuated still further by his strange habit of always wearing mourning clothes) there lay an evil being who used his powers of attraction, his smooth talk and all his other natural abilities to entice and deceive.

Some basic information about Castañeda is also included in the judicial report added to the case file on 28 November 1933, the day he was formally charged with parricide and premeditated murder by means of lethal poisons:

PERSONAL DETAILS OF THE PRISONER
OLIVERIO CASTAÑEDA PALACIOS.

HEIGHT: Five feet nine inches.

COMPLEXION: Average.

SKIN COLOUR: White
HAIR: Black, straight, thick.
EYEBROWS: Bushy.
NOSE: Medium.
MOUTH: Small.
FACIAL HAIR: Thick, but clean-shaven.
FOREHEAD: Narrow.
EYES: Hazel. (Wears tortoiseshell spectacles due to pronounced astigmatism).
CLOTHING: Black suit, three-piece. Bow tie. Cane. Hat.
DISTINGUISHING MARKS: Slight traces of smallpox on cheeks and chin.
FINGERPRINTS: Indelible ink imprints of both left and right thumbs.
NOTE: Also added to file are three photographs of the prisoner, taken from different angles.

These three photographs were pasted to the back of a sheet of paper in the bulky file that was built up day after day following the suspicious death of Don Carmen Contreras on 9 October 1933. The file contains countless depositions by witnesses, forensic evidence, exhumation certificates, letters and other evidence and documents that the judge considered relevant. At the abrupt postponement of Castañeda's trial on 24 December 1933, this file comprised one thousand eight hundred and ninety-two pages.

None of the photographs gives us much indication of the ladies' man whose charms as a relentless seducer had become legendary; the man the Contreras sisters first caught sight of on the afternoon of 27 March 1933 when he appeared at the doorway of his room at the Metropolitan Hotel, weary from dancing to the foxtrot on his gramophone.

The round tortoiseshell glasses lend an artificially solemn look to his youthful face (it should not be forgotten that he was only twenty-five years old at the time). His splayed nose spreads in a rather ugly fashion beneath the bridge of the spectacles down towards a mouth which, though described as small in the judicial report, in fact has a petulant air about it, although the lips are firm enough.

The eyes peer out sullenly from behind the glass lenses at the police camera. They are hooded, beneath high, straight eyebrows. Some said that he shaved his forehead to make it appear higher; above it, his hair is black and thick, combed back off his face.

In his report 'A Fallen Gigolo' for *La Nueva Prensa* of 20 October 1933, Manolo Cuadra can help us complete our picture of the defendant:

> En route to the court, where he is being taken to answer the charges against him, Oliverio Castañeda strides along without ever once lowering his chin, shaven as carefully as in happier days. Nor does he blink at the fierce rays of the harsh noonday sun. His fresh face has benefitted from daily ablutions in the prison courtyard. He walks with a spring in his step, escorted by the vigilant guards, rifles at the ready. If one were not aware that he was on his way to court, one might think he was a new ambassador on the way to present his credentials, his sheaf of documents clutched firmly in both hands.
>
> A question from the journalist elicits nothing more than a disdainful half-smile as Castañeda gently pats the head of a child to move him out of his way. A second question by the journalist, who is pushed roughly aside by the guards, brings a flash of warmth to the accused's eyes as he continues to stride along briskly and jauntily. Desperate to catch a glimpse of him, many people emerge at their front doors. Castañeda responds to their greetings with a slight nod of the head. There are whispers of amazement as he goes by; some of them follow a short way in his footsteps. Many of the women's faces are frozen in astonishment (horrified or contented?). "Seducer," says one when the fallen gigolo is out of earshot. "I wouldn't mind marrying him," retorts another, without a hint of irony in her voice, and closing her eyes dreamily.
>
> Who can reconcile all the conflicting aspects of Oliverio Castañeda's personality? Many people in León are trying to do just that: repressed admiration, fear of the unknown, facile condemnation, self-righteous prejudice —all are to be found in the opinions generally expressed about him. Others attempt to fit him into a variety of

pathological classifications of criminal types. Nature on the one hand, the belief in genetic predestination; nurture on the other, the determining influence, for good or ill, of environmental factors.

Here I should like to quote from an article in the Managua magazine *Caras y Caretas*. In it, Professor Ariel Dorfman, the eminent psychiatrist from the University of Chile, describes the criminal sociopath (society's enemy) in a way that many in León saw as a convincing portrait of Oliverio Castañeda:

"The killer who uses stealthy poison as his weapon is characterised by his love of the shallow banalities of life, by his charm and gracious manners, and by his gift of immediate appeal. However, his divided nature leads him to be brutal when least expected; ruthless in his sarcasm; and destructive when talking about others behind their backs. His behaviour therefore tends to the fantastic, the obnoxious, a need to invent slanderous lies. The most extreme examples of this kind of fantasy involve stories with sexual connotations. At the same time, his own sexual life lacks any real dynamism, and is almost entirely superficial.

"Endowed with a lively and wide-ranging intelligence, the sociopath's capacity for discernment is considerable as long as his reasoning faculty is not impaired by the lure of his fantasies, which he is apt to mistake for reality. However, at no moment will he fall into bouts of delirium or other signs of permanent mental derangement, or indeed betray any psychoneurotic symptoms. Typical character traits include a lack of reliability, of sincerity, and an inability to feel shame or remorse. His social behaviour is without any coherent pattern; this makes him superficial and unable to learn from experience. He is above all egocentric and emotionally stunted: he claims to love everyone, but in reality cannot love at all. He expresses his resentment at the world around him in a concealed, tortuous but calculating manner. He will never become involved in acts of open aggression, with a dagger or pistol in his hand, because he detests the sight of blood. This means that hidden poisons are his preferred weapons of destruction, since they enable him to avoid any confrontation. As such, poison is the logical extension of the many disguises he employs to allow free rein to the basic irresponsibility and superficiality of his interpersonal relationships."

So, a social psychopath of the like of John Barrymore, Maurice Chevalier or Charles Laughton? One last question to this ambassador, this gentleman in black, this screen idol who even in this scorching mid-day heat is not perspiring, but shows all the cool freshness of the magical world of the cinema—for who has ever heard of a star of the silver screen perspiring beneath the studio lights in those warehouses converted into the dream factories of Hollywood's Babylon? And my question is: "Have you seen the film 'Payment Deferred?' What did you make of it?"

Still with a gracious smile on his lips, Castañeda finally deigns to speak to me. "I never go to the cinema. This is farce enough for me." And in mid-street, with the sound of the accused's footsteps and the astonished whispers of the neighbours still echoing in his mind, the journalist notes this response. His sweating hand leaves its mark on the paper before he can write the repentant gigolo's laconic remark.

What of his wife, Marta Jerez? Born in 1913, we already know she was very young when she married one evening in March 1930 at La Merced church in Guatemala City. The wedding was celebrated in a side chapel because the main nave, destroyed in an earthquake in 1917, was still without a roof. She was still very young when she met such a sudden and horrific death in León.

In a letter written from prison on 23 November 1933 to his friend Federico Hernández de León, Oliverio Castañeda recalled that wedding ceremony:

Federico, in the solitude of my cell, nostalgic memories, regrets, distant moments of happiness come flocking to me... Do you, my best man, remember all the problems we had at the wedding? The fact is, I still blame you for most of them, since you were the one who was supposed to have arranged everything with the priest at La

Merced...I can still see our small wedding party (Marta wanted a simple ceremony because her mother Luz was so ill that we were afraid she might die at any moment) standing there outside the locked doors of the church. In the end, you had to go and fetch the priest from his house, where he was already in bed asleep. Then the idiot told us there was no electric light in the church because the fuses had blown during the rosary at seven that evening, as if we were supposed to know! All that was missing was for another earthquake to bring everything crashing down round our ears! Marta was desperately trying not to get her wedding dress ruined on all the planks, buckets, sand and cement left by the builders—don't tell me you had no idea they were working on the high altar when you chose that church for the wedding. Everyone searched for candles, and lit all the ones they could find in the church...so that finally, we were married in semi-darkness. I felt like slapping the priest every time he yawned. Marta thought it was hilarious that I was so annoyed—that was so typical of her, she never let anything get her down. Well, Federico, am I being fair in my memories of you?

As soon as I get out of this trouble—because I am sure that this mess will be sorted out—I intend to take Marta with me from Nicaragua. If necessary I'll dig up her body with my own hands so that she can sleep her eternal sleep in her own country rather than here, where there is no longer any love for us. I would like you to be at my side, Federico, when we can at last lay her to rest in her native land, under the matchless skies of the quetzal.

The only photograph we have of Marta Jerez was taken a month after her wedding at the Estudio Müller in Guatemala City. She donned her wedding dress again for the occasion, changing behind the pasteboard screens painted to represent a brightly-coloured spring garden.

Somebody's impulsive scissors have cut her husband out of the photograph, leaving only the black outline of his suit, an ear, and part of one shoulder. Marta is resting her head against it, her hair swept up under a bridal cap edged with pearls, and a gauzy nuptial veil.

Marta's chief attraction seems to have been her youth, possibly because time had no chance to wither it. In the photograph, her eyes are sparkling in a pale moon face, lit only by her frank, serene smile. She innocently presses her snub nose into the bridal bouquet, intoxicated forever with the vanished fragrance of orange blossom. The silk bows on the bouquet twisted between her fingers stand out against the greys of the painted garden in the backdrop.

Nor, if we consider the photographs of the Contreras sisters, can it be said that they were endowed with any truly striking beauty. According to the birth certificate included in the murder dossier, Matilde Contreras was born on 28 December 1911. She was therefore not quite twenty-two years old when she died on 2 October 1933. She was sent away for two years to the Mission Catholic High School run by Benedictine nuns in San Francisco, California, where she took a course in accounting and typing. A short article in *El Centroamericano* welcoming her back to Nicaragua reveals she returned by boat in December 1930.

She came out officially in León society on 31 December 1930, at the traditional New Year's Ball held at the Social Club. A photograph of her and all the other debutantes of that season is on the society page of *El Centroamericano*. This same oval portrait from the Estudio Cisneros, tastefully misted at the edges, was the one used throughout Castañeda's trial. It appeared once more on the front of the In Memoriam album printed by her grandfather's firm to commemorate the first anniversary of her death.

This album contains an elegy in her honour written by the bohemian poet Lino de Luna, who had been prevented from reading it at her funeral by the driving rain. The following lines give some idea of the poem:

> Matilde died in October, when the burial ground fills
> With the smells of a port: oil and fresh paint...
> With its abrupt caress, heady turpentine
> Offended her passionate love of perfumes.
> What sound did that poor child hear on her tomb
> Beneath the ceaseless lashing of the rain...?
> Who knows but it spoke of cruel hands
> Forcing fresh nails into her drear white casket?

Matilde's most attractive feature seems to have been her languid gaze beneath thick, well-rounded eyebrows. Taken as a whole, however, her face does not appear harmonious, possibly due to the narrow cheekbones and the pinched mouth, a short slash completely lacking in sensuality. Her hairstyle, sweeping the dark locks into two coils on either side of the head, is dated even for 1930, and makes her look older than her years. The blouse she is wearing, closed at the neck with a cameo brooch, makes her look like a schoolmarm. Wearing no make-up or rouge on her cheeks, she looks startled, as if taken by surprise by the photographer's flash, whereas the other debutantes wear practised smiles beneath their costume-jewellery diadems.

The photograph we have of María del Pilar was taken in the Estudio Classeul, near to the Teatro Palace in San José de Costa Rica in September 1933, shortly before she travelled with her mother back to Nicaragua.

María del Pilar was born on 18 August 1918. She had therefore just turned eighteen when the portrait was taken. We have already heard of her happy but fateful stay in Costa Rica from the 22 October 1933 deposition made by her uncle Don Fernando Guardia Oreamuno.

The photograph shows her with one hand stretched out cautiously towards a wooden plinth painted like veined marble, as if she is afraid she might dislodge the vase of white lilies perched on top of it. Her other hand, dangling a sequined bag, is clutching the collar of a long fur coat, beneath which a pair of sling-back dancing shoes is visible. The whole scene creates the impression that she is arriving for a ball somewhere: the studio backdrop suggests a balustrade, with beyond it the tall windows of a palace blazing with lights.

Her hair is curled in tight ringlets, while her full, fleshy lips display all the sensuality that is lacking in Matilde. Though dressed like a woman of the world, she seems to be playacting in her clothes like the child she still is in reality. Her eyes show surprise and amusement; they bulge in a way that is immediately striking, especially since her black eyeliner makes them stand out even more. Perhaps that is why they betray a look of shock that she only half succeeds in brazening out.

Last but not least is the portrait of Doña Flora Guardia de Contreras taken in 1929 at the Estudio Cisneros in León when she was forty years old, having been born in San José de Costa Rica in 1889. By 1933, she had lost none of the fulsome beauty evident from the photograph, and if we are to believe Rosalío Usulutlán's admiration for her, an admiration shared by Doctor Salmerón and the other regulars at the accursed table, she was considerably more beautiful than both her daughters put together.

She is every inch the modern woman: her hair is cropped and swept back from her forehead. Her short crocheted dress is informal and loose-fitting, with a velvet rose embellishing the neckline. She sits in an armless chair with her legs crossed and her hands intertwined over one knee. Her lips are drawn back in a haughty smile that nevertheless offers a glimpse of charmingly irregular teeth.

In 1909, Don Carmen Contreras Largespada, León's most important printer, sent his son Carmen to Costa Rice to find out about the new-fangled electrically-operated Chandler printing press recently imported from the United States by the Lehmann printing company. It was during this trip that Carmen met Flora, and it was not long before he informed his parents of his imminent marriage. The news so upset his mother that she retired to bed for a month.

The cousin of her own spouse, Doña Migdalia would brook no departure from the centuries' old tradition according to which the members of the Contreras family (distant relatives of El Cid and related to the Virgin Mary, as is revealed in the novel *Tiempo de Fulgor*) could only marry among themselves. This rule had been laid down by Belisario Contreras Marino, the first of the family to land on American soil from Spain. Therefore, although convinced of her right to meddle in her son's domestic affairs by choosing both furniture and servants, she steadfastly refused ever to set foot in his house.

When Doña Flora had arrived in León in late 1909 to set up home with her husband, her ailing mother-in-law was quick to proclaim triumphantly that she had been right to oppose her son's marriage to a complete stranger. From the outset, León's leading families considered Doña Flora's conduct far too free and easy. She smoked with a cigarette holder, and despite being a married woman saw nothing wrong with dancing with other men, or going out on her own for an evening's entertainment if her husband had no wish to accompany her. People started referring to her disparagingly as 'that Costa Rican woman', and throughout all her years in León she was regarded as an interloper, despite the pedigree of her family names.

These reservations about her character surfaced once again, camouflaged as expressions of sympathy, after the publication of the scandalous article by Rosalío Usulutlán published in *El Cronista* on 25 October 1933. She was after all a foreigner in Nicaragua, and had opened her doors to another foreigner.

'Far more beautiful than both her daughters put together,' exclaimed Doctor Salmerón when he saw her photograph that same night. He was as usual presiding over the accursed table. He tore the photograph out of the front-page article in *El Cronista*, to keep in the file he was compiling. He had no need to keep the article itself, because he already had a carbon copy of the original.

The phrase lauding Doña Flora's beauty, coined by Rosalío Usulutlán, had pleased Doctor Salmerón from the moment he had first heard it on the evening of 26 September 1933. That was when *El Cronista* had published the same photograph of her to welcome her back to León following her lengthy stay in Costa Rica. On that occasion, Rosalío had also commented that the photograph reminded him of a screen actress, although he could not recall exactly which one.

During the many months when public attentions was focussed on Castañeda's trial, María del Pilar never appeared in a photograph. None of the photographers from Managua, with their up-to-date cameras, succeeded in obtaining a shot of her. Following the scandal unleashed by Rosalío's article she shut herself up in her house. She was seen only by her closest family members, the servants, and very occasionally by the La Fama assistants. Word got round that she had aged overnight, crushed by the bitter weight of her memories, and that before the year was out she would be retreating to a convent in Costa Rica, where she would spend the rest of her days making expiation for the sin of falling in love with a murderer.

So it was that, at her family's request, her testimony to the judicial authorities on 12 November 1933 was given behind the closed doors of her home, on that very same verandah where her sister Matilde had read legal texts out loud to Castañeda late into the night. In this way, María del Pilar was spared the noisy curiosity of the public, the press, and others who thronged the court building to hear the witnesses in the murder trial at first hand.

CHAPTER TEN

Ollie! Ollie! What Have You Given Me?

> We regret to announce the cruel death at two o'clock yesterday afternoon of a distinguished young Guatemalan woman, Doña Manuelita María de Castañeda, the wife of the distinguished gentleman Don Oliverio Castañeda, ex-secretary of the Guatemalan Legation in Nicaragua. Doña Manuelita died of a sudden bout of blackwater fever, following an illness that lasted only three hours. The deceased had, until yesterday, been in perfect health. We extend our deepest condolences to her grieving husband, who is held in high regard in this city.
>
> (*El Centroamericano*, 14 February 1933)

MARTA, whose name is not even given correctly in the obituary quoted above, died in the afternoon of Wednesday 13, 1933. Her funeral took place with unseemly haste the next morning. Nothing further was written about her over the subsequent days, apart from a short article in *Los Hechos*, the weekly newsletter of the Metropolitan Diocese (issue number 7, fourth week of February 1933) with a by-line crediting the canon, Isidro Augusto Oviedo y Reyes, Oviedo the Balloon's brother.

In this article, entitled 'Be Sure Your Accounts Are In Order', the priest extols the spiritual fortitude shown by the young woman in her dying moments and calls for all his parishioners to follow her example:

> Do you imagine, misguided soul, that you can flee this vale of tears unscathed? Even though you fast, do you ever spare a thought of contrition for your deeds? Do you forget that you will be called to account for them in the

Hereafter? Woe unto you, a thousand times woe, if you know not how to prepare your accounts in time, for you will be called to settle your debts before Him.

If, like myself, you had been privileged to be at the bedside of Martita when she was called to the Supreme Accountant, you would have received the most important of lessons. Far from her family, her home, from the land of her birth, she knew peace. All her accounts were balanced: petty cash, capital, up-to-date and totted up, all balanced and above board, ready for payment. The Heavenly Creditor did not warn her in advance, but still, she was ready...for the good debtor the terms of the loan are not painful, and as the guardian angels of her early youth beat their wings to release her from this mortal coil to carry her to Heavenly pastures, where all thirst vanishes and nothing is owed, she smiled joyfully.

Surely this child offers us hope! We are praying for her, but possibly we would do better to pray for you, with your miserly lack of provision, who imagines you can hoodwink Him. He will refuse your dishonest books, your forged receipts, your fraudulent amendments. He will send you directly to the dungeons of Hell, despicable thief, good for nothing fraud.

Requiescat en pace. Amen.

The decision to hold the funeral at such an early hour in the morning, something quite unusual in a city where wakes are generally prolonged affairs, was explained by Doña Flora herself in her first trial statement of 14 October 1933. According to her, Oliverio needed to rest, and it seemed advisable that he should withdraw as soon as possible to the family home, back to the room the couple had occupied until so recently before.

In this same testimony, Doña Flora also informed the court that it was only after the burial that they had received a telegram from the Jerez family. This was signed by the brother of the deceased, Belisario Jerez, and asked for Oliverio to repatriate the body as quickly as possible by air to Guatemala so that it could be buried in Mazatenango.

•

> The witness stated that it would obviously be unjust to blame Oliverio for not complying with this albeit reasonable request from the family since, by the time the telegram arrived, the burial had already taken place. Far from wishing to renege on his duties, he did in fact try to find out whether an exhumation would be possible the next day, only to be discouraged from this course of action after being advised that the bureaucracy involved would be hugely complicated. Nor, as the witness has already stated, had Oliverio harboured any wish to rush the burial. This was a decision for which she took and continues to take full responsibility because, at the time, he was overwhelmed by the tragedy and incapable of organising anything himself.

Despite the fact that this and the many other statements were taken several months afterwards, it is still possible to reconstruct the events of that day. At the time, nobody apart from Don Atanasio Salmerón lent any great importance to these happenings. Unsurprisingly, some witnesses showed some confusion about dates and times, while others lacked objectivity owing to the degree of prejudice that already existed towards the accused.

Of all the statements, that of Oliverio Castañeda is the most complete, although for obvious reasons this was the one which most aroused the judge's suspicions. In consequence it is preferable to return to the one given by Doña Flora, who was at Marta's side almost the whole time. However, between her initial statement of 14 October 1933 and a second one given at her own insistence on the thirty-first of the same month, when she claimed to be less confused and calmer, there is a vast difference. If in the first statement she had been trying to protect her guest, in the second she seemed intent on condemning him.

Doctors, neighbours, friends of the couple, a domestic servant, all agreed to give statements at trial; and although there are more than a few inconsistencies between these numerous statements they form the basis for any attempt to place events in chronological order:

1. Thanks to the statement of Yelba de Oviedo, Oviedo the Balloon's wife, given on 16 October 1933, we learn that on the night before her death, Marta went to the cinema and was feeling well apart from a slight migraine:

> That evening we decided to go to the González Picture House intending to see "Private Lives", starring Robert Montgomery and Norma Shearer, a film that many of our friends had been talking about. My husband was studying for his doctoral exam but at the last moment he decided to accompany us, since he is such a film buff. But Oliverio, whose own exam was only two days away, did not want to come.
>
> Before leaving, Marta complained of a bad headache so I gave her a Bayer aspirin from a small bottle I keep in my bag. On the way we chatted about the outfit she was going to buy in honour of Oliverio obtaining his doctorate. She was so excited about the graduation party, and since their home was so small she was planning to take all the furniture out of their bedroom and store everything at the house of Doctor Ulises Terán, so that they could use it as another sitting room.
>
> We discussed the guest list, which was growing longer and longer, because she did not want to leave anybody out: the examiners, Oliverio's teachers, and his fellow students. I promised her I would bring her a homemade Russian salad and that we would buy some devilled ham and weiner sausages from Cosme Manzo's, which would make things easier. My husband mentioned that Doña Flora would almost certainly send over a few delicacies and some drinks, as would other friends. Marta wanted to surprise Oliverio with some Guatemalan specialities and so planned to arrange the table, as is traditional in Guatemala, with all the food and drink laid out for everyone to serve themselves. She said she didn't want to put out too much alcohol as people would get drunk and things might become out of hand.
>
> We enjoyed the film; Marta's headache seemed to have eased although she did not care for the plot, which was

> about divorce. As we were leaving the cinema, my husband suggested we went for a tutti-frutti sorbet at the Casa Prío; and she agreed. Later we left her at her front door, but we did not see Oliverio again as he was inside studying.

2. After a quiet night, Oliverio Castañeda's trial statement of 11 October 1933 describes how Marta awoke complaining of menstrual cramps and, once again, suffered a copious haemorrhage which soaked her nightclothes, the sheets and the cover. Since she was also complaining of digestive pains, he left their bedroom in search of the maid to ask her for the bottle of sodium bicarbonate kept in the sideboard in the dining-room. Marta herself dissolved the bicarbonate in a glass of water, stirring it with a spoon. This was around eight o'clock in the morning.

In her statement of October fourteenth, Doña Flora confirmed that she saw the empty glass with the spoon in it standing on the bedside table next to a Sacred Heart medallion. However, the maid Dolores Lorente (unmarried, aged thirty) who did not sleep at the house but began work very early each morning, told a different story:

> JUDGE: Please tell the court: Did you take bicarbonate of soda to the room with a glass of water and a spoon to dissolve the medicine?
>
> WITNESS: I did not take bicarbonate and I don't know if they had any in the room. What Don Oliverio asked me for was the bottle of pills that Doña Marta was taking, which I took from the sideboard in the dining-room as he told me to, calling from the door of his room. I handed them to him along with a glass of water covered with a little dish; but no spoon, because he didn't mention a spoon.
>
> JUDGE: Do you remember how many pills were left in the bottle?
>
> WITNESS: There were only three left. Don Oliverio took them out and gave me back the empty bottle, which I took to the kitchen; or I threw it away, I don't remember now.
>
> JUDGE: Do you remember what time it was when you took the pills to Castañeda?

WITNESS: I'd say it was before eight. I started work at seven and had already been about my duties for an hour.

3. According to Castañeda's own statement, he took advantage of a spare moment while the maid Dolores Lorente was preparing their breakfast to go in search of one of his fellow students, Edgardo Buitrago, who was supposed to lend him some books for his exam the next day. He says that after waiting outside in the street for some time, the maid came out to tell him that Buitrago was nowhere to be found. So he returned to his own house close to nine o'clock.

> Once home, he discovered that Marta had stripped the blood-stained bed linen and washed it herself, hanging it out to dry in the patio. This annoyed him, because he felt it was foolish of her to exert herself when she was in such a delicate state. His anger intensified when she answered his call from the bathroom. He saw it as extremely rash of her to be taking a bath after washing the linen, as he was well aware that in the case of menstrual haemorrhage, both exertion and cold water could be fatal.

The maid Dolores Lorente also referred to these events. Once again, she contradicts Castañeda:

> JUDGE: Did you see Doña Marta take the blood-stained linen to wash it, including the bed sheets and the cover?
>
> WITNESS: I would have noticed if she had been washing anything, but she did not do so. The wash-tub is on the patio just outside the kitchen, where at that point I was busy preparing their breakfast. What's more, bed linen is very cumbersome and it takes a long time to wash, especially if it has blood on it. And I didn't see anything on the line, not sheets or anything of the kind.
>
> JUDGE: Is it true that Doña Marta had a bath that morning?
>
> WITNESS: It is true that she went for a bath. The bathroom is also right next to the kitchen and I heard the sound of water. Later Don Oliverio came back and

banged on the door, telling her to hurry up and come to breakfast; he wanted to get on with his studies.

JUDGE: When you went into the bedroom to clean it, did you find any traces of blood either in the bed or in the chamber pot?

WITNESS: There was only urine in the chamber pot, which I went to dispose of in the toilet. I did not see any blood in the bed, although I did not make it myself. Doña Marta always did this personally. The bed was already made when I went in. A few days earlier I had found some undergarments there with traces of menstrual blood. I washed them.

4. Oliverio Castañeda insisted to the judge that when he went to the bathroom door to plead with Marta to come out immediately, she was equally insistent that she felt perfectly well. Aware of how careless she was of her own health and also of the risks she was running, he persisted in his demands, with the result that she cut short her bath. He wrapped her in a towel and took her to the bedroom. He noticed that she was still flushed after the exertions of washing so much bed linen:

> The witness asserts that, while Marta was dressing, and still upset with her rash behaviour, he went into the dining-room to wait for her so that they could breakfast together. When Marta appeared at the table, he was still brooding on all this. During breakfast, the conversation turned to the subject of her haemorrhage. He tried to make her appreciate his concern that these crises were happening every month. He suggested he should fetch Doña Flora and Yelbita to be with her, but she refused. However, the witness states that he insisted and, ignoring her protests that there was nothing wrong and that she felt perfectly well, he went in search of the aforementioned ladies.

Contradicting the statement of Dolores Lorente as to the reality of the haemorrhage, in her statement of October fourteenth, Doña Flora maintained that when she arrived at the house with her two daughters at Castañeda's urgent request, Marta herself confirmed that she had, yet again, bled profusely. She was also complaining of nervous anxiety, for which she gave her a sedative called cuadrolina, made by Parker & Davis. The bottle was sealed and the witness states that she herself opened it.

5. On being cross-examined by the judge on 18 October 1933, Edgardo Buitrago, graduate law student, stated that Castañeda had indeed come to borrow a book, and on not finding him at home had left a message with his mother stressing the urgency of his need for this particular book on Roman Law by Eugéne Petit. However, according to the witness, this visit did not occur on the morning of Sunday, February thirteenth, three days previously. He was certain of this because the reason he was not at home was that he was attending Mass.

If it was not in search of the book that Oliverio Castañeda left the house between eight and nine of that morning, the servant Dolores Lorente certainly knew his destination, although she did not reveal it to the judge, just as she did not reveal that she herself left the house at the same time. This mystery was finally unravelled thanks to the investigations set in motion by Cosme Manzo even before the opening of the trial.

6. Once breakfast was over at around half-past nine, Oliverio Castañeda did indeed go to look for some of his nearest acquaintances to invite them over to his house. As Dolores Lorente recalls:

> JUDGE: Tell us, did Oliverio Castañeda leave the house a second time and did Doña Marta stay in bed?
>
> WITNESS: Yes, he went out, saying that he was going to fetch Doña Flora. But Doña Marta didn't go back to her room; she took a jug from the kitchen and after filling it from the pump in the patio she set about watering the plants in the corridor. She was singing while she was pouring water into the plant pots, a song from her own country; it must have been one of her favourites as I had heard her singing it before. I think it went: "like the moon, silver gardenia, in my serenade, you are like a song…"; she made the sound of a marimba to accompany the words.

In his statement of 14 October 1933, Doctor Ulíses Terán, a forty-three-year-old lawyer, owner of the La Antorcha printers and the Castañedas' next-door neighbour affirmed:

> It would have been after nine-thirty in the morning. I was at the door, I had some parcels of cinema flyers to give to a courier from the González Company, when I saw Castañeda go past. He looked upset and was in a hurry. When I stopped him to ask if something had happened, he told me his wife was seriously ill: she had woken with severe menstrual pains.
>
> I tried to calm him. I told him that such disorders were normal for women and that no one died of such vaginal bleeding. But he shook his head disconsolately and insisted this was a matter of life and death, and then continued on his way as hastily as ever.
>
> I was so anxious because of the alarm apparent in Castañeda, that when the band advertising Scott Emulsion cod liver oil appeared in the street, I stopped the man carrying the Cod to ask him to refrain from making their racket on this block since there was an invalid here. He readily acceded to my request and left the street in silence, together with his accompanying musicians. Followed by crowds of children, the band struck up again a few blocks away.

7. In her statement of 14 October 1933, Doña Flora said that she was standing at the counter of the La Fama shop at around ten in the morning when Castañeda appeared. He had come to ask her if she would do him the favour of staying with Marta, who was unwell again with a heavy bleed and was refusing to rest. He seemed to feel that only Doña Flora, with her authority over the invalid, would be able to persuade her to stop doing so much housework and lie down. Only then could he enjoy the peace of mind necessary for him to resume his studies for his imminent exam. She added that she did not see anything extraordinary in this request, given the strong bond of friendship that existed between the two families, and that she did not detect anything unusual in his manners or his voice.

However, in her later statement of October thirty-first, her recollections were quite radically different:

> The witness now remembers that Castañeda had been deliberately spreading rumours about the gravity of his wife's illness around the neighbourhood. For this reason she wishes to add to her previous account in the following way: when Castañeda left the shop in search of Yelbita Oviedo, the witness returned to her own house to get ready and to let her daughters know what was happening. While she was still in the bedroom, her husband appeared. He was very alarmed, because he had just seen Castañeda in the street, and he had told him that this time Marta could not be saved, that she was without doubt about to die that very day. The witness later became aware that similar tales had been told by the defendant to others of her acquaintance at whose doors he had stopped to announce Marta's imminent death.
>
> Not knowing what was about to unfold, she did not lend any importance to those stories at the time, attributing it all to Castañeda's anxiety, which he had exhibited before in similar circumstances. She said as much to her husband to calm him.
>
> She further maintains that she saw no reason for disquiet when, on arriving at the house with her daughters some twenty minutes later, she found Marta sitting calmly in the corridor giving instructions for lunch to the servant. Quite put out, her first words to Castañeda, who had also just arrived home, had been: "Oh Oli! Why did you bother Doña Flora? I've already told you it's nothing!" It was only after some pleading on the part of the witness that she had managed to convince her to lie down.

8. In her first statement of October fourteenth, Doña Flora rejected, under cross-examination by the judge, the idea that the dying woman had, in her presence, recriminated Castañeda in any way, although this was a persistent rumour in the city. According to this rumour, Marta had repeatedly exclaimed on her deathbed: "Ollie! Ollie! What have you given me?"

However, her brother, Fernando Guardia Oreamuno, claimed in his statement of 22 October 1933 that it was not just a rumour; Doña Flora had told him herself that she had heard the words escape from Marta's lips, shortly before she was overcome by the last of the three fits she suffered, at around one in the afternoon.

Doña Flores did not return to the subject in her second statement, nor did the judge question her about it. However, Doctor Ulises Terán stated on October fourteenth, that the only words uttered by Marta shortly before her final seizure, were as follows: 'Ollie, Ollie, my joy, my life, for you I left everything, my mother, my family, my country...'

With that she was overwhelmed by a paroxysm of fits, each more violent and prolonged than the last. And then she passed away.

CHAPTER ELEVEN

He Wept in the Arms of His Friend

On the morning of 13 February 1933, Oviedo the Balloon was rehearsing for his law exam, pacing up and down in his underwear in front of five empty rocking chairs, one for each member of the board of examiners. The questions were posed by Yelba, with the book open beside her at the sewing machine. Every time he made a mistake, she would stop pedalling and correct him sternly. This would infuriate The Balloon, interrupted mid-flow, and he would protest that he had answered correctly. The two would then become embroiled in a fierce argument.

According to Yelba de Oviedo's statement, given on 16 October 1933, it was in the midst of one of these disputes that Oliverio Castañeda burst in and told them Marta was gravely ill. He was so anxious that he did not want to wait for them, although they only took a moment to dress properly before going out onto the corner of the street in search of a cab. When none passed by, Yelba decided to walk and Oviedo the Balloon had no choice but to trot along out of breath behind her. She maintained that this was around ten-thirty in the morning:

> As I was crossing the road opposite the entrance to the Church of La Recolección, when we were just a block from the Castañedas' house, I heard a terrifying scream carried on the wind in the morning silence. I recognised Marta's voice. At first I thought it was a trick of my imagination, but when my husband finally caught up with me he assured me he had heard it too. I quickened my pace, almost to a run. When I reached the house they immediately took me to the bedroom, where I found Marta writhing in bed, in the midst of a seizure.

This scream must have alarmed Marta's neighbours. However, Ulises Terán, who at the time had been correcting proofs in his office, literally on the other side of the bedroom wall, heard nothing:

> The remainder of the morning passed quietly, and I almost completely forgot my conversation with Castañeda. When my wife brought me the mid-morning drink to my office, where I was correcting the proofs for a new book, "Easter Week in León", prose and verse by Doctor Juan de Dios Vanega, I entirely neglected to mention it to her. I did not hear any noises or anything out of the ordinary on the far side of the wall. Just after half past ten I went out again to get a breath of fresh air, and noticed that there were a great many people going in and out of the Castañeda residence. Seeing Doctor Derbishire's horse and trap tied up outside the house, I decided to go over and investigate.
>
> The living room was in turmoil, and before anyone could explain, Doña Flora de Contreras came out of the bedroom looking very concerned. As she approached me she showed me a bottle of a preparation called Cuadralina, saying "I think Martita has been poisoned with this medicine". She did not say when Marta had been given the medicine, or by whom.

In his statement of 17 October 1933, Doctor Darbishire maintained that in response to Doña Flora's urgent pleas, he arrived at the house at a quarter past twelve in the company of his colleague and student Doctor Atanasio Salmerón, who by chance had been with him in his consulting room. Consequently, Doctor Ulises Terán could not have seen his horse and trap outside the door just after half past ten, but instead the mare belonging to Doctor Filiberto Herdocia Adams, who was already in attendance at the invalid's bedside at the request of Oviedo the Balloon.

Doctor Herdocia Adams, (married, aged thirty-six), explained in his statement of 15 October 1933:

> I was just leaving home on my mare to begin the morning round of my regular patients when I heard shouts from the street corner. Octavio Oviedo y Reyes ran up to me and

urged me to accompany him to an emergency. He gave me no details save that it concerned Señora Castañeda, who was afflicted by an attack of convulsions. I rode on my mare and he trotted alongside until we reached the house.

I found the patient lying in bed, conversing normally, although she did complain of a slight headache and weakness in her lower limbs. This led me to inform her husband and Doña Flora that in all likelihood she had suffered a nervous attack. I also explained to Doña Flora, in order to set her mind at rest, that the medicine contained in the bottle she had shown me, a sedative produced by Parker and Davis, patented under the name Cuadralina, could not result in an overdose even when mixed with other medication or drugs.

Nevertheless, about twenty minutes later, the patient gave us warning that another attack was coming on, begging us to hold down her legs which were beginning to stiffen. This stiffness spread from her extremities (peripheral neuropathy) to her jaw (trismus) until the rigidity had become generalised over her whole body. She then convulsed violently, so that her body arched above the bed and her eye muscles appeared to be in palsy (strabismus). Respiratory failure, by paralysis of the diaphragm, then became evident in the dark tinge to her face (cyanosis).

Once this second attack had passed she recovered, and was able to answer questions put to her even as to the exact whereabouts of certain things I needed. However, when Father Isidro Oviedo y Reyes came into the room, her state began to concern me once more, since she professed not to be able to see him although she could hear his voice. As a consequence I had to revise my previous diagnosis and I expressed my belief to her husband that we were in fact dealing with uremic syndrome.

Doctor Sequeira Rivas, who was able to observe this second attack, concurred with my diagnosis. Doctor Darbishire arrived some time afterwards, accompanied by Doctor Atanasio Salmerón. When he had examined the patient he was adamant in his opinion that it was an acute blackwater fever. I had to agree with his conclusion, as

> did all of our other colleagues who were already present, or arrived later.

In his statement of 20 October 1933, Doctor Alejandro Sequiera Rivas (single, aged twenty-six), described the attacks as a series of seizures of increasing severity, each one separated by a longer interval. He estimated a half-hour gap between the last two, noting that the patient was showing signs of exhaustion and her core temperature had risen to 38°C.

He further recalled that at the same time, following the advice of the doctors present, the patient was given doses of concentrated sulphate of quinine, sulphuric ether, and camphorated oil given via intramuscular injection. She was also given purgatives: orally and rectally as an enema, this last measure being ordered by Doctor Darbishire. In conclusion, Doctor Sequiera Rivas declared:

> At approximately one o'clock in the afternoon, having exhausted all of the remedies that modern pharmacy could put at our disposal, the final crisis arrived. I had just taken a moment to visit the lavatory and it was while I was so occupied that Doctor Ulises Terán, the next-door neighbour, arrived in great haste, rapping on the door of the WC saying: "Hurry up Doctor, the girl is about to die on us!" When I arrived by her side, her face had taken on a deep violet tinge, evidence of asphyxia. She then expired.

As Doctor Darbishire explained in his own statement, he had no hesitation in diagnosing the case as one of acute blackwater fever, not just from the symptoms, but also because he had discovered the patient's history of malaria a month earlier. As we know, this diagnosis was adopted by the other doctors present; however, Doctor Salmerón never shared their opinion.

When, at one in the afternoon, Marta succumbed to the last convulsion, Oliverio Castañeda retired from the bedside in silence. Oviedo the Balloon, clutching an already tear-stained handkerchief in his hands, followed him into the corridor. To his horror, he saw his friend go over to a sewing basket and search for something among the scraps of material.

'I ran to his side, afraid that he would do something stupid,' said Oviedo the Balloon, taking out his handkerchief as if he were about to cry again. This was on the night of 20 October 1933, and he was surrounded by the members of the accursed table in Casa Prío.

'Was he looking for a gun?' Cosme Manzo asked, watching Oviedo the Balloon curiously to see if he really would burst into tears.

'Yes,' replied Oviedo the Balloon, chewing his handkerchief. 'I managed to wrest it from him, and begged him to let me take care of it.'

'Did he offer any resistance?' asked Doctor Salmerón, smoothing down a page of his notebook ready to start writing.

'None,' Tubby replied, unable to hide his discomfort. 'What's more, he said something that took me by surprise.'

'What was that?' said Doctor Salmerón, calmly waiting to take note.

'He said he wanted to hide the gun so that it would not be stolen.' Oviedo the Balloon crumpled up the handkerchief and stuffed it into the sleeve of his jacket. 'He said there was a thief in the house.'

'A theft at that time of day?' Doctor Salmerón laughed and without taking a breath asked: 'Your friend was born to be a movie star. Who, might I ask, would this heartless robber be?'

'Noel Pallais. He was hanging about the house,' said Oviedo the Balloon, trying to laugh too, but it sounded forced. 'He'd turned up some time before the tragedy, with his wife, like many of their friends did.'

'Yes, I remember seeing Noel Pallais among the people there,' Doctor Salmerón agreed after a moment's thought.

'But why would he think that Noel Pallais was going to steal his gun?' asked Rosalío Usulutlán, nudging Oviedo the Balloon.

'Because somebody had already taken advantage of the situation to steal three hundred dollars,' said Oviedo the Balloon. He made as if to raise his arms, incredulous at his own story, but in the end decided not to. 'Oliverio claimed that the maid had seen Pallais do it.'

'Three hundred dollars?' Rosalío Usulutlán plonked his hat on his head as if that were the last straw.

'I'm just repeating what I heard,' Oviedo the Balloon said, shaking his head disconsolately. 'Pallais removed a handbag from the open wardrobe they had been taking out towels and sheets for the invalid from. He grabbed the wallet, throwing it into the air, then pocketed it.'

'Could that really be true?' said Captain Prío in astonishment, his voice carrying over to the table from the cash register at the bar. 'Wasn't it Noel Pallais who suggested we all sign that cable to her family?'

'I don't know, I just don't know,' Oviedo the Balloon said, turning to Captain Prío, confused and worried. 'At the time I believed Castañeda. It didn't seem like a moment when he would be lying.'

Captain Prío was referring to the telegram sent to inform the Jerez family of Marta's death. According to the copy obtained from National Telegraph Office of León included in the case file, this was sent to Mazatenango via Tropical Radio at two-thirty in the afternoon of the day Marta died.

In his statement of 17 October 1933, Oviedo the Balloon described how he went to his friend Castañeda, paper and pencil in hand, in order to take dictation of that telegram:

> The witness states that Castañeda made several attempts at dictating the message, but he eventually gave up, explaining, in a broken voice, that he could not find the necessary words or could even think of where to start such a difficult task; for this reason he begged the witness himself to write it. Seated at his side, Oviedo proceeded to do just as his friend had requested, receiving from him only one instruction, which consisted of mentioning that Marta had died from an acute haemorrhage, attended to the last by her loving husband's care and attention. He then read the cable out to Castañeda, who signed it.

As can be seen from Doctor Ulises Terán's statement of 14 October 1933, it had apparently been Noel Pallais who had suggested that all those present in the house at the time should sign the telegram. They all agreed, so as to leave the Jerez family in no doubt as to the devoted, kind behaviour shown by Castañeda up until her last moments. This was corroborated by Oviedo the Balloon, although he failed to mention anything referring to the alleged theft of money by Pallais.

'Leaving aside the theft,' began Rosalío Usulutlán, taking off his hat again to scratch his head, 'was he or was he not upset? Perhaps not enough to blow his head off...but did he seem distressed?'

'Yes,' said Oviedo the Balloon, nodding solemnly. 'You could see he was upset. In the end, after I had put the gun into my pocket, we embraced and he burst into tears.'

'Did anyone else come to console him?' Cosme Manzo leaned over slyly to ask him.

'Of course, everyone expressed their condolences,' said Oviedo the Balloon, giving Cosme Manzo a sideways glance, and finding him so close that he could see his gold teeth.

'Oh, no, I was referring to the Contreras sisters. What did they do? What did they say to him?' asked Cosme Manzo, breathing all over him.

'I don't recall them leaving the sick-room. They stayed with their mother and the deceased,' replied Oviedo the Balloon, moving away to escape Cosme Manzo's sour breath.

'What I wouldn't give to know what was in that letter,' sighed Doctor Salmerón, throwing his double-ended pencil across the table at Oviedo the Balloon.

'What letter?' said Oviedo the Balloon, dodging it, his jaw quivering.

'The one which Oliverio Castañeda got the maid Dolores Lorente to take to Maria del Pilar Contreras before breakfast that very morning,' said Doctor Salmerón, retrieving his pencil from where it had come to rest next to Oviedo the Balloon's belly.

'I don't know anything about a letter,' said Oviedo the Balloon taking his handkerchief from his jacket sleeve and carefully patting his cheeks dry. He was suddenly pouring with sweat.

CHAPTER TWELVE

The Love-Birds Re-United

OLIVERIO Castañeda took his exam to qualify as a lawyer and notary public on 21 February 1933, a week later than intended. The board of examiners, presided over by the Dean of the Law Faculty, Doctor Juan de Dios Vanegas, who was later to become his prosecutor at trial, passed the candidate unanimously with the much hoped for outcome: a mention of maxima cum laude. The exam dissertation, printed on the highest quality paper by Tipografía Contreras, was entitled 'An Essay on the Origins of the Rights of Man'.

In the Contreras family home, to which Castañeda had moved back on the day of his wife's burial, his success was celebrated that evening behind the closed living-room door. Behind that same closed door, Matilde played the piano at Oliverio's request. Oliverio, who was at first talkative, his old self, joking and animated, but later lapsed into a deep sadness. As the cook, Salvadora Carvajal remembers in her statement of 14 October 1933:

> Don Carmen ordered several bottles of Moscatel from the La Fama store, and everyone sat down to hear Miss Matilde play the piano. Later they made their way to the table for a banquet: the table cloth of finely embroidered lace had been used by order of Maria del Pilar, along with a flower bowl. Don Oliverio drank many glasses of Moscatel, recalls the witness, and also several of a special cognac which Don Carmen kept locked in his closet, with the result that he became completely drunk and maudlin. In the end Don Carmen senior and his son had to carry him to bed between them.

> This ended the celebration, since by now everyone was very upset. Matilde and Maria del Pilar had both burst into tears, devastated at the news that Oliverio would be returning to his native land and that he never wanted to return to Nicaragua ever again, because it was here that he had lost his soulmate, his adored Marta. These words had also had their effect on Doña Flora, and even the witness was touched by so much sadness, which brought a lump to her throat.

If we are to believe Carmen Contreras Guardia's testimony, Oliverio Castañeda must have talked in his sleep that night; tortured by his nightmares. When on 1 December 1933 the judge pressed the witness about other strange aspects of the accused's behaviour, he responded:

> When his wife died and he came to live with us again, my mother ordered me to move into his room because he was afraid to sleep alone. The night he received his diploma-and I should say that the examiners awarded him his title only out of pity on seeing him widowed—he drank more than he should have: something which was not unusual for him. My father and I, disgusted by the spectacle of him slouched drunkenly over the table, had to carry him to bed.
>
> Around midnight he began to toss and turn in his bed and after a while I heard him repeating certain phrases in a confused and anxious tone as if, filled with remorse, he was begging for someone's forgiveness in his sleep. When this was not forthcoming he seemed forced to protect himself, throwing his arms up to shield his face. I got out of bed and cautiously approached him in an attempt to better hear what he was saying. At first I thought it might be something to do with his dead wife because it seemed to me that he was shouting "Marta! Marta!" But later, paying more attention, his shouts sounded more like: "Mother! Mother!"
>
> Awakened by his shouts in the next room my sisters turned on the light and rapped on the wall, begging me to

> wake him from his nightmare. I felt obliged to do so and Castañeda, bathed in cold sweat, came to himself. Once calm, he began asking me with unusual insistence: "Mito, Mito, what did I say? What did I say?"
>
> I reassured him that I had heard nothing, my intention being to let him go back to sleep and see if he would begin shouting again because I had begun to suspect him of poisoning his wife. If it was his mother he was calling for so fearfully, there was even more reason for me to be suspicious. However, nothing else happened for the rest of the night.
>
> The next day I admonished my sisters for forcing me to wake him; if it hadn't been for that, everything might have been resolved sooner and he would not have had the opportunity to go on to murder others.

Oliverio Castañeda did just as he had announced to the Contreras family on the evening they celebrated his legal diploma behind closed doors in their house. He obtained his qualification and after completing some unfinished business in León, he left for Managua from where, on 17 March 1933, he took the weekly Panaire flight to Guatemala. Only Oviedo the Balloon knew he would not be gone for good; according to his previously-mentioned confession at the accursed table, he left him in charge of certain belongings: a trunk, his typewriter, and the Victor gramophone.

We know little of the next three months, which he spent at his mother-in-law's estate, La Trinidad, in Mazatenango. It was then, as he recounts in his trial statement, that the police authorities under the dictatorship of General Ubico forced him to leave Guatemala once more. That is what he claimed in the interview he gave Rosalío Usulutlán while in prison, and what he told Don Fernando Guardia during their train journey to Puntarenas.

In his statement of 22 October 1933, Don Fernando Guardia gave his version of this incident:

> After a frank condemnation of the social elite of León, he confided in me, swearing me to secrecy, that a group of his friends, all in opposition to the government of General Don Jorge Ubico, were amassing a cache of weapons for

an uprising, planned for December of that year. The conspirators did not balk at bloodshed, part of their plan being an attempt on the president's life. From the nature of the plans and the description that he gave of the participants, even without revealing their names, it was easy for me to deduce that this was a despicable Bolshevik revolution.

Several of the ringleaders had visited the La Trinidad estate, where he was enjoying the good life, to ask him to join their rebellion. Pledging them his support at once, he then gave them letters of introduction to several of his contacts in Zapaca, old comrades of General Chacón, inviting them to join their ranks. In addition, he promised to go personally to Chiquimula to ensure the safe passage of the weapons across the border with Honduras, since he had been a student there and was acquainted with the local smugglers. This was a promise he fulfilled.

However, he told me that these goings-on must have come to the attention of General Ubico's secret police. Towards the middle of July a certain Captain Arburola appeared at the estate, sent directly from the capital, to warn him that if he did not leave the country within ten days there would be trouble. On the following day he was summoned to the Prefecture of Mazatenango where he was notified, by order of a telegram which had arrived in the early morning, that his departure was required within forty-eight hours. This forced him to leave for Guatemala City that very day, escorted by a soldier. Once there, he requested a passport to return to Nicaragua, but this was denied without any explanation, and was informed he could only travel to Costa Rica..

From all this, which I had from the man himself, I am led to conclude that we are dealing with a truly dangerous individual, capable of killing in cold blood, and equally capable of participating in illicit, anti-government activities. I don't doubt that his insistence on obtaining a passport to Nicaragua is connected to plots against the government of this country. His opposition to Doctor Sacasa is well known; "that puppet is as short on ideas as he is on trousers", he said to me during our train journey.

Castañeda arrived at Puntarenas on 22 July 1933 on board the steamboat Usumacinta. He was met at the port by Carmen Contreras Guardia, who had been in San José since May. In a letter sent to Oviedo the Balloon dated the following day, he writes:

> Fair winds have brought me without incident to these shores, my dear Montgolfier; but since then, nothing but drama, as I must now tell you of. My brother-in-law dutifully came to greet me at the dockside. The lady in question is here with her mother. Did I know this? Or did I not? I'll leave you free to exercise your insatiable curiosity, as insatiable as your appetite; perhaps it was the "little birds" and let's leave it at that. Since the tête-à-tête last night, of which more later, I can confirm that I am truly happy. An opportunity to re-make my life, formalise my little flirtation, and return to Nicaragua to settle down. What's that you say Montgolfier? You'll be my Best Man? Warn Yelbita, hopefully we will soon be celebrating, and trusting that it won't cause too much pain to my father-in-law's pocket, for I will tolerate only the best, they'll have to get out the Veuve Clicquot. None of your poor man's local rubbish.
>
> I took a room in the Pensión Barcelona, close to La Sabana. Cheap, clean; the owner, Doña Carmen Naranjo, is very refined, she writes poetry which she likes to read to her guests; and as I am also a poet I arm myself with my own offerings. As they say in León: if you read me yours I'll read you mine. If you screw me I'll screw you.
>
> Barely unpacked, an urgent telephone call. The mother inviting me to dinner, obliging me to go to her brother's house at the ends of the earth. For obvious reasons, this gentleman didn't need to be begged. Housekeeping had already left for the day, but Doña Carmen herself offered to press my suit. To her I extend my sincerest thanks.
>
> I invite you to accompany me, flying through the sky in an air balloon of your own invention. Use the spyglass and from your vantage point among the clouds, see me crossing the road. Anxious to reach the tram stop at La Sabana airport, I strike the paving slabs with the metal

tip of my umbrella, like a blessed blind man whose pockets are filled with the alms of love; watch me approach the tram carriage still empty of passengers. Joyous lamps tinge its windows yellow. I board, I am master of the tram. Why doesn't it start now, pulling away with a screech of brakes? Who else are we waiting for, driver?

Other good citizens board, wrapped up in their winter attire. Lovers, married couples, they do not know the happiness of yours truly. I am filled with the desire to ask these couples who are making themselves comfortable on the shiny seats in the back rows: Ladies and gentlemen! What is this? Can you tell me? Where are you going with such complacency? Aren't there better places: circuses, variety shows, ice-cream parlours, etc, where that elusive happiness awaits you, as it awaits me? But compassion stopped my impulse. No, that happiness exists only in my own breast.

And off goes the tram. It passes down Paseo Colón, it clatters, bell clanging, along the stretch of closed shops on the Avenida Central. I hail the lights in their windows, I give my compliments to the manikins, the trappings of fashion strike me as excellent: a toast to ladies' fashion, invented to provide enchantment for the lady in question! Now you climb, fair tram, up the Cuesta de Moras to leave me at last among the elegant bungalows of the Amón neighbourhood.

Cast out some ballast from your balloon and move a little to starboard, so that you have no difficulty in following me. Watch me open my umbrella before I start walking beneath the sodden cypresses lining the footpath. Your faithful companion now arrives at the wooden, two-storied villa hiding its outline behind the acacias in its garden. I have already opened the iron gate, set within a wall covered in bougainvillea, and stride up the gravel path which takes me to the steps of the porch. The tin sheets on the roof of the villa flap in the sudden rain shower as if they were about to break free and fly though the air. Mind your head, Montgolfier!

I close my umbrella and ring the doorbell beside the coloured panes of the door. I hear hurried footsteps coming from somewhere inside, resounding on the wooden floor, as if they were resounding in my heart. When the door opens it is the lady in question herself, body and soul. I will pause to describe her to you: pink sweater, pleated skirt, of an even paler pink; a beautiful sky-blue scarf in her hair, the perfect adornment for her perfumed curls. Her tanned complexion gives off a healthy glow provided by the gentle caresses of the fresher air in San José, and her eyes: oh her eyes! They seek me out, sparkling, full of life. I have seen her Montgolfier, she has looked at me: today I believe in God!

She smiles, and there seems to be something melancholic about her shyness; incredulous, she studies me before throwing herself into my arms. She closes her jet-black eyes as she is about to kiss me, teetering in her high heels. So much more a woman than ever, she's wearing heels, and I...I would sacrifice all my love to her whims, I would give my life.

On tiptoes, closing her eyelids made up with blue eye-shadow. She wants to and yet does not want to wake from this cherished dream in which yours truly arrives at this very door in the endless rain. But he withdraws, suddenly cautious, Montgolfier: do you see, from your vantage point in the clouds? Other footsteps approach, hurrying and welcoming, from the depths of the house which has an odour, now that I become aware of it, of frying butter and floor disinfectant. And now there is no kiss; those tanned arms, for which I would do anything, fall to her sides, because who should appear but...her mother.

Return to the port side, Montgolfier, you won't be able to see anything through the roof however hard you try. An intimate supper, polite conversation and unambiguous signals on the part of the visitor, skilfully designed to demonstrate there are only two beings seated at the table who could save one another if they fell...all the others, an uncle, a brother in law,...her mother: are no more than the supporting cast. I oblige them to play their roles; requiring them to converse, to speak, to comment, their words according to my script. I don't want any mistakes, presumptions, or vain hopes on anyone's behalf. Do you hear me, Montgolfier, not anyone, present or absent.

Supper finishes. Alone in the one moment that circumstances allow, I slip my graduation ring onto the finger of the lady in question. She squeezes my hand. Mission accomplished. Yours truly says his farewells. Tomorrow, today for you, I will return, I write this letter even before boarding the tram once more; the campaign is carefully planned and intensive. I will not lose any opportunity to be by the side of the lady in question, until the day we depart, together, for Nicaragua.

In his statement under oath of 18 October 1933, Oliverio Castañeda also referred to his stay in Costa Rica. I have here his answers to the judge on the matter:

JUDGE: If you confirm that the Carmen Contreras Guardia was waiting for you at the port of Puntarenas, surely this means that you had given him forewarning of your arrival?

ACCUSED: I sent him a telegram advising him of my departure for Costa Rica, but without explaining the circumstances which obliged such an impromptu trip. He had the good manners to travel to the port to meet me and accompany me by train to the capital.

JUDGE: Does this mean that you had regular correspondence with the young Contreras, and indeed that you knew his postal address?

ACCUSED: That is correct. We had developed a sincere friendship in León. That he was able to attain his dream of pursuing his Law degree at the University of San José, in a Faculty that even boasts European professors and an excellent library, is thanks to my tireless appeals to the better nature of Don Carmen, who initially was very reluctant to incur such an expense.

JUDGE: Despite this, you were unaware that for a number of weeks past Doña Flora de Contreras had been in Costa Rica, accompanied by Maria Pilar, her daughter?

ACCUSED: I was completely ignorant of this. The fact that I knew Carmen's postal address did not give me the right to inconvenience him with my letters and distract him from his studies, so recently begun. For me it was a welcome surprise to learn from his lips, after exchanging greetings, that Doña Flora was in Costa Rica for the season, visiting family and on business; and that the youngest of her daughters was with her.

JUDGE: Miss Rosaura Aguiluz, manager of the León post office, affirms in her testimony of 17 October 1933, that while you were in Guatemala, you maintained an intense exchange of letters with Señorita Matilde Contreras. I quote: "On a great many occasions, she came in person to the post office to collect airmail letters postmarked Mazatenango, sent by Doctor Oliverio Castañeda. On those occasions she would post letters of her own to the same Doctor Castañeda, which judging by their weight in grammes, must have contained a great many sheets of paper. Señorita Contreras had also warned her never to send the letters to her house with the postman, as usual, but she herself always came by to collect them", unquote. I now ask you: is it not logical to assume that you came by the information about her mother's trip through these letters?

ACCUSED: You should bear in mind, your honour, that Miss Aguiluz appeared in court to testify of her own accord. As a result, when she takes great pains to stress the "great many occasions" and the "great many sheets", she is merely demonstrating her "great love" for gossip. We did, it is true, exchange a few letters, polite and written in a style appropriate between affectionate friends. Matilde had no need to shroud this exchange in any form of secrecy, as Miss Aguiluz maliciously contends. Nor did Matilde at any point in these letters give me any news of the trip taken by her mother and sister, perhaps for the simple reason that their dates did not coincide with the opportunity to mention that trip.

JUDGE: Once in San José, you stayed in the house of Don Fernando Guardia, where Doña Flora and her daughter were also staying?

ACCUSED: Nothing of the sort. I found lodgings in the Pensión Barcelona owned by Doña Carmen Naranjo, located opposite the tram station near La Sabana Park. On arriving at San José, I said goodbye to Doña Flora's son at the train station.

JUDGE: When was the first time you saw Doña Flora and her daughter after your arrival in San José?

ACCUSED: That same night. A little after I had arrived, I received a phone call at the pension from Doña Flora, inviting me to supper at her brother's home. I barely had time to take the necessary items for a change of clothes out of my suitcase in order to comply, out of politeness, with the invitation.

These answers by Oliverio Castañeda were the subject of close analysis by those present at the 'accursed table' on the night of 20 October 1933, in Casa Prío.

'Not even Saint Peter would believe a word of that,' said Cosme Manzo as he handed Doctor Salmerón the copy of *El Cronista* where the trial proceedings were published.

'Of what?' asked Captain Prío coming over from behind the counter, drying his hands after washing up some glasses.

'Several things,' said Doctor Salmerón. He opened the paper, shaking it out energetically before peering at it short-sightedly. 'Firstly, that they expelled him from Guatemala for conspiracy; and secondly, that he knew nothing of the arrival of the Contreras women in San José. He was after one of the ladies. Or both.'

'And what's wrong with that?' Oviedo the Balloon jerked himself out of his doze. 'He was a free man, without ties.'

'The love-birds reunited,' said Rosalío Usulutlán, drawing the bow across an imaginary violin.

'On that we can agree, my friend,' replied Doctor Salmerón sharpening his double-ended pencil with his penknife. 'He found out about the trip from Matilde's letters, then ran after the other two.'

'He was in such a hurry to greet them personally that he took the first boat,' Cosme Manzo said, savouring the words as if he had a candy in his mouth: 'a true gentleman never wastes time.'

'Remember that bit in *Payment Deferred*?' said Captain Prío, returning to the counter to arrange the clean glasses. 'Maureen O'Sullivan sent letters to the poisoner Charles Laughton. Those letters were never found by the Boston police. They searched for them high and low but they never appeared.'

'Quite right,' Rosalío Usulutlán said, jabbing his finger in the air for emphasis, 'they were safely with his buddy Ray Milland. We only find out at the very end, when the two of them talk in the prison cell, after the priest gets sent away, rejected. The poisoner, unrepentant, did not want his spiritual succour.'

'They never proved anything against Charles Laughton,' said Oviedo the Balloon, who was sprawled over the table with his chin resting on his arms. 'What could he be repentant about if he wasn't guilty?'

'Charles Laughton has nothing to do with it! What they did to that poor Matilde, may she rest in peace, using her as their go-between!' said Cosme Manzo, pursing his lips as if the candy had suddenly turned sour.

'It's not so simple, Manzo, my friend,' said Doctor Salmerón raising his newly sharpened pencil with a professorial air, 'the human heart is unknowable. And those letters: we will never read them.'

'The strains of the overture to the opera Coriolanus can be heard. Beethoven: opus sixty-two,' said Captain Prío. He held a glass up to the light and then misted it with his breath. 'The two friends take their leave of one another. As they say: until we will meet again in Heaven.'

'Only you, Captain, would know about opera in this shit hole of a town,' Doctor Salmerón said, leaning over the table to blow away the pencil shavings. 'What can you tell me about all those letters, my esteemed legal scholar? Will we ever read them?'

'One day, perhaps,' said Oviedo the Balloon said, chewing his nails carefully, his gaze fixed on the square outside 'Never give up hope.'

That gaze, fixed on the plaza, looked sadly towards the dark shapes of the laurel bushes which even the electric glare from the street lamps failed to illuminate. He had attended three showings of *Payment Deferred*. While Charles Laughton and his faithful friend Ray Milland play out their final conversation on death row, the electric chair appears intermittently on the screen, lit by a stark white light. Much like a barber's chair, its only distinguishing features are the leather straps used to restrain the condemned.

Day is dawning. The hour of execution draws near, and Ray Milland remembers the letters. Charles Laughton paces up and down the cell, then returns. He begs him to keep the letters safe in a show of eternal friendship. And once again he protests his innocence. They embrace.

The lights in all the houses of Payne County, close to the prison, flicker and almost go out: Charles Laughton is being electrocuted. And so, while the farmers kneel in prayer, Ray Milland departs, hunched in his raincoat, until he is no more than a speck in the distance of the grey dawn.

CHAPTER THIRTEEN

Like the Plot of a Movie

OF ALL of the doctors assembled around the bed of Marta Jerez on 13 February 1933, the only one who had not been expressly summoned was Doctor Atanasio Salmerón. That lunchtime he had just happened to be visiting his old teacher Doctor Darbishire. When one of the Contreras servants arrived urgently requesting the old man's attendance at the dying woman's bedside, Doctor Salmerón reluctantly agreed to accompany him.

Throughout the whole episode, Doctor Salmerón stayed at a prudent distance from the sickbed. He dared not intervene in the hurried consultations taking place between his colleagues, nor did he give any opinion when Doctor Darbishire imposed his diagnosis, despite being in complete disagreement with him.

Once it was all over, the older man offered to drive him home in his buggy, back to the San Sebastián district where he lived and also had his practice. It was during this journey that, for the first time, Doctor Salmerón plucked up the courage to outline his principal objections to the diagnosis. In particular, the absence of specific features generally associated with comas brought on by blackwater fever: frequent vomiting, sensations of cold, shivering and above all an exceptionally elevated temperature. In the case of the recently deceased, her temperature had never exceeded 38°C; a rise in temperature which, in his opinion, was only due to the muscular effort involved in the convulsive spasms.

Doctor Darbishire listened politely and attentively as he drove the buggy, the reigns held firmly in his hands. When they reached the house, he stopped the horses and as his friend and student descended, invited him back to his surgery that night so that he could expand on the theories he had just outlined. That way they would be able to draw some satisfactory, scientific conclusions, just as they used to in the good old days.

'Do you think we are dealing with some kind of physiological collapse? Poisoning due to uremic syndrome, for example, as Doctor Herdocia Adams believed?' asked Doctor Darbishire, pulling on the reins as Doctor Salmerón recovered his bag from the back seat.

'I prefer to discuss my suspicions with you in private. I will see you tonight.' Doctor Salmerón smiled up at him, his eyes half-closed against the glare of the sun.

'Don't tell me you suspect foul play?' said Doctor Darbishire, returning the smile with his head to one side.

But Doctor Salmerón only tipped his hat in farewell.

As he trotted off again, Doctor Darbishire lifted himself from the seat to smooth the folds of his cape more securely beneath him. A stiff breeze characteristic of the season had sprung up, blowing dust and rubbish from the street into his face. He shook his head in exasperation: as ever, his brilliant former pupil was prone to ridiculous flights of fancy; he had an excellent clinical eye, but was led astray by his feverish imagination.

He knew that even as a student Doctor Salmerón had been an expert in toxicology and that he was also very learned concerning the pathological personality traits of the criminal mind, having read all manner of treatises on the subject, in particular those cases involving poisoning. Indeed, he always had something new to say on these issues which he managed to bring up whenever they met.

He reflected that the situation in the sickroom that day had not provided the best opportunity to come up with an accurate, well thought-out diagnosis. The presence of so many doctors at the bedside of such a gravely sick patient was the product of a long-standing and ill-judged local custom among the well-to-do. These families were never satisfied with the professional opinion of one doctor, and the wealthier they were, the more doctors they required at the bedside.

That unfortunate foreign girl had been accorded this traditional honour; useless in her time of need. Three or four doctors had been called, none of whom had previous knowledge of her medical history. He himself had added to the confusion by bringing along his old student, who apparently was now proposing to complicate matters still further by contradicting his diagnosis. Despite all these negative circumstances, however, Doctor Darbishire still stood by his own clinical judgement; he felt it was well-founded considering the patient's previous symptoms of malaria.

As was his custom, that evening Doctor Darbishire ate alone, with only his Alsatian dogs for company. The dining-room was behind a sky-blue partition at the end of the verandah. The garden outside was a jungle after years of neglect. Fruit tree branches were forcing their way through cracks in the crumbling planks, and the bough of a lemon tree poked in through the dining-room window, its leaves brushing the back of his chair at the head of the table.

Doctor Darbishire ate his own small supper with bored distaste. He fed his dogs directly from the fork, sharing out the portions equally and calming them, because there was always more than enough to go around. He himself never touched the desserts, but served them directly to the dogs from the bowl. Over the years the dogs had developed a sweet tooth, and in particular Esculapio, the dog who had been so cruelly poisoned on the street a few months earlier.

Doctor Darbishire's three daily meals were sent to him courtesy of his godson Captain Prío on a wooden tray covered in a cloth. Since the death of his second wife, the doctor had not employed any domestic help, and the stove remained cold in the abandoned kitchen. His one servant, whose only duty was to keep the consulting room clean, was called Teodosio, a deaf mute from the orphanage run by Father Mariano Dubón.

His first wife had been a nurse from the Salpetrière hospital. They had married shortly after he had qualified as a doctor in Paris. After only two months in León she had fled back to France without even unpacking her wedding trousseau. Sleeping beneath a mosquito net in their oven of a bedroom had been an unbearable purgatory for her. She couldn't stomach the horror of spending the rest of her life swatting at the mosquitoes, gorged with blood, which constantly swarmed through the air. His second wife, a first cousin, had died a few months after their wedding. She had been pregnant at the time and fell victim of a fatal bout of blackwater fever.

Although different in many other respects, the doctor and his disciple shared a solitary lifestyle. They both rented consulting rooms alone, he because he had been widowed twice (his French wife had been declared dead from the moment she left) and his former student because he had reached a point in his life where he had decided to renounce marriage; having pulled out of more than one prolonged engagement at the last moment, afraid of joining the list of cuckolds among his acquaintances.

On hearing the sound of the door knocker Doctor Darbishire stood up, forgetting to take the napkin from his neck. The pack of hounds, upset by the interruption to their dinner, followed him to the door, barking. Doctor Salmerón was very punctual. Taking him by the arm, Doctor Darbishire led along the verandah to the pair of rocking chairs they usually sat in.

Although it was almost seven in the evening, a rosy glow still lingered in the sky. Doctor Salmerón could barely contain his impatience as he sat and waited for his old teacher to light the kerosene lamps hanging from wooden posts along the verandah. The old man always insisted on using a single match, despite the risk of burning his fingers.

As he sat marshalling his thoughts, Doctor Salmerón could not help observing that there was a perfectly good electric light hanging above them which would have been a far better option than laboriously lighting each and every kerosene lamp: and with a single match.

Ever since his student days, when Doctor Darbishire had allowed him to come and study here late, and even sometimes to stay the night, Doctor Salmerón had grown accustomed to his teacher's eccentricities. For the most part they did not bother him, although this could not be said of many of his fellow students and members of the faculty: the way he exaggerated the sound of his "r's" and, in the heat of his enthusiasm, unexpectedly began breaking into French, made him a source of mirth.

Nor did it seem outlandish to Doctor Salmerón that his friend chose to wear that old-fashioned Cordoban cape, fastened with a gold chain. What he could not understand was his excessive attachment to the dogs. He spoke to them in French and on Saturdays would take them for a drive in his buggy. He let them follow him everywhere, including to the lavatory, where he was happy to answer the calls of nature right in front of their snouts with the door wide open. If they misbehaved, he punished them by refusing to speak to them for days.

His only other gripe against the old man, and in this he was alone, concerned his life-long presidency of the Brotherhood of the Holy Sepulchre. The duties of this post required the old man to march at the head of the annual Good Friday procession, bearing a banner and enduring heat and fatigue in equal measure. This Doctor Salmerón regarded as ridiculous. However, all this odd behaviour in no way diminished the respect he and everyone else in León had for Doctor Darbishire's clinical abilities. They all considered him not only an outstanding physician, but also the city's finest surgeon.

Doctor Salmerón was approaching forty. His hair was already greying, and its bushy bristles were resistant to any attempt to tame them. This and his small, almond-shaped eyes and sallow skin suggested mixed-race ancestry. The son of a laundress in the San Sebastián neighbourhood, he owed his doctor's diploma to the many nights she spent ironing shirts until past midnight, at the cost of rheumatism and insomnia. The city's well-to do clientele had never allowed him to forget his humble origins, or indeed his position as the head of the accursed table. As a result, he practised medicine among the poorer districts, where the sick would come to him on pack animals or carts. Unlike the majority of his colleagues, he did not have his own horse and buggy, or even a good mare to take him on his rounds.

Doctor Salmerón sat perched anxiously on the edge of his chair, balancing the rocker with his weight. He felt uneasy about leaning back as he would normally have done in his old teacher's home. He repeatedly shot worried looks at his host, looks that were a mixture of submission and defiance. When Doctor Darbishire was finally ready to listen, he took his small, hard-backed Casa Squibb notebook from the pocket of his crumpled linen suit, stained here and there with iodine. Still too nervous to sink back in the comfortable depths of the rocking chair, he leaned forward, arms on his knees.

'I have some questions for you, sir,' said Doctor Salmerón, moistening his finger tip and leafing through the notebook.

'My, my, a judicial enquiry,' joked Doctor Darbishire, wiping his pince-nez on the lapels of his jacket, as if he were the one about to read from the notebook.

'You told me you attended Señora Castañeda for the first time about a month ago.' Doctor Salmerón raised his eyes from his notebook. 'That was for menstrual irregularities, rather than malaria, wasn't it?'

'Heavy menstrual haemorrhaging. Prolonged bleeding and persistent pain in the ovaries,' said Doctor Darbishire, waving his pince-nez. 'I prescribed Apiolina pills. She had symptoms of fever which drew my attention, so I sent a blood sample for analysis. I suspected malaria.'

'The test confirmed your suspicions,' Doctor Salmerón said, running his fingers through his hair as he glanced down at the pages of his notebook.

'An examination under the microscope revealed the presence of the malaria parasite,' said Doctor Darbishire, putting his pince-nez back into his pocket and resting his hands on the curve of his belly. He rocked gently in his chair. 'Everyone in León carries them in their blood.'

'You then gave her some Pelletier tablets, but her husband asked you to change the prescription, didn't he?" Doctor Salmerón fished in his shirt pocket for his double-ended pencil: red at one end, blue at the other. 'That's what you told me this morning on our way to the house.'

'Yes, he came to see me. He didn't trust patent medicines,' Doctor Darbishire explained, bending to flick a grain of rice off one of his boots. 'He wanted me to make something up from my personal pharmacy. I prepared some capsules for him: one gram of quinine sulphate, one of antipyrine, and two grammes of sodium benzoate. A course of treatment lasting one month.'

'Which was due to finish today, the day of her death,' interjected Doctor Salmerón, underlining something in red in his notebook. 'If she had been taking the medicine regularly the symptoms of malaria would have cleared up. In any event, the concentration of quinine in her system would make a fatal episode of fever highly unlikely.'

Doctor Darbishire stopped rocking. The condescending smile

he had been wearing since the start of the interrogation vanished from his face.

'What do you say to that, sir?' Doctor Salmerón pressed him, tapping the notebook with his pencil.

'It is highly unlikely,' agreed Doctor Darbishire, 'but I have no idea if she did indeed take the pills daily as I prescribed. I told you, I didn't see her again until today.'

'Well sir, when you were called on to attend this lady once more, it was not because of a recurrence of the malaria,' said Doctor Salmerón, who was now the one rocking happily. 'The emergency was, once again, a menstrual disorder: just like the month before.'

'That's true,' admitted Doctor Darbishire, looking concerned and grasping the arms of his rocking chair.

'If we consult the calendar, her period would have been due any day now,' said Doctor Salmerón, his head bumping gently against the headrest of his chair as he rocked to and fro. 'So there is nothing untoward in her husband's alarm, is there? Did the patient herself have the opportunity to mention she was suffering another heavy vaginal bleed?'

'No, by the time I arrived she was already in the grip of those convulsions and so I concentrated on that,' said Doctor Darbishire, drumming impatiently on the arms of his chair. 'You were there with me.'

'Of course I was,' said Doctor Salmerón, flicking back through the pages of his notebook, 'and I heard the husband saying he thought his wife had put herself in mortal danger by taking a cold bath.'

'Well, that can't be the first stupid comment you've heard in your time,' said Doctor Darbishire, thumping the armrests of his chair before folding them on his lap. 'It's part of our job to put up with the ignorance of desperate families.'

'Yes,' Doctor Salmerón began. He was on the edge of his chair again, but now due to excitement rather than nervousness. 'We both heard how all the couple's friends said that Castañeda himself had gone to fetch them because wife was dying. Dying of a haemorrhage.'

'He seems to be a very highly-strung young man,' said Doctor Darbishire, his hands trembling to illustrate his point. 'When I first treated his wife, it struck me that he was very nervous and that this just made the situation worse.'

'But this anxious young man's wife did not die of a haemorrhage, she died in the midst of extreme convulsions.' So saying, Doctor Salmerón, by now almost completely out of his seat, was about to emphasise his concluding words by tapping his colleague on the knees with his notebook, but thought better of it. Doctor Darbishire sat silently twisting the white gold wedding band on his finger, a memento of his second marriage.

'If anyone questioned the fact that the young woman who died today did so of a menstrual haemorrhage,' Doctor Salmerón said, dragging his chair closer to his companion, 'who better to corroborate it than you, sir?'

'What of it?' said Doctor Darbishire, who now seemed lost in contemplation of his wedding ring. 'Can you imagine the fuss if I were to suggest examining her?'

'Yes, but just suppose you were to make an examination. Without your evidence to back him up, the song and dance that young man made wouldn't count for anything,' explained Doctor Salmerón, closing his notebook, which was in danger of becoming illegible, smudged by his sweaty palms. 'It would be exposed for what it was: crying wolf. A lie.'

'Where are you going with all this, my friend?' Doctor Darbishire asked with a puzzled frown. 'You must forgive me for being slow on the uptake.'

'Well, first you will have to let me bore you with a few other details,' said Doctor Salmerón, drying the back of his hand on his trousers before opening his notebook once again. 'If the young Castañeda had really thought the haemorrhage was so bad, wouldn't it have been more sensible for him to have come straight to you, as you had already treated his wife once before? According to what he told us, the first attack was at eight in the morning, but you weren't called until midday.'

Doctor Darbishire stared at him, chewing the soft, white hairs of his moustache. He nodded gravely.

'Instead, he ran to fetch Doña Flora, knowing that at some point, but not too soon, she would send for you: and that's what happened,' said Doctor Salmerón, trying to catch the old man's eye, but failing. 'He knew he could also count on his other friends to summon their own doctors: which also happened. The more the merrier. But let's leave that aside for one moment. For now, the key player is you yourself.'

'Me?' said Doctor Darbishire through his moustache. He was irritated at his student's insistence on placing him at the centre of the drama.

'Yes, you.' Doctor Salmerón replied. He was becoming impatient and seemed on the point of throwing his notebook aside, as if he no longer needed it. 'You had already treated the patient, you were her personal physician. Your diagnosis therefore had more authority than anyone else's. Doctor Herdocia Adams had diagnosed uremic syndrome but when you arrived and said blackwater fever, he immediately demurred to you. From then on any contradictory suggestion wouldn't even have been considered.'

One of the Alsatians loped over to Doctor Darbishire's chair. When he reached out to stroke its head, the other dogs started to emerge from the shadows.

'Well, even if we accept all that, I am still at a loss,' said Doctor Darbishire, settling back in his chair. Surrounded by his pack, he seemed more comfortable.

'The husband raises the alarm. With tears in his eyes, he runs to tell all their close friends that his wife is gravely ill again.' Doctor Salmerón pointed his pencil at the old man. 'It's nothing serious, they reassure him. Nevertheless, they all turn up at the house and the patient does indeed die; but of a series of fits. And, because you have already been treating her for malaria, no one is surprised that your diagnosis attributes the cause of death to blackwater.'

'But she really did suffer from malaria. The laboratory tests prove it.' Doctor Darbishire waved his hands in the air to emphasize his words.

'Let's allow that your course of quinine didn't cure her,' Doctor Salmerón said. He put his pencil behind his ear and tried to soothe the old man. 'But remember, that wasn't why the husband raised the alarm. So we must accept that there was a haemorrhage: did you see any bloodstained sheets?"

'I'm not a detective!' Doctor Darbishire cried, jumping to his feet so quickly that he inadvertently stepped on the tail of one of his dogs, who howled in pain. 'If I'm told that a patient has bled profusely, it's not my job to go looking for bloody sheets but to treat the cause.'

'Begging your pardon, doctor, but when we entered the sick room that wasn't exactly the reason for our being there,' said Doctor Salmerón, trying to pat the injured dog's head, but rapidly withdrawing his hand when it growled at him. 'What state did you find her in? She was in the midst of a fit, and not the first one she had suffered that morning.'

Although he did not like the sound of this at all, Doctor Darbishire felt obliged to sit down again. The dogs had picked up on the tense atmosphere and closed ranks around him.

'My conclusions, sir, if you would care to hear them.' Doctor Salmerón stuffed the notebook back into his pocket.

'About time, too,' Doctor Darbishire said, adjusting his pince-nez and forcing a smile. 'Let's hear them, it can't do any harm.'

'Our highly-strung young man poisoned his wife. He timed it to coincide with her problematic menstrual cycle.' Doctor Salmerón reached to his pocket for his notebook, then decided to carry on from memory: 'That way he had the excuse to go off in search of all their friends who already knew of her illness.'

'Poison. Of course, I should have expected as much.' Doctor Darbishire sighed sadly. 'You're an incurable case, my friend.'

'Yes sir, poison.' Doctor Salmerón insisted, although he was stung by his old teacher's cutting remark. 'Lock-jaw, cyanosis, asphyxia, convulsions. A set of symptoms not unlike malaria and as he hoped, you arrive and pronounce: blackwater fever.'

'And what type of poison, may I ask?' Doctor Darbishire stifled a yawn, attempting to convey his complete disdain.

'Strychnine, doctor, to judge by the symptoms,' replied Doctor Salmerón, annoyed but attempting to hide it. 'The same strychnine used a few months ago to poison your Esculapio.'

The dogs whined and growled as they gathered at their master's feet.

'How can you know that?' said Doctor Darbishire, clinging to the arms of his chair as if he was in the middle of an earthquake.

'Because that night Castañeda was with his friend Oviedo,' explained Doctor Salmerón, pleased to see he had shaken the old man. 'The two of them poisoned your dog together. If you don't believe me, ask Rosalío Usulutlán: he saw them.'

Bewildered, Doctor Darbishire shooed the dogs away, slapping their haunches with his palm. They resisted his efforts until he scolded them and they finally slunk off.

'These allegations of yours are very serious,' said Doctor Darbishire, rocking vigorously back and forth in his chair. 'Only an autopsy would be able to tell us the truth.'

'So ask for one. You were her personal doctor,' said Doctor Salmerón, leaping up from his chair so suddenly it kept on rocking.

'I have no right to. It would cause a scandal,' Doctor Darbishire replied, also rising to his feet and confronting his former pupil. 'What is more, you heard Doña Flora, the funeral is to be held as early as possible tomorrow morning.'

A hot breeze shook the leaves and bushes in the abandoned garden. Frustrated, Doctor Salmerón looked for his hat on the wall rack. Next to it, in a heavy oval frame, was a portrait of Doctor Darbishire's second wife.

'If that young man remains in León, be prepared for further deaths,' Doctor Salmerón said, grabbing his hat clumsily.

'How so, my friend?' Doctor Darbishire enquired, smiling broadly as he accompanied his colleague to the door. The Alsatians had once again emerged from the shadows to surround the old man, almost tripping him.

'Oh, take no notice of me,' said Doctor Salmerón, marching down the passageway without a backwards glance.

'You shouldn't fill your head with all those movie plots,' said Doctor Darbishire, putting his arm affectionately around the other man's shoulders. 'You seem to have been carried away by the suspense of *Payment Deferred*. Real life is very different. Nothing ever happens in this city.'

'I wish you a good night,' said Doctor Salmerón. He stepped down into the street, turning at the last moment to give the old man a curt handshake.

PART TWO

Evidence for the Prosecution

In the orchard I will die,
Deep in the rose garden they have killed me.
I went for to pick roses, mother
I found my love in the orchard,
In the orchard I will die,
Deep in the rose garden they have killed me.

Spanish Ballad

CHAPTER FOURTEEN

The Cod Dancer Outside the Scene of the Crime

IT WAS the evening of 26 September 1933. Dressed in only his flannel long-johns, the journalist Rosalío Usulutlán was lying immobile on Doctor Atanasio Salmerón's examination couch. He was staring fixedly at the dark water stains on the ceiling made by the rain as it leaked in through the roof tiles. Outside came the muffled sound of a rainstorm.

The doctor was digging his hands into different places of the journalist's belly. As he probed the region of the gall-bladder, Rosalío the journalist gave a prolonged groan. Doctor Salmerón told him to get dressed and then went over to the hand-basin where he washed his hands thoroughly using the pink cake of anti-bacterial Lifebuoy soap.

'You haven't taken any notice of me! You are still on the spicy food and the fat,' said Doctor Salmerón, taking the threadbare towel from its peg to dry his hands. 'I've told you that if those gall-stones don't dissolve I'll have to slice you open!'

'Did you know, doctor, that your friend Charles Laughton is back in town?' said Rosalío, sitting up to put on his vest. The sweat covering his bony torso gleamed under the intense light from the lamp above the couch.

'Oliverio Castañeda?' said Doctor Salmerón with an expression that was both pleased and puzzled.

'The very same, living and breathing,' said Rosalío, edging himself off the high couch so that he could jump straight into his shoes.

'When did he arrive?' asked Doctor Salmerón. Without taking his eyes off the other man, he walked over to his desk. He sat heavily, making the chair creak beneath his weight.

'This morning, at Corinto. Cosme Manzo saw him when he was

collecting some goods from the customs house,' said Rosalío, smiling broadly at Doctor Salmerón as he buttoned up his trouser fly. 'He had just disembarked from the steamer and was having breakfast at the Lupone Hotel. You'll never guess who with!'

'The Contrerases?' said Doctor Salmerón, leaning back in his chair and making it groan again.

'They all came together on the same steam ship: him, Doña Flora, and María del Pilar,' said Rosalío. He finished dressing and adjusted his hat as if he were in front of a mirror.

'Why the hell didn't you tell me this before!' cried Doctor Salmerón, scrunching up a sheet of paper and aiming it at Rosalío's head.

'Because you probably would have wrenched my gall-bladder out with your bare hands,' said Rosalío, backing away while coyly protecting his nether regions with his hands.

'I told you so,' said Doctor Salmerón, rubbing his hands gleefully, 'I knew he had unfinished business here! Tonight we drink that bottle of cognac!'

At this point it is necessary to explain to the reader the importance of this bottle of cognac:

After Doctor Salmerón had unsuccessfully expounded his theories to his old teacher Doctor Darbishire, the accursed table had made the Castañeda case their sole topic of conversation for several weeks. However, in the absence of any new information and with Oliverio Castañeda's departure from León—supposedly for good, despite Doctor Salmerón's best efforts to convince them he would return, their discussions tailed off. In one of these sessions Doctor Salmerón had gone to the extreme of making a wager with Cosme Manzo: a bottle of cognac, to be paid on the day that Oliverio Castañeda returned to the city. If after one year he still hadn't turned up, Doctor Salmerón would lose the wager.

According to what Rosalío had just told him, it now seemed as though his prognosis had been correct. On the morning of September twenty-sixth, Oliverio Castañeda had disembarked from the steamship *Acajutla* in the port of Corinto. It was also true that Doña Flora de Contreras and her daughter María del Pilar had also returned to Nicaragua on the same ship.

This was a simple coincidence, according to the evidence Castañeda gave to the trial judge on 11 October 1933:

I decided to return to León as in Costa Rica I had met a gentleman, a Cuban by the name of Don Miguel Barnet, who had suggested we collaborate together on the publication of an annual directory which would contain all manner of information about the countries of Central America. Given my connections in Nicaragua, both my contacts in government circles and those in the world of business and industry, it seemed natural that we should begin our enterprise in that country.

By chance, Doña Flora Contreras and her daughter were also making preparations to leave at around the same time, and for this reason when it came to booking tickets we ended up on the same steamer. It was a coincidence that I would almost say was inevitable, because the steamship makes the journey between Puntarrenas and Corinto only once a month.

My business partner sailed with me, and we had decided to book a suite at the Metropolitan Hotel. However, during the crossing Doña Flora insisted on convincing me to stay in her house; my old room was still empty. Her winning argument was that I would only have to pay the family a token rent, and what's more everyone would be delighted to have me back. In the face of such amiable arm-twisting I felt obliged to capitulate. I accepted her invitation to return and install myself once again beneath the roof where I had previously received so much delightful hospitality.

The offer was formalised by Don Carmen at the train station itself. He intimated that he would be glad to have me by him while he was finalising the contract with the Water Company which was still being held up by the municipal authorities. My partner was not pleased by the distractions this would present for our own project, and he took a room in the Metropolitan Hotel.

However, if we are to believe the testimony of Señorita Alicia Duquestrada, (a twenty-three year old spinster and domestic servant) the question of hospitality had come up not during the sea crossing, but some time before. In her statement, given on 19

October 1933 at her own home in the presence of her father, Don Esteban Duquestrada, she revealed how Matilde Contreras had voiced opposition to the idea of Oliverio Castañeda returning as a guest of the house:

> JUDGE: Did Matilde Contreras express any opinion to you, her close friend, with regard to Oliverio Castañeda returning to live in the house? And, if so, when did she do this?
> WITNESS: Yes, she confided in me. Don Carmen received a letter from Doña Flora telling him of her expected return date, which also mentioned that Oliverio Castañeda would be accompanying them and to make his old room ready. When Matilde heard this, I can tell you, she really was not pleased. She told me so on the same day the letter arrived. She had just got back from a nine-day retreat at La Merced, praying for the soul of Doña Chanita, Pallais's widow.
> JUDGE: Can I then assume that the family were already prepared for Castañeda's stay? The accused has testified that arrangements were only brought up during the voyage, not before.
> WITNESS: I stand by what I said, as Matilde told me it was all in the letter sent by her mother from San José.
> JUDGE: And upon what basis did Matilde object to receiving Castañeda as their guest once more?
> WITNESS: She told me that it was entirely thoughtless of her mother, and that the gossip in León about her sister and Castañeda would be dreadful. Everyone would think that they were coming back together, because they had become close in Costa Rica. She wanted to avoid such an awkward situation and said she was going to do everything she could to make sure he stayed away. In fact, she was of a mind to talk to her father that very night.
> JUDGE: Did Matilde intimate she was aware that Castañeda had already been in Costa Rica for some time and had been in the habit of making regular visits to her sister María del Pilar?
> WITNESS: Matilde wasn't unaware of this. María del Pi-

lar had written to her in great detail and she showed me the letters. She knew that Castañeda had been making daily visits to her uncle's house, where María del Pilar was staying with her mother. It was from those letters that she also knew about the trips she had made with him to the Irazú volcano and the estates at Aserrí and Curridabat; to parties at the Unión Club, and gala performances at the National Theatre, where they listened to the great tenor, Melico Salazar, dressed as a clown, singing "Ridi, pagliaccio".
JUDGE: In these letters you saw, did María del Pilar give the impression of being very much in love?
WITNESS: From the letters, she seemed very happy, but she never spoke of an affair, although she was always mentioning Castañeda, speaking very highly of him: how attentive he was, how amusing, and other praise of that sort.

Matilde never carried out her threats to do everything possible to stop Oliverio Castañeda from returning to live at their house. It is also probable that she never spoke to Don Carmen either. In fact, as one of the servants, Salvadora Carvajal, said in her statement of 14 October 1933, on the day that they were due to return, Matilde was cheerful and full of enthusiasm from the moment she woke:

> On the day of their return, Miss Matilde woke in good spirits, although Doctor Darbishire had to prescribe her quinine as she was getting hot and cold chills. She kept busy, organising the whole household into sweeping and mopping, paying special attention to Don Oliverio's room because she had heard that he would be arriving on the same train. She herself went into the garden to cut flowers with the secateurs, even though Don Carmen scolded her for getting wet; it had rained the night before and the plants were dripping. She didn't take any notice and just blew him kisses. Once she had gathered the flowers, she put bunches of them into vases which she placed on the chest of drawers in the bedroom, on the piano and on the little tables in the corridor. When she had done all this, she sat at the piano and practised some pieces until about five o'clock, when the train was due. Then she went to the train station in the car with her father to wait for the travellers.

At around eight o'clock everyone was seated in the dining-room, at the table adorned with a vase of gladioli courtesy of Matilde. Everyone, that is, except for María del Pilar, who had retired to bed with the excuse of still feeling sea-sick from the voyage. Don Carmen raised his habitual glass of Moscatel, and stuttered through a toast. Then, according to Salvadora Carvajal's statement, Oliverio Castañeda stood up and responded with a long and florid speech, interrupted several times by applause and laughter from those present.

At the same time, in another part of the city, at the accursed table in Casa Prío another toast was taking place; instead of Moscatel it was cognac, in payment of the wager. Once the first toast was done, Doctor Salmerón proceeded to reopen the investigation which he had been forced to set aside. He re-outlined the arguments which he had set before Doctor Darbishire. To conclude the briefing, he updated everyone concerning the last entry he had made in his Casa Squibb notebook: something that until then only he and Cosme Manzo had been aware of.

Doctor Salmerón had hoped to give the details of this incident in the evidence he gave before the trial judge on 28 October 1933. However, he was prevented from doing so, for reasons which will become clear later. As we shall also see subsequently, it came to light in public along with many other sensational revelations when Oliverio Castañeda finally mentioned it himself, during the defence which he presented on 6 December 1933.

For the moment, however, it was still a secret. Cosme Manzo, a successful business man whose grocery store was close to the city market, was, as the reader may recall, the sole distributor in León for Scott Emulsion cod-liver oil. As part of his advertising campaign for the product, he organised a weekly 'Cod Parade', as Doctor Ulises Terán mentioned in his testimony of 14 October 1933 concerning the death of Marta Jerez.

The five-metre-long cod was made out of a framework of metal rods, overlaid with panels of silver painted card. Inside the belly of the fish was a hollow for the cod-man who made it dance, to music provided by a band that would follow him through the streets, along with swarms of children and curious onlookers. At the end of the procession the cod would always be stored at the back of El

Esfuerzo, Cosme Manzo's store. Its presence there has been noted before, head downward against the wall.

The incident which concerns us was related to Cosme Manzo by the cod-man, Luis Felipe Pérez, a few months after it happened. On the morning of 17 August 1933, when he had gone to retrieve his cod-fish outfit at the shop ready to begin the day's procession, he ran into an old acquaintance: Dolores Lorente. She was buying a few yards of cloth, and seeing her reminded him of the incident. This was to be the last time that he led the cod dance because a few days later he was stabbed to death by a shoemaker during a barroom brawl in the Zaragoza neighbourhood.

Manzo immediately told the story to Doctor Salmerón, who recorded it in his Casa Squibb notebook under the title 'What Oliverio Castañeda did before breakfast the morning his wife died':

> I was waiting for the band at the entrance to La Recolección church, so that we could begin the parade. We always left from there so that we could join the road that goes up to the university, follow that road until we got to the Institute on the corner, and then double back on ourselves past San Francisco church until we got to Calle Real, going past the Cathedral. Then we'd split up in front of the store.
>
> The sun was already quite high, it must have been about eight in the morning. Just then, a young-looking man in a black suit arrived at the church porch and stopped to wait in the doorway. I thought he must be there for some remembrance mass, but no. A short while later, a woman appeared. I knew who she was, but I didn't say anything. We were neighbours when I lived in the Zaragoza neighbourhood. We fell out over a fighting cock of mine which strayed into her yard. She wrung its neck and put it in the stew pot. Her name was Dolores Lorente, a cook. She went up to the mourner and took a piece of paper or letter that he gave her. She left, heading north and a bit later he left too, in the same direction: off towards the university.
>
> The brass band had got drunk the night before, playing at a wake in Chacra Seca. They took ages to arrive. So the parade began late, probably shortly after nine in the morning. As we went down the road I saw the same

> young man in mourning coming out the door of a house. It was the house next to the one with the giant torch painted on it. The owner of the printers told me that there was a sick person inside, so I should not do the cod-dance. I respected his wishes and stopped, and so did the band. We walked on for a stretch without making any noise.

'But the fellow who used to dance the cod is dead, right? He got killed a month ago in a bar in Zaragoza, didn't he?' Rosalío Usulután said, clipping Cosme Manzo round the head with his hat. 'How are you going to prove to me that the story is true?'

'Are you calling me a liar?' Cosme Manzo retorted, snatching the hat from Rosalío.

'Oh ye of little faith! Why doubt it?' said Doctor Salmerón, taking the hat out of Cosme's hands and returning it to Rosalío. 'The man was beaten to death, but the bearer of the love letter is still alive.'

'I know about this Dolores Lorente,' said Captain Prío. He took out his pack of Esfinge cigarettes and, after lighting the only one left, went on: 'The world of cooks holds no mysteries for me. She used to work for the Castañedas.'

'Yes, and she now works for me. I could bring her over,' said Cosme Manzo, displaying his gold teeth as he grinned triumphantly at Rosalío. 'Need any more proof for your pudding?'

'You should have said so from the start!' Rosalío Usulután said, drawing his chair up noisily alongside Cosme Manzo. 'A thousand pardons, Don Cosme.'

Doctor Salmerón clapped his hands for silence: 'Now let Manzo finish his story in peace.'

'I persuaded Luis Felipe to forget about his wretched fighting cock, I even offered to pay for it,' said Cosme Manzo, stretching himself and spreading his arms wide to indicate this act was of no importance. 'I told him to fetch this Dolores Lorente so that we could have a little chat together. She was able to tie up the loose ends of the story.'

'Who was the letter for?' Rosalío Usulután asked, tugging humbly at Cosme Manzo's shirt sleeve, concerned that even now he might not reveal the mysterious destiny of the letter which had been handed over in the doorway of the church.

'Well, it wasn't for another man!' said Captain Prío, throwing his unfinished cigarette to the ground and grinding it out with the heel of his boot. 'If Castañeda went to the trouble to meet the servant in the doorway only half a block from his own place, it can only have been because he didn't want his wife to find out about the letter.'

'Was the other woman Doña Flora by any chance?' Rosalío Usulutlán said tentatively, craning his neck.

'Hot and cold,' replied Cosme Manzo, folding his arms, enjoying Rosalío's discomfort. 'You're getting close. Dolores Lorente took the letter and went to look for Woman X in La Merced church. This Woman X was waiting on her knees in one of the pews. Just as she had done on other occasions."

'One of her daughters then,' said Rosalío Usulutlán, directing a pleading glance towards Doctor Salmerón.

'One of the two,' said Doctor Salmerón, laughing and signaling with his pencil at Cosme Manzo to carry on.

'Ever since Castañeda had gone to live in that house he had been using the servant to send letters to Woman X every morning. Always at the church. And she would reply via the same means,' Cosme Manzo said, unbuttoning his shirt to stroke the medallion hanging round his neck from a thick gold chain. 'That was the last of them. As we know, he returned to his old rooms in the house after that. There was no need for more letters.'

'Matilde Contreras?' said Captain Prío, searching in vain for cigarettes in his shirt pocket. 'She always prays at the Merced church.'

'Not her. Which only leaves one, so she is Woman X,' said Doctor Salmerón, holding the bottle of cognac up to the light before serving himself. 'And now, Manzo my friend, let's make a fresh wager.'

'María del Pilar Contreras?' exclaimed Rosalío Usulutlán, turning in horror to Captain Prío. 'I would never have guessed. It seems like only yesterday she was playing with dolls on the porch of her house.'

'Some doll!' said Cosme Manzo, mocking him, 'you'll die a holy innocent! What do you want to wager on now, doctor?'

'That León will soon see another sudden death from blackwater fever,' said Doctor Salmerón, clambering to his feet to propose a toast. 'If no one dies, I pay. Cheers!'

'What are we celebrating?' a voice asked from the doorway. It was Oviedo the Balloon, on his return from a film-show at the Teatro González.

CHAPTER FIFTEEN

An Esteemed Lady on a Trip Combining Business and Pleasure

THE photo-engraving of Doña Flora de Contreras, taken by Cisneros Studios, appeared in the evening edition of *El Cronista* on 26 September 1933. Alongside it was the gossip column which carried an announcement of her return from Costa Rica:

> The virtuous and esteemed Doña Flora Guardia de Contreras is returning to León today after a well-earned rest, staying with her relatives in the Costa Rican capital. She is accompanied by her attractive daughter, Señorita María del Pilar Contreras Guardia. According to the latest news, during her stay she also secured the import of several new shipments destined for her prestigious emporium, La Fama. We are sure that these will soon be on show in the window displays of said emporium, and given the exquisite taste of this distinguished business lady, we shall be treated to a consummate exhibition of all the latest feminine couture. On her arrival at the Pacific Railway station she will be met by a select group of close family and friends.

Nowhere in the article, or in the rest of the newspaper, is mention made that Oliverio Castañeda was travelling with them. *El Centroamericano*, the only other newspaper in León, was similarly silent on the matter in its welcome column.

The photo-engraving certainly caught the eye of Rosalío Usulután. That night, as they were toasting the wager with the bottle of cognac, he showed the newspaper to the regulars at the accursed table so that they could admire it and admit he was right. In fact, he admired it so much that he used it much later, with disastrous consequences, as part of his scandalous reportage published on 25 October 1933.

'Not bad for forty!' said Doctor Salmerón, gently stroking the picture.

'Forty-something, doctor,' Cosme Manzo corrected him, running his tongue over his gold teeth.

'More beautiful than her two daughters put together,' said Rosalío Usulutlán, standing with hands on hips to challenge anyone to disagree with him.

'You're right, of course you are,' Doctor Salmerón hastened to agree.

'She looks like a famous film star, but I can't remember which one!' mused Rosalío, staring at the newspaper and looking perplexed.

He continued to gaze at the page, unable to tear his eyes away from the haughty beauty that seemed immune from the ravages of time. We can also see how Doña Flora was portrayed by Manolo Cuadra in his piece of 28 October 1933 entitled 'Dramatis Personae'. Rosalío did not think much of this man or his writing, although this was probably influenced by professional jealousy.

> The swan-like neck, the enticing brilliance of the olive green eyes; the high arched brows, gracefully pencilled in, delineate the smooth curve of her forehead. Seated on a straight-backed chair, there is majesty but also a touch of vanity in her informal, youthful bearing; all the more remarkable since the lady in question is fast approaching that crucial line of forty springs.
>
> Let us beg her to rise from where we see her seated in the photo-engraving so that we can see her walk, tall and svelte in her high heels, as she does when she goes to the shelves in search of a bolt of cloth in her shop (for indeed, she runs her own fashion store). She knows how to unroll the cloth on the counter with grace and confidence. She strokes the silk so gently with her bejewelled hands, preserving that distance and exoticism that the ladies of León,

> I am told, so admire and yet resent. They resent how she manages to be so glamorous even when she is merely at work in the shop. They are insulted by the subtle waft of her perfume on the air—an unknown brand—she guards her secrets jealously and her own perfume is not offered for sale in her shop.
>
> The readers of the *Nueva Prensa* will have to content themselves with this analysis. It is based solely on a photo-engraving but it is all we have to go on. Despite our best efforts to catch her at home, we have not had the opportunity to meet the lady face to face. However, according to reliable sources in León, our conclusions are not far from the truth. Is she very beautiful? Indeed she is. Does her beauty arouse female envy? Certainly, most certainly. Is her haughty demeanour a cause of resentment? This is also undeniable. Does her status as a foreigner aggravate these feelings of animosity and resentment? Of this there is no doubt.

However, the initiates of the accursed table had not convened for the purpose of admiring a portrait of the lady who had returned from her trip combining business and pleasure. Having exhausted the topic of the codfish-dancer and with the last of the cognac gone, they were preparing themselves for the second half of their agenda. Captain Prío served a round of Campeón rum, the rum of champions, distilled and bottled by Don Enrique Gil, with its sepia label bearing the likeness of the boxer Kid Tamariz.

As we know, Oviedo the Balloon was a great lover of the cinema. Only very special circumstances, such as killing dogs or a game of dice in the back room at Cosme Manzo's, could make him miss a film. That night, true to form, he arrived at Captain Prío's after a showing of *Emma* at the Teatro González; a story of sublime, self-sacrificing love, starring Marie Dressler. Cosme, who lent Oviedo money for gambling purposes, wielded considerable influence over him, and had insisted he join them at the end of the evening. Doctor Salmerón wanted to question him.

The interrogation turned out to be a success. Thanks to The Balloon's excellent memory and the delight he took in recounting the details of his raucous escapades, Doctor Salmerón managed to get a complete list of all the dogs poisoned on 18 July 1932, including Esculapio, Doctor Darbishire's dog. When it came to this last poisoning, Oviedo was particularly enthusiastic, leaping to his feet and throwing himself to the floor of the bar (by that time closed to the public), in a vivid re-enactment of how he had defended himself from the beating at the time.

Tipsy from the Campeón rum, which he liked to mix with Kola Shaler, The Balloon reminisced about his other adventures together with Oliverio Castañeda. He had been so eager to see Oliverio that, as soon as he heard of his return, he had rushed over to greet him at the Contreras' house that very evening. Of course he had always been sure that Castañeda would return, why else would he leave behind his trunk of books, his typewriter and the gramophone? Hearing this, Doctor Salmerón scribbled in his notebook: 'Left behind belongings. Never intended to leave permanently. Return was planned'.

Once The Balloon had gone, already half drunk, Doctor Salmerón began the task of organising the information according to what interested him most: the exact number and size of the poison doses used on the killing spree. He started with the first three, destined for dogs around the water pump that were administered in the presence of Don Carmen Contreras, and ending with those dished out later that night, street by street, door to door, until they climbed back up onto their carriage. Doctor Salmerón tallied up the number of dead dogs to a total of twenty.

Oviedo had also informed them that the strychnine was obtained through the Argüello drugstore, with the authorization of the U.S. police authorities. He later confirmed this in his testimony to the judge on 17 October 1933, and was supported by evidence given by the pharmacist, Doctor David Argüello, in his witness statement of 19 October 1933.

It was almost one in the morning by the time Rosalío Usulutlán finally took leave of his cronies. Doctor Salmerón had charged him with a mission of the utmost importance. For this reason we shall stay with him through the next morning, that of the 27 September 1933; a day that saw him take a trip to the Argüello drugstore.

The court records inform us that the Argüello drugstore was

situated on the Calle del Comercio. This street was in fact a succession of grocery stores, pharmacies, hardware shops and other businesses situated to the south side of the Municipal Market. The hall itself was an old adobe building occupying an entire block at the back of the Cathedral. To the north, the Calle Real stretched as far as the doors of the Calvario church.

The Argüello drugstore was halfway down the block, between the Kaiser hardware store, with its frontage covered in sawdust and strewn with half-assembled wooden crates, and La Santa Faz, the makers of candles and oil-lamps, which announced its business with strips of candles hanging over the door. Cosme Manzo's establishment, El Esfuerzo, with its prominent red-and-blue sign, stood at the western end of the block.

The drugstore was very easy to pick out owing to a billboard high on the wall above showing a naked, blond infant with a disproportionately large head holding a bottle of Laxol as if it were a toy. There was a wooden grille across the doorway containing little windows, through which customers were served after hours.

Rosalío pushed open this grille, leaving behind the intense humidity of the city street which, in the suffocating heat of day, was packed with trucks, horse-drawn carriages and the occasional automobile carving its way through the strolling pedestrians. Also left behind were the bustle and cries of the market traders, the stench of rotting fruit and vegetables, and the even more pungent odour of cold grease coming from the open-air stalls where strips of lard were hanging drying among clouds of flies.

By contrast, inside the drugstore there was a freshness like entering the cool shade of a cave. The air was sweet with the scent of magnesium citrate, vanilla essence and eucalyptus. Display cabinets, painted red and edged with elaborate, funereal braid, reached up to the ceiling. The articles on show behind their glass fronts were ranged in careful order: from their upper reaches where chamber pots and enema syringes could be seen, to the rows of medicine bottles made of tinted glass or porcelain.

A barefoot youth was polishing the floor, tiled in a pattern of red and blue diamonds. Careful not to slip, Rosalío made his way to the nearest assistant, who was leaning on the counter with his elbows as he leafed through a copy of the *Bristol Almanac*. As instructed by Doctor Salmerón, Rosalío asked for a vial of strychnine, to kill dogs with, and as predicted at the accursed table the night before, he was asked to wait while the assistant disappeared through a narrow doorway between the shelves. Poisons had to be dispensed by the owner of the drugstore in person, who, as we already know, lived with his family behind the shop.

Doctor Argüello appeared after a few minutes. He was in the middle of taking his ten o'clock refreshment, a glass of barley water, which he raised by way of greeting.

'Aha! Don Chalío,' he said. He was chewing an ice-cube which he slipped back into the glass before enquiring: 'What makes you want to turn words into deeds?'

'The dogs in La Españolita are getting out of hand!' replied Rosalío. He was not a good liar, and could not suppress a nervous glance outside.

'You need authorization. You of all people should know that.' Doctor Argüello ran his tongue carefully around his mouth in search of stray grains of barley. 'You were the one who ruined my sales of the yellow powders.'

'They were worse than useless!' said Rosalío, taking hold of the brim of his hat with both hands to pull it further over his face, as if to conceal his identity.

'Yes, I know they don't work,' Doctor Argüello agreed readily.

'And how many dogs could you kill with one of those little bottles of strychnine?' Rosalío asked innocently, stepping back from the counter, hands in his back pockets.

Sympathetic and eager to help, Doctor Argüello began to search among the keys that he carried on a heavy chain at his waist. He selected a tiny key and went over to the drawers at the bottom of the display cabinet. He opened one and took out a small cylindrical phial which he held up to the light to inspect its contents.

After this visual examination he raised the bottle to his ear and listened to the noise it made when rattled, trying to make some calculations in response to the journalist's question. After a moment's further hesitation he finally decided to break the seal around the neck of the bottle and called Rosalío over to the dispensing area next to the enormous cash register.

Rosalío watched through the window of the dispenser, which

was not unlike a confessional, as Doctor Argüello put on his spectacles and then some red rubber gloves, before removing the tiny cork stopper from the bottle and emptying the white powder it contained onto one of the pans of a pair of weighing scales. Taking a spatula, he divided the powder into little piles.

'Twenty-five doses, each of one gram and a half,' announced Doctor Argüello, without taking his eyes off the scales. 'The phial contains thirty-seven and a half grams.'

'Twenty-five. Assuming each dose is enough for an adult dog,' said Rosalío, leaning over hands on knees, so that the pharmacist can see him through the little window.

'More than enough,' said Doctor Argüello, placing a funnel into the bottle, 'any more would be a waste.'

'And what about a person?' asked Rosalío, laughing in a way that sounded unconvincing even to him.

Doctor Argüello looked at him over the top of his spectacles which had slipped down on his nose, so sternly that the journalist was terrified.

'A person? The fatal dose for a person is the same as for a dog. A gram and a half," said Doctor Argüello, grinding his teeth as if still chewing the ice from his glass. 'The only difference is that a person would take longer to die, about three hours. A dog would be dead much more quickly.'

'I suppose that's because a dog's digestive system is more sensitive,' said Rosalío, straightening up.

'I suppose so,' replied Doctor Argüello, spooning the poison into the funnel and back into its phial.

When he gave evidence on 17 October 1933, Oviedo the Balloon was jostled and pushed by the crowd in the court room, and was so nervous that his hands shook visibly as he held his water glass, refilling it again and again. However, he did not hesitate to confirm that there had only been twenty doses of strychnine in the batch he had acquired, with the authorisation of Captain Wayne, at the Argüello Drugstore. And, in court, far away from his weighing scales and spatula, the pharmacist himself had said the same thing.

The trial judge did not have access to the findings of Rosalío's enquiries of that morning. The striking discrepancy in the number of doses was recorded in the Casa Squibb notebook along with all the other evidence amassed in Doctor Salmerón's secret investigations.

As Doctor Argüello locked the poisons safely away again, he mentioned that it would be the anniversary of his mother's death on October third, and that he had written an acrostic dedicated to her memory which he would like to see published in *El Cronista*. Rosalío was happy to go along with this.

While waiting for Doctor Argüello to re-emerge from the depths of the pharmacy with his poem, the journalist's attention was caught by the Gillette razors advertising stand on the counter. He smiled to himself, noting how much Doctor Argüello, with his beautifully groomed moustache, resembled the man in the advert. But his eyes were drawn to another advert: on the glass of the window through which he had just watched the pharmacist at work calculating doses of poison, was a sticker from which the eyes of Maureen O'Sullivan gazed back at him. With her close-cropped hair, the Metro Goldwyn Mayer star, the lead actress in *Payment Deferred*, was recommending Bayer's caffeine-asprin for feminine cramps. Rosalío tapped his forehead as a thought struck him.

'It came to me just then, doctor,' Rosalío later explained, tapping his forehead again, 'Maureen O'Sullivan is the one Doña Flores reminds me of. Except that she's much younger, of course.'

'So there are five doses unaccounted for,' said Doctor Salmerón, quickly jotting this down and then fixing Rosalío with a look. 'That leaves our Charles Laughton with four.'

CHAPTER SIXTEEN

An Alarm Bell Nobody Heard

THE WINTER of 1933 was the wettest ever seen in the Pacific region of Nicaragua, especially in the western departments. Between the months of July and October the rains caused constant interruptions to the trains running between León and Corinto, due to undermining along the tracks. The telephone and telegraph poles running parallel to the rail lines also suffered considerable damage. Many of the roads to the areas around León were completely impassable. Crops were ruined; the maize and sugar cane harvests were badly hit in particular. Hundreds of cattle and horses perished by drowning. When the waters finally receded towards the middle of November, the rain gauge at San Antonio sugar refinery in Chichigalapa recorded an amazing twenty inches of rainfall.

In the city of León, clouds of insistently buzzing mosquitoes invaded courtyards, kitchens and verandahs from early evening onwards. In the centre of town the houses reeked of Flit and it was impossible to sleep anywhere except under a finely meshed mosquito net. When the houses were closed up at night, the atmosphere became unbearable: even these rains were unable to mitigate the extreme heat.

On the morning of 30 September 1933 the paths of Doctor Darbishire and Doctor Salmerón crossed at the San Vicente Hospital. The former was just leaving after visiting his private patients, while the latter had been making his rounds of the public ward. It had not rained all morning, but the sky was clouded to the west and threatened rain. The two exchanged a few pleasantries about the weather and the plague of mosquitoes; but Doctor Darbishire knew full well that the real topic of conversation had not yet been broached.

Only a few days earlier, Doctor Salmerón had turned up again at the surgery on Calle Real, along with his Casa Squibb notebook. He had brought information and alleged evidence, the outcome of his most recent investigations into what he had begun to call the 'Castañeda Case'. All this had taken Doctor Darbishire by surprise: for months now he had considered the whole affair long forgotten.

On that occasion, Doctor Darbishire had patiently listened to his former pupil as he expounded on his latest findings: the number of dogs poisoned on 18 July 1932, the true number of doses contained in the phial of strychnine obtained by the poisoners from the Argüello drugstore. He had also listened patiently to the tales of love letters and other intrigues. They had parted cordially enough, but Doctor Salmerón's thesis that Oliverio Castañeda had kept back some of the poison had been met with nothing more than reluctance from the older man.

Now Doctor Darbishire had the distinct impression that his student, dissatisfied with their previous discussion, was trying to steer the conversation back to the same topic, although he did not dare to do so directly. Standing with his Cordoban cape folded over his arm and clutching his hat, Doctor Darbishire thought to himself how amusing it was that he was the one considered eccentric and not Doctor Salmerón. Here was a man who when he got an idea into his head could never let it go.

The old man was feeling in a good mood that morning; and he decided to have some fun. What he was about to tell his colleague went against the grain. In the same way, Castañeda rubbed him up the wrong way. His dislike of the man stemmed from the moment he had heard from Doctor Salmerón himself, how that brash and pretentious individual had been involved in poisoning his Esculapio.

This aside, however, he still refused to give any credit to his friend's detective fantasies, for although he had adorned them with details and organised them in a logical way, they were still fantasies. In the abstract they might seem reasonable, but in the cold light of reality—the stultified, uneventful reality of León—they lost all meaning. León was not the place for romantic trysts or the kind of mysterious crimes that had become so popular since the arrival of cinema. It was too much like the plot of *Payment De-*

ferred, which happened to have its first screening on the night that Esculapio died.

'I have a new patient,' said Doctor Darbishire, spinning his hat between his fingertips, 'your friend, Oliverio Castañeda.'

Doctor Salmerón loosened his tie but did not respond.

'If you'd like to hear about it, come and sit with me.' Doctor Darbishire said, taking him by the arm and leading him to one of the benches in the hallway, which was still empty of patients and visitors. 'He turned up yesterday in my consulting room.'

'Don't tell me that Oliverio Castañeda has malaria,' said Doctor Salmerón, allowing himself to be led and then sinking wearily onto the bench.

'No, of course not. Our lady-killer has halitosis, and is very worried about it!' said Doctor Darbishire, crossing his legs and arranging the folds of his trousers carefully. 'I prescribed a course of liver salts and regular mouth washes with Listerine.'

'Bad breath?' cried Doctor Salmerón, scarcely able to contain his amusement. 'He came to you for that?'

'The fact Oliverio Castañeda suffers from bad breath is not what I wanted to tell you,' said Doctor Darbishire, blithely jiggling his leg, 'But that in your honour I asked him about the state of affairs at the Contreras residence.'

Frowning, Doctor Salmerón turned his head slowly. His oriental eyes narrowed to slits.

'I gave him some good advice,' Doctor Darbishire went on, cupping his knee in his hands. 'I told him he should marry María del Pilar. Because since he is living in their house again, the rumours going around are bound to reflect badly on his hosts. Besides, he would be getting a good bargain.'

'So you finally acknowledge that the love interest exists?' Doctor Salmerón said, turning back to face the old man again. 'Remember the last time I told you about the codfish-man.'

'Wait a moment, my friend, we're not at the accursed table now!' laughed Doctor Darbishire, uncrossing his legs. 'All that about letters at the church, I don't buy it. I'm no expert in the ways of scheming lovers. What I do know is there are lots of comments flying round León.'

'Well then, you'll have to excuse the accursed table,' said Doctor Salmerón, wiping saliva from his mouth on his sleeve, 'or accept that the whole of León is an accursed table.'

'I don't know,' said Doctor Darbishire, still chuckling to himself. 'I have just been hearing all the tittle-tattle at the Club, my patients are all full of it too. I can't believe everything I hear, but the return of the young widower to that house was a great indiscretion on his part, and also of those who took him in. I simply pointed that out to him.'

'And what did he say?' asked Doctor Salmerón, peering at him intently.

'That it was all just the idle gossip of people who had nothing better to do,' replied Doctor Darbishire, mimicking Oliverio Castañeda's disdain. 'And that having just recently lost a model wife, beautiful, rich and with a European education, he was not going to get hitched to an ignorant child with frizzy hair, with whom he could not appear in Guatemalan society without blushing.'

Despite the levity with which Doctor Darbishire was treating the subject, he was somewhat taken aback by his own daring, and was annoyed at himself for betraying professional secrets.

'That deals with María del Pilar. But what about Matilde? Did he say anything about Matilde?' Doctor Salmerón asked, so excited now that he stumbled over his words.

'He brought up the subject himself. He told me that he knew full well of all the rumours concerning his love for Matilde, but that there was nothing to it,' replied Doctor Darbishire. He was still smiling, but could not look his friend in the eye. 'According to him, Matilde is a well-educated, spiritual girl, but without any physical attractions. He is not interested in her either.'

Doctor Darbishire was about to continue, but like a man who has foolishly strayed too close to the edge of a precipice, he backed off, not daring to reveal the most shocking part of the story: that Castañeda had, without a trace of shame, also revealed that he was aware of the gossip surrounding his relationship with Doña Flora. The old man had no wish to hear anything more, and so had cut him short. He had no wish to hear any of Castañeda's explanations.

'That man thinks very highly of himself,' said Doctor Salmerón, nodding his head knowingly.

'His only concern was that he would disappoint Don Carmen,'

Doctor Darbishire resumed cautiously, wishing he had never begun this conversation.

'Disappoint him?' said Doctor Salmerón, instinctively fishing for the Casa Squibb notebook in his pocket, only to find that he already had it in his hand. 'Why would that be?'

'Well, it's obvious that Don Carmen, a man of limited intellectual capacity, would welcome someone such as him to run his business as his son-in-law,' said Doctor Darbishire, so embarrassed by now he started to examine his clean, well-manicured nails. 'But Castañeda said he wasn't going to fall into that trap. On the contrary, he was not going to spend longer than he had to in that house, where the only thing they were interested in was money.'

'My friend, you know that when we speak in confidence my lips are sealed,' said Doctor Salmerón, who knew him better than anyone and had noticed the change in his demeanour. He squeezed his hand affectionately saying, 'This isn't the first time we've discussed our patients.'

'His last words to me were,' Doctor Darbishire said taking out his pocket watch, as if by showing that he was in a hurry he could distance himself from what he was saying: 'In that house they worship the golden calf and I will not pray at that altar.'

'The golden calf...what a hypocrite, he certainly prays at that altar,' said Doctor Salmerón. A disdainful expression crept over his face and, still clasping the old man's hand, he went on; 'The first thing he did when he arrived was to try to bribe the municipal authorities to secure the new water contract. That contract is daylight robbery.'

'I don't get involved in such things," said Doctor Darbishire, standing up and about to wrap himself in his cape. 'I know nothing of business. I hoped that by telling you all this I could set your mind at rest, not alarm you further.'

'Set my mind at rest!' Doctor Salmerón said, not moving from the bench.

'Next week he is leaving for Managua,' said Doctor Darbishire. He adjusted the clasp on his cape and stuck out his chin like a cock preparing to fight. 'It appears he is writing a book, something to do with the geography of Nicaragua. He has no intention of returning to León.'

'All this about leaving and not coming back remains to be seen,' said Doctor Salmerón, rubbing his shoe as if getting rid of some spit. 'He still has work to do here. And he has plenty of strychnine.'

There he was again with the strychnine. The old man felt another surge of pity for his student: so brilliant, so well-qualified, and yet living in such poverty. He was saddened at the sight of his student's shabby shoes and ragged socks crumpled limply around his ankles.

'Can I give you a ride?' asked Doctor Darbishire, turning towards his student. He put his hand on Doctor Salmerón's shoulder, leaving it there until his student moved to get up.

Usually, when they left the hospital together they would travel out in the buggy and he would drop Doctor Salmerón off in the square outside the train station. Doctor Salmerón liked to take breakfast at one of the many food stalls set up among the mule drivers and labourers all waiting for the morning trains. He would then begin his rounds in the Ermita de Dolores neighbourhood, an area notorious for prostitution, traipsing on foot through the streets full of ditches, weeds, and foul-smelling puddles.

Without answering, Doctor Salmerón rose to his feet and followed him to the exit. The horses harnessed to the buggy were lazily munching the grass growing up through the paving stones thanks to the recent rains.

'Leave me at San Juan Park,' said Doctor Salmerón, one foot already on the running board. 'I have an appointment to see the fair ladies at the sanatorium.'

'Oh, I won't hear of it, I'll take you directly to the sanatorium. It's no trouble, I'm going that way myself." Doctor Darbishire untied the reins of the buggy.

'Where are you headed?' asked Doctor Salmerón, slotting his bag under the seat, simply out of politeness.

'I'm going to see the Contreras family. Matilde has symptoms of malaria which I don't much like,' said Doctor Darbishire. He gave the horses a feeble tap with the whip, but this was enough to get them going. 'Don Carmen brought her to see me. Night sweats, shivering, loss of weight, yellowing to the whites of the eyes.'

'When was this?' asked Doctor Salmerón, gripping the edge of the canopy above him and turning to face his teacher, eyes wide with surprise.

'About a week ago. I sent a blood sample off for analysis and it came back positive. Malaria for a change,' said Doctor Darbishire holding the reins carelessly as the buggy bowled over the potholes in the road.

'And what did you prescribe?' Doctor Salmerón pressed him, forgetting all pretence at politeness.

'The usual, except that I doubled the dose of quinine sulphate,' said Doctor Darbishire, relaxing his hold on the reins as the horses settled into a comfortable trot.

'In capsules?' asked Doctor Salmerón, hardly able to believe what he was hearing.

'Of course, I prepared them myself, in my own pharmacy,' Doctor Darbishire retorted, irked by the curt tone of the questions.

'You mean to say that you made up the prescription three days ago when you first saw her?' asked Doctor Salmerón, incredulous, his voice choked.

Doctor Darbishire kept his eyes on the horses. His look hardened, and he did not reply.

'How many capsules?' Doctor Salmerón spat the words out so vehemently that a spray of saliva hit Doctor Darbishire's cheek.

'A box containing sixty tablets, with six to be taken daily, two after each meal,' Doctor Darbishire told him. Keeping the reins steady with one hand, he wiped his face with the other. As the horses quickened their pace again, he went on: 'If necessary I'll increase the dose of quinine further. And please don't raise your voice to me.'

Out of the corner of his eye, Doctor Darbishire saw his colleague's lips moving as he made hasty calculations, staring up into the canvas roof of the buggy as though he was praying.

'Seventy, six a day. Seven days: so she has enough left for three more days,' calculated Doctor Salmerón turning in his seat so rapidly that the buggy lurched to one side. 'Withdraw the tablets. Today! Goddamit!'

'Goddamit nothing! I can't go play around with my patients,' cried Doctor Darbishire, unfurling the whip to urge the horses on. 'And please stop going on with these childish fantasies of yours.'

'Childish fantasies?' said Doctor Salmerón, grabbing hold of his hat which was about to blow away as the buggy speeded up.

'Remember me when you get an emergency call in three days' time. Just you remember me.'

'I always remember you,' said Doctor Darbishire sarcastically. He wrapped the end of the whip round his hand as there was no longer any need for it.

'Drop me here!' Doctor Salmerón said abruptly, grabbing his bag. Without waiting for the buggy to come to a halt he leapt down into the street, just managing to keep his balance.

Doctor Darbishire stopped the buggy a block down the road, next to the railway station and looked back. He could not make out his former pupil. The seven-thirty train from Chinandega gave several long whistles as it pulled in. Separated from the rail track only by a pine hedge, the street had filled with smoke.

Doctor Darbishire's buggy continued on its way: to the home of the Contreras family.

CHAPTER SEVENTEEN

A Letter of Condolence

León, 4 October 1933
Don Carmen Contreras Guardia,
San José, Costa Rica

DEAR Mito,

I don't have time to write at length. I need all the time I have to console your parents and sister, who are so deeply affected by the terrible thunderbolt that has struck our house. That thunderbolt struck with such precision, directly over my own head. As far as I am concerned, Matilde's one way trip to oblivion hit me in the same way as the death of my own Martita. I have given myself away, I fear. What else could I lose in my life, what other calamities could ambush me on my journey? Fool that I am to ever have thought that such trials only come at the end of life, when you can expect nothing else.

The pillars of León society have gathered round us to distract us from our pain with the show of consideration dictated by custom. Don Carmen and Doña Flora have been very content with the demonstrations of sympathy and expressions of sincere condolence that have made our immense suffering bearable. But as you might well point out: there are no balms capable of soothing these wounds. You would be right, there are none.

How did these cruel events unfold? It is not something I wish to tell, but I feel I owe that much to you. On October second, I arrived late for dinner because I had been delayed working with the mayor and councillors sorting out the finer points of the new contract with the Water Company (which I might add in passing is going very favourably for your father).

Matilde, whom we, my dear Mito, affectionately knew as Mati, was waiting for me on the verandah. After scolding me for my lateness, she ordered my supper and sat at the table with me while I ate. Once I had finished, Don Carmen came to sit and talk with us. I told him about the council meeting, which had been very heated and difficult, and then we discussed the evening papers. Doña Flora and María del Pilar arrived later, back from visiting little Monchita Deshon, and joined the conversation. What a peaceful scene of after-dinner companionship; the sign of a happy home. But happy for how long?

When we left the table, Mati retired with me and we sat at some distance from the others on two of the easy chairs just along the verandah. If only I had known that this was to be our very last conversation! She was always so anxious to learn, an enemy of frivolity inclined instead towards philosophy and politics, religion, the transcendence of self...the sublime qualities of music, the harmonies of poetry. I am not embarrassed to admit, Mito, that I am proud to feel that I was in some ways her mentor; nurturing her as one nurtures a delicate flower. She was the prize rose in the garden of her home; she stood out from all the others.

Around ten-thirty we all went to bed. I went first, followed by María del Pilar and then Doña Flora and Mati; Don Carmen was last. I was tired after a day spent in meetings with various different councillors, attempting to get them to agree the terms of the draft contract I had carefully prepared; a copy of which will be in your hands shortly so that you can peruse it.

It would have been around five minutes past eleven when I was wakened from a profound sleep by the sound of raised voices. It was Don Carmen calling to me: 'Ollie! Ollie! Get up, get dressed, open your door, Mati is not well!' You can imagine my alarm and the speed with which I dressed. In no time at all I was out of my room and awaiting orders from your father. He told me to get Doctor Darbishire without delay. At that moment a downpour started, so heavy that we had to stand close together in order to hear one another.

At first, Doña Flora told me it was not yet necessary to fetch Doctor Darbishire. The convulsions which had unexpectedly disturbed Mati's sweet dreams appeared to have passed. Assuming they had passed, we were discussing the possible causes of these convulsions, when all of a sudden a fresh attack took hold of her. Now there was no time to lose. In a frenzy, I fought with the telephone trying to get hold of the operator to obtain Doctor Darbishire's number. By now every moment counted, and so I wanted to ask him to get ready while I came to pick him up. Finally the operator answered, but he couldn't hear me over the fury of the storm. Then, seeing that your father's car had broken down, I rushed out into the deluge, forgetting both my umbrella and my cape. I ran, jumping across the flooded streets with my heart in my mouth, all the way to Buitrago's garage to hire a car.

I will leave aside all my adventures on the way, and say only that I finally arrived at the surgery. I beat desperately on the door. After much persistence on my part, I managed to raise Doctor Darbishire and he opened the door. He went to dress and get his bag. He took what seemed an age, while I waited in anguish. Oh, the cruel ticking of the clock...if only someone had the power to detain your fatal rhythm! He came out of the house and we returned in the car, I think I hit 60 km/hr...we stepped over the threshold of your house just as Don Carmen arrived, accompanied by Doctor Alejandro Sequiera Rivas, who now lived opposite, where Chepe Chico used to live. More doctors appeared, soaked by the rain. They all considered the case. Another attack overwhelmed her. They passed judgment: acute blackwater fever. The life of our afflicted beauty was not to be saved, they told us.

Nevertheless, they did not give up. They prescribed. I kept the hired car running: they needed drugs, someone had to get them and that someone was me. Captain Anastasio J. Ortiz arrived and offered the loan of his car, for our convenience; I paid off the chauffeur and told him to be on his way. We drove in search of a late-night pharmacist: the Argüello drugstore, and flew back with the medication. The news: she was in the same hopeless state. We ran in search of her grandfather, her uncles, little Monchita Deshon, Doña Alicia, Nelly and later Noel Pallais and his wife, Don Esteban Duquestrada, his wife and daughter, and several other friends and acquaintances. The rain did not ease up, and yet they all came, one by one.

When I returned with Tacho Ortiz after completing these tasks,

Mati had already been taken into the arms of God. She had known that her time was near and had prayed fervently, exclaiming with Christian piety: 'I'm dying, I'm dying. Oh, Sacred Heart of Jesus, most holy Virgin, I welcome death, but give me time to prepare!'

She passed away at one in the morning. María del Pilar was the first to realise she had gone. She ran to her parents' room to tell them. As I write, the house is full of pain, weeping, confusion and so many people: the parlour is full, the corridor, everywhere. Excuse the tumult of my thoughts, it is for you to give them some order. Doña Flora has been so brave, as has María del Pilar. But not so Don Carmen. He has taken it hard. He is so plainly overcome, refusing even to eat. For him, the memory of his sweet girl is the only thing that exists. I feel, and I will try to make Doña Flora see, that she needs to take immediate steps concerning the health of your father. We cannot afford any further tragedy in this unfortunate household.

We laid her out in her own clothes on her bed in the room where she passed away, until the coffin ordered from Rosales funeral parlour arrived. The grave was dug the following day, with the intention to erect a beautiful mausoleum later. The funeral mass took place at three. The passing bell rang throughout the day, and at half past four a select assembly accompanied her to the Cathedral. The mass was sung with great solemnity, with the Archbishop himself, Monsignor Tijerino y Loáisiga, officiating. The canon, Father Oviedo y Reyes, gave an inspiring eulogy, recalling all of Mati's virtues, likening her to the flowers of the fields from the Song of Songs. The sky had been overcast all day, as if the weather wished to join us in our grief; as soon as we entered the Cathedral the heavens opened. The rain continued without pause until the burial at the cemetery.

She was taken from the house on the shoulders of Don Leonte Herdocia, some others and my own. From the Cathedral she was carried on the shoulders of Guillermo Sevilla, Raúl Montalván, some others and my own. She was lowered into the grave by Bernabé Ballardes, your father, myself and some others.

We received telegrams from the president, government ministers, friends and family in Managua, Granada, Chinandega; condolence cards came from the Club, the town council, the Archbishop's office, etc. I am collecting them all together to make an album, or Book of Remembrance. Your father has approved the expense, and we will get it printed at your grandfather's. It will include a photograph of Mati, thoughts and poems, one of which I have composed, and another by Lino de Luna. He asked to recite it at the graveside, before Mati was buried, but it was raining too hard.

I have included my own here. Don't look for any merit in it, since it has none apart from the painful sentiments with which it was written:

> A blaze of roses smothers the deathly shroud,
> Their buds bespoiled by so much sobbing.
> Weep your doleful tears, failing roses, cry out aloud!
> All is tears; I cannot cease...my weeping.
>
> Pale Death did enter here with capricious tread,
> Deeply asleep, Mati ne'er gave a start.
> Anguished I listened as the sly steps approached her bed,
> Engraving their path, sweet child, on my heart.
>
> Hark! I hear another step, soft and more merciful,
> You hear it too; your hour of need draws nigh.
> Midnight footsteps: heralding angels so blissful,
> They are come Mati to take you on high.
>
> A blaze of roses, the white roses of October,
> On snowy plumage angelic hosts flew.
> Their beating wings protect what the shroud will cover,
> You who in life, no evil ever knew.
>
> Without your gentle hands to make the piano sing,
> We mortals will not hear its sound again.
> Midnight footsteps: all music now has taken wing,
> Silence...
> In October skies, an *Angel* is playing.

The contingent from Chinandega has just arrived: Don Juan Deshon and his wife Doña Lola, María Elsa Deshon and Angelita Montealegre. They are all weeping a great deal and making quite an impression on your father; every show of sympathy, every word of condolence seems to renew the anguish he feels as the bereaved father. You should have seen how much he cried as he read my poem. I have to confess, Mito, I never thought to see your father, who is such a strong man, so diminished both physically and mentally.

Shedding hot tears, all the young ladies of León came to place wreaths and bouquets of flowers at the foot of the white coffin: Estercita Ortiz, Sarita Lacayo, Nelly y Maruca Deshon among others. It was these flowers that inspired my poem. The young men of our troubled circle, who shared the joys of Matilde's life and tasted the sweetness of her being also cried inconsolably: Noel Robelo, René Ballardes, Julio Castillo, Enrique Pereira, and many more. I have tried, here and there, to comfort them as best I can, but my heart is not in it; I too need comfort. It is rare to see so many flowers on a tomb. Perhaps it is because she was such a young girl, virginal, adored and adorable, who deserved to go to her rest amidst the perfume and music of heaven. This is what I tried to say in my poem. *El Centroamericano* wishes to publish my offering, Don Carmen is all for it; but I want to preserve it for the Book of Remembrance. What do you think?

Just imagine, Mito, the night before she went to sleep, never to awaken, she had been playing the piano with that sweetness only she could bring to the keyboard. That is why I mention the piano in my poem. She sang too, and laughed a great deal. The Sunday before I gave a dinner in honour of a few friends of mine from abroad: an Italian gentleman named Franco Cerruti, you may have heard of him as he is well respected as a businessman in Costa Rica, and a Cuban by the name of Miguel Barnet, my partner in the project to publish a book on Nicaragua. By the way, this project is on hold at the request of your father who wishes me to concentrate solely on the Metropolitan Water Company affair. He has no room in his head for any other thoughts at present.

Enough of that, I was telling you how Mati played so beautifully and what's more, among the happy talk of outings, parties and politics, I was gratified to hear my guests extolling her many virtues. I include three cuttings about the funeral from the newspapers. When everything around here has calmed down and the attention I must devote to your parents allows for it, I shall take the opportunity to write with further details. Your cable was read by everyone and it is still wet with the tears that fell upon it. I propose to distract Don Carmen as much as possible so that he does not succumb to grief. But you must recognise, it is a heavy task for me alone. If he gives way, where will this excellent family find strength?

Make your heart a bulwark and write some words of courage to your father; try to lift his spirits. While I am here I promise not to leave him alone. I had planned to go to Managua today, before we were overtaken by these horrible events. I had thought to spend a month there and then go on to other towns, gathering information for my book; but don't worry, all of that is forgotten now, as duty calls me to be by your father's side. I will stay here. I will find excuses to soothe my business partner's displeasure.

You must rise to the challenge of this situation, the likes of which you will never have experienced, owing to your youth. Put aside your own suffering, and write a letter of comfort to your father and use your filial affection to distract him from the anxiety that has overpowered him. We must at all costs exorcise the void that threatens your beloved father's soul.

I will say goodbye here, Mito; your father is calling for me. Matilde was a child of God, and God has seen fit to reclaim her. That is the nature of death and only the heart can interpret its meaning. When the bitter winds of sorrow have eased and when our hearts are once again at peace in our breasts, then we may reflect. I hope that your brotherly heart and mine, which I feel is no less brotherly, now lacerated with bloody thorns will one day escape their prison of pain and heal their wounds. I do not know how long it will take, I really do not know…

With fondest embraces, you are always in my thoughts and I beg you to have patience and forbearance. Your sorrowful friend, I remain as ever yours,

Affectionately,

Ollie

PS: I insist that you do not forget to write to your father. You must forgive my need to press this point, but it is better to be safe than sorry. Ok.

CHAPTER EIGHTEEN

Secrets of Nature

Señorita Matilde Contreras Guardia

Gentle and virtuous Señorita Matilde Contreras Guardia, León has still not recovered from the painful upheaval caused by the terrible news of your death. Your final journey, as you know better than any, came to an end at one o'clock yesterday morning despite the diligence of the doctors gathered at your bedside. The cruel malady attacked cunningly as you slept, and vanquished science; yet again the blackwater fever, which has long reigned over this city, cried out in victory.

As soon as they heard the sad news, the numerous friends of your esteemed family abandoned their beds without a care for the ferocious downpour and came in all haste to your heartbroken home, where they showed their heartfelt grief at your departure. Sweet, innocent child, only hours earlier you were so content, unaware that Death was already weaving your white shroud. How could you have known that your virginal soul had been selected and that your immaculate brow would soon be crowned with lilies?

Your departure for the House of God has left us with nothing but sweet memories. You were pure, and your soul emanated the exquisite perfume of its many enchantments. Among these was music: you played on the piano with such accomplishment.

Now you have fallen into an eternal sleep. Even the inconsolable sobbing of the many people who mourn your passing cannot break your virginal slumber. But mourn you they should, for even the short path that you trod through this life is sown with the incorruptible roses of honour and the jasmines of virtue.

In the Cathedral solemn prayers were offered for the eternal rest of your soul, and your remains were taken to the Guadalupe Cemetery. Undeterred by the rain, you were accompanied by a considerable, yet select cortege which extended for over a block, marching in silence behind your coffin; which was of course, white in recognition of your unblemished youth.

You received such a wealth of floral tributes that the gardens of León are now bare. However, we must add just one more bloom: the humble forget-me-not. This we lay reverently at your tomb.

At this delicate moment, we should like to extend our sympathy to your bereaved family and especially to your parents, the respected businessman, Don Carmen Contreras, and the esteemed Doña Flora Guardia de Contreras. We also extend our condolences to your siblings, the young student Don Carmen Contreras Guardia, presently in Costa Rica, and Señorita María del Pilar Contreras Guardia, and beseech them to comfort their parents at this difficult time.

(*El Cronista*, 4 October 1933)

UNDER A darkening sky that announced the imminent storm, Rosalío Usulutlán had been stationed since before four o'clock on the sidewalk outside the La Rambla store on the corner opposite the Cathedral. He was waiting for the funeral cortege of Matilde Contreras to pass by, hoping to pick up some first-hand accounts for the tribute he intended to print in *El Cronista* that very day, but although he was there in a professional capacity, it has to be said that he too had been moved by the tragedy.

However, once the cortege had entered the Cathedral, and he began his journey back to the newspaper office, hugging the walls to avoid the worst of the rain which was already starting to fall with a vengeance, his reasons for having been there did not seem so solid. He felt a sense of shame and overwhelming self-pity.

Surrounded by his family, Don Carmen had shuffled along behind the funeral carriage, his hands touching the window, reluctant to be parted for a moment from the pure, white casket whose zeppelin-shaped outline was all but obscured under a mass of flowers. Giving in to an inexplicable feeling of urgency, Rosalío had rushed into the street from his place on the sidewalk among the other curious onlookers. He had pushed his way through the crowds of mourners, who were now walking hurriedly, watching the weather, to give his personal condolences to Don Carmen.

He had doffed his hat as a sign of respect and had compelled Don Carmen to remove his hand from the carriage window to shake it. As the cortege had gone on towards the Cathedral, Rosalío Usulután had stood there, smiling inanely until the last of the procession, the clerks, the members of the accounts department, the shop girls and errand boys from La Fama had passed him by. At that point, the first thunderclaps exploded, rebounding off the rooftops.

He could not prevent himself from feeling humiliated. That rich fellow was no friend of his, and never had been. He had no reason to give him any condolences. During his campaign against the Municipal Water Company, whenever he had seen Don Carmen in the street he had been given the cold shoulder. Don Carmen had connived with the paper's owner to get him sacked, and through consistent pressure and machinations managed to get him banned from pursuing the topic. Rosalío had been forced to write the accusatory pamphlets, printed sometime in January: it was then that he had received Don Carmen's surprise visit. It was the first time in many years that he and Don Carmen had spoken.

Later he had accepted money from Oliverio Castañeda to hand over the pamphlets. He knew it was Don Carmen's money and from then on he had made every effort not to cross paths with him: avoiding the street of his house where he usually saw him at the door, as well as the Social Club where he would see him sitting with his associates in the afternoons. He could not bear the possibility of meeting his gaze and detecting in it any sign of disdain or mocking.

Now, as he jumped over the rivulets of water gushing down the streets, the journalist tried to reconcile his conscience. He had acted out of Christian piety; not servility. Don Carmen had been too distracted by woe to acknowledge his condolences. His intention to write a gossip piece for the front page, which was already drafted and typeset in the print room, was not a source of shame. Nor was the obituary he now proposed to add. Moreover, he had already made the decision; to backtrack now would be unbecoming. He put his hand on his heart beneath his oil-skin rain coat: the pity he had felt for that young woman since the morning when he heard the passing bell toll was real and intact.

Later, seated at his Underwood typewriter he examined his conscience one last time. His purpose was true, he was not deceiving himself; he really did care that the life of that young woman, in the flower of youth, had been so cruelly cut short. He began typing the obituary, using two fingers, pecking at the keys like a pair of chickens eating maize; it would appear in the paper without fail. Once it was finished, he handed the text to the typesetter who worked silently as the rain lashed the roof. Still in need of a picture for his piece, he went to look for one in the drawer containing the engraving plates, trying to find the photograph taken for Matilde Contreras' coming out in society.

After some time looking through all the plates, each one mounted on a wooden block, he finally found the one he was after. He blew off the dust. He knew her face very well, although he had only ever seen it from afar: seated in a wicker chair at the doorway of her home watching the evening draw in, or conversing with her sister and sometimes at the Bishop's palace when she played piano at the charity events for Padre Mariano Dubón's orphanage.

Just then he heard something at the front door: it was the sound of a coin striking it, almost inaudible over the noise of the rain. The typesetter answered the door; then he heard voices. The typesetter called to him and he went over, the block still in his hand. In the doorway stood the assistant from El Esfuerzo, shivering with cold and holding a piece of sacking over his head for a hood: Cosme Manzo required his presence at the shop, the others were waiting for him.

The urgency of that request suddenly reminded him, with a sense of dread, of Doctor Salmerón's warnings. He thought back to how, when he had left the sidewalk to offer condolences to Don Carmen, he had seen Oliverio Castañeda at close quarters, grief-stricken as he walked alongside the funeral carriage. He remembered also how he had stood alone, in the middle of the street, among the droppings left by the horses all decked out in their funeral caparisons, watching through the clustering umbrellas as the funeral procession came to a halt outside the Cathedral. Castañeda had been first in line to carry the white coffin.

Now there was to be an emergency session of the accursed table at Cosme Manzo's store. He imagined how Doctor Salmerón had most likely arrived first and settled himself down where the cardboard Codfish was kept among the sacks of rice and cans of paraffin and how he was probably at that very moment excitedly going through his Casa Squibb notebook, where there were now surely many new entries. Cosme Manzo meanwhile would no doubt be pacing up and down impatiently, waiting for him. In his obituary he had written that Matilde Contreras had been the victim of blackwater fever. Now that he was expected to go and see them he wondered if he would have to retract this assertion. He had also made a great deal of her virginal chastity: most likely they would also take a dim view of that.

Peering round the half-open door he debated with himself while Manzo's assistant waited for him to give a response. He was not going to take anything out. He was also not in the mood to enter into speculation concerning the possibility of poisoning. It all seemed totally absurd and besides, Oliverio Castañeda was no enemy of his. Why should he want to conspire against him? And another thing, this emergency meeting he was being called to was starting to look dangerous: Doctor Salmerón was not going to be content with simply boasting about how his calculations had been correct and that his predictions were all coming true. He would be after blood; he was sure to come up with a plan to unmask Castañeda. What would happen if an investigation were opened and he were asked to testify?

He dismissed the assistant, telling him that he still had work to do at the newspaper office, and that he would come along later, if he could, but that the others weren't to wait for him. He closed the door and went back inside, instructing the typesetter to say he wasn't there if they came looking for him again.

It is clear from reading the obituary reproduced at the start of this chapter that Rosalío Usulutlán did not retract the assertion that Matilde Contreras died of blackwater fever. Not only does this fit in with his resolution not to change anything he had written, but it was also totally in line with the diagnoses of the doctors who attended the patient, Doctor Darbishire being foremost among them. It should also be noted that he also retained the repeated references to the chastity of the deceased.

However, he did renege on his decision not to attend the emergency session that Cosme Manzo had invited him to. Half an hour after the assistant had been dismissed, he ventured out into the still pouring rain and headed for El Esfuerzo store. He took with him, wrapped in the folds of his waterproof coat, a book belonging to Oliverio Castañeda. This book had been given him by Castañeda that night in January when he had gone to retrieve the pamphlets from the Christian Brothers' printers and he had been entreated to keep it safe at all costs.

The book was a volume entitled *The Secrets of Nature* by Doctor Jerónimo Aguilar Cortés, edited by the widow of Charles Maunier in Paris, 1913. It was not exactly a toxicology textbook, but it did contain descriptions of the properties of certain alkaloid-containing plants: some beneficial to health, others fatal.

In the fly-leaf of the book was a stamp from the Chiquimula Hospital. Oliverio Castañeda's name was inscribed on the first page, underneath the title, and on the line below a date had been written in the same handwriting: 4 April 1920. It was probably the same Oliverio Castañeda who placed a photograph of his mother, Luz Palacios de Castañeda, between the pages. According to available information, she died in that very hospital in May 1920.

As he prepared to leave the offices of *El Cronista* to attend the meeting, Rosalío Usulutlán remembered that Oliverio Castañeda had not been by to collect this book on his return from Guatemala and that it was still locked away for safekeeping in a desk drawer. He figured that it could be immensely valuable in the hands of Doctor Salmerón, especially now that there had been another fatal poisoning. Needless to say, the photograph would also be of great interest.

The last point to be made is that the book also passed through the hands of Doña Flora de Contreras. As we shall hear later, she said as much in her statement given on 31 October 1933, in which she also describes the photograph.

CHAPTER NINETEEN

Her Fingers Caress the Keyboard for the Last Time

On the night of Sunday 1 October 1933, Matilde seated herself at the Marshall and Wendell grand piano, for what was to prove the last time. As he related in his letter to Carmen Contreras Guardia, dated October fourth, she was entertaining Oliverio Castañeda's dinner guests. The cook, Salvadora Carvajal, was required to give details of this dinner in her statement of October fourteenth, taken while she was being held in prison. Because the case concerned a possible poisoning, the judge required her to give an account of what food had been prepared that night and who had a part in its preparation. In describing the soirée she also recalled some of the pieces Matilde played:

> That night Oliverio invited some guests to dinner. They were all strangers to the house. Doña Flora informed the kitchen well in advance and she and Miss María del Pilar helped organise everything. They asked for two fried chickens, which I bought live from the market. I killed and plucked them myself. Also, pureed potatoes, some chayotes, rice with tinned peas from the shop, refried beans and three bananas baked with cinnamon. They had coffee with green papaya candies. I expect they had wine, but I wouldn't know about that as I wasn't serving at table. That was Leticia Osorio's job, with the help of Bertilda Cáceres, the indoors maid.
>
> Leticia began to clear the plates and cutlery from the table at about ten o'clock. I could hear the sound of voices from the dining room and later, applause. It was then that

> I heard the piano which dear Matilde plays so beautifully. The pieces that night were of quite a sad turn, very moving. Bertilda and I were washing up, but we stopped to go and listen at the kitchen door. Leticia sat on the bench and every so often she would say "lovely", "lovely" until she toppled over asleep and I had to get her to bed, half dragging her.

Salvadora Carvajal also mentioned that it was unusual for the Contreras family to receive guests. However, as we know these were Oliverio Castañeda's friends: one was his business partner in the project to write a book about Nicaragua, the Cuban Miguel Barnet, and the other a recent acquaintance, the Italian Franco Cerutti. The latter had been resident in Costa Rica for a number of years. The owner of a marble business on the Paseo de los Estudiantes, he was visiting León on one of his regular trips to drum up business among the wealthy families for his memorial headstones.

The Costa Rican papers were full of speculation about Castañeda during his trial, and Cerutti entered the debate at one point by writing an article for *La República*. This appeared in the edition of 27 November 1933. A copy of the paper was added to the case file and was used as part of the defence presented by the accused on December sixth. It was during this defence that the accused chose to reveal many events which had until that point remained hidden.

Cerutti's article, entitled 'A Casual Bystander', contains many details about that Sunday evening. Its main points are included here:

> I met Barnet at breakfast in the dining room of the Metropolitan Hotel, where I was staying, as usual. Meeting him again was a real pleasure since I had not seen him since we had parted at the port of Havana in July 1929, after enjoying the long crossing together from Genoa. He explained his reasons for being in León and promised to introduce me to his associate, to which end he sent a waiter to the house across from the hotel. His associate duly arrived and we began talking most amiably; there was an immediate understanding between us. We ordered some drinks and talked further.
>
> The associate was a young Guatemalan gentleman, a

lawyer by profession. Oliverio Castañeda. He loved to recite poetry, which he did with great feeling, clasping his hands together, his voice laden with emotion. His favourite verses concerned star-crossed lovers; I recall one about two rivals that ends with a duel fought with machetes. For me it was quite terrifying; spine chilling. He also recited a poem dedicated to his dead mother. As I remember, it was a madrigal or a sonnet of his own composition which brought him to the edge of tears as he performed it, such was the depth of his emotion. However, he knew how to lighten the tone of his recital with a seasoning of more playful verses; popular at the student rallies in his native Guatemala and replete with some quite colourful references to priests, nuns and queers. This repertoire was undoubtedly risqué but genuine nevertheless.

The warmth of feeling between us led to a dinner invitation at his lodgings. After this he excused himself, saying that he had business to see to his host, who was also his client. Without further delay the waiter was sent across the street again in search of the aforementioned gentleman.

We did not have to wait long before this gentleman arrived and was duly introduced. Castañeda rather embarrassedly informed him about the dinner invitation. The older gentleman mumbled something, slightly put out, and then smiled grumpily. A while later, he and his young lodger departed, to talk business.

I remarked to Barnet that this amiable young man had a great deal of nerve taking the liberty of inviting us to dinner only to notify his patron afterwards, and in such an off-hand manner. Barnet replied, his eyes full of mischief, that indeed I was right. Only Oliverio Castañeda, he said, was capable of getting that tight-fisted man to lay on any kind of hospitality; his reputation was such, that despite his pre-eminent position in León, even the Sisters of Mercy never wasted any time with him. He did hint that there might also be another factor at work: a possible wedding on the horizon might also have helped smooth matters.

That night I had the opportunity to observe to what

extent the young Castañeda had made himself at home in that house. His words were acted upon by the family as much as by the servants. The head of the household, although reserved, seemed very attentive to the needs of his young lodger, going out of his way to meet those needs. At times he seemed almost deferential, like a servant, I would say. Everyone laughed at his jokes and his brilliance, praising him with unseemly enthusiasm. To a casual observer, he appeared to have an unusual degree of influence over each and every one of his hosts.

Barnet had spoken of a wedding on the horizon. This seemed entirely natural, as my friend had informed me: here was a young man who had been recently widowed. However, he seemed to bestow his attentions equally on both daughters of the household, without favouring either, while at the same time not stinting on flattery directed at the lady of the house. It was artfully done; watching him perform these feats of gallantry was like seeing a trapeze artist at the height of their powers.

At Castañeda's insistence, the elder daughter agreed to play for us. When she seated herself at the piano, an instrument which she played passably well, Castañeda placed himself at her elbow and set about play acting as if he were the conductor of an orchestra. The lady of the house enjoyed the show, as was evident from the contented glances she sent in the direction of her husband. However, the younger daughter, who had seated herself alone at the furthest end of the room, looked on with obvious annoyance. She seemed to sense that although Castañeda was acting as if it were all a game, he was clearly enthralled by the playing of the pianist.

After a time, Castañeda seemed to remember himself and, emerging from his reverie, made a tiny, almost imperceptible gesture as if to blow a kiss at the sulking girl. That kiss seemed to have the power to dispel whatever dark thoughts were tormenting the poor girl and her eyes, wet with tears, immediately brightened.

Later, the after-dinner conversation turned to other topics, and the young Castañeda requested that I go to my hotel room to fetch my catalogue of headstones so that his host could look through them. I complied, but not without reservations, as I felt it inappropriate. Don Carmen went through the photographs politely, but without any mention of a commission. At a quarter past eleven we took our leave, principally at the instigation of Barnet, who had to be away early the following day on a trip to Managua.

On the morning of Tuesday, October third I made ready to check out of my hotel since I needed to take a train to Corinto. As I left I could not help noticing the strange goings-on at the house opposite: rows of chairs had been placed on the sidewalk outside the door and there was a constant stream of people coming in and out. I decided to investigate and was told by one of the staff at the hotel that one of the daughters of the house had died suddenly. As I had so recently been honoured with the hospitality of that household, I felt obliged to go in and offer my sincerest condolences.

At the wake I met my great friend Rodemiro Herdocia, a handsome and graceful man who was a florist of incomparable skill; on a par with any in Padua, Florence or Rome. Rodemiro told me that the parents of the deceased had retired for a while and he proceeded to guide me over to where the younger of the two daughters stood surrounded by a group of young ladies. In this way I discovered that it was the elder daughter, the pianist, who had passed away.

The younger daughter was so wrapped in her grief that she did not seem to recognise me. At that moment though, Castañeda appeared out of one the rooms and was able to remind her of our recent meeting. I had to leave at that point and since then I heard no news from him until I saw his name in the papers.

I am writing these lines because I am at a loss to understand how such a fine young man of such good character could be responsible for this chain of horrible murders. I can only trust that justice will shine its light on this case and he will be exonerated. As I believe he must be.

Late in October 1933, by the time the cook Salvadora Carvajal was released from prison and Rosalío Usulutlán went to see her at her house in Subtiava, the contents of Oliverio Castañeda's luggage were already public knowledge. His trunk had been requisitioned by order of the judge, and the papers had by then published a list of all the titles of the records among Castañeda's possessions. These became instantly popular in the dance halls throughout León and the rest of Nicaragua.

The pieces became part of the standard repertoire for every dance-band and one song in particular, 'True Love Is a Once-in-a-Lifetime Thing' was to be played as part of a concert performed by the Municipal Band in Plaza Jerez on Sunday 29 October 1933. The song was withdrawn after an open letter of protest, entitled 'Grief Mocked', appeared in the diocesan paper *Los Hechos*, signed by the canon, Augusto Oviedo y Reyes, on behalf of the archbishop, Doctor Onesífero Rizo.

Among the many instructions Doctor Salmerón gave Rosalío prior to his interview with the cook was to ask whether 'True Love Is a Once-in-a-Lifetime Thing' had been one of the tunes played by Matilde on the night of Sunday, October first.

However, the cook could not remember, as she did not know any of the songs by name. So Rosalío took out his harmonica and there in Salvadora's smoke-filled shack, gave a performance of the song which was so familiar from being played at all hours on the radio.

'That's it!' said Salvadora with a toothless grin. 'That night was the last time I heard it!'

She repeated the melody herself, humming gently as if lulling a baby to sleep in its cradle.

CHAPTER TWENTY

A Clandestine Meeting in the Stock Room

NIGHT HAD already fallen by the time Rosalío Usulutlán arrived in the vicinity of the city market. The rain had begun to clear but there were still torrents of water washing down the cobbled Calle del Comercio, sweeping banana leaves and other rubbish with them. The thunder was now a distant rumble way out to sea. All of the shops were closed, except for one; the door of El Esfuerzo stood slightly ajar, the thin beam of yellow light making flickering reflections on the wet sidewalk. Rosalío poked his head around the door. The assistant who had come to find him earlier at the newspaper offices was selling a packet of epsom salts to a solitary, rain sodden customer.

The assistant motioned Rosalío through to the stock room at the back of the store, from where he could hear the sound of muffled coughing. As he walked through the shop he noticed Doctor Darbishire's hat and cape draped across one of the counters. This observation gave him a bit of a start as the old man was not in the habit of coming out so far from his home. Even stranger was the fact that he had not seen a horse and buggy at the door, which meant that he must have come on foot in the pouring rain.

A few moments earlier, Cosme Manzo had been no less surprised when his assistant had brought him the news that an old man was at the door, asking for Doctor Salmerón. Doctor Salmerón, far from being startled, seemed quite overjoyed. He waved his arms theatrically at Manzo, indicating that he should let Doctor Darbishire through. When Manzo refused, Doctor Salmerón practically pushed him out to receive his guest.

In the end then, Manzo did invite the old man in. He even managed to show some degree of hospitality by bringing him the seat from his office, which was just a corner of the shop screened off with a metal grille, like a cage. He offered the seat to the old man with a curt gesture, brushing it with his handkerchief. Doctor Salmerón very pointedly remained standing.

This was exactly how Rosalío found them when he arrived. Doctor Darbishire was suffocating in the oppressive atmosphere in the stock room, heavy with the scents of paraffin and pig fat. He had removed his heavy black cashmere jacket, which he had worn to the funeral and was attempting to dry with his handkerchief, as well as his trousers and shoes.

The journalist's arrival did not seem to disturb him. He merely glanced up without bothering to greet him. It did not seem to occur to the elderly doctor that his presence in their den was in any way extraordinary, or indicated any complicity on his part. As far as he was concerned, he had been looking for his colleague and, knowing that this was where he would be, he had been obliged to meet him there. That was all.

Doctor Salmerón had also removed his jacket and rolled up his sleeves, as if preparing to lance an abscess. Keeping his distance from Doctor Darbishire, he kept glancing at the others as if to caution them: if the old man has risked catching his death of cold walking through the streets in this incessant deluge it's because he did not want his carriage to be seen outside the store. And, given that this was the first time Doctor Darbishire had taken the initiative to seek him out after their angry exchange of a few days earlier, he surmised it could be no small matter that had brought him.

Rosalío Usulutlán went cautiously over to where Cosme Manzo was seated, far from the glare of the light bulb hanging above the two doctors' heads, on a box of Estrella laundry soap in the corner by the Codfish of Scott's Emulsion fame. As he made room for him, Manzo, with his finger pressed to his lips, warned him that he must not say even half a word.

'My friend, I want to consult you over a few issues concerning the young Castañeda,' began Doctor Darbishire, his voice barely reaching the two witnesses in the shadows, obliging them to lean forward in order to hear. His tone was deliberately professional, appropriate for the discussion of a clinical case between two colleagues.

'Yes, sir?' Doctor Salmerón said, remaining motionless, respectfully detached.

'You know me well. I am not an alarmist, but nor am I negligent,' said Doctor Darbishire, smoothing his jacket out over his knees, 'I wanted to apprise you, if you will permit me, of certain aspects of this case which have struck me.'

Although he was trying to hide it, the old man was clearly worried by something. His ruddy face, criss-crossed by blue veins, was furrowed with deep creases across the brow.

'What aspects are we talking about?' asked Doctor Salmerón, scratching his bare arms as if troubled by an itch.

'The symptoms for a start,' said Doctor Darbishire. Feeling a sneeze tickle his nose, he half closed his eyes and put his hand in front of it. 'The young Contreras woman presented with symptoms very similar to those of Señora Castañeda. Do you remember those symptoms?'

'They both died of blackwater fever. It would be logical that their cases should be similar,' said Doctor Salmerón, his lips, thick and shining in the light of the bulb, pouting in an expression of indifference.

'Can we leave aside the play-acting, my friend,' said Doctor Darbishire. He still had his hand over his nose, although the urge to sneeze had vanished. 'You needn't play the role of the offended party with me. I accept that you did warn me and I did not listen. That is why I am here now with you: to discuss the case in all seriousness. It is possible we are dealing with a maniac.'

'Very well then, let's examine the case,' Doctor Salmerón said, biting the cuticles of his thumb nail.

'I have already told you about the symptoms,' said Doctor Darbishire, finally sneezing and covering his mouth with his hand. 'Repeated attacks, each one worse than the last. Paralysis of the lower extremities, loss of consciousness, loss of control of the eye muscles, lock-jaw. I tried to prise her teeth apart with a spatula: it was impossible.'

'Strychnine,' declared Doctor Salmerón still chewing his nail.

'Here are the remaining tablets from the treatment I prepared for Matilde,' said Doctor Darbishire, searching in the pockets of his jacket folded in his lap, 'I think they should be tested. There are two left.'

Without moving from where he stood, Doctor Salmerón extended a hand to take the little pill box. It opened like a drawer, and he took out the two tablets, examining them with a casual air.

'What could be done with the tablets?' asked Doctor Darbishire fidgeting with his jacket, trying to find a better place for it but failing. He kept it on his lap.

'I know someone who could run some tests on them in complete confidentiality,' said Doctor Salmerón, dropping the tablets back into the box, which he then closed. 'The technician, Absalón Rojas, who works at the laboratory in the Faculty of Pharmacy.'

'Oh, no, that won't do,' said Doctor Darbishire, holding out his hand to take back the pill box. 'What happens if the tests come back positive for strychnine?'

'We would have some evidence. What more do you want?' said Doctor Salmerón, thrusting the box back into Doctor Darbishire's open palm.

'But evidence against whom? Against me, the one who prepared the same medication for both patients, who then died in similar circumstances!' cried Doctor Darbishire jabbing his chest with his thumb.

'You are joking of course, my dear friend. Who would suspect you?' said Doctor Salmerón, lowering his head as if searching for something on the floor, and laughing. 'You have simply been the unwitting agent of this criminal.'

'It would be better if I just handed them over to the judge,' said Doctor Darbishire, slipping the pill box back into his jacket pocket. 'Let him decide whether our suspicions are valid or not. That way we can put an end to all this speculation.'

'And if there's nothing untoward in them?' asked Doctor Salmerón, thrusting his chin forwards challengingly.

'Well then, it would just show I needn't have listened to you,' said Doctor Darbishire his eyes wandering round the room as if in search of his frustrated sneeze. His gaze came to rest on the Codfish's silver tail, shimmering in the light of the bulb. The rest of the fish was shrouded in shadow, as were the two witnesses seated on their soap box.

'No, it would be worse than that,' said Doctor Salmerón, following the old man's gaze. He could make out the Codfish's tail and was amused to see the outlines of his two friends, sitting very still, hunched up in the darkness. 'For the judge to order the tests he would need first issue a court order to start criminal proceedings.'

'Isn't that what you want?' asked Doctor Darbishire as he tried to estimate the size of the codfish. It seemed far smaller stowed here head down and motionless than it did out on the street.

'If there is nothing in the tablets, the criminal is going to feel secure and confident to carry on poisoning, without risk of discovery,' explained Doctor Salmerón, peering at his friends' hiding place. He saw the coffee-coloured shape of Rosalío Usulutlán's hat move closer to the bulk that was Cosme Manzo. 'And you would lose the trust of the Contreras family forever when they found themselves the focus of a scandal, provoked by none other than their family doctor.'

'But if there was a criminal hand in this, wouldn't there have to be poison in the tablets?' asked Doctor Darbishire picking up his jacket and shaking it out, 'or are you now contradicting yourself?'

'No, I am not contradicting myself,' said Doctor Salmerón. He caught sight of the flicker of a match in the dark corner: Cosme Manzo was giving Rosalío Usulutlán a light. 'Who's to say that the undoubtedly talented Oliverio Castañeda wouldn't take the precaution of poisoning just one of the tablets?'

'Just one? I don't understand,' said Doctor Darbishire who could now see the glowing end of a lighted cigarette, fixed in the invisible mouth of Rosalío Usulutlán. He motioned towards the corner of the room, warning 'You over there! You'll set fire to the fish! Don't you know how easily cardboard burns?'

The cigarette end wavered up and down in the darkness. Doctor Salmerón could just see his friends as they leapt up in fright and disappeared behind the stacked soap boxes. Then he heard something fall and crash onto the floor, and the fish-tail disappeared.

'When he poisoned his wife there were no tablets left,' said Doctor Salmerón, trying his best not to laugh as Manzo re-appeared making rude gestures at Rosalío, blaming him for the fish's fall. 'This time there are, but I am practically certain they won't contain any poison.'

'So?' said Doctor Darbishire, nonplussed by his own inability to follow the argument. He was also becoming aware of his colleague's attempts to hold back his laughter and this was making him even more uncomfortable. 'May I remind you that this is not a game.'

'I've already told you, the poison was in only one deadly tablet,' said Doctor Salmerón, finally suppressing his laughter, but still keeping an eye on the performance in the corner. Rosalío was now trying to stand the codfish upright. 'Russian roulette, my friend. There was only one bullet in the revolver.'

'In that case,' said Doctor Darbishire lifting his jacket like a worthless rag, 'what is the point in testing the pills even in secrecy?'

'So that you and I can verify that we are dealing not with an amateur but with a master of his art. Anyway, tests are worthless now in the case of Matilde,' said Doctor Salmerón. He saw the tail of the codfish lift up, then he heard another noise as somebody tripped up, and he could no longer contain himself.

'What's going on!' cried Doctor Darbishire getting to his feet in anger, 'if you can't listen to me properly we shall have to continue this another day!'

'Sit down my friend! An analysis of the gastric juices, urine, saliva,' said Doctor Salmerón, wiping the tears of laughter from his eyes. 'Why didn't you take any samples of the gastric juices from your patient last night? Why didn't you catheterise the patient?'

'I wasn't prepared,' said Doctor Darbishire, putting on one arm of his jacket.

'And if you had suspicions last night, why didn't you order an autopsy?' asked Doctor Salmerón turning his back to the corner with the writhing codfish so as to avoid laughing again. 'Why did you come to tell me all of this only after the burial? You had all of the morning, from dawn until noon, to find me. I wasn't in hiding. If you could find me here, you could have found me anywhere.'

'Everything is so simple for you. Do you know how these pious people would react to the suggestion of cutting up the body?' said Doctor Darbishire, putting his arm through the other jacket sleeve without getting up from his seat. 'The body of a young woman, a virgin? Thank goodness you're not asking me to exhume the body. That would certainly be something to see!'

'Well, it's the only thing that would stop that man. I will cut off both my hands with your scalpel if you don't find strychnine in the body,' said Doctor Salmerón, holding out both his hands to his old friend.

'I'm not having anything to do with you,' said Doctor Darbishire, standing up and smoothing out his jacket. 'I'll let the judge decide what he wants to do with the tablets.'

'Magnificent. And the next victim will be Don Carmen Contreras,' said Doctor Salmerón. The abscess lanced, he rolled his sleeves back down. 'Is Don Carmen suffering from malaria?'

'Who isn't in this stinking dump of a place?' Doctor Darbishire said, ducking to avoid hitting his head on the electric bulb as he walked towards the door.

'Well don't prepare him any quinine tablets!' advised Doctor Salmerón jokingly, buttoning up his shirt cuffs.

Without turning, Doctor Darbishire made a gesture in the air as if startled by a mosquito in his ear. Then he was gone.

'Do you think he will give the capsules to the judge?' Cosme Manzo asked, looking towards the doorway where the old man had disappeared.

'No, he won't hand anything in,' said Doctor Salmerón, glancing at the fish one last time. It was now correctly positioned against the wall. 'And you two are a pair of clowns. You'd do well in the Atayde Circus.'

'It's just like him to decide to start smoking. He never smokes and then all of a sudden he's pestering me like a louse, begging for a cigarette until I give him a light!' Cosme Manzo complained, pointing an accusing finger at Rosalío who was now hobbling towards them.

'And why is Don Carmen next?' asked Rosalío looking hurt and rubbing his knee.

'For two reasons,' said Doctor Salmerón, staring at him disapprovingly. 'He sleeps without a mosquito net, and he is in the way.'

CHAPTER TWENTY-ONE

Pointless Regrets

DOCTOR Darbishire left the stockroom in such a state of irritation after their futile discussion that he forgot to pick up his cape and hat. On his way home along the Calle Real, his annoyance lifted with every step he took. In its place he felt the familiar sense of pity towards his former student.

Ever since his days in the Faculty he had tried unsuccessfully to separate him from the band of dissolute characters he liked to surround himself with. A set of resentful, poorly educated individuals whose only entertainment was gossip and slander. How could a talented man like Doctor Salmerón be satisfied to set himself up as the king of such a dunghill?

And what about himself? By going to the stock room at the back of Manzo's shop he had voluntarily exposed himself to the risk of contamination. With great effort he resisted the urge to sniff his clothes, which now seemed to him impregnated with the pervasive stench of urinals. What was worse, he hadn't even managed to rid himself of the regrets that had been haunting him since the middle of the previous night. Quite the reverse: his interview with Doctor Salmerón had only succeeded in deepening them.

What was the cause of these regrets which, as his annoyance receded, now struggled to compete in his breast with the pity he felt for his old student? As the reader will already suspect, it was the certainty that Doctor Salmerón could have prevented the agony of Matilde Contreras's last moments, and her death at midnight.

There was something else, too. As he had watched over her, in the throes of the penultimate fit, clutching the edges of her coverlet with her fingers, the dying girl had begged for the forgiveness of her mother and sister. That prayer, drowned out by violence of the downpour that had been hammering down on the roof of the house, had pursued him throughout the day as he had listened in his consulting rooms to the funeral bell tolling hourly from the Cathedral; and at lunch time with his barely touched bowl of soup in front of him, that entreaty had seemed unbearable.

What if that young girl really had been poisoned? What if the poisoner now came to possess her sister as a reward for his crimes? Wouldn't that plea seem all the more appalling? And hadn't Doctor Salmerón warned him? And he, through his own laziness, was now accomplice to these foul deeds.

For this reason he had gone, fruitlessly it now seemed, in search of his old student after the burial. He had called first at his home, and on discovering he was at Manzo's had not hesitated to follow him, despite the humiliation he felt at appearing there. When he'd at last found him in that dingy back room, there he had stood, looking for all the world like a robber chief hatching secret plans among his cronies.

What were the words with which Matilde Contreras begged for forgiveness on her deathbed that so disturbed Doctor Darbishire's peace of mind? Oliverio Castañeda told Carmen Contreras Guardia, in his letter of 4 October 1933, that in her last moments Matilde had only been able to utter words of Christian piety. The testimony of the child Leticia Osorio recorded on the October nineteenth, however, sheds a necessary light on events:

> The witness confirms that she was awoken at about twelve o'clock at night and that it was María del Pilar who called her because Señorita Matilde was very ill and her help was needed. The witness put on her dressing gown and went directly to Señorita Matilde's room where she found her in the midst of a very unpleasant fit, writhing on the bed, her face purple and her eyes wide open and staring. When she had recovered, she heard Matilde say the following words: "Blessed Virgin, I die with joy, but please grant me a little time to prepare!"
>
> Later, when Doctor Darbishire came into the room, brought by Don Oliverio, Matilde was overwhelmed by an even worse attack; and when that had also passed, the

witness recalls her saying these further words: "Mother, I am dying, I beg the forgiveness of you both. I beg your forgiveness. And yours too, my dear sister, forgive me."

Doctor Darbishire was not a man who liked harbouring doubts, and regrets were even worse. To relieve his feelings he would have liked to go over the events of that tragic night, blow by blow, with Doctor Salmerón, from the moment he had heard the knocking at his door above the sound of the driving rain. If only they had been able to sit, as of old, just the two of them, in the courtyard of his consulting rooms, without the presence of those scoundrels: to recount all that he knew, all that he suspected, and everything that had happened.

Doctor Darbishire furnished the details of that night in the testimony he gave before the judge on 17 October 1933, parts of which we have heard before. Unfortunately, contrary to what might be expected, his statement conceals his suspicions and many other fundamental points. Nor does it reflect the intense feelings of doubt and remorse which had begun to plague him.

Another thing he failed to mention was his attempt to find the judge at his home on Saturday, October seventh, in order to convey those suspicions to him. This intention was frustrated because the judge was absent. He certainly did not mention anything about his long consultation with Doctor Salmerón that same Saturday, which we shall examine later. He also said very little about the unhappy chain of events in which he found himself involved on the morning of October ninth, when the fate of Don Carmen Contreras began to unfold.

JUDGE: Tell me, at what time on 2 October 1933 did you receive the call to attend your patient Matilde Contreras, and who made that call?

WITNESS: It would have been around eleven thirty at night when I heard knocking at the front door. It was difficult to make out due to the noise the rain was making as it poured down on the city. I went to answer, but I could not see anyone, and so returned to my room. The knocking continued and again the same thing happened, so I assumed that there was some kind of joker at work. I answered the door one last time and found the young gentleman Oliverio Castañeda wrapped in an oilskin, beneath an enormous umbrella with a stone in his hand. He explained that when I didn't answer he had gone across to the grounds of San Francisco church in search of a pebble he could use to make a louder noise.

JUDGE: Did he have a hire car waiting with him at the door?

WITNESS: I must confess that, yes, there was a car, but due to the rain I didn't see it, since its lights were off and it was dark in colour. In any case, it was not parked outside my consulting rooms but outside the house of Doctor Juárez Ayón. It only drove up when we were ready to go.

JUDGE: How much time do you think was spent in this sequence of knocks at your door?

WITNESS: About ten minutes in total.

JUDGE: Do you consider that those ten minutes made a vital difference to the case you were called to that night at the Contreras family home?

WITNESS: In all honesty I could not say. Between the time it took to answer the door, what I needed to get dressed and the journey in the car which Don Oliverio had at his disposal, it must have added up to around half an hour. In any event, the case was a hopeless one.

JUDGE: Did Oliverio Castañeda say anything to you during the journey in the car?

WITNESS: He seemed upset and frightened when he told me how Don Carmen had come to fetch him from his room, in a state of alarm. Thinking there must be a burglar in the house, he had got up and armed himself with his revolver. Then in the passageway Don Carmen had told him to go back to bed, that it was nothing, that Matilde had been sleeping on her left side which had put pressure on her heart. Moments later, however, before he had had time to undress, Castañeda told me the alarm had been raised again and he was sent to fetch me. "It's all so dreadful, Doctor," he kept repeating, "I fear for Matilde's life, she looks as if she has the same thing as Marta did before I lost her."

JUDGE: Can you confirm whether, in actual fact, the patient did present the same symptoms as did the deceased, Marta Jerez de Castañeda?

WITNESS: I can say that, as in the other case, she presented the symptoms of blackwater fever, for which reason I made the diagnosis as I did. It was also on the strength of the patient's previous medical history, which as in the previous case, I was also aware of: I had treated them both for malaria. The other doctors who the family called that night, among whom was Doctor Sequeira Rivas, were all in complete agreement with my opinion.

JUDGE: Did you suspect any criminal intent?

WITNESS: I had no reason to suspect anything of the sort. In my professional life I have seen and treated innumerable cases of malaria which have degenerated into such crises, most of which proved fatal. The death of my own wife is a case in point.

JUDGE: In her statement on October fourteenth of this year, Doña Flora Contreras asserts that on your last visit to the patient you mentioned your intention to exchange the quinine capsules made by yourself for a commercial preparation, which in the end you did not do. Can you tell me your reasons for considering this change?

WITNESS: It was a comment I made in passing, but it was not really my intention. I believe that my treatment, based on the tablets I prescribed, was entirely adequate.

JUDGE: Doña Flora also asserts that the night of the death, you were very concerned as to whether the patient had taken her tablets; indeed, that you asked to see the box to make sure there were two left. What was your reason for doing this?

WITNESS: My intention was to check that the patient had been taking her medicine regularly. Sometimes families are careless.

As we can tell from his evasive responses, Doctor Darbishire seems to have been determined to keep silent about his doubts. He also fails to inform the judge of how he surreptitiously pocketed the box of pills. These had been fetched by a diligent Doña Flora, as if amidst all the rush and confusion that reigned in the sickroom, this was what her daughter's life depended upon.

It was Doña Flora in her statement of 14 October 1933 who revealed the doctor's preoccupation with the tablets. It was only the witness's poor memory, or indeed her understandable confusion about the matter, which allowed Doctor Darbishire to escape suspicion.

> When questioned by the authorities concerning the circumstances surrounding the death of her daughter Matilde, the witness responded saying that the daughter in question had been suffering from malaria and had been receiving treatment from Doctor Darbishire, the family doctor. She also said that since Matilde was very careless, she herself had taken charge of ensuring that the tablets were taken, administering them together with something to line the stomach such as a glass of barley water or warm milk. The treatment comprised six tablets daily, these tablets having been prepared by Doctor Darbishire in his dispensary: two with breakfast, two with lunch and two before bed.
>
> She said that after his last visit to the patient, during which he observed that the fevers continued unabated, Doctor Darbishire had suggested substituting tablets for a recently imported commercial medicine which was very effective. The opportunity to do this did not arise, and the doctor did not mention it again.
>
> On Monday, during the day, her daughter seemed well, very happy and had talked to her friends about the previous night's dinner because she'd been so pleased by all the compliments she'd received from the guests about her magnificent piano recital. The witness can vouch for her daughter's improved health and mood because when she was suffering fevers she tended to be downcast and wrapped herself in a sweater even though it was hot; something which she did not do on that day.
>
> The witness stated that at seven o'clock that evening

she decided to visit the young lady Monchita Deshon who was ill at the time. She had been meaning to visit for several days and asked her daughters to accompany her. Matilde, however, told her that she would prefer to stay in and await Oliverio's return. He was expected very late that evening, having been tied up with Water Company business at city hall since midday, and she wanted to give him his dinner. As a result it was only María del Pilar who accompanied her.

She said that on her return at around nine-thirty that night she found her husband, Matilde and Oliverio, who had just finished eating, all seated in the dining room. They were reading through and discussing the papers. Her husband greeted her with the news that all the discussion surrounding the new contract had been finished, having reached a deal which was very favourable to the Water Company, and that it would soon be signed.

The witness said that at around ten o'clock that night she gave Matilde an Alophen pill. Since it was the right time she also gave her the tablets prescribed by Doctor Darbishire for her malaria. These were administered with a glass of barley water which she had prepared personally since the servants had already gone to bed.

She said that when she took the medicine and the drink to Matilde, she found her talking with Oliverio in the courtyard. Oliverio was joking that the tablets were also a beauty aid and because of the effect they obviously had he'd decided to ask Doctor Darbishire to increase the dose. Her daughter had laughed at this as she swallowed the tablets one by one.

They all went to bed, her husband being the last to retire as he was in the habit of walking round the whole house including the shop, to ensure there was nothing out of place and that all the doors were locked. The witness also stated that when she entered her bedroom it was already raining hard.

She recalls that it must have been a quarter to twelve when María del Pilar raised the alarm because she had heard Matilde screaming. She and her husband went immediately to their daughter's room, where they found Matilde rigid and unconscious. She says that her husband attempted artificial respiration and that as soon as her daughter came to, she grabbed the witness' hands crying "Mama, mama, I am dying!"

Her husband reassured their daughter that there was nothing to worry about and recommended she turn onto her other side to relieve any pressure on her heart. No sooner had they returned to their own room than María del Pilar came running for help once more. By this time they realised that matters were serious because Matilde was now convulsing, clenching her jaw and fists. Without wasting any more time, her husband sent Oliverio to fetch Doctor Darbishire.

The witness referred to how, while waiting for the doctor, she and María del Pilar applied Vicks Vaporub to the legs and chest of the patient and woke the servants, telling them to boil up some water in case it was needed. She stated that when Doctor Darbishire finally arrived, driven in the car by Oliverio, he diagnosed acute blackwater fever. The diagnosis was confirmed by Doctor Sequeira Rivas who arrived at the house a few moments later.

Doña Flors further stated that Doctor Darbishire questioned her persistently as to whether Matilde had taken her quinine tablets that night and that she responded that she had herself given them to her. She says that he asked her repeatedly for the box of tablets and that when she found them and showed them to him there were only two remaining tablets, those for breakfast the next morning; proof that she had indeed been diligent in treating Matilde as instructed.

Pressed by the judge, the witness stated she thought she saw the box of tablets on the bedside table, where Doctor Darbishire had left them. However, when the room was later cleaned in preparation for laying out the body, she is less certain as to where the box of tablets may have ended up.

We already know where the box of tablets ended up. Doctor Darbishire put them in his pocket, and on the night of October third, after the clandestine appointment with his colleague in Cosme Manzo's stock room, he took them back to his consulting room. His bag, however, which he had left in his consulting room, contained something that was perhaps far more important.

The objects in question were a pair of haemostats, which had, clamped within them, a wad of cotton wool. Without revealing his intentions to anyone, Doctor Darbishire had swabbed the inside of Matilde's mouth to obtain a sample of her saliva. Owing to the unpleasant turn taken in their discussion, he concealed this from his colleague. Now that he had been assured that the poison might have been contained in a single tablet, this sample of saliva had become the test of whether murder had indeed been committed.

Doctor Darbishire switched on the light as he entered the surgery and took out the pair of haemostats from his medical bag: the wad of cotton was still secure between their jaws. Placing them on the glass-topped writing desk, he took the box of tablets from his pocket and set them to one side. He sat for a while, gravely contemplating the objects in front of him.

By the time he made his way to his bedroom he had made a firm decision to go to the judge the following morning; as soon as he had finished his rounds of the San Vicente hospital. He was resolved to be entirely frank and to hand over the haemostats with their wad of cotton and the remaining tablets.

He undressed, throwing his clothes over a chair. Let Justice decide. As he lay in bed he remembered that he had left his cape and hat at Cosme Manzo's shop. He gave a start of disgust at the thought and sat up in bed once more.

He would send Teodosio to get them as soon as it was morning. He lay down again but found it impossible to sleep. It felt as if he were lying on a bed of nails.

CHAPTER TWENTY-TWO

Odd Behavior at the Wake

IN THE midst of the deluge that engulfed the whole of León on the night of 2 October 1933, the Contreras family's friends and relations began to arrive at the house. They gathered there owing to the diligence of Oliverio Castañeda who, in the company of Captain Anastasio J. Ortiz, had dedicated himself to doing the rounds of the dwellings of those he considered closest to the family, as related in his letter to Carmen Contreras Guardia.

While his companion stayed in the vehicle, Castañeda would knock urgently at their doors until the sound of his rapping resounded throughout their houses. The witnesses later recalled how, trembling beneath his enormous umbrella in the dark porches of their rain-drenched homes, he would gabble the news of Matilde's imminent death.

Some of the witnesses asserted that Castañeda even told them the death had already occurred, in advance of the actual event. This of course later contributed to the suspicions raised against him. The testimony of Graciela Deshon, president of the Daughters of Mary, is typical in this respect. On 16 October 1933, she stated that:

> Castañeda gripped me firmly by the shoulders, which struck me as a bit too familiar, shouting: "To hear this you need to be strong, my dear Chelita; Matilde, our angel, who delighted us with her music, has flown heavenwards, back from whence she came." But the scoundrel was lying to me. When I arrived at the house, I found Matilde alive and surrounded by her doctors, who were doing all they could to save her.

In the preliminary hearing on 1 December 1933, Oliverio Castañeda answered the judge's questions on this particular matter:

> JUDGE: At midnight on the night that Señorita Matilde Contreras passed away, without being asked, you went about calling on various people at their homes so as to gather them at the family house. You informed some of these people that Matilde had already died, despite the fact that this had not yet occurred. From this I can only conclude that you were absolutely sure that she would succumb because she had been poisoned.
>
> ACCUSED: It is true that as a gesture of friendship I did gather those people who were closest to the family. I never considered that this was unwelcome, quite the opposite. Later, during the wake both Don Carmen and Doña Flora thanked me for having gone ahead. Unfortunately she now seems to have turned against me, or she would confirm this.
>
> As to your other accusation, I never gave anybody the impression that Matilde was already dead. Any who says otherwise is lying, most likely due to the hatred against me that permeates the atmosphere of this city. The only thing I was able to tell them was that Matilde's condition was serious, that she was victim of a series of terrible fits. That was the truth.
>
> JUDGE: Upon what basis did you assure them that Matilde's condition was so serious? Had you been present in the room to witness any of these fits?
>
> ACCUSED: I knew it because this is what Don Carmen told me when he came to my room and asked me to go to fetch the doctor. The second fit came upon her as we were talking in the corridor, about to return to bed in the impression it had all been a false alarm. Later, when all the relatives and doctors were going in and out of Matilde's room, they referred to the fits and sent me for the medicines necessary to alleviate them. Out of discretion I did not go into her room, even once. I limited myself to assisting in whatever way possible from outside.
>
> JUDGE: In a statement given on 14 October 1933,

Doña Flora asserts that everyone had gone back to bed when the second fit came on. Why do you persist in your story, as related in your letter to Carmen Contreras Guardia, that you were still talking in the corridor when the new crisis arrived?

ACCUSED: Because it is the truth, and I don't see that this detail has any importance. What's more you should bear in mind that Doña Flora's state of anxiety at the time might well have caused her to forget the exact sequence of events.

JUDGE: I have in my hand your letter to the young Carmen Contreras Guardia, dated the 4 October 1933, in which you wrote that you heard Matilde on her deathbed, saying certain things. How can this be the case if you never, at any point, set foot in her bedroom?

ACCUSED: I did not need to have heard them directly as they were recounted to me by those of her family who were in the room. You should remember that at that time, before the rumour machine was set in motion against me, I was an esteemed and trusted member of the household.

Matilde's close friend, Alicia Duquestrada, gave a statement on 19 October 1933. By special dispensation of the judge it was taken at her home, and in it she referred to that night:

> As soon as Castañeda had been to call us we got ready to go but my father wanted to wait until the rains had subsided a little because the streams of water coursing down the streets were quite strong and he was frightened they would overturn the buggy. As the rain showed no sign of ceasing, I threatened to walk to the Contreras' family home, which made him change his mind. We arrived without any mishap.
>
> It was approaching one o'clock, and we found the house lit up as if for a party. In tears, I ran to Matilde's room and found that everything had been taken out, only the bed was left where she lay dressed in a white satin dress, one which she never wore because it was too loose around the shoulders. On her head she was wearing an

embroidered veil like a bride on her wedding day.

In the kitchen, the female servants were heating water to make coffee and to wash the cups and saucers that with Oliverio Castañeda's help they were taking off the shelves in the shop to bring into the house. He approached me as he was coming back from one of these trips to the kitchen. Embracing me tightly, he said between his tears: "Have you been to see her already Alicia? Go and look at her one last time. She looks as if she is about to smile at one of my jokes."

The judge had no further questions at this stage, but the witness expressed her wish to add another piece of information, and to this end she said:

Oliverio Castañeda had many books, some of which he used to recommend to Matilde. He sometimes let me read them too and as my father has now explained to me, I realise that they were intended to pervert our virtue and our religious beliefs.

Only a few days before Matilde died, he gave her a cyclostyled copy of one of these books. According to him, this was the only way he could get hold of it because it was forbidden by the Pope and persecuted by the priesthood. When I was visiting Matilde one afternoon, Castañeda appeared and asked: "Have you read that little book yet? Why don't you lend it to Alicia?" Matilde did just that and I took the book home but did not read it until today, thank God.

The night of the wake, during the conversation that I have already mentioned, he reminded me of the book and asked: "Read it Alicia, and take care to return it to me. Don't let anyone see you read it; it should be a very intimate experience and you should read it alone." Now, as directed by my father, I shall give it to you, your honour. My father insists it is full of corruption. It was written in France and is nothing but perversion and tales of immorality which I cannot even imagine.

(At this point the father of the witness, who was present while the statement was being recorded, handed over the item in question. The book comprises one hundred and thirty-two single sided, typewritten pages. On the front page the work has been annotated with the title "Gamiani" while what is actually printed gives no indication as to the content of the book, indeed it suggests something quite different: "The martyrdom of Santa Águeda and other poems by Santiago Argüello".

Without wishing to be considered as experts in the matter, both the presiding judge and the court secretary charged with recording the statement concur that the work is a Spanish translation of "Gamiani", originally written by the French author, Alfred de Musset.)

The last journey Oliverio Castañeda made in the car was to fetch Rodemiro Herdocia. By profession a florist (unmarried, forty years old), his skill and physical attributes were, as we have already heard, admired by the Italian sculptor Franco Cerutti. Rodemiro set aside the whole of his ample back yard in the San Felipe district to the cultivation of araucaria, water lilies, irises and all manner of flowers for the production of funeral wreaths and garlands. He was also in the business of assembling biers to support coffins, as well as the rental of chairs for wakes.

On 18 October 1933, the florist made the following statement:

When asked about what he remembered from the wake of Señorita Matilde Contreras, the witness replied:

Doctor Oliverio Castañeda woke me in the middle of the night. He told me the terrible news from the Contreras home and requested that I construct a bier for Matilde and send a hundred folding chairs; the ones I rent out. I roused my two young assistant gardeners who live with me and asked them to harness the horses to the cart so that we could begin transporting the chairs and other necessary items.

I thought it very strange indeed that while I was expressing my anguish at the fatal turn of events, Doctor Castañeda kept making all sorts of inappropriate jokes, which were in very poor taste considering the tragic circumstances. I tried to make him see this, but he just answered me with further double entendres, which was very typical of his behaviour.

Once at the home of the deceased and when everything had been prepared, we awaited the coffin, which had been ordered from the Rosales funeral parlour. I went out into the corridor, where I found Castañeda chatting in the company of several people. I needed to enquire whether any funeral bouquets were required for the bier as I would have to send my assistants back to the garden to cut the flowers. I thought it best to ask him as he seemed to be in charge of arrangements.

He did not answer me immediately as he was in the middle of a heated argument with one of the gentlemen in the group, Don Esteban Duquestrada, about the time of the burial. Don Esteban was of the opinion that, with the approval of Don Carmen, it had already been decided that it should take place at four o'clock in the afternoon after a service in the Cathedral. He was going to speak with Monsignor Tijerino y Loáisiga about it that very morning. Castañeda on the other hand was insisting that the funeral should take place in the morning according to Doña Flora's wishes.

One of the other gentleman present at that discussion, Don Evenor Contreras, was of the same opinion as Castañeda; but Don Esteban was very emphatic in his opposition. As I was in need of an answer, I asked again about the flowers. Castañeda gave me a very strange look, quite frightening in fact, and replied: "You're the one surrounded by rosebuds, Rodi." At this he guffawed so loudly that everyone around was quite put out. Eventually, Don Esteban turned to me and said in a very serious tone: "Yes, my friend, order the flowers."

During the same conversation, Castañeda also insisted on transferring Matilde's body to the coffin without delay. Barely had the casket arrived from the Rosales funeral parlour than she was laid out in it and the lid sealed. "Doña Flora finds it repugnant that people come to view the body," he said, "and I agree with her, it is just morbid curiosity."

Taking advantage of a lull in the rain, my assistants and I went to the garden to cut all the flowers we needed while it was still dark. It was about three in the morning and the only light we had was from a few fluorescent lamps.

> We took the flowers by the armful from the cart and into the house of mourning until all available vases and other receptacles were filled. Tired and exhausted, I sat down on one of the chairs we had set out along the corridor. There were already a great many people there, congregating for the wake, talking and drinking cups of black coffee. Thanks to the conversations I overheard I realised that there were already rumours about Doctor Castañeda doing the rounds among the guests.
>
> These rumours painted Doctor Castañeda as the master poisoner. They said that his late wife had tormented him with her jealousy and that he had poisoned her with strychnine. That her jealousy had been justified, since after her death he had made it clear he was in the market for a new wife and that since Matilde had been in his way it was not surprising he had now poisoned her too.
>
> I moved out of earshot, as I could not bear to hear any more. I was astounded that people were repeating such accusations only yards away from the dearly departed Matilde and while the family were grieving, as yet untroubled by the possibility that her death had been the result of criminal intent born of carnal desire.

When the judge enquired whether Rodemiro Herdocia knew the names of any of those present when these rumours began circulating, the witness cited Doctor Alejandro Sequeira Rivas. The judge questioned the doctor about these allegations when the latter gave testimony on 20 October 1933:

> I can say that, among those present at the wake, there was a certain amount of disapproval for the behaviour of Oliverio Castañeda. They considered it inappropriate for example that he was going from group to group trying to enliven the conversation with his jests. Although I barely knew him, I felt I had to approach him and caution him to moderate his behaviour, reminding him that he was a guest in the house and the family might well be offended. To me, he seemed a little under the influence, although I couldn't smell any drink on him.
>
> Nevertheless, I must be honest and say that the only

> rumours that I heard concerning an alternative cause for the death of Marta Jerez, whom I attended in her hour of need, came from the lips of Rodemiro Herdocia. He was going round spreading these rumours among all the people in the neighbourhood and on the street outside. I never gave any credence to any of it, since Herdocia is a well-known gossip. As to the accusations of criminal intent in the death of Matilde Contreras, I attended her through that fatal illness in my professional capacity, and can vouchsafe that no one made any comment at the time, least of all to Herdocia himself.

That same day, October twentieth, the judge recalled Rodemiro Herdocia so as to clarify his prior statement:

> Warning him first to be aware that he would be charged with perjury should he not tell the truth, the presiding judge, the Chief Criminal District Prosecutor, proceeded to interrogate the witness, Rodemiro Herdocia, concerning his previous statement. The aim of these questions was to determine the origin of the rumours that had circulated during the wake for Señorita Matilde Contreras, which according to other reliable witnesses had come from Rodemiro Herdocia himself.
>
> The witness admitted that he had been the one who had made the comments in the presence of other guests at the wake. He said that he had been repeating the allegations made by Cosme Manzo in his shop a few days before, when the witness had been there on an errand to buy a length of chintz to make a curtain for the picture of Jesus the Redeemer which he had in a shrine at his home.
>
> On the occasion in question, Manzo had told him that Doctor Castañeda was a master poisoner. He also said that he poisoned dogs for fun—although this was just to practice, his real purpose being to eliminate certain persons in order to release himself from the tangles of his love-life. This was the reason why he had given strychnine to his wife; it would not be surprising if he went on to poison other members of the Contreras family since they were all on his list. And, according to Manzo, he would not stop

> until he succeeded in marrying one of them and getting his hands on Don Carmen's fortune.
>
> According to the witness, Manzo told him that Doctor Castañeda enjoyed his murderous task because he was something of a demon lover; he had all of the Contreras women at his feet and completely under his spell. He also mentioned certain letters which had been written by these women to the poisoner, which were not exactly letters to the Infant Jesus. Manzo said that when these letters came to light, the whole of León's polite society would be trembling in its sanctimonious boots because they still believed in virginity.

Cosme Manzo appeared to give his statement on the following day, 21 October 1933. The fact that one of his associates had been called to shed light on the salacious gossip, in particular concerning the letters, must have been a cause of alarm for Doctor Salmerón. He did not panic, however, and even convinced Rosalío Usulutlán to publish an article reporting the scandal which appeared in *El Cronista* a few days later, on 25 October 1933.

The judge appears to have been satisfied by Cosme Manzo's denials, although it is unlikely that he believed them, knowing full well Cosme was an associate of the accursed table. This being so, he must have guessed that the ultimate source of the allegations reported by the florist must be Doctor Salmerón, whom he resolved to interview later.

Cosme Manzo's testimony is included here, his script having been discussed in advance with Doctor Salmerón:

> The witness energetically denies all the imputations made by Rodemiro Herdocia and calls on him to substantiate his words with proof. The witness considers every part of what has been said to be wholly defamatory, and reserves the right to lay charges of slander before the court. He accepts that the aforementioned Herdocia has been to his shop on many occasions as a client, but states that there has never been any friendship between them, which might lead him to take him into his confidence, least of all concerning matters about which the witness has no knowl-

edge. The witness considers himself to be a sober person, committed to his business interests and not in the habit of indulging in idle gossip.

The witness further maintains that he does not know and has had no dealings with Oliverio Castañeda. He has, however, read about Castañeda in the press, and has heard certain rumours about him being repeated across León. As a result, he is aware of the charges made against the man. The witness would also like to make clear that he has never had dealings with the Contreras family either, and knows nothing of their private lives. This is all that the witness has to say.

The statements which have been cited, as well as others that appear in the judicial records, all coincide in their account of the impertinent behaviour displayed by Oliverio Castañeda at the wake for Matilde Contreras. The testimony of Don Esteban Duquestrada, given on 18 October 1933, also corroborated that of the florist in describing how the accused was very keen to see the body placed in the coffin and for the burial to take place very early in the morning.

The prisoner himself acknowledged this last point and gave his reasons at his arraignment:

JUDGE: Would you elaborate on why you were so insistent that the body of the deceased should be buried early in the morning? Why could it not have waited until the afternoon as is more customary, and indeed as was the wish of the family? I can only presume that you needed to hide the evidence of your crime by trying to make it difficult for the body to be subject to an autopsy.

ACCUSED: And I can only reply that your honour presumes incorrectly. In the first place it was only a matter of an opinion I expressed to Don Esteban Duquestrada, and not of a particular insistence on my part. Don Esteban had been given charge of the funeral arrangements, and I was afraid it was going to rain heavily that afternoon, as indeed it did. I don't need to give you proof that there was a great rainstorm over the whole of León that afternoon.

JUDGE: You did also insist that the body of Señorita Contreras be placed in the coffin immediately. There are several witnesses to this. I am forced to believe that this haste on your part also hints at the same objective: to avoid anyone seeing the body and making any observations that might incriminate yourself as the author of her death.

ACCUSED: I don't quite understand how the mere observation of a corpse, either inside or outside a coffin, could allow anyone to come to that kind of conclusion. I must repeat that as before this was nothing more than my stating an opinion. The statement of Rodemiro Herdocia to which you are referring is malicious in every sense. I am astonished that your honour would give such weight to the allegations of someone so easily led and fickle in nature owing to the peculiarities of his personal proclivities.

When Rodemiro asked me about the flowers I in turn asked him whether the coffin had arrived from Rosales funeral parlour. When he told me that, yes it had arrived, I went to Don Esteban and said: "Well, I suppose we may as well place her into the coffin now." And Don Esteban agreed with me. In this case as in the instance of the time of the funeral, I had no reason to mention Doña Flora, whose opinion had not been sought. It would seem your honour that everything that I said and did that night, which above all else was a time of grief—even the simplest smile, the most innocent word, a statement about whether it was raining or was hot—is going to be used against me.

The courtroom was full to bursting and Castañeda's supporters could be heard fervently applauding and shouting encouragement. The judge was once again forced to order the clearance of the public gallery as he had done earlier that day after the violent exchange between the accused and the witness Carmen Contreras Guardia.

Oliverio Castañeda took a linen handkerchief from his pocket to wipe his neck, then removed his spectacles and mopped his brow. After a moment's pause he rose to his feet and turned towards the gallery to acknowledge the applause and cheers with a courteous nod of the head.

CHAPTER TWENTY-THREE

A Fruitless Search for a Missing Judge

IT WAS the afternoon of 7 October 1933 and Doctor Atanasio Salmerón was just leaving the house of the Chief Criminal District Prosecutor, Doctor Mariano Fiallos Gil. He was putting his hat on when he saw his one-time mentor, Doctor Darbishire, on the far side of the street, looking as though he were about to cross over. It seemed as if he too were on his way to see the judge, but startled at the sight of his old student, he beat a hasty retreat, wrapping himself in the folds of his voluminous cape. With a faint grin of pleasure on his lips, Doctor Salmerón followed and caught up with him.

They had not seen each other since the night after Matilde Contreras' funeral the previous Tuesday, when they had argued in Cosme Manzo's stock room, but this new chance meeting showed they could not postpone the opportunity to thrash out their differences.

'He's not here. He's gone to his ranch at El Sauce,' said Doctor Salmerón, grabbing his mentor by the elbow.

'And when will he be back?' asked Doctor Darbishire, slowing down and adjusting his pince-nez. He looked at his student with an air of concern.

'Monday, on the seven a.m. train. Are you going back to your consulting rooms? I'll accompany you if you like,' said Doctor Salmerón, taking him by the arm in order to walk with him the few blocks separating them from the consulting room on Calle Real.

At this point we have to leaf back through a few pages of our calendar of events:

On the day after Matilde Contreras' funeral Doctor Darbishire set out for the hospital earlier than usual. He did not even bother to take his customary bath with sprigs of rosemary that morning as he wanted to catch Doctor Salmerón before he began his rounds. Doctor Salmerón, however, was nowhere to be found, either in the corridors or in the waiting room where he sat for quite some time on one of the benches, killing time by going through some medical records.

He returned to his consulting room at around eight o'clock. He was worried that his student was avoiding him. He was even more concerned that the haemostat with its wad of cotton had gone missing from his desk where he had left it the night before.

He went to look for Teodosio. He found him at the far end of the yard throwing the dirty water from his mop-bucket over the plants. Terrified by the reprimand he received, the youth managed somehow by means of signals to explain that in the course of his customary duties cleaning and disinfecting all the used instruments, he had taken the haemostats and placed them in their appropriate drawer. The cotton wad had been disposed of in the latrine, along with some other dressings, gauzes and dirty bandages.

Now all Doctor Darbishire had left was the little box of quinine tablets. Careful that an accident should not now befall these, he placed them in a locked drawer in his writing desk. However, he realised that this resolved little. He could not forget his colleagues' certainty on one particular point during their discussion the previous night; at the time it had struck him as just another indication of his colleague's idiotic fixations, but now it seemed obvious: only one tablet had contained the poison. Visiting the judge now seemed pointless.

He did not receive any calls for medical assistance from the Contreras family over the following days. This allowed him to comfort himself in the knowledge that at the very least, no potential murderers would be using medicines prepared by him to claim any more victims. In addition, as Doctor Salmerón had not re-appeared, he could be thankful that he did not have to deal with any more of his murderous theories.

On Friday morning, on the pretext of being in the neighbourhood as he was completing his home visits, he turned his buggy in the direction of the Contreras residence. He hoped that this would further put him at ease, but in the event and contrary to his hopes, what he found only gave him more cause for alarm. As a result, he found himself that Saturday afternoon on his way to see the judge with the box of tablets in his jacket pocket. However, it seemed that it was his destiny to fall into the hands of the ever-present Doctor Salmerón.

We can now return to the mentor and his student as they walk side by side:

At the junction with Calle Real they met Doctor Darbishire's buggy, driven by Teodosio. The horses were trotting along at a brisk pace; the canopy was down and the dogs were in the back, out on their usual Saturday afternoon drive. The old man waved his hat wildly to greet his dogs; they however took no notice of him, sitting snugly ensconced in the buggy.

When they arrived at Doctor Darbishire's home, he immediately invited his student through into the dining room. The old physician was not a connoisseur of liquor, but he know that Doctor Salmerón was partial to a tipple now and then, and so he took two tumblers from the sideboard and brought out a bottle containing some fire-water, a gift from one of his patients in Malpaisillo. He ventured into the abandoned kitchen in search of salt and a knife and finally he went to the window where the lemon tree pushed through, and cut some fruit from one of its branches.

'I have so many things to tell you, sir,' said Doctor Salmerón, cutting the lemons eagerly and wincing as some of the juice squirted into his eye.

'Let me begin,' begged Doctor Darbishire as he poured a measure into the cut-glass tumblers; one for his student and one for himself. The sediment disturbed at the bottom of the bottle swirled in a dense cloud. 'I have far more to tell you.'

'I know. You were at the Contreras' place yesterday, and met Doctor Segundo Barrera there,' Doctor Salmerón said, smiling and pointing the knife at him.

'So now you've become a spy, have you, my friend?' asked Doctor Darbishire, grinning back as he put the corn-cob stopper back in the bottle.

'My account is from the horse's mouth, he himself told me about the incident this morning in the surgery,' said Doctor Salmerón, laying down the knife as carefully as if he were returning a scalpel to the instrument trolley.

'There was no incident,' said Doctor Darbishire spreading his hands in front of his disciple, 'my patients are free to choose another doctor. I cannot chain them to me!'

Doctor Salmerón felt the urge to laugh, but he contained himself. The old man seemed genuinely hurt, and he did not want to offend him.

For the benefit of the reader, it is necessary to retrace our steps yet again and accompany Doctor Darbishire on the day he made his courtesy call to the Contreras family:

That Friday, at around eleven o'clock in the morning, he strode confidently into the house, as he was accustomed to do. He was intercepted by a rather flustered Doña Flora. She politely offered him a seat and sent for some refreshments. However, despite this show of affability she was unable to hide her obvious embarrassment. He had intended to ask after the health of the members of the household, but before he had the chance, he heard coughing coming from the half open door of one of the bedrooms at the end of the corridor; in fact it was the same room where, not too long ago, he had attended to Marta Jerez. Oliverio Castañeda was sitting at the head of the table in the dining room. He was working diligently at his typewriter and he barely acknowledged the guest, greeting him with the merest inclination of his head.

'Doña Flora explained, with some anxiety in her voice, that Don Carmen was now sharing that room with Castañeda,' said Doctor Darbishire, carefully raising his brimming glass, 'and that she was now sleeping in with María del Pilar.'

'Removing temptation, what a wise decision! Your health, sir!' said Doctor Salmerón, draining his glass at one go.

'But guess why she was so anxious,' said Doctor Darbishire shrugging his shoulders and keeping them hunched as if to accentuate his disdain: 'Doctor Barrera was there. At that moment he came out of the bedroom carrying his medical bag. He then walked over to Castañeda and stopped to talk with him.'

'Did you go over to say hello to Doctor Barrera?' asked Doctor Salmerón. He had refilled his glass and was holding it to his lips.

'Don't play the fool, my friend,' said Doctor Darbishire severely as he smoothed his moustache with his fingers. 'Let's get straight to the point: when Don Carmen started complaining of fevers in the evening, his elder sister María took matters into her own hands and decided to call Doctor Barrera. Don Carmen had not been keen, but his sister insisted. Doña Flora took sides with his sister.'

'I see. Malaria of course?' said Doctor Salmerón downing his drink and making a face, 'Then we must be prepared for another case of blackwater fever.'

Doctor Salmerón was aware of the history between his two colleagues. They had fallen out over a matter of professional rivalry and had not so much as exchanged a greeting since. When they met at the Contreras' house, Doctor Segundo Barrera was so conceited that he had not deigned to look at the other man, and in his hurry he did not even bother to take his leave of Doña Flora.

Although Doctor Darbishire was hurt to find that he had been replaced by his principal detractor, when he realised that Doña Flora was about to give him all sorts of excuses, he stopped her.

'As you must understand, my first impulse was to leave the house at once,' said Doctor Darbishire. Then he lifted his chin in an attitude of pride saying, 'but as the servant had already brought the refreshments I did not want to upset the lady. I stayed and had my drink in a civilised fashion; although to me it tasted like bile.'

'I don't wish to stir up trouble, sir,' said Doctor Salmerón, wiping his mouth with the back of his hand, 'but the situation is very serious. I won't hide anything from you: Doctor Barrera is feeling very smug to have poached one of your patients, especially one so illustrious as Don Carmen Contreras.'

'The insufferable fellow,' said Doctor Darbishire, smiling but blinking back his evident bitterness.

'Don't worry about that. When I say the situation is serious, it is because it will be very difficult to get him to alter his prescription,' explained Doctor Salmerón. He poured some salt onto a slice of lemon and sucked on it. 'For that to happen we would have to risk telling him of our suspicions.'

'Change it? Why?' asked Doctor Darbishire, startled.

'Don't tell me that you don't know what Doctor Barrera ended up prescribing?' Doctor Salmerón said as he helped himself to another drink, taking care not to disturb the sediment at the bottom of the bottle. 'Wasn't that why you were on the way to see the judge?'

'No, I had other reasons—I'll explain later,' said Doctor Darbishire, now gravely concerned. 'Tell me, what medication did he prescribe?'

'Quinine and antipyrine, in tablet form just as you prescribed for Matilde Contreras. And indeed for Marta Jerez,' said Doctor Salmerón, studying the sediment as it settled back at the bottom of the bottle.

'A course of how many tablets?' asked Doctor Darbishire, sitting forwards and spreading his hands across the table, just managing to avoid spilling his as yet untouched glass.

'Nine daily over fifteen days. He must have begun taking them yesterday,' Doctor Salmerón said. After hesitating a moment, he poured himself another drink.

'And did Doctor Barrera tell you all this quite freely, or did you interrogate him?' asked Doctor Darbishire, nervously stroking the table top with his hands.

'Of his own free will. As I said, he is over the moon to have this patient,' replied Doctor Salmerón closing his eyes, and knocking back his drink. 'He gave me a blow by blow account of the medical examination. He was just like a child with a new toy.'

'What a mess! That man is capable of anything,' said Doctor Darbishire, taking a sip from his glass, but barely wetting his lips.

'Doctor Barrera?' asked Doctor Salmerón, vigorously rubbing his cheeks, which have turned bright red. Feeling the heat, he unbuttoned his shirt at the neck and loosened his tie.

'Don't play games. I was talking about Oliverio Castañeda,' Doctor Darbishire rebuked him, tutting with disapproval, 'you turn everything into a joke. When I say that he is capable of anything, it's because of something he said to me.'

'So you stopped to speak to Castañeda?' asked Doctor Salmerón, glassy-eyed. By now he had got through almost a quarter of the bottle.

'It was Castañeda who accosted me,' said Doctor Darbishire. He moved the bottle slightly towards himself and out of his former student's reach. 'He came over to Doña Flora to let her know that he was going out to get the medicine, and I took advantage of the moment to take my leave. We ended up going to the door together. All of a sudden he took me by the arm and dragged me off to a corner, apparently to take me into his confidence.'

'And what did he tell you?' asked Doctor Salmerón. He undid his jacket and fanned himself with the lapels.

'He told me that he was very sorry for what had happened to me and that neither he nor Doña Flora approved of Doctor Barrera,' said Doctor Darbishire, replacing the stopper so firmly in the neck of the bottle it seemed he wished to close it forever. 'He said that it had to do with Don Carmen's family who were sticking their noses into everything from medical issues to matters of business.'

'He knows how to look after his interests,' said Doctor Salmerón. He reached over to get hold of the bottle once again, but stopped, 'he talks as if he were lord and master!'

'He gave me the Water Company contract as an example,' Doctor Darbishire went on, keeping a close eye on the bottle, but not making any attempt to retrieve it just yet. 'He complained that he had taken such pains to organise everything, acting as Don Carmen's trusted advisor and lawyer, and that now everyone was trying to get in on the act, poking their noses in and trying to make changes.'

'But why would he tell you all this?' asked Doctor Salmerón taking the stopper out of the bottle and disingenuously sniffing it, 'you are not party to any of this business.'

'He wanted to ask me a favour,' replied Doctor Darbishire, drumming his fingers on the table top, and idly following their movements, 'something that Doña Flora did not dare to do.'

'What favour?' enquired Doctor Salmerón, seizing the opportunity to serve himself another drink quickly while the old man was distracted.

'To re-examine Don Carmen, in order to reassure Doña Flora,' said Doctor Darbishire in disgust.

'And did you re-examine him?' asked Doctor Salmerón, who was now sipping his drink more slowly.

'Of course not! What sort of a man do you think I am? Do you think I have no dignity?' cried Doctor Darbishire making such a wild gesture with his hand that he inadvertently knocked his pince-nez off his nose. 'I thanked him for his trust in me, but told him that I was in a hurry. He still had me by the arm, and propelled me into the corner. Then, peering all round him, he lowered his voice still further.'

Doctor Salmerón leaned back in his chair and blinked hard. Doctor Darbishire was not sure whether this was a sign of interest or the effect of all the alcohol he had drunk.

'He told me that what ailed Don Carmen was not physical but psychological,' said Doctor Darbishire, examining the lenses of his pince-nez against the light before putting them back on. 'According to him, Don Carmen was in an acute state of nervous breakdown, the victim of a severe and life-threatening depression.'

'Life-threatening depression?' said Doctor Salmerón slurring his words and half closing his eyes.

'Now that they share a room he knows he wakes frequently and goes walking along the verandah in the dark,' Doctor Darbishire said, standing up and placing the bottle at the far end of the table. 'The previous night he said that when Don Carmen didn't return for some time he had got up to look for him. He says he found him in Matilde's now empty room, lying in her bed sobbing.'

'Suicide,' said Doctor Salmerón nodding his head slowly, 'he is preparing the ground for a fake suicide.'

'Now you see why I decided I couldn't wait any longer and that I had to make my suspicions known to the authorities,' said Doctor Darbishire, heaving a great sigh.

'Do you realize what an intricate web he is weaving for us?' said Doctor Salmerón, who now had his eyes tight shut and was speaking with long pauses between his words. 'Once again we have a suspected case of malaria. He has the tablets and one of them will surely contain strychnine. He is preparing everything for another case of blackwater fever.'

'Then why the suicide?' said Doctor Darbishire, raising his voice to startle his pupil out of his doze.

'He is setting the scene for a suicide just in case,' said Doctor Salmerón, trying unsuccessfully to open his eyes, 'a father, driven mad with grief by the death of his beloved daughter, who then takes poison.'

'All very well, but then Castañeda cannot be given all the credit,' said Doctor Darbishire taking the knife and purposely letting it fall so that it clattered against the bowl of salt, 'Don Carmen's sister served him the opportunity on a plate when she got involved.'

'That's where you are wrong, sir,' said Doctor Salmerón waking suddenly at the sound of the knife falling, his eyes lighting immediately on the bottle.

'Wrong?' said Doctor Darbishire peering at his companion over the top of his pince-nez.

'Who do you think went to get Doctor Barrera on behalf of Don Carmen's sister? It was Castañeda himself!' said Doctor Salmerón. He stretched his arms as if about to yawn, then grabbed the bottle, hugging it to his chest. 'It was he who drove the doctor to the house and even carried his bag for him!'

'So the sister knew nothing about it?' Doctor Darbishire said in alarm, not just about what he was hearing but because Doctor Salmerón was spilling liquor everywhere as he tried to pour it.

'Yes, of course she knew,' said Doctor Salmerón trying to steady the bottle, unwilling to abandon his efforts to refill his glass. 'It was Castañeda who told her that the situation was dire and who recommended that she call Doctor Barrera.'

'Why pick Doctor Barrera?' asked Doctor Darbishire. Despite his irritation with his pupil for drinking so much, he took the bottle very politely and filled his glass for him.

'Because by taking you off the case he managed to engineer it so that no single hand was responsible for the preparation of the tablets. That way the scent is more easily lost,' said Doctor Salmerón, ceremoniously raising his glass in a toast.

'But...he asked me to examine the patient. What if I had accepted?' said Doctor Darbishire, getting to his feet. He replaced the stopper once more and returned the bottle to the sideboard.

'He knew full well that you would not accept, sir,' said Doctor Salmerón, bobbing his head inanely while he watched with amusement as Doctor Darbishire put the bottle away. 'He found out about the rivalry between yourself and Doctor Barrera. Knowing the answer, he asked you the impossible. The arch manipulator covers himself yet again.'

'Alright, but he can't have counted on the tablets. Doctor Barrera might well have prescribed a commercial medication,' Doctor Darbishire protested, bolting the door of the sideboard.

'Wrong again, sir!' said Doctor Salmerón, his eyes gleaming with drunken mischief. He looked at his old teacher with a mixture of pity and affection and went on: 'He himself convinced Doctor

Barrera that he should prescribe a treatment based on a custom preparation just as before, and not a commercial medication.'

'He asked Doctor Barrera to make up the tablets?' said Doctor Darbishire rushing back to the table.

'Instead of going to the pharmacy, he went directly to Doctor Barrera's consulting room,' Doctor Salmerón confirmed emphatically. 'He convinced him and then stayed to watch as the tablets were prepared, praising him to the skies for his precision in mixing all the ingredients. Your friend Doctor Barrera was deeply flattered, and put even more effort into his work than usual.'

'The poor dupe,' said Doctor Darbishire. He was trying to show compassion but his voice trembled with fear. 'Snared like a little bird.'

'Don't worry about it, I have it all covered,' said Doctor Salmerón, speaking as if his tongue had swollen and no longer fitted in his mouth.

'Got it covered? In what way?' enquired Doctor Darbishire, supporting himself on the table as he settled back in his chair, his eyes glued to his former student.

'I have informed Captain Ortiz of the situation. He is going to put the house under discreet surveillance,' said Doctor Salmerón, smiling to himself as if it were all some great prank. 'And I have committed myself to mounting a permanent guard from the bar at the Metropolitan Hotel.'

'I can't believe what you're telling me!' said Doctor Darbishire, getting up suddenly and coming round the table to glare at his student.

'Yes, undercover surveillance with secret agents, and I at a moment's notice will rush in with this tube here,' said Doctor Salmerón, patting his jacket pocket, 'to take a sample of the victim's stomach contents.'

'You're talking nonsense,' said Doctor Darbishire grasping his friend by the shoulders: 'How do you imagine you can prevent a crime by calling in the National Guard!'

'It's not nonsense. It is a plan. That is how they caught Charles Laughton; don't you remember?' said Doctor Salmerón, laughing and slowly licking his lips. He tried to stand up, but his head lolled against the back of the chair.

'If you're on such good terms with the National Guard, why did you want to see the judge?' said Doctor Darbishire, turning his back on his friend and walking away, annoyed.

'Because sir, I, like Oliverio Castañeda, have more than one string to my bow,' said Doctor Salmerón, seemingly amused by his own joke.

Doctor Darbishire retraced his steps. He was about to say something but realised that his student was snoring peacefully, his badly shaved chin covered with greying bristles, nestling on his chest.

'I've never heard such nonsense!' said Doctor Darbishire, looking about him as if in search of help, 'Now he thinks he's a detective in a movie.'

PART III

Collecting the Evidence

Leave me, sorry enemy,
Evil, false, base traitor,
I'll not be your friend
Nor marry you, no!

The Ballad of Fonte-Frida

CHAPTER TWENTY FOUR

Public Rumours of a Criminal Hand

On MONDAY, 9 October 1933, on the sudden death of Don Carmen Contreras, one of the most celebrated cases in the judicial history of Nicaragua began. It is to the many complex events surrounding this trial that this book is devoted.

His death occurred close to nine in the morning of the aforementioned day, exactly one week after Matilde Contreras had met a similar fate. The circumstances surrounding each case were very similar and equally unusual. The only difference was that in the second instance, death was even more sudden, occurring only half an hour after the appearance of the first symptoms.

The Chief Criminal Prosecuting Judge for the District of Léon, Doctor Mariano Fiallos Gil, arrived at the house in person just one hour later. He was accompanied by his secretary, the poet Alí Vanegas, who proceeded to write the court order setting a preliminary hearing at the very table in the dining room where not long before Oliverio Castañeda had sat to type up the letters of condolence that were to appear in Matilde's Funeral Garland:

> Having been alerted to the death in suspicious circumstances at approximately nine in the morning of Don Carmen Contreras Reyes, a married business man domiciled at this address, and also being aware of the rumours circulating concerning criminal intent, the Chief Criminal Prosecutor hereby decrees:
>
> By the authority granted him under Article 127 of the Penal Code, he orders that an investigation be opened and that due diligence be taken to facilitate the proper investigation of these events.

As an initial precaution, the judge authorised the removal of the body to the morgue at San Vicente Hospital so that an autopsy could be performed. His orders were carried out by midday. By the time the body, covered from head to toe by a striped bedspread, was lifted by the stretcher bearers onto the floor of the supply wagon provided for the purpose by the National Guard, a veritable multitude of onlookers had gathered around the house.

Doña Flora judged this measure barbaric and unnecessary and protested vociferously. She was not alone in voicing opposition. At midday, only moments after the body had been dispatched to the hospital, Captain Anastasio J. Ortiz arrived with two National Guardsmen. They were armed with Springfield rifles and were intent on arresting Oliverio Castañeda. Both Doña Flora and María del Pilar tried to stop them, first with entreaties and tears, and then by physically barring the way between Castañeda and his would-be captors.

It was not until six in the evening that Captain Ortiz finally managed to detain the suspect and even then the opposition he encountered from the widow and her daughter was no less determined. The body had by this time been brought back from the hospital, and the house, already full of mourners, was then invaded by a stream of curious onlookers, turning this new event into a public scandal.

Captain Ortiz had returned to the house accompanied by a squad of soldiers. According to the statement he gave on 27 October 1933, he deployed several of them round the doors and, pushing rudely past the two women, penetrated to the depths of the house in search of Castañeda. He discovered the suspect locked in the bathroom, so drunk that he had to be dragged out.

If the judge ordered a preliminary hearing, this was because there was not sufficient evidence in the rumours circulating to directly charge Castañeda. Therefore, when the National Guard captured Castañeda he was detained on a charge of sedition, a ruse sanctioned by the judge to prevent Castañeda's escape while the investigation proceeded.

We will hear subsequently of how the judge personally became a witness to the unusual power of the rumours spreading across the city that morning. For now, however, let us concentrate on the testimony of Demetrio Puertas, a bookkeeper in the employ of C. Contreras & Co., who was later cross-examined concerning events of greater importance towards the end of the trial. His first deposition given on 17 October 1933 recorded that:

> Just after nine o'clock, the witness was returning home in the Calvario neighbourhood because both the office and the shop had been closed on account of the sudden death of their owner. As he walked through the city market he heard the stall holders gossiping about how a gentleman, one of the wealthiest in León, had just been poisoned by his son-in-law at his own table; his breakfast chocolate laced with strychnine, its taste disguised because chocolate is always slightly bitter, and that only a week beforehand the poisoner had given strychnine to the daughter of the same gentleman; it had been in a sorbet which he had spoon-fed to her saying, "Eat it, it's so good. If you want more I'll give you more!"

That night, Doña Flora de Contreras, seeing that her efforts to save her house guest had failed, sent an urgent telegram to the Chief of Staff of the National Guard, General Anastasio Somoza García:

> DOWNCAST SUFFICIENTLY BY LOSS HUSBAND AND STILL NOT RECONCILED DEATH DAUGHTER UNJUST IMPRISONMENT YOUNG OLIVERIO CASTAÑEDA SIMPLY INCREASES MY SUFFERING AND ANXIETY AND THAT OF FAMILY. ENTREAT YOU MERCIFULLY ORDER IMMEDIATE RELEASE. IN HOPE,
>
> FLORA DE CONTRERAS, WIDOW.

The telegram was dispatched, the wake went ahead, and the rumour mill kept turning in ever greater circles. While all this was going on, in his cell inside precinct XXI prison, Oliverio Castañeda received his home-cooked supper, prepared for him under the watchful eye of María del Pilar. The dishes and bowls were delivered to the prison on a silver-gilt tray covered by an embroidered cloth by little Leticia Osorio, as she recalls in her deposition of 19 October 1933:

> While Don Carmen was laid to rest in his casket in the main room and with the house full of people, Señorita María del Pilar was pestering the women in the kitchen, who were already busy making coffee for everyone, to get Don Oliverio's supper ready. The chauffeur, Eulalio Catín waited outside for me to take me in the car. I sat in the back with the tray on my lap. They also sent him some bedclothes and his toiletries, tucked inside a pillow case, and on a hanger was a change of clothes she had ironed. She put a note into his jacket pocket which she wrote sitting on his bed as I waited for her to give me all the items to take over.

According to the prison's visitor register, these little consignments continued over the following days, the return address being annotated sometimes with the name of María del Pilar, and others with that of Doña Flora. In his revelatory letter of 6 December 1933, Oliverio Castañeda requested that this record be added to the court dossier.

Besides the three daily meals, drinks and items of freshly ironed laundry, as well as a china vase and bunches of flowers, the record listing the gifts received on different dates included many other objects:

3 pairs of new Pyramide socks
½ dozen new handkerchiefs of the same brand
1 new Esterbrook fountain pen
1 bottle of Parker ink, blue
1 block of lined writing paper
1 bottle of 4711 eau de cologne
1 jar of Murray hair cream, 3 oz.
1 bottle of Listerine mouth wash
6 sachets of Doctor Kemp tooth powder
3 cakes of Reuter scented soap
1 pot of Heno del Campo perfumed talc
1 stainless steel Figaro razor, with case and matching shaving brush
3 rolls of Scott toilet paper

Doña Flora acknowledged the existence of these consignments in her first deposition, given on 14 October 1933, well before Oliverio Castañeda requested that the record be made official:

> The witness states that food parcels were sent to Oliverio Castañeda from her home to the prison over a number of days, as were other necessary items for his comfort and personal hygiene. She has since been notified that the authorities have forbidden these consignments and, as of yesterday, they have been stopped.
>
> The reason given for her actions was that she considers the imprisonment of the young Castañeda to be wholly unjust. She continues to regard him as an honourable person of good intentions, whose reputation is now suffering irreparable damage.

Why and on what grounds were these consignments stopped? In his deposition of 27 October 1933, Captain Anastasio J. Ortiz explains it in the following manner:

> Out of consideration for the Contreras family who insisted on helping the accused, sending him his meals and other gifts, I authorised the governor of the XXI to allow them, provided their contents were logged. Even bunches of flowers were allowed in, although this was quite out of the ordinary.
>
> However, on the afternoon of October thirteenth, the governor called me on the phone at headquarters to inform me that there was a horse and cart at the gates and that they were carrying a cargo comprising two trunks, a dressing table complete with a mirror and a marble topped table all intended for the accused, Oliverio Castañeda, and delivered courtesy of the Contrerases. Faced with this situation I felt it necessary to consult my superiors in Managua. They gave me strict orders not only to send back the cart and all the goods on it, but also to prohibit, henceforth, the entry of any kind of food, flowers or perfumes.
>
> On being advised of these orders, the accused threatened to go on a hygiene strike and he did in fact spend

> two or three days without bathing, shaving or changing his clothes. As the newspapers have reported, he went around in just his shirtsleeves. However, he himself broke off this peculiar strike of his own free will.

On October twenty-fifth, *El Cronista* carried an article on its front page entitled 'No Smoke Without Fire', and audaciously published the now famous photoengraving of Doña Flora de Contreras. Rosalío Usulutlán was responsible for the article, which cost him his job as staff reporter at the newspaper. As we have seen, the article unleashed quite a society scandal in the city of León.

Although Rosalío changed the names in his report, some of the details he used were already public knowledge: for example, Doña Flora and her daughter's opposition to Castañeda's detention, and the gifts of flowers and perfumes which the pair of them had sent to the prison. More than anything else, even the recklessness of publishing the photograph, what provoked the scandal was that the report dared to make conjectures about the amorous entanglements of the drama's protagonists. These details, discussed at that infamous gossip-shop, the accursed table, now spilled out into the public domain.

The author of the report tried to justify his actions by penning a further article. However, *El Cronista* no longer wanted to publish his work, and *El Centroamericano* would not touch it either, but *La Nueva Prensa*, a Managua daily, did eventually pick it up and published it in its edition of 29 October 1933.

Manolo Cuadra, a poet who worked as a journalist for *La Nueva Prensa*, was sent to León to cover the case. He took it upon himself to send the article to Managua and also wrote a brief covering note, which appeared at the beginning of the article, praising the courage of his colleague who at that point was under threat of arrest.

The article was entitled: 'In self-defence: the merit of public rumour':

> A judge, invested with all the majesty of the law, has initiated a criminal process based on sections of the Penal Code of 1894, which provides for a criminal investigation to be carried out on the basis of public rumours which

suggest that a crime, or series of crimes, may have been committed. And with good reason. After the death of Don Carmen Contreras, rumour spread like wildfire, disturbing the previously tranquil city of León.

The stench of this rumour hung in the air and it continues to stink. It is palpable; you can cut it with a knife. If you look about you on the street and pick any two people in the distance, talking on a corner or in a doorway, you can be sure that they are engrossed in a conversation about the cause not only of the most recent death, but of the previous deaths that led inexorably to this last one. You can also be sure that they are speculating about the tale of passion that lies or may lie behind these violent and mysterious deaths: a tale of repressed love, jealousy and misplaced emotions. This is where rumour begins and points its thousand fingers: naming names and deeds that until this point had been hidden by the delicate veil of secrecy.

Should the journalist have remained silent? Or to the contrary, protect his readers' right to know through the printed word what is being spoken of publicly in ice-cream parlours, billiard halls and cafés, at every cock fight, in drugstores and linen shops, in train stations and even in churches? Be silent, and deprive the story of the benefits of a journalistic treatment when it is spreading so furiously by word of mouth, commented upon by carters, barbers, porters, herders, shop assistants and doormen in public offices?

Be silent, yes. Hush up the very thing that is the subject of unedifying, sotto-voce comments by the high and mighty, who act so offended but know better than anyone what is going on. They talk about it, and not without relish, during their soirees at the Social Club. My dear sirs, the scandal is to try to silence me, a terrible punishment for simply having brought to public knowledge deeds which this chronicler has certainly not invented.

In my article, that is now so condemned, I did nothing except give credence to public rumour, and for this I am told I may face prison and have even been threatened with

> excommunication. The Judge himself has opened a criminal investigation on the basis of these rumours. He had no other evidence to hand, should he then be persecuted for his zeal? No, he should be praised.
>
> The nature of my job meant that I was present in the home of Señor Contreras shortly after he died, and I was witness to many of the events which my pen later described. These events were interwoven with other opinions, commentaries and revelations. I felt it prudent to protect the identities of those concerned by using pseudonyms, but this anonymity does not make their contributions any less valid. There have been many revelations, and conjecture has been rife. Everyone in the city, from every social class, even our infant school children, know the twists and turns of this infamous case by heart. I do not deny the salacious nature of the story. It is not however the doings of my pen that make it so but the doings of those involved.

Rosalío Usulutlán was not lying when he described the level of public interest and the power of gossip; he took the subject further in later publications. Throughout the day and well into the night, the city of León was consumed by rumour. People congregated in every available public space to discuss the events and the emotional tangle behind them. Ever growing crowds gathered on the streets surrounding the house itself, provoking a complaint from the owner of the Metropolitan Hotel, Don Lorenzo Sugrãñez. He sent a letter to the authorities to the effect that the rabble outside the house was prejudicial to the free movement of traffic and the convenience of his guests.

Similar groups congregated outside the courthouse, the judge's home, and at the prison, receiving fresh rumours and passing them on. The largest crowd, however, was the one that formed in the grounds of the university at around six in the evening, when a package arrived from the morgue at San Vicente Hospital. The package contained samples taken from the digestive tract of the victim, and were destined for the laboratory in the Faculty of Pharmacy where they were to be tested.

Barely an hour later, Doña Flora penned her telegram urgently requesting the release of Oliverio Castañeda. She later retracted this request on 17 October 1933 in a new message, sent as before to the Chief of Staff of the National Guard, General Anastasio Somoza García:

> WISHING NOW NOT IMPEDE LEGAL INVESTIGATIONS CONCERNING CAUSE DEATH HUSBAND AND DAUGHTER AND REALISING EXTREME GRIEF OVERWHELMED REASON PREVENTING PREVIOUS RECOGNITION PROBABLE CRIMINAL INTENT BEG YOU NOT TO ACT ON TELEGRAM SENT FEW DAYS AGO REQUESTING RELEASE OF ACCUSED. SINCERELY, FLORA DE CONTRERAS, WIDOW

The writing of this telegram was recalled by Leticia Osorio in her statement of October nineteenth. Twice a distraught and tearful María del Pilar snatched it from her mother's hands in order to destroy it. And twice her mother wrote it again.

CHAPTER TWENTY-FIVE

Do Not Tremble or Weep

1 THE DAY he died, Don Carmen got up before dawn, as was his custom. The servant Salvadora Carvajal was busy in the kitchen stoking the wood stove in order to heat his bath water when she saw him go past, wrapped in an old sheet, shuffling along in the worn-out shoes he used for slippers. She recounted the scene in her statement given on 19 October 1933:

> I waited for him to finish his business and then brought him a bowl of water which he took from me without so much as a "good morning". He was the sort who don't speak to servants.
>
> Don Oliverio, another early riser, came into the kitchen to ask for a cup of coffee. He complained about being kept awake on account of Don Carmen's restless night. Apparently Don Carmen had been getting up a lot, and when he did sleep had been tossing and turning in bed. As a joke he said to me, "Tonight, make room in your bed for me, Doña Yoyita. You can warm me up and I'll sleep soundly."

When the judge cross-examined the accused at the initial hearing on 1 December 1933, he had a great many questions concerning the events of that night:

> JUDGE: Is it true that you told the servant, Salvadora Carvajal, that you had been kept awake on account of Don Carmen's restlessness during the night before he died, telling her he had been getting up a lot and tossing and turning in bed?

ACCUSED: I told her that I had been kept awake as it was true that Don Carmen had got up on several occasions during the night, but I never at any point mentioned tossing and turning in bed. She must have been confused about this point and I think you should ask her the question again.

JUDGE: How do you sleep at night? Do you sleep well or do you suffer from insomnia?

ACCUSED: I sleep well and do not suffer from insomnia. This is because I have a clear conscience.

JUDGE: Then how do you know that Don Carmen had a bad night?

ACCUSED: Because in order to secure the door that opens onto the courtyard, Don Carmen was in the habit of placing a heavy bench against it. Every time he got up to go out he had to move this bench, making a great deal of noise. In addition, the hinges of that door creak loudly when it is pushed. He would also turn on the room light when he got up and it stayed on until he came back to bed. One does not need a troubled conscience to have difficulty sleeping through all that palaver.

JUDGE: I duly note all the comments concerning your conscience and also that you make them entirely on your own initiative. Now tell me, for what reason do you think he kept getting up?

ACCUSED: I can't tell you exactly what his reason was. I imagine he felt stifled and that he went out to take some air in the courtyard or perhaps to answer some pressing call of nature. Or possibly he was simply feeling anxious and couldn't sleep. I didn't ask him so I will have to leave you to choose an answer.

JUDGE: Did it occur to you, who are so avowedly attentive, to get up and follow him? To find out what ailed him?

ACCUSED: Why thank you for recognising my attentiveness! At least I have one virtue in your eyes.

JUDGE: I advise you not to make comments that are not directly relevant and confine yourself to answering my questions.

ACCUSED: In that case, my answer as to why I did not get up and follow him is because, unlike on other occasions, he did not ask me to. On other nights, distressed by the loss of her daughter, Doña Flora had woken, sobbing; at his request I accompanied him to the room where she slept with María del Pilar and waited at the door while he administered a sleeping draught to her.

That night, when I noticed him opening the door the first time, I asked: "Is Doña Flora unwell?" and he responded: "No, my friend, go back to sleep. Thank you." I deduced from this that it was most likely he who was sick.

JUDGE: What type of sickness would this be? Please elaborate.

ACCUSED: I would elaborate if I only could. I said "most likely", which does not represent a categorical diagnosis. If someone is constantly getting out of bed and can't get to sleep it is not generally the case that they wish to contemplate the stars in search of relaxation and amusement.

2. Let us now turn to the morning of Monday, 9 October 1933. You could say it was a peaceful morning, the start of a normal day for a family in mourning where everyone still spoke in hushed tones and even the kitchen chores were carried out in silence. Oliverio Castañeda accepted an invitation to accompany mother and daughter to the church of La Merced to hear the seventh of nine daily masses dedicated to Matilde. It would not have seemed strange to any passers-by to see this party of two women in mourning, heads covered by their lace shawls, with the young stranger who himself always wore black walking between them, taking a leisurely stroll in the direction of the church.

They returned for breakfast and this is what the cook, Salvadora Carvajal, had to say on the matter:

> They came back from mass and Don Carmen was waiting for them in the dining room. They had oranges, which I peeled and served to them myself, and they also had bread and butter and milk which they had with a few drops of coffee essence. After the dirty dishes had been collected,

the young María del Pilar came to the kitchen to get a glass of water so that her father could take the quinine tablets Doctor Barrera had prescribed.

In the initial hearing, Oliverio Castañeda responded to the judge's questions about that breakfast:

JUDGE: In her second deposition, given yesterday, 31 October 1933, the widow Doña Flora de Contreras affirms that, during that breakfast, you addressed her in the following terms, and I quote: "I see that Don Carmen is extremely ill and you must be strong to hear what I am about to say: I fear that he is not long for this world. But do not tremble or weep, for you have at your side a man who will look after you and support you." You may have a copy of the text to see where I am quoting from, if you wish.

ACCUSED: That will not be necessary, your honour. I am confident of your ability to read, although I am not so confident about the abilities of Doña Flora to accurately recall events or intentions. First of all, you must allow me to recover from my surprise. If these statements, none of which passed my lips, had any semblance of truth, then she should not have delayed so long before revealing them!

It is true that, like every other morning, I went with her and María del Pilar to the masses being said for Matilde's soul. And the same as every other morning we all breakfasted together, conversing on all sorts of topics. But I say to you that none of that nonsense could ever have escaped my lips—for the simple reason that Don Carmen was there with us!

Ask her about it, ask the servants about it and you will discover that Don Carmen waited for us to get back for breakfast and he came to sit with us at the table. It would have been easier for her to construct these lies if she had put them in a more believable setting: during any one of our many, more private, meetings. However, as we can see, she has been poorly advised.

JUDGE: Doña Flora also affirms that, again at the breakfast table, you further told her, and once again I quote: "Last night, Don Carmen asked me to take charge of his office and has given me authority over all his business dealings. However, before I can accept, I need to get your blessing." According to the witness, no such proposal was ever made to you by Don Carmen.

ACCUSED: I have never mentioned any such thing to Doña Flora, and I must remind you again that Don Carmen was present at the breakfast table. Doña Flora is right about one thing though and that is that such a proposal never existed. What Don Carmen did suggest, on the Sunday evening, and I might add, in her presence, was that I should have my desk moved next to his on the corridor where the Water Company has its offices. He wanted to leave all aspects of the contract in my hands and he urged me not to leave for Managua.

Don Carmen was a man of few words and few friends, and when we returned from mass I did make a comment to Doña Flora to the effect that I had been flattered by his offer. This was not because it was in any way beneficial to myself—I would come out the poorer because it meant abandoning my book project—but because it had come directly from him. It was such a rare show of trust on his behalf.

3. A little before eight in the morning, Don Carmen went to his desk to begin work. While the servants were still busy clearing up, Castañeda took his typewriter from his room and set it up at the head of the table in the dining room and began working on the Funeral Garland for Matilde.

Later on, Don Enrique Gil called. This gentleman, a liquor manufacturer who lived in the neighbouring town of Chichigalpa, offered the following insights into the morning's events when he gave his deposition on 21 October 1933:

The witness declares that on October ninth of the current year he took the train to this city with the intention of coming to offer his condolences to Don Carmen and family. He has been a friend of the family for many years, and his reasons for not undertaking the journey previously are not relevant.

He adds that he reached the house just after eight o'clock in the morning and that his friend, who emerged from his office to receive him in the dining room, seemed greatly touched by his visit. They talked about the tragedy and the witness says that he attempted to comfort his friend by talking of other subjects and reminding him of the pleasant times they had recently spent together when he visited Chichigalpa a few days earlier in the company of Don Esteban Duquestrada.

As the witness was preparing to leave to attend to some business in the city concerning the distribution of "Campeón" Rum, Don Carmen said that he would like to show him the album he was making in remembrance of his late daughter. To this end he got up and walked over to the dining table where Oliverio Castañeda was seated at his typewriter; they exchanged a few words and then he returned with the album in his hands.

It is not clear what happened in the few moments that it took to leaf through the album, among whose typewritten pages was a poem by Castañeda dedicated to Matilde, but all of a sudden Don Carmen began to complain of a strange pain in his body. The witness says that he called to Doña Flora, who had just come in from the shop, and explained what had happened, advising her to take Don Carmen for a lie down in bed. They led Don Carmen between them as his legs were so stiff that he was finding it difficult to walk.

In order to get to the bedroom they passed by the dining room table where Oliverio Castañeda was sitting, typing. He showed no sign of alarm, indeed he did not even turn his head to look; he just continued working away, undisturbed.

When they got Don Carmen into bed, he complained that he had no feeling in his legs and they were stiffening even more, at which point he was overwhelmed by a strong convulsion. Doña Flora was very alarmed by this and she begged the witness to fetch Doctor Darbishire.

The witness left the room in haste and headed out to the street. As he passed Oliverio Castañeda once again he noticed that he was still deep in his typing, as if he were completely unaware of events. Once in the street he saw a carriage and hailed it; he was about to get in when he saw Doctor Atanasio Salmerón, whom he knew by sight, rushing towards him from the direction of the Metropolitan Hotel, bag in hand.

Out of breath, Doctor Salmerón enquired whether anyone in the house was sick, to which the witness replied in the affirmative, going on to explain what had happened and the mission he had been charged with. Doctor Salmerón replied with the following words: "Go and find Doctor Darbishire, I will take care of this until he arrives."

4. The judge was very interested in finding out why Oliverio Castañeda had not moved from where he sat typing throughout the events described by the witness. At the initial hearing, the accused responded in the following way:

JUDGE: Based on your previous statements I must conclude that you felt yourself to be among one of Don Carmen's few friends, despite the considerable age difference between the two of you.

ACCUSED: Yes, I had that honour. The trust between us was such that, for safekeeping, I gave him all of the money I received in my allowance from Guatemala. When he died, there were three hundred pesos of mine in his safe; which out of discretion I have not sought to reclaim from the family.

JUDGE: Would you say that Don Carmen was a strong man who could endure life's troubles?

ACCUSED: I would say so, without any doubt. I have never come across such a stoic man as he. He never complained about anything; only the death of his daughter was able to affect his spirits. This cast him down. His physical health, however, was as robust as ever.

JUDGE: Why then did you not get up and help him when on the morning of his death he was taken past you, supported in the arms of Doña Flora and Don Enrique Gil? You went on with your typing as if nothing were happening. If you were such close friends, was this not a dereliction of duty? If you considered him to be so strong would not the fact that he required support to help him walk not be something that caused you to suspect a grave infirmity?

ACCUSED: I have to confess that I did not notice because I was so engrossed in copying out the messages of condolence for Matilde's death. I was taking such care and attention over this task that I completely forgot everything else around me.

JUDGE: Don Enrique Gil said that he went to get medical help after Don Carmen's first convulsion and he hurried passed you again. Were you still so engrossed that nothing registered? Would nothing have been able to distract you?

ACCUSED: When Don Enrique Gil left the bedroom to go out to the street I didn't notice that either. You should be asking him why he didn't see fit to let me know what was happening. If he passed so close and in such alarm, wouldn't it have been logical to stop and ask me for help? At the very least so that I could have shown him to the telephone in order not to waste time!

In her deposition of October fourteenth, Doña Flora confirms that Castañeda did indeed carry on typing as she helped her husband to bed, assisted by Don Enrique Gil. She put his lack of attention down to his poor eyesight, and justified it further by explaining how he was always like that when he was typing: to the extent that he would even forget mealtimes and would leave any refreshments brought by the servants.

However, in a second deposition, referring to the same episode, and to which the judge attached great importance in his summing up, she said:

JUDGE: Previously, you stated that when you took Don Carmen to his room, Castañeda did not move from the seat where he was typing. Could you confirm this?

WITNESS: I confirm it. I would also say that it would have been impossible for him not to notice that we were

> carrying my husband to his room: the table was in our way and so we brushed past him; you can see for yourself where it is. It was not until Doctor Salmerón arrived that he noticed what was going on. This was after my husband had already suffered his first fit.

5. There were further changes. In her first deposition, Doña Flora gave a version of the events of that morning which coincided, save for a few details, with those given by other witnesses. For example, she asserts that the quinine tablets prescribed for her husband by Doctor Barrera were kept under lock and key in the sideboard to which she alone had access and that María del Pilar had asked for these keys when she went to get the medication at the end of breakfast.

However, in her second deposition of 31 October 1933, she amended this statement in the following way:

> JUDGE: Could you confirm that you were present when Don Carmen asked María del Pilar to get his medication at the end of breakfast?
>
> WITNESS: Yes, I was present; it was I who reminded him that it was time to take it. He then asked my daughter, María del Pilar, to bring the box of tablets from his bedroom. The pills were not in any sideboard, as I mistakenly said before; they were on the bedside table to which both Castañeda and my husband would have had access.

6. In her first deposition, Doña Flora did not say anything about the judge's decision to order an autopsy on her husband's body, but later she made the following comments on the subject:

> JUDGE: When I came to your house on the day that your husband died, Oliverio Castañeda assured me you were opposed to the idea of an autopsy on the body. Why was this?
>
> WITNESS: I had no reasons, only the ones that he gave me. When you arrived that morning and explained that the body needed to be taken to the hospital, he came into the bedroom and said: "Señora, the body of your

husband will be subjected to a savage violation. They will saw open his skull and extract his brain, they will cut open his stomach to take out his intestines, his spleen, his liver. He will be unrecognisable. They will fill him with sawdust and old newspapers and once they have done this they will stitch him up with a sacking needle." It was for those reasons that, at first, I opposed the autopsy, which I now see was so necessary.

These assertions were put to the accused at the initial hearing:

> JUDGE: The day that I went to the house where these events took place, you came to tell me that Doña Flora was opposed to the autopsy I had ordered. From her deposition, which you can read now, it appears that it was you who instigated this opposition in the widow. Your reasons for doing so are more than clear; an autopsy would uncover evidence of a crime.
>
> ACCUSED: Evidence of a crime has in no way been uncovered, because the tests to which the internal organs have been subjected are null and void because they were not rigorous or scientific. As to Doña Flora's decision to oppose the autopsy, that was all hers and never interfered with by me. It was made based on her Christian principles, and I simply passed it on to you. Her statements concerning the fears that I had regarding how her husband's body would be treated are an invention on her part, for which I feel sorry for her.

7. Doña Flora was presented with a further set of questions once the judge had finished his interrogation. The prosecuting attorney, Don Juan de Dios Vanegas, who was present throughout the proceedings, asked that certain questions be asked of the witness in her capacity as the claimant. This petition was granted:

> Question 1: Aware as she is that she is required to tell the whole truth, is the claimant sure that the accused made certain remarks beside the bedside of the deceased, and can she clarify what these remarks were?

Answer: He said that we should not make any noise so as not to disturb my husband. I didn't give this any thought at the time but later I found out that strychnine poisoning makes the victim very sensitive to sound; from this I concluded that he already knew the cause of my husband's illness.

Question 2: Aware as she is that she is required to tell the whole truth, is the claimant certain that the accused seemed unconcerned in the period following the death of the victim?

Answer: Indeed, his behaviour was quite off-hand, as if nothing had happened. He did not show any sign of distress and he maintained this demeanour right up until the moment that Captain Ortiz arrived to detain him at midday. In fact he was so unconcerned that he didn't even resist, telling us that he was being arrested for his politics and that we should not worry, as his contacts in Managua would obtain his immediate release. Later he continued with this devil-may-care attitude, taking to the bottle to such an extent that when the authorities finally did arrest him, they found him locked in the bathroom, completely drunk. I had never before seen him in such a state.

Question 3: Aware as she is that she is required to tell the whole truth, is the claimant sure that she only sought to defend the peace of her home when she opposed the arrest of the accused?

Answer: That is so. I only opposed his arrest due to the outrage inflicted upon my home by this event and because I was completely ignorant of his culpability, about which I now have no doubt.

Going back to Oliverio Castañeda's initial hearing, we can see his response to the statements made by Doña Flora in answer to her attorney's questions:

JUDGE: According to Doña Flora, you asked everyone to be quiet around Don Carmen, from which she concludes that you already knew that the dying man had ingested strychnine. I refer you to several toxicology texts to support the hypothesis that victims of strychnine poisoning are hypersensitive to noise and to light.

ACCUSED: First, you should explain the legal basis upon which the prosecuting attorney was allowed to interview a witness in the absence of the accused, that is, myself, as required by the Criminal Code as it currently stands. This alone is more than sufficient cause to render both the questions and their answers impermissible.

However, I would like to be generous and cooperate with your inquiry, your honour. So, I will say to you: when I went into the dying man's room I made every effort to be caring and attentive to him, and I am not exaggerating when I say that he breathed his last in my arms. I would have liked to have had it in my power to save him, and not simply to have been able to ask for quiet. He died without any medical attention, as Doctor Salmerón's interfering cannot be counted as such.

I will add one other thing: what manner of murderer, disposed to poison their victim, is likely to bother to rid them of noise nuisance?

JUDGE: I will leave aside your anomalous conduct after the death of your victim, something that Doña Flora also mentioned. However, I should like to ask: what made you start drinking in those tragic circumstances? Did you perhaps feel that all was lost and you were attempting to avoid the consequences of your crime with the help of the bottle?

ACCUSED: I did not drink a drop of alcohol that day. It is also untrue that I was found locked in the bathroom in a state of inebriation as I have read in Doña Flora's illegal responses and in the deposition given by Captain Ortiz. You would do better to attend to the testimony of little Leticia Osorio: her innocent nature frees it from the taint of lies and manipulation, and gives it weight. You will then see that all I have said on the matter is the truth.

The deposition given by Leticia Osorio on 19 October 1933 does in fact support what Castañeda said. At the same time it gives her version of the events leading up to his arrest:

The guards came at around twelve o'clock asking for Don Oliverio and when he heard their voices he shut himself in his room. The guards entered the verandah, where María del Pilar met them and asked them what they were doing there and who had given them permission to enter. Don Tacho Ortiz, their commander, said that he had orders from his superiors and that Don Oliverio should give himself up. At that moment Don Oliverio appeared with his hat in his hands and said to the captain: "Don't make a fuss Don Tacho, I'll come with you." Turning to María del Pilar he told her: "They have come for me because of my politics; they may try to force me to leave Nicaragua. Goodbye."

María del Pilar embraced him, holding him tight, and then Doña Flora came in and said: "What is this outrage? Respect my grief, Tacho!" "There is no outrage, Señora, this man must come of his own free will or I will not accept responsibility," said Don Tacho. María del Pilar cried harder and Doña Flora, who by now was also weeping, kept repeating: "He is not leaving here." Then Don Tacho called to his guards who had surrounded Don Oliverio with their rifles pointed at him, and said: "Let's go; I don't want any drama." He said to Don Oliverio: "It won't do you any good shielding yourself behind women's petticoats!"

A little later in the afternoon, Don Tacho came back with more guards and Doña Flora and María del Pilar argued with him again: "If it is for political reasons then it is Guatemalan politics," Doña Flora told him. "This is not political, this man is a criminal. Why you defend him I don't know, he intends to kill you, too," Don Tacho said, growing angry. "Lower your voice, people are listening," pleaded Doña Flora, crying again. "Well then let me take him, if you don't there will be an even bigger scandal because I will take him come what may." Don Tacho then shouted even louder, "Where is that good-for-nothing?" The guards went through the whole building: "Here he is," called one who had gone right to the back of the house: "He's locked himself in the toilet." They brought him out, guarded by two soldiers. They pushed María del Pilar and Doña Flora aside using their rifle butts; then they took him out right in front of everybody. The women shut themselves in their room and wept. I heard Doña Flora say that she was going to complain to Managua and that Don Tacho would end up the prisoner once General Somoza found out what he'd done.

When questioned by the judge, the witness affirmed that she didn't see Don Oliverio drinking any alcohol, and that she does not know if he was drunk or not when they took him. However, she did say that she heard Doña Flora comment that he was in no way drunk and that this was a slander made up by Don Tacho, who, on seeing them taking him out of the toilet, had said: "Here comes the drunkard, he must have something to celebrate!"

8. In conclusion, here is Doña Flora's answer to the last question put to her by the prosecuting attorney. It concerns a matter about which the judge, strangely, did not see fit to interrogate the accused during the initial hearing:

> Question 4: Aware as she is that she is required to tell the whole truth, is the claimant certain that if the accused was knowledgeable about the effects of certain poisons, this was due to the fact that he had in his possession at least one book on the topic? Could she also please explain how she came to know about the existence of this book?
>
> *Answer:* It is true that he had such a book in his possession. While he and his wife were still living with us, a few weeks before the death of Marta, I noticed Castañeda leaving his room with a book in his hand. He went over to where my daughter Matilde was sitting on the verandah, darning some socks. I went a little closer to find out what the book was, and he told me: "You cannot imagine how fascinating this book is. From its pages you can learn how to eliminate people and do them all kinds of harm without leaving any traces." Alarmed, I took the book which was called *The Secrets of Nature*, and as I recall I admonished him for attempting to teach Matilde about that kind thing. I kept the book for safe-keeping.

> A portrait of Castañeda's mother was tucked between the pages; it was very yellowed and discoloured with age. It is a photograph that sticks in the memory, your honour. It is a picture of a woman, still young but looking gaunt, sitting up supported on pillows in a hospital bed; her long straight hair is falling over the sheets. Standing by her bedside are some doctors in white overalls and a nun holding a tray of medical implements and medication.

As the reader will remember, Rosalío Usulutlán knew of this photograph. At the very moment that Doña Flora was giving her second statement it was already in the possession of Doctor Atanasio Salmerón, tucked between the pages of the book which the journalist brought to Cosme Manzo's stock room on the evening of Matilde Contreras' burial.

CHAPTER TWENTY SIX

An Unwelcome Visitor

WHEN DOCTOR Atanasio Salmerón appeared at the door to the dining room which opened on to the verandah, Oliverio Castañeda was still deep in his typing. Eventually he looked up in order to scrutinise the uninvited guest, continuing to type as he did so until the carriage return bell tinkled, indicating the end of a line.

Doctor Salmerón came in carrying his medical bag, and walked in the direction of the bedrooms. He had no idea which one to enter as he had never been to the house before. Castañeda leapt from his chair to bar the way.

'Did he seem frightened or just surprised?' asked Rosalío craning his neck. He was holding a metal advertising plate for a brand of anisette called "The Monkey" which Captain Prío was about to fix to the wall beside the bar. It was the night of 11 October 1933.

'He grabbed the chair he had been sitting on and placed it down in front of him,' said Doctor Salmerón, seated at the table watching the other two at their task. 'Adopting a very haughty tone, he asked me what I was doing there, as if I were some kind of thief. He made me so angry I pushed him out of the way. But he followed me and managed to cut me off again. I shouted at him to get out of the way, and at the sound of our voices, Doña Flora came out of one of the rooms.'

'She must have been surprised,' Cosme Manzo said, trying to signal to Rosalío that the sign was askew. 'Take it down a little to the right.'

'She was surprised to see me in the house, she was surprised by the shouting and the scuffle, but she wasn't going to boot me out at that point. I was the saving angel. "Come through, he's dying," was all she said to me,' Doctor Salmerón explained, raising himself slightly in his chair to take a quick look at the poster. 'It's too low now.'

'And Castañeda?' Captain Prío asked, his mouth full of tacks, just about to hammer in the first of them. 'What did he say then?'

'That man is a true artist. He took off his glasses and rubbed his eyes as if up until then he'd had no idea of what was going on,' said Doctor Salmerón, resting his hands on the table, still half standing he waited for the first hammer blow. 'He went over to her and put his arms around her, reproaching her: "Why didn't you call me? I would have gone to get Doctor Darbishire myself." And with that he strode into the bedroom.'

'He must have been aware of everything while he was typing,' said Cosme Manzo, going to the aid of Rosalío and holding the lower edge of the poster; 'I bet he had calculated how long it would take Gil to get to Doctor Darbishire's consulting room and how long it would take him to return with him. That is, if he was there at all.'

'He didn't need to worry about that; the dose of poison he'd put in the tablet was stronger than before. There wasn't going to be time for anything.' Doctor Salmerón said, wincing at the sound of the hammer.

'What about María del Pilar Contreras?' Rosalío managed to ask before giving a howl of pain. The metal advertising fell to the floor with a resounding crash.

'You cry baby. Show me your finger,' said Cosme Manzo, grabbing Rosalío's hand. 'She must have been in the bedroom. How could she not be, she was the apple of his eye.'

'She was in the room already. She was massaging Don Carmen's legs. She didn't seem upset; she seemed to think that it was just a passing problem,' said Doctor Salmerón, going over to examine Rosalío's finger; he had refused to show it to Cosme Manzo. 'She asked me if I thought it could be some kind of indigestion. But it was Don Carmen himself who told her in no uncertain terms that it was not indigestion, as he had not eaten anything rich for breakfast and had barely eaten any supper, just a glass of milk and a bun.'

'So he was conscious at that point,' said Captain Prío, picking up the advert from the floor and shaking it to clean it. 'Did he seem calm?'

'He didn't seem frightened, just in great pain. "I don't know what the matter is, my legs feel very strange, it's as if I have a cramp," he said as I unbuttoned his shirt to listen to his chest with my stethoscope,' said Doctor Salmerón forcing Rosalío's hand open. 'He wasn't talking to me though, but to Castañeda, who was cradling his head. You idiot, you nearly lost a nail! Get me some surgical spirit, Captain.'

'And then another attack came on,' said Cosme Manzo peering across to see Rosalío's finger which had turned bright red. 'If there isn't any surgical spirit we'll have to use the Monkey Anise.'

'He began to shudder. It was dreadful. The convulsions were frighteningly violent. He was writhing on the bed like someone possessed by demons,' said Doctor Salmerón. He let go of Rosalío's hand and went back to the table, 'The lot of you together can't even manage to bang in a nail.'

'Was that the last attack?' asked Rosalío, protecting his injured finger with his other hand. 'I'm going to put some ice on this.'

'He'd had a small fit when they first got him to bed. This was the second and the last,' Doctor Salmerón confirmed, making himself comfortable on his chair. 'Put whatever you like on it, you're making such a fool of yourself!'

'And how did you manage the gastric catheter?' asked Captain Prío, examining the metal poster carefully before placing it on the wall again. 'Come and get hold of this, Don Chalío.'

'No chance, you can smash someone else's finger!' said Rosalío. Hunched over the ice-box and turning away, he gave him the finger with his good hand.

'I quickly took off my jacket and rolled up my sleeves, ready to do battle,' said Doctor Salmerón, getting up to act out the scene. 'I had to find a way of inserting the tube; it looked as if I was going to have to break his teeth. In the end after quite a battle I managed to get his jaw open with the aid of a spatula. I asked for a jug and María del Pilar ran to the kitchen to get one.'

'And Castañeda? Did he try to stop you?' asked Cosme Manzo, who was now holding the sign. 'Be careful not to hit me, Captain.'

'No. While I was struggling with the catheter he only reproached me, telling me that I wasn't helping the invalid in any way. That was for Doña Flora's benefit. He never moved, he just sat stroking

Don Carmen's forehead,' said Doctor Salmerón shrinking back in anticipation of the hammer blow.

'Well, it didn't really do him much good,' said Rosalío, blowing on his finger before applying the ice-cube he had wrapped in his handkerchief.

'Don't mess with me, nothing would have saved him at that point,' said Doctor Salmerón, giving Rosalío a withering look. 'When I removed the catheter I listened to his chest with my stethoscope. His heart beats were very faint and irregular. Soon afterwards he died.'

'And at what point did Castañeda ask for everyone to be quiet?' Cosme Manzo asked, screwing his eyes closed as Captain Prío hammered.

'That was before I inserted the catheter,' replied Doctor Salmerón, wincing with every hammer blow. 'He propped him up with pillows and demanded silence. "I know your game," I thought to myself. You know what you gave him.'

'So then he died. And there was the battle for the jug,' said Cosme Manzo. He was now holding the sign with one hand as it was already fully secured on the other side.

'Well, it wasn't really a fight,' said Doctor Salmerón as he got to his feet. The sign looked as if it was going to stay in place. 'While I did up my cuffs and looked for my jacket to put it back on, Castañeda, cool as anything, took the jug and gave it to one of the servants who had come running into the bedroom on hearing the shouts from the women. Very calmly and in a low voice, he gave instructions to tip the contents down the lavatory. Equally calm, I grabbed my bag and followed her out onto the verandah.'

'And Castañeda followed you,' said Rosalío. He was swinging his hand like a censer as he went over to look at the sign, which was now in place on the wall. 'What a stubborn monkey. He never lets go of that bottle!'

'Yes, he came after me. But I already had the jug again; the servant had given it to me without any fuss,' said Doctor Salmerón, also going over to take a look at the monkey who was indeed hugging the bottle close to its chest. He caressed its enamelled surface with his fingers and remarked, 'Acting like the master of the house, he rebuked me: "why didn't you let her throw out that disgusting mess?"'

'But he didn't try to take it off you?' said Cosme Manzo, taking his turn to stroke the surface of the metal sign; his fingers lingered over the label on the bottle that the monkey was guarding. On that label another monkey guarded another bottle.

'No, he didn't. I told him I was going to hand the jug over to the authorities because Don Carmen had died of poisoning,' Doctor Salmerón explained proudly as he returned to the table, walking backwards to admire the monkey, who stared back at him defiantly. 'Giving the impression that he couldn't believe his ears, he turned his head to one side as though to hear me better. He told me that I was not only a busybody but also rude, and that my presence was not required. I answered back, saying that he didn't have to worry, I'd be going directly, but that I would be taking the jug with me. I was ready to kick him if he so much as tried anything.'

'And he didn't try anything,' said Cosme Manzo coming to sit next to Doctor Salmerón. He dried the back of his neck with his red linen handkerchief. 'You owe me a glass of Monkey Anise, Captain.'

'There's no Monkey Anise here,' Captain Prío told him, stowing the hammer in a drawer under the bar. 'If you want I can get you a beer.'

'He wouldn't have dared!' said Doctor Salmerón. He held his arms close to his body and mimed a dodge as if he were still protecting the jug, 'Least of all at that moment, because Doctor Darbishire came in. Seeing him, Castañeda changed completely and went to greet him, all sorrowful, his arms open wide to embrace him, saying: "Would you believe it, Doctor, this is a terrible state of affairs. Another death in the family. You should give us all a blood test as it seems that everyone in this family is infected with some killer microbe." Doctor Darbishire did not answer him. He saw the jug in my hands and understood that I had no intention of relinquishing it.'

'If you've got no Monkey Anise, why the hell have you stuck that sign up, Captain? Was I injured for nothing?' said Rosalío, showing Captain Prío his bruised, purple finger.

'Didn't Doctor Darbishire say anything to you? Didn't he support you?' asked Captain Prío, shooing Rosalío away with an irritated wave of his hand. 'I put it up because I like the monkey and because it's my wall.'

'His exact words to me were: "Sit down Doctor. The judge is on his way. Give him that receptacle. Do whatever he tells you to."' So saying, Doctor Salmerón rose from the table and with a leisurely gait, strolled across the room as if he were Doctor Darbishire himself making his way to the sickroom, from which the sound of crying could be heard.

'So you and Castañeda were alone again,' said Cosme Manzo blowing the froth from the top of his beer.

'No, he went after Doctor Darbishire, as if the word "judge" had never been mentioned. He poked his head into the sickroom and kept repeating: "That's a dreadful thing to happen, don't you think? This good and noble man, dead, struck down so suddenly,"' said Doctor Salmerón. He retraced his steps to confront the monkey again and clasped his hands across his chest. He was again transported to the moment, protecting the jug.

He remembered how he had suddenly felt so weary and out of place standing on the verandah of that house, where he had never before set foot and was never likely to again. Everyone there seemed hostile and strange. He leaned against a pillar and his hopelessness increased when he saw the rocking chairs ranged against the wall, turned over with their rockers in the air; prevented from rocking and definitively denying him the right to sit down. Abandoned on the table in the dining room, his medical bag looked similarly out of place there, as were his cracked and dusty shoes. He could even smell the acrid scent of his own sweat, and that disgusted him too, as if his own body was telling him that he didn't belong there. Once again he listened to the wails of mother and daughter coming from the sickroom and these disconsolate cries seemed like a raging wind blowing through the house, forcing him, the intruder, out onto the street.

He hugged the jug close to his chest and braced his humbly shod feet on the mosaic floor. He was not going to lose this battle now; he would not leave until the judge arrived.

'You'd be a rotten coward to run now, just when you have that son of a bitch right where you want him,' he told himself, and raised his chin in a gesture of proud defiance, which nobody was able to witness on the deserted verandah.

CHAPTER TWENTY-SEVEN

A New Judge Comes on the Scene

THE TRAIN from El Sauce reached León in the morning of October ninth with more than an hour's delay. It was around eight-thirty when Judge Fiallos disembarked to begin what was going to be the most nerve-wracking day of his life. His luggage was a pair of cowhide saddlebags which he hoisted over one shoulder; one of his farm hands followed close behind him carrying several stems of bananas. Both of them were enveloped in the smoke from the locomotive.

Captain Anastasio J. Ortiz, his neighbour for many years, had been watching out for him on the platform for some time. As he began to push his way towards them, the other passengers and hawkers scattered in fright. Dressed in his army fatigues, his U.S. Marines Stetson pulled right down over his ears with its strap under his chin, Captain Ortiz looked like someone left behind by the recently departed occupying troops. His blue, piggy eyes and ruddy complexion helped support that impression.

The two men began talking as soon as they were close enough, leaving the station swiftly via the warehouse, Captain Ortiz following in the wake of Judge Fiallos' long, energetic strides. Judge Fiallos sent his boy off in a horse cart with his saddlebags and bananas, paying the driver from a little coin purse he had with him. Captain Ortiz waited for him with the engine running at the wheel of the Departmental Command's Ford convertible, another legacy of the Marines. By the time they drove off it must have been around nine in the morning.

As the reader will probably remember, Doctor Atanasio Salmerón had stormed into the Contreras residence in accordance with a plan that he had supposedly agreed with Captain Ortiz. Supposedly, because in the deposition that he gave on 27 October 1933, of which we have already seen parts, the latter denies any complicity on his part:

> On Saturday October seventh Doctor Salmerón came to my home in the early hours of the morning. He wanted to tell me about his suspicions concerning Oliverio Castañeda, whom he held responsible for the death of his wife and by the same means, the death of Señorita Matilde Contreras. I found his arguments to be quite incoherent, and although he talked of evidence he was only prepared to reveal this at his discretion, and so I gave him little credibility.
>
> He also proposed a covert operation on the Contreras family home, where he was convinced another death would soon take place. It was an operation that he wished me to take part in. I didn't give him an outright refusal but I politely declined. In addition to the insubstantial nature of his theories, my lack of interest in his operation was also due to his reputation as a rumour-monger who spreads falsehoods about honourable, respectable people, presenting these as irrefutable facts. The libels printed in the newspaper *El Cronista* concerning the present trial are a case in point. They are written by Rosalío Usulutlán, but I am quite certain that they were inspired by his intimate buddy, Doctor Salmerón.
>
> Although for the reasons I have outlined I had no wish to involve myself with him in any way, this does not mean that I was not prepared to take my own measures. I considered it prudent to wait for your return, your honour, so that we could discuss the situation together, which as you are aware, is exactly what has happened.
>
> I was prompted to act in this way because Doctor Salmerón mentioned that Doctor Darbishire was well acquainted with the machinations of Oliverio Castañeda, and was aware of the danger he posed to the Contreras family. Doctor Darbishire is someone whom I hold in great esteem, and indeed consider to be a person of very high moral standing. For this reason, when we met at the station and after I had given you a brief outline of the case, I advised you to go directly to find him.

At that moment, around nine in the morning, Doctor Darbishire was in his surgery engaged in a minor operation which had turned out to be more complicated than he had anticipated: draining an abscess in the left armpit of Canon Isidro Augusto Oviedo y Reyes. The root of the abscess was very deep and despite having had several doses of anaesthetic applied to the area, the cleric was still letting out little moans of pain. The doctor was obliged to leave his patient on account of the insistent knocking at his door which made the window frames in the surgery rattle. Greatly annoyed, he answered the door with his scalpel still in his hand. He was preparing to reproach the unwelcome guest when he saw that it was none other than Don Enrique Gil.

Bemused, he listened to his message, and after dithering for a moment retraced his steps, and threw the scalpel onto the instrument tray. His aim was so bad that the knife hit the floor, but he ignored the accident and grabbing some scissors and a gauze dressing which he doused in Mercurochrome he placed it onto the still-moaning priest's open wound. From the door, on his way out again, he told the priest to keep the dressing pressed onto the wound until his return. Quite forgetting Don Enrique Gil and without stopping to remove his white coat he headed towards the coach house.

He set off from his house in the buggy at full tilt, and it wasn't until he reached the corner of Casa Prío that Captain Ortiz was able to catch up with him, although he had chased him the full length of the block, hooting his horn. At this point we should turn once again to Captain Ortiz's deposition:

> On the sidewalk outside the consulting rooms we came across Don Enrique Gil and it was he who apprised us of recent events, including Doctor Darbishire's hasty departure and whose buggy we just glimpsed driving off down the Calle Real. We set off in pursuit and eventually caught up with him. He was very angry and I now realise why. He protested that we were preventing him from reaching his destination. I offered to drive him as the car seemed like a faster way to travel, but he was unwilling to accept, and I opted to let him go on his way.

> Doctor Darbishire had barely set off again when both yourself, your honour, and I became aware that the street sellers parading up and down the sidewalk outside Casa Prío were gossiping about how Don Carmen Contreras had just died of poisoning. I rushed out to question them and they told me that this story was being repeated on every street corner. As you will remember, this convinced us that it was now more than necessary to formulate a plan and put it into action as quickly as possible.

Judge Fiallos had not shaved or changed his clothes in the previous two days. His crumpled grey linen suit was stained with banana juice and flecked with mud. Despite this, he lost no time in asking Captain Ortiz to take him to the court house to complete the requisite paperwork before going to the scene of the crime.

On their journey to the court house, Captain Ortiz told him of his intention to immediately telephone Managua to obtain authorisation for the arrest and detention at the precinct XXI jail of Oliverio Castañeda on charges of sedition. In his opinion, these were not unreasonable grounds for his arrest, although the main point was to stop him from escaping while criminal investigations were underway. Later in the day, Judge Fiallos was troubled by doubts, the origin of which will be revealed later, and he reproached himself for having allowed this measure to be taken, as it was entirely illegal.

When Judge Fiallos's car arrived outside the court house they sounded its horn loudly. His secretary, Alí Vanegas, came over to greet him, leaving his associates on the sidewalk where he had been discussing recent news among the bystanders who had just come out of the 'Amores de Abraham' barbers and the Titanic Billiard hall.

He had not yet issued the decree ordering the initial hearing but Alí Vanegas, who knew all the procedural dodges far better than he, assured him that it could be added to the dossier at a later date. For his part, Alí was extremely enthusiastic about the case as it promised to be quite a sensation.

Judge Fiallos arrived at the house accompanied by his secretary a little before ten o'clock. Making his way through the horde of people in the main living room, he found himself on the verandah, but before he had the chance to enquire after the whereabouts of any of the relatives of the deceased, he was confronted by the sight of Doctor Atanasio Salmerón: immobile, clutching the jug defensively to his chest, his strange presence completely unchallenged. When Doctor Salmerón saw Judge Fiallos he solemnly walked over to him and handed him the jug as if it were some form of gift.

At that moment Doctor Darbishire came out from one of the bedrooms, on his way back to his surgery. He was able to offer some explanation as to the value of the jug's contents as evidence. In consequence, Judge Fiallos ordered his secretary to write out a receipt for Doctor Salmerón, a copy of which was added to the official case dossier that was formally opened a few moments later when the court secretary took dictation of the decree ordering the initial hearing at the dining table.

Doctor Darbishire and his former student left together, having been informed that they must remain available to give testimony to the authorities as and when required. Moments later, Judge Fiallos asked for Don Esteban Duquestrada, whom the reader will recall was a close friend of Don Carmen, in order to request that he talk to the widow concerning the immediate removal of the body to the morgue so that the autopsy could take place.

As we already know, this gave rise to the first moment of tension in the house. Doña Flora flatly refused to leave the bedroom where the body was being dressed and Don Esteban returned without an answer. A short while later it was Oliverio Castañeda himself who appeared to inform the judge that the widow had received the news of his presence in the house with some disquiet and although he was welcome as a friend of the family, he was not so welcome to carry out official investigations which she had not authorised. Taking Don Esteban and Don Evenor Contreras, brother of the victim, as his witnesses, Judge Fiallos warned Castañeda that he risked arrest for perverting the course of justice if he continued to obstruct their investigations. He asked Alí Vanegas to read him the relevant articles in the Penal Code.

While Castañeda retreated to the far end of the courtyard to sit and sulk at his typewriter, Don Esteban went once again to try to persuade Doña Flora to accept the autopsy with good grace;

indeed, Judge Fiallos was entitled to order the removal of the body by force if necessary. A few sobs were heard, but it did not take long before Don Esteban reappeared at the bedroom door and gave the nod that consent had been obtained.

At about a quarter to twelve, the corpse was loaded onto the National Guard's supply wagon, which had been put at the service of Judge Fiallos by order of Captain Ortiz. The latter was already at the house awaiting the removal of the body so that he could lead his guards in to arrest Oliverio Castañeda. Judge Fiallos, accompanied as ever by his secretary, got into Don Esteban's car and followed the wagon to the hospital. Four enlisted soldiers armed with rifles stood on the running boards of the wagon to guard the body. Their progress was very slow owing to the throngs of people along the route.

Under the watchful eye of Judge Fiallos, the jug containing the stomach contents had been sealed. The operation had taken place in the offices of C. Contreras & Co. using a half page of a folio sheet of paper, secured with a length of buff tape otherwise used for banding bank notes. The seal was signed by Judge Fiallos and Alí Vanegas, who then took this piece of evidence personally to the Faculty of Pharmacy at the University. The Director of the Chemistry Laboratory, Absalón Rojas, received the jug and with it a judicial order naming him, from that moment, as the expert witness in matters of chemistry.

By three-thirty in the afternoon the pathologist, Doctor Escolástico, had completed the autopsy. The documentation, completed in the morgue, records:

> The presiding forensic pathologist confirms receiving a body, which was divested of all clothing and placed upon the dissecting table. Proceeding to an external physical examination: the body is that of a male, of the white race and approximately fifty years of age. The body presents with complete rigor. There are no mutilations or other physical defects or scars. Skin colour is extremely yellow and there are marked patches of cyanosis on the thorax, each one about the size of a cent coin. The face also shows the same bluish discoloration (cyanosis); the pupils of the

eyes are dilated and, when examined under strong light the conjunctiva appear blocked.

Taking the scalpel myself, I began the dissection of the body. Making the initial incision from the upper thorax to the lower abdomen, the whole region was dissected and opened to reveal the internal organs. I immediately proceeded to a physical examination of the stomach, and seeing no abnormalities I removed the organ by means of the technique recommended by P. Marcinkus.

I then explored the spleen and was able to determine that it was normal. I then carried out an examination of the intestines and found them to be undamaged and without any sign of lesions. I removed a section of the duodenum of approximately one foot in length. Next I examined the liver and the gall bladder and was able to establish that these were also normal. I extracted a section of the right lobe of the liver and the gall bladder in its entirety, again following Marcinkus. I then proceeded to remove the right kidney, which appeared to comprise healthy tissue.

I then turned to the examination of the organs contained within the rib cage. I was able to determine that the heart and the large blood vessels leading to it were normal. I removed the heart, according to the technique described by M. Sindona, ready for its subsequent examination. The lungs, both the right and the left, showed signs of cyanosis on their anterior and posterior surfaces which can be attributed to asphyxia.

My next concern was the brain, which I removed from the cranial cavity with the help of a Calvi saw. A superficial examination of the organ showed that it was normal, as were the longitudinal sections that were cut from the left hemisphere and preserved for future investigation.

From an external examination of the organs described it is not possible to infer a cause of death except to say that the lungs do show signs of asphyxia. As a result, these organs should themselves be dissected before any chemical tests are carried out for the purpose of toxicology which the presiding pathologist deems necessary.

On concluding the dissection I ordered my assistants

> to pack the body cavities with embalming materials and to suture the incisions. As a final action, the body was injected with a solution of formaldehyde sufficient to preserve it for up to forty-eight hours. All of the organs and parts of organs removed were placed into glass vessels without the addition of any preservative solution.

It was reported that crowds of townspeople maintained vigils at various points in the city late into that night. In his article, splashed across the front page of *El Cronista* the following day beneath the headline "A Great Commotion Engulfs The Ancient City", Rosalío Usulutlán compared the atmosphere to that of a religious festival:

> Our beloved León is shaking its age-old mane: it bristles, it stirs...Maundy Thursday, Corpus Christi...only these major festivals of the Catholic faith when the faithful make their pilgrimages to the various altars around the city seem to offer to this chronicler the same spectacle of fervour and coming together. Driven on by a strange will, the public is pushed from one place to the next and, not satisfied with remaining in one place, that same common will impels them move on to somewhere where fresh news or a new event may occur.
>
> Here, however, Christian faith has been substituted by a pagan urge; a surge of current that has shocked us out of the humdrum drowsiness of day-to-day existence... Sensation is all the rage, among those who ask the questions and those who respond, the need to know and to comment unite both the big players and the little fish, those in suits with those in shirtsleeves, the powerful and the dispossessed. Such is the power of news when it galvanizes us...

Judge Fiallos was still at the morgue, where the autopsy was being finalised. Just before four in the afternoon, Absalón Rojas appeared to bring him the results of the chemical tests on the stomach contents. These results dealt a blow to his spirits, and as soon as he could he telephoned Doctor Darbishire from the hospital to relay them.

Rojas used the opportunity to present the judge with a request to requisition the refrigerator at Casa Prío due to the fact that the laboratory did not possess the necessary facilities to keep the tissue samples in a good state of preservation. Rather than make a formal requisition, Judge Fiallos wrote a letter to Captain Prío on behalf of Rojas, a copy of which appears in the official court dossier:

> León, 9 October 1933
> Captain,
> I respectfully beg you to place the refrigerator found at your establishment at the disposition of Absalón Rojas. It will be returned to you at the earliest opportunity. I count on your kind cooperation.
> Sincerely,
> Mariano Fiallos Gil

At five o'clock in the afternoon, the two-door Kelvinator refrigerator powered by kerosene burners and emptied of its previous contents of bottles of Xolotlán beer was hoisted onto a horse and cart. It was transported to the Faculty of Pharmacy accompanied by a crowd of curious onlookers.

CHAPTER TWENTY-EIGHT

The Dogs Take Up Against Doctor Salmerón

When doctor Darbishire appeared at the door dressed in his white coat, which he was wearing only because of his haste that morning, an expectant murmur rose from the crowd filling the street. Doctor Salmerón kept as close to him as he could, and the crowd parted to let them through. He seated himself in the buggy with Doctor Darbishire and without exchanging a word they set off for the consulting rooms on Calle Real, pursued most of the way by a swarm of children.

The dogs leapt joyfully onto the sidewalk when Teodosio, the deaf and dumb boy, opened the door to them, but the old man made no move to pet them as normal. Canon Oviedo y Reyes was no longer there; Teodosio communicated by signs that Adelina and Midgalia, the priest's two spinster sisters who lived with him, had come to find him. They were bringing him the latest news about the poisoning, but when they found him abandoned on the operating table they decided to take him with them, with his dressing clamped under his arm and wrapping him in his cope as he was unable to put his cassock back on.

There was a long silence between teacher and student as they rocked on their chairs on the verandah, which was baking in the midday heat. Every so often they exchanged a furtive glance. All that could be heard was the creak of the rocking chairs and the grackles flapping around the lemon tree and strutting calmly across the tiled yard, indifferent to the presence of the dogs dozing in the shade.

Doctor Salmerón knew that his old teacher's silence was the silence of guilt. If only he had been more determined, if only he had rolled his sleeves up, the criminal could have been stopped in time.

He was feeling smug but he bit his tongue because, in the presence of the vanquished he wanted to be magnanimous in victory. He appraised the old man from where he sat in his rocker: he seemed more decrepit than ever, his spirit crushed by defeat. He wanted to finish him off, but held back and pushed harder to rock back and fro.

At that point the waiter from Casa Río turned up with lunch and Doctor Darbishire motioned for him to leave the tray on a little table against the wall beneath a portrait of his second wife. He couldn't eat and he didn't invite Doctor Salmerón to partake of the dishes either. He had noticed that his student had been examining him closely: he was overwhelmed, ashamed. He felt the weight of events suddenly upon him, as he went through over and over how to begin the discussion he needed to have to unburden himself. Perhaps he should suggest a detailed written report, signed by them both and sent to the judge in which they could enumerate all the hypotheses, all the logical deductions, that Doctor Salmerón had laid before him with such intelligence, starting with the death of Marta Jerez. He could complete the report with the conclusions he had formed now that he could see the whole picture clearly. Doctor Salmerón had made such a precise note of the minutiae of events in his notebook that it would not be a difficult task to compose such a report.

He was also feeling uncomfortable about the thought of having to lay the whole truth before the judge, because he would undoubtedly be called as a witness. He was tormented by the idea of appearing in the crowded court room and being forced to confess what he saw as his negligence. He hoped that owing to his age and position in society he would at least be able to demand that he give his statement in his own home.

Stationed on the sidewalk, Teodosio had managed to garner the latest news from the street. He poked his head into the verandah to let them know that Don Carmen Contreras had been taken to the hospital and that Oliverio Castañeda had escaped arrest by the soldiers as a result of the uproar created by the women of the house. The old man did not want to know, and dismissed the boy gruffly. Doctor Salmerón on the other hand was encouraged by these new developments, which seemed to add yet more credibility to his theories. He got up from his rocker to have a look at the lunch tray;

taking the cloth off, he began to pick at the food with his fingers which he licked after every mouthful. As he lingered, undecided whether to move away or not, one of the birds flew onto the table, landing at a prudent distance from the tray.

'Sit and eat if you want,' said Doctor Darbishire, finding in that moment a way to break the silence. His words sounded strange to him, like a baby's first garbled attempts to speak.

'I'm not hungry,' replied Doctor Salmerón, swallowing hard. He raked his greasy fingers through his hair and then took out his pocket watch to check the time. It was after one o'clock.

'Do you have to leave already?' asked Doctor Darbishire, startled. The last thing he wanted was to be left on his own for the rest of the day.

'They should be working on the rib cage by now,' Doctor Salmerón mumbled with his mouth full. 'Why don't you call the hospital to find out?'

Doctor Darbishire rose obediently and went into the entrance hall where the telephone hung on the wall. After a while he returned with the news that the autopsy was half completed and would be finished by three o'clock. Doctor Salmerón, who had returned to his rocking chair, already had his Casa Squibb notebook open on his knees.

'There is one detail about the first murder, that of his wife, which we should consider now that the judge will be needing our opinion,' said Doctor Salmerón, going through his notes line by line with a grubby finger.

Doctor Darbishire made himself comfortable, arranging the folds of his white coat and folding his arms. He felt as if he was once again entering that treacherous swamp he so detested, but he had run out of arguments to avoid it.

'When our murderer ran out into the street seeking his friends to raise the alarm, his victim was fit and healthy at home, engrossed in household chores,' Doctor Salmerón looked up from his notebook and into the eyes of the older man. 'We heard this mentioned a great deal on that day. Doña Flora was insistent in her assurances that when she arrived with her daughters, Marta was well. It was only later that she suffered the first fit.'

'But as you will also remember, when he went out to call on

everyone it was because of her menstruation and not blackwater fever,' said Doctor Darbishire, noting how humble he sounded repeating these old arguments back to his student.

'Ah, but wouldn't it have been better to have had his alarm justified from the outset with the presentation of convulsions?' Doctor Salmerón responded, pointing with his double-ended pencil. 'Nothing could have been more convenient than to have had the servant meet Doña Flora at the door saying: "My mistress is having a fit!"'

'You mean to say that our murderer miscalculated the time it would take for the poison to take effect,' said Doctor Darbishire shrinking back into his rocking chair, further accentuating his submission; he wasn't even surprised now that he had taken to calling Castañeda a murderer.

'Exactly, my friend,' said Doctor Salmerón waving his notebook energetically; 'and this is the mistake that is going to cost him dearly. It is going to be obvious from all the witness statements given by everyone who came to the house, called there by him.'

'It seems odd that a professional murderer would make such a miscalculation,' Doctor Darbishire commented, blinking to try to feign interest, 'if his intention was to justify his urgency in calling his friends.'

'Even the best tricksters mess up sometimes,' Doctor Salmerón gloated, giving his rocking chair a triumphal push. 'Castañeda is an expert poisoner. But that time he deliberately didn't use his system of Russian roulette. That morning, when he gave his wife her last three pills, he knew they were poisoned. The pantomime had been prepared in advance, and for that reason parts of it failed.'

'So we have an expert who can fail, because it's not a profession he could learn from books. Why, he's not even studied pharmacology,' remarked Doctor Darbishire, now smiling more warmly.

'Ah, but books are exactly where he learned to poison,' said Doctor Salmerón, leaning forward with an air of mystery. 'In order to prepare the poisons he administered to his victims he took account of their age, weight, sex and state of health. I have in my possession a book on deadly poisons which had fallen into his hands.'

'A book? What book?' asked Doctor Darbishire, also leaning in.

'It's called *The Secrets of Nature*,' replied Doctor Salmerón, finding the entry in his notebook to show the old man. 'At the beginning of this year he asked Rosalío Usulutlán to look after it for him, who knows why. When he returned to Guatemala he forgot to reclaim it.'

'So what conclusion have you come to that can explain his mistake?' said Doctor Darbishire, who had not been able to read the entry. 'You would expect that he would know his wife better than anyone; he should have been able to prepare a dose of strychnine for her that would take effect when he wanted it to.'

'He judged her to be more susceptible than turned out to be the case,' said Doctor Salmerón, going over to the little table again and using his notebook to scare off the grackles that had taken possession of the tray. 'Because of that he decided not to run any more risks. Matilde Contreras suffered for one hour exactly; in the case of Don Carmen, a fit and robust man, the quantity of strychnine in the deadly tablet dispatched him within half an hour.'

'It must have been that when he poisoned his wife he didn't have much experience,' said Doctor Darbishire thoughtfully, following in the steps of his student, hands clasped behind his back.

'Of course he did. He had already poisoned several people,' Doctor Salmerón said, ladling a spoonful of beans onto a piece of tortilla. 'He began at the age of fourteen, poisoning his own mother.'

Doctor Darbishire stopped in his tracks, then returned to his rocking chair like a convalescent afraid of exerting themselves too much.

'The book I mentioned was taken from Chiquimula Hospital,' explained Doctor Salmerón placing a hand under the tortilla, ready to catch any beans that might fall as he was eating. 'His mother was a patient there for several months in 1920, suffering from cancer. He poisoned her while she was in the hospital, so that she would not continue to suffer.'

'How do you know she had cancer? What is all this about him poisoning her?' asked Doctor Darbishire. He kept his rocking chair immobile, feeling it was somehow too fragile.

'In between the pages of the book I found a photograph of her. It shows her in a hospital bed,' said Doctor Salmerón, busy stuffing the remains of the tortilla into his mouth.

'And from that you draw the conclusion that he poisoned her to end her suffering?' Doctor Darbishire was incredulous; he closed his eyes and shook his head.

'No, I draw that from the confession he made to his friend, Oviedo the Balloon, and which Oviedo repeated to Cosme Manzo,' said Doctor Salmerón, sucking his teeth and then spitting. 'When the book came into my possession I studied it, and analysed its possible relationship with the photo. Then I asked Manzo to find out what Oviedo the Balloon knew about the mother.'

'You mean to tell me that Castañeda was brazen enough to confess to Oviedo that he poisoned his own mother?' cried Doctor Darbishire, impatiently thumping the arms of his rocking chair.

'Of course not,' said Doctor Salmerón covering the tray with the cloth again. 'But he did confess to him that he had never been able to rid his mind of his mother's terrible suffering. She had a malignant tumour in her lumbar spine, and not even the largest dose of morphine could numb the pain.'

'And you have filled in everything else,' said Doctor Darbishire, not wanting to argue or get angry now, his voice just sounded sad.

'One: his mother was suffering and he could not bear to see her suffer,' said Doctor Salmerón raising his finger to denote the first point of his argument; 'two: he appropriated a book which describes the properties, doses and effects of alkaloid plants; and three, he keeps a photo of his mother in that same book.'

'And he poisoned her when he was fourteen?' said Doctor Darbishire, pulling a face like someone swallowing a purgative. 'You do realise that we are talking about a child?'

'A child who is highly intelligent and devoid of morality,' said Doctor Salmerón, serving himself water from the jug which had come on the lunch tray. 'The natural born criminal of whom Lombroso speaks, my friend.'

Doctor Darbishire watched him take a mouthful of water and swill it around his mouth as he walked to the railing at the end of the verandah, where he spat it over a patch of begonias growing in the garden.

'Moreover, the book contains a chapter justifying euthanasia using alkaloids, as they prevent any suffering by provoking a lethal slumber,' said Doctor Salmerón while still leaning over the begonias. 'He must have stolen the alkaloids from the hospital dispensary. He put her to sleep like a little sparrow.'

'What a repulsive affair,' Doctor Darbishire said, his brow furrowing once more. 'You must forgive me, but my mind refuses to credit such a thing.'

'I'll bring you the book tomorrow so that you can read it, then you will be convinced,' Doctor Salmerón said, coming back to his seat, and patting his belly in satisfaction.

'Don't trouble yourself. Take the book to the judge. Why would I want it?' said Doctor Darbishire, waving his hands and shaking his head.

Just then the telephone rang. Doctor Salmerón looked at his pocket watch again and Doctor Darbishire opened his white coat to take out his own: it was almost four o'clock. He hurried off to take the call.

When he returned, Doctor Salmerón was waiting for him, his notebook open in his lap, ready to continue pulling together the few loose ends that still remained. However, the demeanour of the old man was not lost on him; he did not any longer seem to be revolted by what he had heard. Quite the reverse, in fact: he was glaring at him.

'That was the judge,' said Doctor Darbishire burying his hands deep in his pockets.

'And what did the judge have to say?' asked Doctor Salmerón, closing his notebook.

'I have some bad news for you,' replied Doctor Darbishire. He went over to his rocking chair and grabbed its backrest.

'They didn't do the autopsy?' Doctor Salmerón exclaimed, getting to his feet, confused.

'The autopsy is done. They are drawing up the report. Later they are going to send the internal organs to the university laboratory,' said Doctor Darbishire. His hands were trembling so badly they made the whole chair shake.

'And that's the bad news?' Doctor Salmerón snickered.

'The tests on the stomach contents in your jug came back negative. Completely negative. There are no traces of poison,' said Doctor Darbishire gripping the back of the chair so tightly in his hands it seemed as if he wanted to snap it in two.

'Don't joke with me, my friend,' said Doctor Salmerón, forcing himself to laugh again.

'Make fun of your own foolishness, I won't stop you,' said Doctor Darbishire. He pulled his chair aside, dragging it by its backrest, 'you have landed me in the dirt. Laugh at that too.'

'Don't be put off by this setback, sir. Sit down,' Doctor Salmerón said, clearing his throat with great difficulty, 'the important thing is the autopsy. The examination of the internal organs will tell us the truth.'

By now, the dogs had finished their nap, and they raced into the garden in pursuit of the birds, which scattered in fright. The old man shouted at them, trying to bring them to order.

'Sit down? So that I can hear more drivel? Because of you I am in it up to my neck. Why I ever got involved with you I shall never know!' said Doctor Darbishire, his voice trembling as much as his hands. 'I committed a terrible error supporting you in front of the judge, getting the contents of that jug analysed. And now I'm stuck playing the fall guy in your screen drama.'

'We have only just begun, my friend,' Doctor Salmerón said, suddenly feeling exhausted. One of the dogs pushed its way in between his legs, but he couldn't be bothered to move.

'Go and eat shit. *You* have only just begun,' Doctor Darbishire said, walking towards the hallway and standing there stiffly in silence.

'Do you realise you are insulting me, sir?' asked Doctor Salmerón picking up his hat with dismay.

'No, I'm bidding you farewell. Haven't you noticed I'm showing you to the door?' replied Doctor Darbishire, who stumbled slightly as the dogs moved in to keep a tight guard around him.

Doctor Salmerón rammed his hat onto his head and hurried towards the hall. He did not stop to look at the old man as he passed him by.

'And all that about Castañeda poisoning his mother, they wouldn't believe that even at the accursed table!' Doctor Darbishire shouted after him as he reached the threshold.

'Old fool!' Doctor Salmerón shouted back as he opened the door.

He had to close the door quickly behind him because the pack of hounds was hot on his heels, barking loudly.

CHAPTER TWENTY-NINE

An Eventful, Anxious Day

IT WAS not quite dark yet but the street lamps had already been switched on when Don Esteban Duquestrada's car pulled into the grounds of the university from the direction of the Recolección church. When the assembled throng outside the main university building spied the car, a swarm of people surrounded the vehicle and blocked its path. The focus of interest was the gleaming jars being guarded in the back seat by Judge Fiallos and his secretary, Alí Vanegas. The car parked with difficulty in front of the Faculty of Pharmacy which had been locked from within and was now guarded by a National Guardsman.

While Alí Vanegas took charge of unloading the jars with the help of the university porters, Judge Fiallos strode into the building. The crowd assailed him with questions, but in the midst of all the excitement no one noticed the look of deep worry etched on his face.

In his hand he had the expert-witness report which established the negative results of the tests on the stomach contents. As soon as the autopsy had finished he had seized the first opportunity to leave the morgue and go straight to the hospital director's office. There he had made a telephone call to Doctor Darbishire to pass on the findings of the report, asking, as we know, for these developments to be kept secret.

The source of his concern was this fundamental section of the report:

> The seal on the jug was broken in the presence of the witnesses listed at the end of this report. Transferred into a sterilised measuring cylinder, the contents comprised 250 cc of gastric fluid, clear in appearance and acidic in nature.

> A sample of 100 cc was taken from said fluids and this was subjected to the F. Carlucci-Schultz method for the extraction of alkaloids. The results were negative.
>
> A sample of 60 cc was taken from said fluids and this was subjected to the Casey-Bush method, which tests for small traces of strychnine. The test was negative for strychnine.
>
> The remaining fluids will be preserved until such time that the proper authorities decide what should be done with them.

At ten that night the tests were suspended until the following day; further doubts came to haunt the judge on top of those he had expressed to Doctor Darbishire over the telephone. With the help of Absalón Rojas, Doctor Escolástico Lara had begun a physical examination of the contents of the other vessels. His first priority had been an examination of samples under the microscope. These also turned out negative, as he recorded in his report:

> The organs listed below were sectioned using a scalpel in order to ascertain their internal state. They were also tested for their reactions to acid. The following results were obtained:
>
> Jar 1: right kidney. Very congested and has a normal odour: not that of almonds or ammonia. Vermilion in colour, blood is red. Acidic.
>
> Jar 2: Stomach and part of the intestine (duodenum). Has a normal odour: not that of almonds or ammonia. Whitish in colour. Filled with liquid, the remains of a citrus fruit juice. Strongly acidic. The mucous membrane has become almost completely detached and the serous membrane has suffered some damage; signs of haematoma on some regions. The intestine is empty and does not contain any mucous. Its colour is reddish, it has a normal odour and is strongly acidic.
>
> Jar 3: Heart and part of the spleen, very congested. Normal odour, blood is red and strongly acidic.
>
> Jar 4: Gall bladder: normal odour, normal colour. Blood is brown and acidic.

Jar 5: Liver: extremely congested. Normal odour, normal colour. Blood is brown and strongly acidic.

Jar 6: Section of the Brain: moderately congested, slightly soft; normal odour, normal colour. Blood is red and moderately acidic.

The organs were also subject to an examination under the microscope, for which tissue samples of the appropriate dimensions were prepared from each organ. The presence of crystals indicating strychnine or any other alkaloid were not detected. The techniques used in these tests follow the work of J. Kirkpatrick with modifications by her student Eagelburger.

So what had been proved that day? Nothing. Judge Fiallos had known nothing of the affair until his arrival in León that morning and it still struck him as the right decision to have gone to find Doctor Darbishire immediately. If the family doctor had confirmed that Don Carmen Contreras was indeed in imminent danger then they could have ordered precautions be adopted, such as the immediate confiscation of any medication being taken by Don Carmen.

However, with the sudden death of Don Carmen, the rumours in the streets had forced him to act precipitously and he had not had the chance to reflect on the consequences of allowing Captain Ortiz to proceed with the detention of Oliverio Castañeda. This was slowly dawning on him as the two of them conversed in the corridor outside the laboratory. Close to nine that evening Captain Ortiz had come to let him know that Castañeda had finally been locked up in a precinct XXI cell.

'There is nothing in the stomach contents,' said Judge Fiallos, passing Captain Ortiz the report which was written on pink paper; 'and up until now they haven't found anything in the internal organs.'

'Rojas must be tired. It should wait until morning,' said Captain Ortiz returning the page after folding it into four.

'It's not a question of tiredness!' said Judge Fiallos, rubbing his eyes. He himself felt exhausted. 'If the tests keep coming back negative, then the case is closed. Castañeda must be released.'

'You're over-stressed; we have only just got started,' Captain Ortiz said, lifting his Stetson to scratch his head. 'I'm not going to let that smooth talker out any time soon.'

'You can't put someone in jail for being a smooth talker,' said Judge Fiallos, stuffing the report into his shirt pocket.

'Smooth talker, slanderer. According to the gossip, he's bedded all of the women in this town, married and single,' said Captain Ortiz, taking off his Stetson and shaking it out forcefully. 'He's like a scorpion lurking in a pile of clothes!'

'We are talking about scientific tests, and the tests keep drawing a blank,' Judge Fiallos said, rubbing his stubbly chin. 'Even Doctor Darbishire washed his hands of the affair when I read him the report, placing all the blame squarely on Doctor Salmerón. He doesn't want to hear any more about it.'

'That idiot Salmerón is another slanderer,' Captain Ortiz said, slapping his leg with his Stetson. 'I should lock him up, too.'

'Exactly. If it had just been Doctor Salmerón's word, I wouldn't have dared lift a finger,' said Judge Fiallos, half closing his eyes, enjoying the breeze which was coming from the enclosed courtyard. The acrid smell from the chemical tests was still in his nostrils.

'Tomorrow they should test it on some dogs,' suggested Captain Ortiz adjusting his chin strap before putting his hat back on. 'If the dogs die, then the organs contain poison.'

'That is what they are planning,' said Judge Fiallos. Alí Vanegas stuck his head around the door to the laboratory and the judge motioned him to wait, saying: 'but if nothing happens then you and I will look ridiculous.'

'Ridiculous is how the widow will look after making an exhibition of herself in front of everyone,' said Captain Ortiz, stretching his neck to accommodate his chin strap. 'She's already given everyone in this town more than enough to talk about.'

'Well, if Castañeda turns out to be innocent, it will look like she had every reason to have opposed his forceful removal from the house,' said Judge Fiallos, grasping the egg-shaped marble doorknob, 'and you will be the one seen as responsible for the scandal, not her. They need me inside.'

'Me, responsible? That's rich, all I've done is help you!' said Captain Ortiz, moving towards the door and stopping the judge from closing it behind him. 'Whatever the outcome, if nothing turns up, the least we can do is deport that man to Guatemala. Ubico can deal with him.'

'That's another matter. If I close the case, you will have to allow me to set him free,' said Judge Fiallos, pushing the door gently so that Captain Ortiz was forced to let it go.

When their day was done, Alí Vanegas and the judge walked the two blocks back to his home, hounded most of the way by the busybodies who were still lingering. As they walked along, the judge warned his secretary not to discuss the day's tests with anyone, as any speculation unleashed on the streets would prejudice the credibility of the following day's results.

Later, as he ate, surrounded on all sides by his family and friends, he spoke very guardedly about the case, taking care to deny that the tests had even begun.

However, the company was more interested in talking about the circumstances of Oliverio Castañeda's capture and how he was publicly torn from the arms of Doña Flora and her daughter. They also seemed to take it for granted that the stomach contents and the internal organs contained poison, a certainty which Judge Fiallos, staring intently at his fork, could not share for the reasons outlined above.

Later that evening as he undressed for bed, alone because his wife was still sleeping in with their firstborn son, his thoughts returned to Oliverio Castañeda. They had been students together in the Law Faculty, graduating within weeks of each other. The man was certainly arrogant and a teller of tall tales in which he was the romantic hero with women throwing themselves at him from all sides. Although the judge had never shunned him completely, he had always kept his distance in class and in the corridors.

He had assumed that Castañeda had gone back to Guatemala for good and had been surprised to meet him in the billiard room at the Social Club a few days earlier. He remembered now that he had been among the very few from their year who had gone to the funeral of Castañeda's wife, and that before leaving Castañeda had sent him a note thanking him for that gesture and extolling his gentlemanly behaviour.

During their regular little chats at court, Alí Vanegas had occasionally touched upon the goings-on between Castañeda and the Contreras women, giving the whole thing a very saucy slant; that it had started while his wife was still alive and that he had enjoyed playing their jealousies against one another without caring that they all had to live under the same roof. These stories had come back to Judge Fiallos that morning when they had gone to find Doctor Darbishire. He had never given them much credit because he was acquainted with Castañeda and he also knew the tendencies of his secretary who, when not talking about literature, liked to amuse himself by collecting gossip from billiard halls and bars, all of which had as a general rule originated at Doctor Salmerón's accursed table.

Stretched out on his back in bed and dressed only in his pyjama pants, the judge reflected on his own role. In the morning, when he had taken the first depositions, he had felt engaged by the novelty presented by this case. Throughout the day he had continued to enjoy the sudden notoriety he had attained despite the fact that he had no real vocation as an attorney or indeed a career in the judiciary.

To get a better picture of the personality and aspirations of the youthful Judge Fiallos (he was born in 1906, the same year as Oliverio Castañeda, and was therefore just turning twenty-six) we must interrupt his uncomfortable reflections and turn to an article by Manolo Cuadra. The article is entitled 'Judge Fiallos and All the Other Poets' and was published in *La Nueva Prensa* on 14 October 1933:

> After a train journey which in a more civilized country would have taken half the time, we find ourselves in León: the cradle of liberal thought and the spiritual birthplace of Rubén Darío. We have been sent by the editor-in-chief of this newspaper with more chores to complete than pesos in our pockets, and determined not to allow ourselves to be swept up in the sensational happenings which have captured the public imagination and converted this proud metropolis into a mecca for the national press.
>
> An innumerable number of poets are caught up in the already infamous Castañeda case. It could not be otherwise, since we find ourselves in a city of poets: from the

accused to the presiding judge, his secretary and the lawyers. I should also add myself to the list as, although I am disposed to accomplish my delicate task with rigour and dedication, I am more avant-garde poet than chronicler. I am however satisfied to be a soldier of the press, having been wise enough to hang up the trappings of my mercenary days when in an evil hour I was recruited by Sparta to fight in my native Greece against the Helot nationalists...but that is another story.

Poets, poets, everywhere...among the papers confiscated from the trunks belonging to the accused there were many poems of a romantic nature. Alí Vanegas, the judge's secretary, writes poems in the avant-garde mode; he has read them to us and informs us that there is a book on the way. The word on the street is that his father, Juan de Dios Vanegas, about to give evidence against the accused, has also tapped into the fountain of inspiration and is heir to the modernist movement of which León was a stronghold. And Mariano Fiallos, presiding judge: also a poet.

It is he to whom we wish to dedicate ourselves on these few pages, even though the recent tragic events call us with their electrifying insistence, like the Morse code that called to us in less honourable times when we were camped out on the mournful mountains of Segovia. We know Judge Fiallos from last year when he came out in support of León's ill-starred fighter, Kid Tamariz. He is an expert in matters of boxing as am I. But I chose to support Kid Centella, the most dangerous contender as far as his protégé was concerned, although it is only gentlemanly to concede my man as not in the same class.

Kid Tamariz was at his glorious peak, on the point of completing a string of fifteen knockouts, when we saw him fall. That tragic night in the ring at Campo de Marte in Managua he deserved better luck, but was knocked to the canvas by a treacherous punch from Kid Centella which caught him square on the head and deprived him of his mental faculties. He now wanders the streets of León in a daze, launching his famous deadly jabs at thin air; always on guard, he ducks and weaves defensively in a frenzy of wasted energy. The youngsters who follow him around applaud heartlessly. The promise of his past has evaporated, leaving only its image in the lively representation of his likeness printed on the labels of Campeón Rum.

In a world of his own, the poet of the ring, the precision of whose upper-cuts was pure harmony; in a world of his own Alfonso Cortés, chained to the bars of a window overlooking the Calle Real, his head spinning with the clamour of the heavenly spheres turning on their axes; and left in a world apart by alcohol in eternal tragic bohemian revelry, Lino Argüello, "Lunatic Lino", poet of dead brides who never were, "except in his pleasant, ailing dreams". Solitary, skulking in the streets and wretched liquor bars, and since tragedy finds a warm welcome in his soul, he has recently sung of the death of Matilde Contreras, the Ophelia, crowned with white lilies, in Castañeda's drama.

Returning to Mariano Fiallos: he is an amiable poet who sings of the comforts of family life. He is a narrator of homely tales, in love with the homeland, a land of scorched Pacific plains and of volcanoes whose ancient, haughty peaks interrupt the landscape: "raw with age and solemn with myth" as Darío says. He is a musician who is not only a consummate pianist but also adept at the guitar, comfortable playing both long recitals and more intimate serenades. He does not abuse the pleasures of bohemia, and in his good-natured company one might equally well discuss Hölderlin and Babe Ruth, García Lorca and Primo Carnera, Johann Sebastian Bach and María Grever, the pessimism of Nietzsche and the length of Greta Garbo's legs...

The last time we spoke was shortly after the fall of boxing's Icarus, Kid Tamariz. On that occasion he confided to me that he had accepted the position of Judge, effective on his graduation. He said that this was only from the necessity of his recently married state and that he would give it up as soon as he got his chair at the Faculty of Law, promised to him by the Dean of Faculty, the father of his poet-secretary.

During the few weeks that he has been in post he has

had only trivial matters to deal with: knife fights provoked by local rivalries in the neighbourhoods surrounding León, arguments at cock-fighting rings that have occasionally ended in shooting, minor robberies at grocery stores, pilfering of church collection boxes. The inscription on the wall of his courtroom makes it clear that he has not forgotten his primary calling; behind his desk are a few lines of Terence, copied in Gothic script by Alí Vanegas, which he considers to be his motto: "Nothing human is alien to me."

The cases that pass across his desk are useful only in that they give him fodder for the characters and plots of his stories. The same can be said of his weekend visits to the ranch which he inherited from his father, El Socorro, close to El Sauce in the Zapata valley. The property is a black hole for money, but he gets the opportunity to play at being the gentleman farmer; talking with the farm hands and peasants in order to learn the secrets of common speech, just as I learned them from Caliban, while at the same time listening to the twisted words of Ariel, during the war in the Segovia mountains.

He already has a title for the book of stories he intends to publish: "Scorched Horizon"; as I have a title for mine: "Opposing Sandino in the Mountains". In the loneliness of his office when there are no litigants, or on his tours of inspection to the countryside aboard his beaten-up Ford which he has baptised "Blue Bird" in homage to Maeterlinck, he and his secretary turn to talking of books and their literary preferences rather than the penal code. The "Blue Bird" also takes other routes... I have been its passenger.

This is the man who sits in judgement over Castañeda and this is how I wish to introduce him to the reader. I had barely wiped the dust from my travelling hat and unpacked my meagre possessions at the Chabelita rooming house, whose walls must accustom themselves to the scratching of my pen and the spleen of my nocturnal soliloquies these next few weeks, before I set off for the courtrooms in search of the latest news and to shake the honest hand of Mariano Fiallos.

Our meeting was brief since he needed to complete some paperwork concerning the court hearing. As a little hors d'oeuvre I started an entertaining chat with Alí Vanegas and I am certain that the gravity of the matter in hand will not prevent the judge from sharing a main course conversation with me...and indeed the chance to enjoy a joy-ride aboard our accomplice in the act: Blue Bird.

Despite his fatigue, Judge Fiallos still found it impossible to sleep. He heard the neighbourhood cocks crowing and got up to check the time on the glowing phosphorescent hands of his alarm clock on the bedside table. It was only just one o'clock; daybreak was still some hours off. He lay down again, but as he did so he heard a loud knocking at the front door. He got up somewhat alarmed and went out into the passageway pulling on his bathrobe. His wife meanwhile was trying to hush the baby, who had been woken by the disturbance and was crying loudly. One of the farmhands who had been spending the night on a truckle bed in the hallway came to meet him, lighting the way with a torch. The boy handed him an envelope which had been left at the door. The judge tore open the envelope and asked the boy to bring the torch closer so that he could read what was in the letter:

León, 9 October 1933
His Honour Chief District Criminal Judge,
Dear Doctor Fiallos,

My honour and professional reputation are at stake. In the case of a negative result in the tests carried out on the stomach contents taken from the victim before he died, it is necessary that you take these same liquids and inject them into a dog. This has not been done yet. According to my sources, these key experiments will take place tomorrow morning. You must inject a dog. If the dog dies, an outcome of which I am certain, this will confirm that I was correct, as indeed I know I am. If not, then the weight of public outrage will be on my head.

Do this and as always I remain at your service and will do everything to support you.

Yours,
Atanasio Salmerón
Doctor and Surgeon

PS: Your secretary Alí Vanegas has informed our common acquaintance Rosalío Usulutlán that there are 90 cc of the stomach contents still remaining. This is sufficient to complete the experiment I request.

Judge Fiallos was seized by an urge to tear the letter to pieces and throw it to the four winds. He was disgusted by the affront and even more disgusted with Alí Vanegas, whom he had expressly warned not to tell anyone about the test results. It was his duty, however, to keep a full record of all documents related to the case and add them all to the court dossier, even if they did represent such an impertinence as this.

Doctor Salmerón's letter did find its way into the court dossier. Bound into the bundle is a page from Doctor Salmerón's prescription book with his letterhead showing the address of his clinic and its opening hours.

'What's going on?' asked Judge Fiallos's wife who had come to the door of the bedroom with the still sobbing infant.

'Nothing,' Judge Fiallos replied, putting the letter into the pocket of his bathrobe. 'Just a mad man loose on the streets sending me letters at midnight.'

CHAPTER THIRTY

Sensational Experiments at the University

ALTHOUGH the morning of October tenth dawned cloudy and with the threat of rain, throngs of curious onlookers gathered undeterred from the early hours around the university. The university, which stood next to the church of La Merced, was a traditional wood-framed construction on two storeys. Within its walls were housed the Faculties of Law, Medicine, Surgery and Obstetrics and, occupying the west wing of the first floor, the classrooms and laboratories of the Faculty of Pharmacy.

A crowd of street sellers had installed themselves on the sidewalks and around the plaza at the entrance to the main hall, where the body of Rubén Darío had lain in state for ten days in 1916. With their stalls, tents and carts they gave this august, century-old hall of academe the feel of a busy marketplace. This is just what Rosalío Usulutlán manages to capture in his article: 'Sensational Experiments at the University', which appeared in *El Cronista* on October eleventh.

In contrast, the Contreras residence was abandoned. The body of Don Carmen was still unburied, the funeral was due to take place at four in the afternoon, and although only a few blocks away it seemed isolated from the events unfolding at the university. The only visitors were a few women dressed in mourning, and not even the sombre tolling of the cathedral bells every hour beneath the rain laden sky seemed able to give the onlookers cause to remember that the bereaved family even existed.

Rosalío Usulutlán's story offers us the following insight into the happenings of that morning:

> The first to arrive was the judge, Doctor Fiallos who went in at seven-twenty armed with an umbrella and oilskin

cape. A few moments later appeared his secretary, Alí Vanegas, followed by the forensic pathologist, Doctor Escolástico Lara. They met with Absalón Rojas inside the laboratory where, helped by some of his students, he had been charged with organising and sterilising the glassware and other instruments to be used in the tests.

In the courtyard beyond, the cats and dogs required for the experiments were already chained up at a convenient distance from one another and in the care of a porter. This is according to the word on the street, as this reporter and indeed all other members of the press were prevented from gaining access to the building. We are also aware that frogs were collected that morning on the banks of the river Chiquito by the porters.

At around eight o'clock the great and the good of public life began to arrive in their carriages and automobiles. Each one had to wait while the National Guardsman stationed at the gate knocked on the door with his rifle to attract the attention of Alí Vanegas. The secretary peered out of the window and then went to consult the judge. If permission was granted, the door was opened.

These goings-on leant an air of farce to proceedings which culminated in some extreme shows of disrespect on the part of the loafers and vagabonds with whom those waiting to be admitted had to share the sidewalk. The crowd shouted mocking and scurrilous names at them, and those who did not gain access were sent on their way with whistles of derision. At one point a mango stone, thrown by anonymous hands, hit Vanegas on the head when he imprudently leaned too far out of the window.

Among those citizens who were granted admission by the judge were the City Mayor, Doctor Onesífero Rizo; the president of the Western Appeals Court, Doctor Octavio Martínez Ordónez; Canon Isidro Augusto Oviedo y Reyes; the director of the San Vicente Hospital, Doctor Joaquín Solís; the chief of the León's Public Health Department, Doctor Rigoberto Sampson; in addition to other well-known doctors and pharmacists of the city. It was thanks to these people that the public was kept up to

> date with the progress of the experiments, because the judge could not prevent them from passing on news of events through half-open windows to friends and family posted outside the building. These whispered confidences served this chronicler so well, and indeed all the rest of his colleagues of the fourth estate.

The first analyses completed by Absalón Rojas are described in the official report included in the court dossier:

> CHEMICAL ANALYSIS OF THE INTERNAL ORGANS
>
> At 8:40 in the morning I commenced the chemical analysis of the internal organs. To this end all of the organs were ground into a fine paste, this being divided into four equal parts: the first to test for volatile poisons (alcohol, ether, chloroform, phenylamine, etc); the second to test for acids (sulphuric, nitric, oxalic, picric and phenylic acid, etc) and metals (cyanide, arsenic, antimony, mercury, etc); the third to test for alkaloids (for example, strychnine); and the fourth to be kept in the refrigerator in the case that any tests needed to be repeated.
>
> From the results of the tests done on the first two samples using the distillation technique developed by E. Abrahms, I can conclude that there were no traces of volatiles; using the set of organic reactions suggested by Secord and Allen nor were any acids or metals detected. This demonstrates that yesterday's result showing high levels of acidity in all of the organs was a consequence of contamination by gastric fluids as a result of mishandling.
>
> Using the third sample I attempted to extract alkaloids using Ether in the manner described by North-Singlaub. I obtained a yellow substance which was comparable in colour to picric acid but this did not yield any of the characteristic reactions of alkaloids. Nor did sublimation of this substance in a Poindexter retort enable me to obtain the characteristic reactions of strychnine. I preserved the sample for further chemical and biological analysis.

By now it was already close to midday. These latest results had been communicated to the curious onlookers via the windows by the witnesses within and they were growing restive. Speculation was rife and there were some who began to shout out, stridently demanding the freedom of Oliverio Castañeda. This too is recorded by Rosalío Usulutlán:

> One of the women, who had just sold the last of her stock of meatballs in sauce, approached one of the windows, knife in hand, her head protected from the sunlight by a wide-brimmed straw hat. In language that does not bear repetition in print, she demanded that the doors of the jail be opened so that the prisoner could leave, and that all of the doctors and know-it-alls should be locked up in his stead. By way of a joke, she went on to offer her services to supply them all with enough food so that they wouldn't go hungry while in prison. This performance was met with many guffaws and the unofficial herald inside promptly closed the window, fearful of becoming the target of a missile.

The experiments continued through lunchtime without pause. Referring again to the official record:

> I proceeded to look for traces of strychnine using iron ferrocyanide, potassium ferrocyanide, sulphuric acid and bichromate of potassium as per the methods of V. Walters. The reactions were all negative.
>
> I continued with a further test evaporating a solution made with chloroform as described in a method developed by Gavin-Tamb. In this case examination under the microscope of the residue remaining after evaporation revealed traces of strychnine in crystal form.

The news was relayed in a haphazard way through the windows and the crowd became excited once more. Shouts in support and against the defendant could be heard along with jokes and applause. The dogs chained up inside began to bark: 'Barks that were met with tasteless jeering,' commented Rosalío Usulutlán, 'as the crowd knew full well what fate lay in store for these hapless canines.'

The experts then proceeded to the long-expected experiments on animals, the results of which also appear in the dossier:

BIOLOGICAL TESTS WITH A FROG

I began the biological tests using a frog, and proceeded in the following way: taking the third portion of macerated internal organs which had been reserved for the alkaloid tests, I placed a quantity of 25 grams into a test tube. This paste was mixed with 10 cc of a 30 per cent solution of sulphuric acid and used 2 cc of this to prepare an intramuscular injection.

The frog was injected in the shoulder and at 1:10 this area was swollen and moist. At 1:12, symptoms of nausea; when allowed freedom it shrank back and vomited. At 1:13, further vomiting but lacking strength. Nausea appeared to pass. At 1:15, responded to touch, little movement. When the bench was struck, little response. Respiratory distress. At 1:17, full-blown convulsion. Unable to jump. Prodded, further convulsions. At 1:19, hind legs outstretched. When flexed, no movement. Unable to recover previous position. At 1:20, hind legs rigid, thorax and abdomen appeared swollen and slightly moist. Front legs became rigid. At 1:21, hind legs limp and stomach soft to touch. Front legs limp. At 1:22, reflexes very weak. At 1:23, no responses. Weak indication of breathing. Agony and final collapse occurred at 1:24. Death of frog.

BIOLOGICAL TESTS WITH A DOG

At 1:50 p.m., I proceeded to inject 6 cc of the same solution into a dog weighing 6 kg and observed the following: at 1:52, symptoms included dilated pupils and an aversion to noise and light. At 1:54, it appeared morose and lethargic. At 1:57, efforts were made to encourage it to move and it did not obey. At 2:00, it vomited and showed signs of respiratory distress. At 2:02, it began to moan quietly and piteously; it vomited again. At 2:03, it experienced its first fit. When checked using a stethoscope its heart rate was found to be accelerated. Its jaw was rigid (trismus). At 2:04, the fit passed. The dog showed signs of exhaustion and its hind limbs became rigid to the touch and unresponsive to stimulus by pin prick. At 2:07, a second fit occurred. All four limbs became rigid. At 2:09, the

> fit passed. The dog became limp all over, its vital signs were minimal and it was unresponsive, even refusing to open its eyes. At 2:12, it experienced a third fit. Its eyes became crossed (strabismus); jaw locked such that it could not be prised open with a spatula (trismus). At 2:14, the fit passed. Breathing, shallow; heart beat weak when checked with stethoscope. At 2:17, agony. At 2:18, the dog died.

The third experiment was carried out on a cat weighing one kilo. Injected at 2:30 with a 4 cc dose of the same solution, it died at 2:50 after presenting very similar symptoms, making it unnecessary to include the experimental report in addition to those already cited here.

When the news circulated that animals injected with the extracts taken from the internal organs were dying, apparently poisoned, it caused a great commotion. This is how Rosalío Usulutlán described the scene:

> All around the building the windows began to open, one by one and little by little with a clattering of blinds and catches. Hearing this, the spectators rushed hither and thither to find a good spot, anxious to hear the news.
>
> Discovering the fatal outcome suffered by each animal in turn, the mob roared like a raging sea and there were some who, shouting at the tops of their voices, called for the guilty party to be made an example of. Banding into factions, some threatened to march on the XXI prison with the intention of showing the prisoner the full strength of popular opinion. Others went about trying to organise a petition which they intended to send to the relevant authorities requesting the application, without further ado, of the ultimate sanction: the death penalty. Nothing came of either of these initiatives.

The tests should have ended there, but Judge Fiallos, now relieved of his doubts, took a last-minute decision to order Absalón Rojas to inject another dog with the remains of the stomach contents collected from Don Carmen Contreras by Doctor Atanasio Salmerón. This surprised Alí Vanegas, still smarting from the reprimand he had received for his indiscretion the previous evening.

This was an act of justice. Early that morning, Doctor Salmerón had presented himself at the door to the Faculty requesting to be admitted. Having been roundly refused by Judge Fiallos, the doctor had had to endure the catcalls of the mob. The judge heard the jeering through the closed windows and it was witnessed by Rosalío Usulutlán, who described the episode in his article, although without mentioning the name of Doctor Salmerón.

The dog was injected at 3:15 in the afternoon and it died at 3:45, after suffering three severe fits.

After this, the official report was written and it was signed by five o'clock in the afternoon. Those present all acted as witnesses, except for Canon Oviedo y Reyes, who had been obliged to leave before four o'clock, as detailed by Rosalío:

> The Very Reverend Canon Isidro Oviedo y Reyes was the first to leave the building. This was on account of his being needed to say mass at the funeral liturgy for Don Carmen Contreras led by the Bishop of León, Monseigneur Tijerino y Loáisiga, and the hour of the burial was fast approaching.
>
> With his arm raised, the canon appeared to be imparting his blessings to the crowd and some even made the mistake of kneeling. Reliable sources state, however, that the position of his arm was the result of a recent operation on his armpit which impeded him from lowering the affected limb.

CHAPTER THIRTY-ONE

Doctor Salmerón Returns to the Fold

ALÍ VANEGAS was in the habit of leaving the door to his student room open until late into the night. This was partly owing to the suffocating night-time heat in León, but also because he liked to spy on the night owls to find someone to gossip with. The room was in the family home of his father, Doctor Juan de Dios Vanegas, on Calle Real. It shared a wall with the equally historic house where Rubén Darío had spent his adolescence and where the poet Alfonso Cortés, on succumbing to the madness of which the reader is aware, was now chained to the railings of one of the balconies.

Sparsely furnished and abandoned to the haphazard breezes of disorder, the room only got cleaned when Alí Vanegas submitted to the demands of his mother who would accuse him, from the other side of the door, of living in a chicken coop. Only then would he open the door to let the servants in. While the women swept all the rubbish out onto the street, his mother, who was unwilling to leave the servants at his mercy, would keep a watchful eye on him, strap in hand. This was also the only time when he was obliged to wear his trousers in the room. His most impressive possession was a metal bedstead so large it was visible from the street, its four posters crowned with cherubic heads and hung with gauzy curtains that were thick with dust.

As the reader will also recall, it was due to his nocturnal spying that he was witness to the hurried retreat of the dog poisoners in a carriage on the night of 18 July 1932. Later that same night, Rosalío Usulután had appeared at the room with his tale about the beating. These were events that the two of them came clean about in their respective depositions once the dog-hunt became an essential part of the judicial inquest opened in November 1933.

For the moment, let us stay with Alí Vanegas. He had left Judge Fiallos at the door to his home and returned to his own room after what had been a tremendously eventful day. As usual, he undressed down to his underpants and prepared to go over some neglected paperwork. However, after a while and finding he could not concentrate, he abandoned the deck chair where he had been sitting, and went over to the trunk where he kept all his books and papers in search of his poetry notebook. He had decided to pass the time by writing up his latest poem, 'Eulogy for an Unknown Woman' and he had just sat down again when Rosalío Usulutlán appeared once again at his door. This time he was there as the messenger of Doctor Atanasio Salmerón.

The last time we saw Doctor Salmerón he was slamming the door of Doctor Darbishire's house in fear for his life with a pack of hounds hot on his heels. His next move, once he had gained the safety of the sidewalk, had been to head off to Casa Prío, his tail between his legs.

As was to be expected on such a momentous day as that one, Casa Prío was full to bursting. Everyone was drinking warm beer, emptied out of the refrigerator in preparation for its relocation to the university. As Doctor Salmerón walked between the tables all he could hear was inane chatter concerning the only subject that seemed to excite everyone: the arrest of the poisoner Oliverio Castañeda after the death of his latest victim. He could take no pleasure from this chatter.

He went straight over to his usual corner and took out his Casa Squibb notebook but did not feel like opening it, and so put it to one side. As his anger subsided, his sense of defeat grew: he'd been cast out like some disinherited son who'd fallen out of favour with the patriarch. It was so out of character for the old man to have uttered such foul language that he stood in no doubt that their friendship was at an end.

Cosme Manzo came in to the bar a good while later. When the refrigerator had been removed there had been a stampede in its pursuit, but now the tables were full again and Manzo circulated, stopping here and there to divulge the details of the arrest. He had just come from the Contreras residence, where he had seen the military operation in which the poisoner had been dragged out, completely drunk amidst the shouts and protestations of the two women of the house as they tried yet again to impede his capture. As he retold the story, he acted out their sobbing and pleading, to the delight of everyone present; everyone that is except Doctor Salmerón, from whom he got only the faintest of smiles.

Manzo didn't seem too worried when Doctor Salmerón told him about the debacle of the tests on the stomach contents. He had spent the day toing and froing from one place to the next, from the crime scene to the hospital, and had been eye-witness to many of the day's events. For him this was only the beginning, and a preliminary result such as the one that Doctor Salmerón had dolefully reported was not a source of concern. The internal organs had not yet been examined, they had not completed the animal tests, and they had not heard the key witness statements. And then there was the compelling evidence contained in the Casa Squibb notebook: how the poison had been obtained, how Castañeda had retained a portion of the strychnine after killing the dogs, the Codfish-man's story, and the book *The Secrets of Nature*. When this evidence was revealed in all its glory, no one would dare to contradict it.

'The special reserve,' said Captain Prío ostentatiously placing two bottles of ice-cold beer on the table. 'I've hidden the ice-box in case you want more.'

Cosme Manzo drank thirstily, straight from the bottle. Doctor Salmerón took his reluctantly.

'Listen, Doctor,' said Cosme Manzo, wiping the foam from his lips on his shirtsleeve. 'One thing you have to remember is that we have Doctor Darbishire in our corner. Anything he says will play to us.'

Doctor Salmerón rubbed his finger across the wet ring left by his beer bottle and did not answer. He was ashamed to have to admit to Manzo that he'd been turfed out of the old man's house with the dogs at his heels, clearly intending to bite him if they caught him.

'Don't tell me the old man has got cold feet,' said Cosme Manzo without lowering the bottle from his lips.

'We can't count on anything from that old curmudgeon,' said Doctor Salmerón, a wave of anger rising inside him. 'He blames me for the fact that they couldn't find any poison in the stomach contents.'

'And he fought with you over that?' said Cosme Manzo, placing the bottle very carefully back onto the table as if not wishing to disturb anyone with the noise. 'That crusty old bastard has always been too proud.'

Doctor Salmerón nodded in agreement and then looked away. His chin trembled. Doctor Darbishire was proud and inconsiderate; never again would he set foot in his house even as a doctor, even if the old man were struck down by an apoplexic fit.

'I bet he even threw you out of the house,' Cosme Manzo went on, scrutinizing Doctor Salmerón, who was still turned away from him, biting the knuckles of his clenched fist. 'I bet he was capable of setting the dogs on you.'

'He did,' said Doctor Salmerón, clenching his jaw as he felt the tears welling in his eyes.

'Your pride is wounded, Doctor,' Cosme Manzo said, taking him firmly by the arm. 'At the end of the day all those rich bastards have their snouts in the same trough.'

'Where's Rosalío?' asked Doctor Salmerón. He grabbed the beer bottle by the neck and took a swig. Manzo was right. They were all the same and he had put their noses out of joint. 'I need to talk to him.'

'That's more like it, Doctor, we are where we are,' said Cosme Manzo, grinning and downing the rest of his beer. 'He's probably at the university. The internal organs are about to be delivered and there is a huge mob outside.'

'Go and get him for me,' said Doctor Salmerón, patting Cosme Manzo on the knee. 'I need him to try to speak with Alí Vanegas to get the lowdown on what's happening in the laboratory, and to tell him it's a matter of life and death that they inject those stomach contents into the animals.'

'I'll do you a deal, Doctor,' said Cosme Manzo while getting to his feet, casually holding the empty bottle in his hand. 'Let's see what you have to say to this.'

Doctor Salmerón was already deep in his notebook but he looked up.

'We've got a can of worms to open,' Cosme Manzo said, resting his hands on the table top and leaning so close to Doctor Salmerón that he brushed his head with his hat brim. 'We need a good story from Rosalío, laying out all the facts we know. The love letters, the scheming and the crying. We'll tip those worms right into their trough.'

'I like it,' said Doctor Salmerón, convinced. He took a moment to think, then cautioned, 'but first we have to sort out the question of the jug.'

Manzo left with his orders just as the bar began to empty rapidly. The locals were off to the university because the internal organs had just been delivered and the experiments were due to start. An hour later he returned: Rosalío hadn't been able to speak with Alí Vanegas at all; the doors to the university were locked and all journalists had been denied access by order of the judge.

It was nearly ten o'clock when Manzo and Rosalío brought back the news that the experiments had been suspended owing to the lateness of the hour and would not begin again until eight the following morning. They had still not been able to get close to Alí Vanegas as the latter had accompanied the judge to his home.

That was how they came up with the plan to send Rosalío to find Alí in his room. And so it was that Alí Vanegas found Rosalío at his door, hat raised in a polite greeting and wishing him a good evening.

'I don't give interviews to the press,' said Alí Vanegas, pushing his bundle of poems to one side.

Rosalío went in search of a stool, moving rapidly, his body hunched over so that it looked as if he were hunting it down. He grabbed it and dragged it close to Alí Vanegas' deck chair.

'Be careful your inspiration doesn't freeze, going around in your smalls!' Rosalío whispered in his ear.

'I keep my inspiration in my balls and I don't want them to cook,' replied Alí Vanegas, fanning himself with a palm leaf. 'The judge has forbidden me, under any circumstance, to talk about the case. If you have come to get anything out of me, your mission will have been in vain.'

'If you want to know anything about the case,' said Rosalío bringing his stool closer, 'you'd do better to ask me, as I know more than the judge.'

'So what on earth are you, my esteemed colleague, doing looking for me at this late hour?' asked Alí Vanegas, tapping him on the leg with his fan.

'I want us to help a friend,' said Rosalío, taking off his hat and covering his mouth with it.

'Well, that all depends on which friend and what help is required,' Alí replied, casting him a sidelong glance. Sweat glistened on the top of his shaven head.

'Doctor Salmerón made a valuable contribution to the tests now underway. He has made it possible to catch the murderer and everyone should be grateful to him,' said Rosalío, taking his hat away from his mouth for a moment and then covering it again.

'What sort of contribution?' asked Alí Vanegas, fanning himself energetically. 'He entered the Contreras residence without permission. He could be facing charges of trespass. There was no poison in his jug.'

'So the dog didn't die?' asked Rosalío, placing his hat on his knees. Using his finger he drew a line in the thick layer of dust on the arm of the deck chair.

'What dog?' said Alí Vanegas, pulling out a hair peeping from the fly of his underpants and holding it up to the light.

'The dog they injected with the stomach contents today in the laboratory!' said Rosalío, making a cross in the dust. 'And don't be such a pig, my friend.'

'If I'd pulled yours out, then I'd be a pig,' said Alí Vanegas, flicking the hair into the air and watching it fall to the floor. 'They haven't injected any animals yet. They've only just started on the internal organs. Tomorrow it's the turn of the dogs, the cats and the other animals. It was the chemical tests on your famous jug that were done and came out negative.'

'Doctor Salmerón has already been told that,' said Rosalío, craning his neck in order to read what Alí Vanegas had been writing, 'but he says that the chemical tests are not the important ones. It's the ones with the dogs that he's interested in.'

'Well then, if he already knows, it wasn't from me that he heard it,' said Alí Vanegas, covering the page with his hand. 'And when you leave here, remember that I haven't told you shit about anything.'

'What he wants you to make sure of is that they inject a dog with the stomach contents. The truth will out!' said Rosalío, spreading his arms wide as if declaiming poetry. 'Is that the elegy you told me about?'

'I am just a simple clerk,' said Alí Vanegas, no longer bothering to cover the page and letting him read it. 'Whatever he wants, he needs to ask the judge himself, if he's brave enough. The judge has had enough of the whole sorry tale of that jug. But he should speak to the judge, there are still ninety cubic centimetres of fluid.'

'Ninety cubic centimetres,' mused Rosalío, taking his stool back to where he had found it.

'You came here to wheedle information out of me,' Alí Vanegas said, stretching out to pass him the elegy, 'and to spy on what I am writing. Read it if you want, enjoy yourself. See this avant-garde gem shine.'

'Better if you read it,' said Rosalío, coming over, hands on hips: 'that sonnet for Sandino that you wrote wasn't bad.'

'Not bad! Perfect you mean, philistine,' Alí Vanegas said making some last changes before beginning to read.

'Not bad: you shouldn't be so vain my friend,' said Rosalío, straightening his trousers. 'You can be sure one person didn't like it at all, and that's Somoza.'

'As if I give a damn about Somoza,' said Alí Vanegas, beginning his recitation in a strange nasal voice: 'You, with your trembling flesh, the unknown who knocks at my door, set upon igniting the white linen sheets of my bed with a smouldering heat, a candle guttering in the hurricane of desire…'

'The unknown: you mean any old whore!' said Rosalío, running for the door. 'Is that why you keep the door open?'

'The whore's your mother!' cried Alí Vanegas leaping after him, but Rosalío had already vanished, leaving behind the sound of his laughter in the street.

This conversation explains how it was that at midnight on 9 October 1933 Judge Fiallos came to hear knocking on his front door.

Rosalío returned to Casa Prío bearing his valuable and encouraging news: that there were ninety cubic centimetres of the stomach contents left, more than enough to inject a dog. He had barely finished speaking before Doctor Salmerón had his prescription book out and was scribbling the note. Cosme Manzo offered to deliver it personally.

'Let's see what happens,' said Doctor Salmerón smiling confidently.

'And you,' Cosme Manzo said, giving Rosalío a fulsome slap on the back, 'get ready to write the story of your life!'

'I need to talk to Rosalío about that,' said Doctor Salmerón, dismissing Cosme Manzo with an impatient wave of his hand.

CHAPTER THIRTY-TWO

Princess of Black Flowers

THE DEATHS of the frog, the dogs and the cats following the injections administered in the university laboratory and their incontrovertible symptoms of poisoning confirmed Oliverio Castañeda's guilt in the public imagination. Although the petition calling for the application of the death penalty never materialised, there was an editorial in *La Prensa* in Managua endorsing this view. It was published on 11 October 1933, signed by the director, Doctor Pedro Joaquín Chamorro Zelaya, and entitled: 'Public Enemy Number One':

> It is a sign of the terrible times we are living through in our republic when the foundations of morality are challenged by these vile and insidious attacks on that most sacrosanct of institutions: the family. Such is the horrendous case that has rocked the city of León. Not only should we praise the National Guard for their prompt action in ordering the arrest of the man guilty of these heinous crimes, as has been proved thanks to the advances of science, but we should also demand that the sombre, vengeful shadow of the gallows be cast over events to expunge the ignominy of this betrayal and barbarity.
>
> We at *La Prensa* are demanding this, not unaware of our Christian sentiments, but mindful of the voice of the public. These crimes are like a pustule, infecting society with evil humours, which must be cauterised, however painful. If the sore is allowed to fester, the infection will spread to the entire body of society, risking its collapse.

On the same day, October eleventh, Judge Fiallos received a telegram from Managua signed by the President of the Supreme Court of Justice, Doctor Manuel Cordero Reyes. This was added to the case dossier:

> UNANIMOUS DECISION SUPREME COURT JUSTICES AWARE HEIGHTENED PUBLIC REACTION ORDER USE ALL MEANS AT DISPOSITION WITHOUT HESITATION COWARDICE INVESTIGATE DEATH DON CARMEN CONTRERAS (R.I.P.) AND OTHERS CONNECTED TO HIM. GUILTY BE SUBJECT FULL FORCE OF LAW FOR SAKE SOCIAL HARMONY AND PROTECTION DECENT HONOURABLE CITIZENS. COOPERATION BY YOU DEMANDED ALL RELEVANT AUTHORITIES WITHOUT DELAY. ACKNOWLEDGE RECEIPT.

Meanwhile, although this did not reach the press, loud voices of disapproval were raised against the widow and her daughter. They were still sending the prisoner consignments of food, bedclothes and all manner of articles despite the results of the laboratory tests. As we know, these consignments were put a stop to by Captain Ortiz on orders received from National Guard High Command. This action was met with applause in an editorial by *La Prensa*, which was careful, however, not to identify the rebuffed senders by name.

Criticism of Doña Flora reached a new intensity when she defended the innocence of the accused, albeit in a round-about fashion in her deposition of 14 October 1933. This defence stirred up the old animosities against her which had circulated in certain sections of León society since her arrival in the city as a newlywed many years earlier.

Despite his infamy as organiser of the accursed table, Doctor Salmerón enjoyed an overnight transformation into a man respected for his intelligence and judgement. He was widely applauded for his spontaneous action of intervening at the crime scene armed with his gastric catheter, ready to extract the stomach contents of the victim at all costs. For this reason and because the whole world had already got wind of his notebook in whose pages the evidence of Oliverio Castañeda's crimes had been collected, a great deal of expectation was building with regard to his forthcoming deposition.

He appeared before the magistrate on 28 October 1933, when the city was still buzzing with the scandal caused by Rosalío Usulután's exposé. As we saw previously, Judge Fiallos could not distance himself completely from the effects of the scandal and he was drawn into a bitter confrontation with his witness. It was because of this and what happened later that the full details of the encounter were never entered into the public record of the trial.

However, we have not yet come to that point. For the moment, Doctor Salmerón's star was rising, and this emboldened him to give some advice to the judge during an interview that he arranged with Rosalío Usulután which appeared in *El Cronista* on 14 October 1933 under the title: 'Opinions of a Man of Science':

> REPORTER: Are there any particular steps that you think Judge Fiallos should take at this stage in his investigation?
>
> INTERVIEWEE: With all due respect to the judge and without wishing to meddle in the delicate legal procedures entrusted to him, I would suggest that he should order the immediate exhumation of the bodies of Señora Marta Jerez and Señorita Matilde Contreras.
>
> REPORTER: Upon what basis do you make this suggestion?
>
> INTERVIEWEE: On the fact that we are dealing with a common thread: a single suspect who has been close to three people who died on different dates but in very similar circumstances and exhibiting very similar symptoms. If we are agreed that the last of these people died as the result of a premeditated poisoning using a toxin disguised as medication, it would not go amiss to verify whether the other two were also victims of the same toxin.
>
> REPORTER: One of these people you refer to, Señorita Matilde Contreras, is not long dead. The former however, Señora Marta Castañeda, has been interred for some time. Would it be possible to find traces of poison in her body after such a long period has elapsed?
>
> INTERVIEWEE: It is possible. Ingested poisons survive for a great many years in the tissues of the victim. Take the famous case of Bouvard, in France. In 1876, the

wife of this legal clerk died suddenly in broad daylight and years later they discovered evidence that she had been poisoned by her husband who had been jealous of his rival, M. Pécuchet, also a clerk. The exhumation took place in 1885 and an examination of the internal organs, using the methods of J. Barnes, was able to establish the presence of strychnine.

REPORTER: Do you not think that disturbing the eternal rest of these bodies would be a sacrilegious violation? Doesn't it violate the teachings of the Holy Catholic Church?

INTERVIEWEE: Not in any way. Justice, hand in hand with Science, should take precedence over sanctimonious obscurantism. Forensic medicine shows us the way, and the judge should use the sanction of the law to apply its procedures.

The judge was already envisaging the exhumation of the bodies, but he preferred to keep this a secret, not wishing to further arouse curiosity and provoke a scandal. Once the laboratory tests had been completed that afternoon he told Captain Ortiz of his plans and asked him to keep the graves under discreet surveillance. When he received the telegram from the President of the Supreme Court, he took the opportunity of acknowledging its receipt to request a special expense account of around 240 córdobas to cover the necessary costs. The breakdown is included here:

Two auxiliary forensic medical technicians: 150 córdobas
Two assistants: 40 córdobas
Detail of four gravediggers: 12 córdobas
Refreshment for gravediggers: 10 córdobas
Alcohol and other disinfectants: 10 córdobas
Transport: 8 córdobas
Contingency: 10 córdobas

On this occasion Judge Fiallos was not angered by the advice Doctor Salmerón offered, even though this risked stirring up debate on the matter, as in fact occurred. However, he was forced to make the decision public because of the doctor's opinions, in conjunction with the fact that, during the interview granted to Rosalío Usulutlán which took place in the jail, Castañeda himself dared to request the exhumation of his wife's body in order to prove his innocence.

This is clear from the statement the judge gave to Manolo Cuadra of *La Nueva Prensa*, published on 16 October 1933 as part of an article entitled 'Princess of Black Flowers':

> We found Mariano Fiallos in a taciturn and melancholy mood this stormy morning when we sought him out to uncover the truth behind the rumours concerning the exhumation of the presumed victims of poisoning in the Castañeda case.
>
> At the foot of one of the columns in the corridors of the courthouse, a blind woman in a simple tunic known as the Miserere by gossips and plaintiffs was singing her sad song. All that remained of her faded beauty was the lifeless gleam smouldering in her strange green eyes, her head bowed over her badly strung guitar. We asked the judge if he was at all disturbed by the strains of the song whose words did in truth seem to wring sadness from every chord: "I believe that in the depths of the grave, we all will wear the same shroud..."
>
> He assured us that it did not. On the other hand, the insistent sound of the rain dripping from the sodden roof tiles was capable of filling even the most stalwart of souls with melancholy. And the judge is not among the stalwart. The case that he has before him is marked by scandal, and yet it seems nothing if not tragic. The falling rain, the pathetic litany of the song, the need to break open the tombs of those women who loved and perhaps died for love...in truth this grey morning has much more to give.
>
> I tear myself away from these reflections to begin my interview. He begins: "I have decided to order the exhumation of the bodies of Marta Jerez and Matilde Contreras, and to this end have requested additional funds to cover the cost. This turn of events should not be a surprise to anyone. It is perfectly normal in cases such as these, and is not in any way intended to excite morbid curiosity

among the public. You may rest assured that I will not tolerate the presence of any persons not directly involved with the process, to ensure that these exhumations do not become a Roman circus."

"I do not wish to enter into scientific debates before having the results to hand," was his answer to a further question. "If there is strychnine present in the bodies and if it persists in corpses that have been buried for some time are questions that can only be answered by means of laboratory examinations and tests. Justice does not offer opinions, it seeks proof."

Strychnine. The lay reader will undoubtedly be grateful for a few learned references as to the origin of its fearful reputation. To this end we have accessed the library at the National Institute of the Western District under the guidance of Padre Azarías H. Pallais, sometime poet and director of the educational staff there. His poetic offerings are always signed "from Bruges in Belgium" where he was ordained, and are full of nostalgia for those days, although now he is to be found behind the walls of the old convent of San Francisco, the location of his school.

Origin and characteristics:

From the Greek "strychnos"—nightshade—the nocturnal princess of the alkaloids, princess of the black flowers, her dark embrace is capable of stopping both the most vigorous and the most feeble heart. She is also the bringer of great gifts; her enchanted breath can extinguish fever and can bring relief as an emetic, just like her sisters in arms antimony and tartar emetic. If she so desires, she may also be a tonic, so skilful is she at playing the subtle chords of the nervous system which are like a lute caressed by her invisible fingers, a skill which she shares with others of her caste: laudanum and belladonna.

Godmother to the grievously ill and the melancholic, comfort of the suicide in their mental torment, the princess of black flowers adorns their shrouds with her funeral garland. Love's avenger, sovereign of jealousies, succour of ambition, mistress of hate, mentor of betrayal, mother of pain, her name which can only be spoken in hushed and reverent tones is deceptive, bringing to mind wisteria, bougainvillea, magnolia, camellia, azalea, forget-me-nots: all early blossoms that the storm will be stripping from their stems in the drowned flower beds of our mist-shrouded gardens on this day of mourning.

She sleeps hidden inside the heart of St. Ingnatius' bean and the *nux vomica*, fruits that are forbidden in the Philippines and across Australasia. When her sleep is disturbed she spreads her funereal wings and flies out across the world bringing the gift of silence, a remedy for weariness and inconsolable sadness, the fatal burns imparted by unrequited love, and if asked she will become the accomplice of the resentful traitor and the hidden hand of revenge.

St. Ignatius' bean is a plant which appears in the tropical spring, festooning the hedges at the roadside with its bunches of black bell-like flowers, each a deep goblet which perfumes the air with a scent more intoxicating than the jasmine that even from afar brings with it drowsiness. When its flowers fall to the ground, blown by the breeze they are gathered by fair maids who weave them into their festive bonnets worn for the nightlong revelries honouring St. Ignatius: how appropriate to celebrate at night with this flower and its retinue of dreams, restlessness and shadows.

The crimson, fleshy fruit is similar in form and size to a pear, although it has nothing of the pear's sweetness, being repellent in its bitterness. Tightly packed inside are the seeds: hard-shelled and rounded, they are light brown and the size of a hazelnut.

The *nux vomica* hangs between the leaves of the luxuriant and exalted tree which gives it life. It is well protected by these prickly fronds, as if warning of the dangers of intimate acquaintance. Its seeds are flat and hard. They have an acrid smell and their shells are dark tinged with grey. The seeds are tasteless and only gain their bitterness when subjected to intense heat, when they also change colour from dark to shining white.

Deadly Effects:

The princess of black flowers arrives on silent feet and

announces her presence in the bosom of the victim, who is seized by a terrible sense of anguish that explodes into a terrible scream of desperation. It is as if in that scream the victim is overcome by a premonition of all the catastrophes and woes of the world.

The body of the victim is then helpless in her embrace: unable to speak, muscles are rigid, the head arched backwards and the face pale. Little by little the jaw clenches tight. The extremities spasm in pairs, becoming more violent with each episode as the victim struggles to break free from her implacable, constricting arms.

At some point all the muscles of the limbs and the body contract. The victim, lying rigid on their back, cannot move, their facial expression grotesque, eyes bulging, gasping for breath. Death appears imminent, but after a time the muscles relax and the head slackens. The contractions cease and the rigidity seems to pass, ushering in an ominous period of calm: the princess concedes a truce and loosens her embrace.

Remission is short in duration, however, and the victim is soon overwhelmed by another embrace more violent than the last. The convulsions come with such intensity that the victim's body is lifted up and arches over the bed. This condition, opisthontonos, reaches its maximum intensity as trismus sets in, then the limbs tense and convulse, turning the soles of the feet inwards.

In this state the victim cannot articulate sounds, and finds it ever more difficult to breathe. The heartbeat becomes irregular and their eyes stare and bulge. Reason flees the extreme nature of these paroxysms; the victim is immobilised and insensible as if dead.

This second death agony is not the last. A new interval of calm allows the re-establishment of circulation and the victim recovers some consciousness, but no liberty of movement. In time the victim suffers a burning thirst that burns the throat and heralds the onset of new convulsions, coming one after the other, each more violent than the last. The embrace now tightens.

The senses of the victim are heightened to the extent

that even the slightest touch or noise can provoke further fits. There is one last feeble attempt to escape the embrace, much shorter than the last. The princess then relinquishes her grip, casting her floral tribute of black flowers onto her victim's bosom. Her shadow has prevailed, covering all.

I read Mariano Fiallos my notes concerning the princess of black flowers. They were in my folder, ready and waiting to be attached to this dispatch. He listened to me, sombre and silent. The rain continues its dismal refrain, the arpeggios of the singing have stopped. I leave, and as I cross the courtyard I see that the blind girl is sleeping at the foot of the column, hugging her out-of-tune guitar.

By confirming his intentions, Judge Fiallos unleashed a heated debate. Foremost among those who protested were Canon Isidro Augusto Oviedo y Reyes, who expressed his opinion in an article entitled 'Stop this sacrilegious violation', which appeared in *El Centroamericano* on 17 October 1933:

Enough is enough! This inveterate free-thinker who we have never seen set foot inside the hallowed precincts of a Catholic church has rashly dared to state his opinion that the mortal remains of two esteemed devotees of the Catholic faith, who surrendered their souls aided and comforted by the Holy Mother Church, must be wrenched from their tombs and disturbed from the peace which they enjoy at the side of the Almighty. I must be silent concerning the name of this man, although the discerning reader will know to whom I refer. This godson of Voltaire and Galen sits enthroned in magisterial authority over the events that have afflicted the city of León. He has decided for himself how the case should be investigated: even if this is at the cost of the values and beliefs of the faithful and their pastors.

Enough is enough! I thought that I had heard it all except that the foreign defendant, who would do better to keep quiet out of respect for decent society and the family who generously sheltered him, has publicly expressed his wish to see the body of his sweet, unassuming wife, his in

> the eyes of God, violated in order that the aforementioned character can prove his innocence. Oh Lord, what times we live in and what things we must witness!
>
> And yet it appears this was not enough. I could barely believe my eyes when I read the latest declarations of Doctor Fiallos in *La Nueva Prensa*. In an interview given to some pencil-pusher who finds amusement in turning the words of the litany into coarse rhymes, he makes it clear that, using the powers vested in him, he will order and sanction the exhumation.
>
> He says that he does not want to create a Roman circus, as if that means anything. For an act to be barbarous it does not require witnesses. To commit an outrage it suffices that the Almighty sees the impious act and condemns it.
>
> It would not go amiss for his honour the judge to examine his own conscience and as an act of contrition reassess his intentions. Or will he demonstrate his allegiance to those Masonic rites which go against the faith that he inherited from his elders? What say you, judge? Speak, so that we know what we can expect.

Doctor Juan de Dios Darbishire gave his deposition from his own consulting room, at midday on 17 October 1933. The article by the canon was already in circulation, but the judge had no suspicion of how quickly the doctor would align himself in this debate. He was even less prepared for how evasive and unforthcoming the doctor would be, right from the start, deliberately concealing details of events of which the judge knew he had first-hand knowledge.

Although the death of the dog after it had been injected with the stomach contents showed that his student had been correct after all, Doctor Darbishire was not yet prepared to alter the stance he had taken from the moment of their abrupt parting on the afternoon of Don Carmen Contreras' death. Quite the contrary, he seemed intent on being entirely confrontational from that moment on, as is reflected in his statement.

His views can be deduced from reading his article 'In Search of Scientific Truth', published in *El Centroamericano* on 19 October 1933, which had already been sent to the newspaper before his interview with Judge Fiallos, a fact which he also hid:

In the search for scientific truth it is always wise to distance oneself from those emotions which will cloud the judgement. It is in this spirit that I would like to express some of my own opinions with the hope of establishing the basis for justice.

The recent toxicological analyses that have taken place in the laboratory at the Faculty of Pharmacy and whose results have caused such a stir on being made public are, I feel, dubious from the outset. Tests on animals like this are old-fashioned: these methods date from 1863 and have been largely side-lined due to the introduction of more modern techniques in toxicology. This is clearly evident from a brief consultation of the work of F. Moreau and A. Arnoux, to mention but two of the most illustrious contributors to this field, both of whom are professors at the Institute of Higher Studies in Criminology at Bordeaux.

The practice is fraught with huge errors. There is a simple principle, which has very strangely been ignored in the present case: when a person dies, toxic substances named ptomaines form in the tissues of the cadaver, and these, when injected into another person or an animal, produce effects similar to those of poisons, including symptoms such as convulsions.

In addition, ptomaines have similar chemical properties to plant-based alkaloids, a fact that leaves those poorly instructed in the field open to making grave errors. From this we can surmise that the process of investigation reliant on physiological tests on animals does not provide results with any merit whatsoever. Quite the reverse, they open up the possibility of painful miscarriages of justice, such as happened in the case of General Calvino, who died in Rome in 1886: tests on dogs mistook simple ptomaines for arsenic, and the error led to false accusations of political conspiracy. Or take the case of Montereau in 1893. This time the analysis confused morphine with ptomaines, and led to an innocent man being sent to the gallows for the murder of his lover, a certain Madame Moreau.

In both of these cases, dogs received injections prepared using substances recovered from internal organs, the analysis of which had supposedly detected these poisons, but there was nothing more than ptomaines. In this case however, the situation takes a more serious turn when we consider the fact that the previous analysis of the material used to inject the dogs gave doubtful and contradictory results.

This is not the end of it. Even in these old methods to which I refer, long since disregarded by modern science, they did take certain measures that were not taken here. Strychnine is known to act only on the grey matter of the medulla oblongata and the spinal chord, whereas veratrine, for instance, acts on the muscles without affecting the nervous system. In this way the material injected into the dogs should have been taken from the brain only and not a mixture of all the organs extracted. Thus I ask, what scientific argument can be made to support the hypothesis that Don Carmen Contreras or the injected animals died of strychnine poisoning?

I would now like to turn to the examination of the stomach contents taken from Don Carmen moments after his death by Doctor Atanasio Salmerón. I should like to remind my colleague, who seems to have forgotten, that one of the symptoms of strychnine poisoning is trismus: the contraction of the jaw muscles. In this case it would have been impossible to introduce the gastric catheter via the mouth without breaking the patient's teeth, something which my esteemed former student seems not to have found necessary.

I have the highest opinion of Absalón Rojas. I believe that he proceeded in good faith and I have no wish to damage his professional reputation. However, he should be aware of the fact that here in León we are not blessed with the most up to date laboratory or the best equipment and instruments. This does not reflect poorly on Absalón Rojas but speaks of the backwardness of our country.

Finally, I would like to say something about the proposed exhumation of the body of Señora Castañeda and that of Señorita Contreras. Medical history has something to say about this, from the mouth of the famous toxicologist Lautréamont, it is a cautionary tale to keep in mind in order to avoid blundering into error. The case involves a trial that took place in Bavaria in 1896 in which a veterinary surgeon named F. J. Strauss was accused of having poisoned his sister with strychnine in order to inherit the family fortune. When the body was exhumed four months after death, it was examined by a pharmacologist named Kohl. His results showed the presence of strychnine. However, two professors by the names of Blüm and Biedenkopf questioned this finding, and to demonstrate that it was false they injected seventeen dogs with strychnine. The animals were buried and then exhumed eight months later. When their remains were analysed, no strychnine was found in any of them using any of the chemical tests. Yet these animals had been injected with pure strychnine! It was all too late for the poor veterinary surgeon who had already surrendered his head to the guillotine.

In this way it behoves Judge Fiallos to think awhile on this instructive story and take care before upsetting the deeply held religious feelings that are the foundations of our society. I would not see his reputation besmirched because he has been taken in by the irresponsible counsel of certain individuals who under the pretext of science seek to fuel the sort of sensationalism worthy only of the make-believe farces confected in Hollywood to which, unfortunately, they are addicted.

The night that this article appeared, Cosme Manzo read it aloud to the members of the accursed table who were gathered at Casa Prío.

'Look how he has signed it: "Ex-inter at the Pasteur Institute, Paris, honorary member of the Medical Association of Philadelphia, United States, and three times president of the Board of Medical Regulators, León,"' said Cosme Manzo, imitating Doctor Darbishire's slight French accent.

'And look, they've included the photograph of his first Holy Communion!' said Rosalío Usulutlán taking the paper and handing it to Doctor Salmerón. 'That microscope must be the first one that ever made it into Nicaragua!'

Doctor Salmerón opened the paper and, bending over it, began underlining in red those passages that most irritated him.

'Reply to him in *El Cronista*,' suggested Rosalío Usulutlán, making an energetic mime of writing on the palm of his hand.

'Why waste our powder shooting down that vulture?' asked Cosme Manzo, shifting impatiently in his seat. 'We need to open up the can of worms. That will really put the wind in the sanctimonious old goat. It's a miracle that he didn't mention the Brotherhood of the Holy Sepulchre in his string of titles.'

'The article is ready,' said Rosalío Usulutlán, looking to Doctor Salmerón for the go-ahead. 'I'll publish it when you give the word.'

'Both, we need both,' Doctor Salmerón said, folding the paper carefully and putting it in his pocket. 'First I'm going to give him my reply. I'm the one who's going to settle that old fool's hash.'

CHAPTER THIRTY-THREE

Two Coffins are Surreptitiously Delivered to the National Guard Barracks

On the morning of 20 October 1933, Judge Fiallos woke in a foul mood. He had been suffering with a cold for the last two days and, as he had not been able to bathe again, he dressed uncomfortably. The night had been stifling, and now even the chafing of his clothes against his skin irritated him.

At the breakfast table he managed only a few sips of coffee and a morsel of French bread. His wife urged him to eat more, warning that he would feel worse with an empty stomach; in order to avoid entering into a pointless argument, he did not answer. The smell from the fried eggs on his plate turned his stomach, and the bread that he was still trying to chew as he left the table felt like a dry rag in his mouth.

As he reached the front porch of his house, the messenger boy from the Telegram Office arrived on his bicycle sounding his bell. He handed over a telegram. Leaving his wife to sign the receipt, the judge continued on his way, reading as he walked: *Supreme Court of Justice convened assess costs exhumation authorise no more fifty córdobas to be collected from Regional Finance Department.*

This telegram did not improve his mood, and realising that he would have to add this to the case dossier too, he stuffed it impatiently into his pocket along with the scrap of toilet paper he had been using to wipe his nose. In the face of such stinginess he might as well beg for contributions from passers-by on the street corner.

Although Judge Fiallos' bad mood owed a great deal to his cold, this was not the principal cause. His investigation had recently run into difficulties, most notably over the exhumations. The drastic cut in resources available as a result of the Supreme Court decision was one thing, but it was child's play in comparison to his other problems: namely interference from the National Guard in the matter of the exhumations and other no less serious matters.

The issue had been brought to his attention by Alí Vanegas on the previous afternoon. He realised that it required immediate action, and for that reason he decided that instead of heading for the court house, where he was in the habit of going before eight o'clock in order to go through the lists of witnesses and prepare the questions for the day's interrogations, he made his way to the police barracks of the National Guard in search of Captain Ortiz.

The barracks were situated in Plaza Jerez, opposite the Gónzalez Theatre. He found it a great effort to get up the stairs to the second floor of the building, where he could already hear Captain Ortiz somewhere inside verbally abusing some butchers from Telica who had been brought in for slaughtering female cattle out of season. When he saw Judge Fiallos in the doorway, Captain Ortiz tried to speed up the paperwork, imposing a fine and sending them on their way to pay it at the Finance Department. The butchers left with a recruit to whom they would need to hand over the receipt for payment of the fine before they could be freed.

Captain Ortiz wiped the sweat from his brow with the shirtsleeve of his khaki uniform, then picked up his plate of fried eggs from his desk; it was still steaming hot, and he began to eat standing up. Judge Fiallos did not sit either.

'You look like death,' commented Captain Ortiz, walking round the office with plate in hand. 'You ought to be in bed.'

'I only got up because I need to talk to you,' said Judge Fiallos hoarsely.

His mouth still full, Captain Ortiz stopped chewing. His tiny blue eyes disappeared under a deep frown.

'I would like to know who authorised Usulutlán to interview Castañeda in prison,' Judge Fiallos said, pausing to blow his nose on his scrap of toilet paper. 'I have only questioned him once as a witness, and there he is giving his ridiculous opinions about the investigation.'

'He's a prisoner of the National Guard: ours, not yours,' said Captain Ortiz, chewing contentedly once more. 'I have here a telegram from Doña Flora in which she asked General Somoza to keep him in jail. If she didn't ask your permission, it's because it is not yours to give.'

'Which means that you can do what you like with him? I'm just here for decoration?' said Judge Fiallos, swaying on his feet. In front of the desk were two metal chairs, but he dismissed the idea of sitting down.

'I have my orders from Managua,' said Captain Ortiz, dipping a piece of bread into one of the egg yolks; 'Castañeda is held by order of General Somoza, and he decides what happens to him.'

'And I suppose it was Somoza who decided which questions Usulutlán would ask the suspect,' said Judge Fiallos, fighting the urge to cough.

'Nobody gave Usulutlán a list of questions,' said Captain Ortiz, thumping his plate down on his desk.

'Of course they did. And they were written in your handwriting. Usulutlán showed them to Alí Vanegas yesterday in the court house when he came to give his deposition,' said Judge Fiallos, wringing out his scrap of toilet paper. He realised that he would soon have no option but to sit down, 'and they were written with the intention to discredit the laboratory tests.'

'You have to recognise that here in León we don't have the equipment or the chemicals that can give any guarantee,' said Captain Ortiz, studying his plate as if debating whether to carry on eating or not. 'You know what Doctor Darbishire said in his article.'

'Darbishire has already said something new. Did you also speak to him and ask him to write that stuff?' asked Judge Fiallos, moving towards one of the metal chairs, but stopping himself from grabbing onto the back for support.

'No, I haven't sunk to that level,' replied Captain Ortiz, holding his glass of lemonade up to the light before taking a gulp; 'that old grouch just wants to get even with Doctor Salmerón after their fight. But that doesn't mean that what he says isn't correct.'

'It's all just opinions, of which there are many,' said Judge Fiallos, his eyes locked on the plate smeared with the yellow egg yolk. He had no alternative but to grab the back of the chair. 'One thing I do know for certain is that the National Guard want to take the investigation to Managua, and that they are planning the illegal exhumation of the bodies.'

'Who told you that?' asked Captain Ortiz, breaking the yolk of his second egg.

'It was something else Usulutlán told Alí Vanegas,' replied Judge Fiallos, relaxing. Still resisting the urge to sit, watching Captain Ortiz with his runny egg yolk, he couldn't help being reminded of pus: 'the National Guard put in an order for two coffins at the Rosales Funeral Parlour and brought them here the night before last.'

'You believe Usulutlán?' asked Captain Ortiz, licking the egg yolk off his fork and depositing the clean utensil onto his plate. 'Next thing we know you'll be pulling up a chair with those reprobates at the accursed table.'

'I am under an obligation to find out everything pertaining to the case. I do not collect gossip, I take statements,' said Judge Fiallos, shaking his head but not letting go of the seat, trying to ignore the nausea engulfing him. 'That is why I must ask the owner of the funeral parlour to give a statement.'

'General Somoza just wants to help, to make sure that there is proper evidence,' said Captain Ortiz, striding towards the window. He rested against the window ledge and, legs braced, let off a string of resonant farts. 'The laboratory at the Ministry of Health in Managua has up-to-date equipment; here there's nothing. We may not like it but Castañeda is right.'

'So this is an army of occupation, same as the Yanks,' said Judge Fiallos. He shivered and hugged himself, 'and Somoza thinks he has the right to wipe his arse with the law.'

'You're getting all worked up about nothing. If it weren't for the National Guard, Castañeda would be home free in Guatemala,' said Captain Ortiz, returning from the window with a spring in his step. 'What's your problem with them doing the laboratory tests in Managua?'

'I'm the one who decides what should happen in this trial,' said Judge Fiallos, banging the desk top with his fist. Hearing the cutlery clatter on the plate he started, surprised by his own forcefulness. 'If you exhume those bodies I'll go to the press.'

'I'll do you a deal,' said Captain Ortiz, hoisting himself onto his desk after clearing a space among the files.

Judge Fiallos collapsed into a fit of coughing. He realised he was going to need a car to get home.

'You do the exhumation, I won't get involved,' said Captain Ortiz. As he swung his legs he noticed that one of his boot laces was undone and he put his foot on his desk to tie it up again. 'But as for the internal organs: we divide them up and send half to Managua and examine the other half here.'

'What does Somoza want?' asked Judge Fiallos, rounding the desk and slumping into the captain's chair without thinking. 'Does he want Castañeda busted out of jail, or convicted? What happens if the results obtained in Managua are negative? Castañeda gets set free, even if we find evidence of poison here?'

'I'll let you into a secret,' said Captain Ortiz, doing up his other boot lace. 'Ubico has been in contact with Somoza asking for Castañeda's head. He considers him a political threat. What's more he holds Castañeda responsible for the death of his nephew in Costa Rica.'

'That explains why Usulutlán asked the question about Rafael Ubico,' said Judge Fiallos, feeling quite at ease in the chair. He felt as if he never wanted to move again.

'You could say that,' Captain Ortiz said, getting down from his perch on the desk and taking a few steps to check that his boots were nice and tight. 'Don Fernando Guardia will be getting the details of that case to you; they are already on their way from Costa Rica. He was the one who persuaded his sister to send that second telegram. He is a very serious-minded fellow.'

'But you still haven't answered my question,' said Judge Fiallos, feeling his feverish cheeks. 'Getting the internal organs sent to Managua is just what Castañeda wants. Instead of making sure he's convicted, the National Guard are doing him a favour!'

'Don't be so naïve!' Captain Ortiz chided him, stowing the breakfast plate and utensils into a desk drawer. 'In Managua, Somoza can make sure the results come out positive. That's why he's in charge.'

Judge Fiallos' ears were stuffed up from his cold and the captain's words sounded muffled and hollow. The chair suddenly felt uncomfortably hard. He thought of the quiet darkness of his room and was overcome by the desire to get back to his own bed, to lie down between its clean and recently ironed sheets. At that moment he would have happily lain down fully dressed.

'So we have a deal, then?' Captain Ortiz shouted after him as he was already on his way to the door, walking carefully as he was a little unsteady on his feet.

'I don't do that kind of deal,' said Judge Fiallos as he reached the stairs, 'but I'm glad of the favour you've done me.'

'Favour? What favour?' asked Captain Ortiz catching up with him and barring the way.

'Releasing me from the case. Now I can resign, as of today,' Judge Fiallos said, skirting round him and starting down the stairs. They seemed much steeper than he remembered. As he descended he had the sensation of floating, his feet didn't seem to touch the steps.

'Mariano!' Captain Ortiz called, leaning over the balustrade.

Judge Fiallos continued his descent, not bothering to turn. He thought to himself that he would soon be in the Plaza Jerez where he would undoubtedly be able to flag down a car.

'This conversation never happened,' said Captain Ortiz, leaping down the stairs two at a time, 'and you can forget that nonsense about resigning!'

Judge Fiallos was crossing the hallway when Captain Ortiz caught up with him.

'For fuck's sake, you can't even take a joke!' Captain Ortiz exclaimed, grabbing the judge by the arm.

'Then give the order for the coffins to be returned to the funeral parlour,' said Judge Fiallos, pausing at the doorway and turning to face the captain. A blast of hot air from the street caught him and he felt ready to drop. 'Next time don't be so crass. The bodies must be reburied, it's only the internal organs that we need for the autopsy.'

'What date did you set for the exhumation?' asked Captain Ortiz, lowering his voice to avoid being overheard by the numerous petitioners on the benches lining the hall.

'The twenty-fifth of October. And I need you to keep a close watch. I don't want any gawpers,' said Judge Fiallos, shading his eyes with his hand. The sunlight streaming through the doorway was too bright for his eyes.

'Not even me?' asked Captain Ortiz. A woman approached, trying to attract his attention, but he motioned her to go away.

'Invite Somoza as well if you like,' Judge Fiallos said, smiling for the first time, although his head felt as if it was about to explode.

CHAPTER THIRTY-FOUR

Strychnine to Poison a Parrot

FEELINGS were running high both in support of and against the accused, and as the trial progressed the members of both camps became more and more outspoken. The depositions of all the witnesses, almost without exception, were recorded verbatim by the press and became the subject of every conversation all over Nicaragua.

The interview that Rosalío had managed to get with the prisoner in his cell was printed in many newspapers across Central America. While he was still able to publish, Rosalío's articles on the details of the trial were just as good as those of the dailies in Managua, which had posted their star reporters to León, among them Manolo Cuadra. As we know however, Rosalío was summarily dismissed from *El Cronista* after his scandalous exposé of October twenty-fifth; of which more later.

Everyone was engrossed in the trial, and the court received numerous messages offering information and advice of various kinds. Sometimes the messages were anonymous, while others were signed with either real or assumed names, and Judge Fiallos was obliged to verify the precedence and authenticity of each and every one of them. New witnesses came forward voluntarily to give evidence and he also had to investigate all of them. The press speculated ever more wildly about the motivations and circumstances behind the murders; except when they were vehemently denying that the murder had ever taken place, and among the letters sent by readers there were stories which claimed to expose previously hidden cases of other poisonings which they urged the judge to add to the charges listed against the accused.

Letters from mediums, spiritualists and palm-readers also found their way into the case dossier. One such is the following, dated 23 October 1933 and signed by Maestro Abraham Paguagua, a well-known medium based in León:

> In the presence of witnesses who are prepared to vouch for the truth of what they saw and heard, I called on the spirit of Don Carmen Contreras to appear. Several attempts failed to summon him but instead his daughter appeared, weeping and distraught. She clearly stated that Oliverio Castañeda had poisoned her by giving her a cup of coffee laced with strychnine. He took the poison from a sachet that he kept in his trouser pocket and he put the poison into the coffee while no one was watching. She said that Oliverio's pockets must be searched. She begged us to pray for her soul and she wants her mother to know that she is well and that she should not worry about her and that she should ensure that masses are said for her every day, that she doesn't want them to be sung. Also that she should donate alms for Father Mariano Dubon's charity work.

There is also a letter, signed by a certain Rosuara Madregil and sent from the Central Post Office in León on October twenty-fifth:

> Doctor Castañeda was besieged by the women in the Contreras household and he could not bear the situation any longer. He warned María del Pilar the last time that they were together on one of their many secret trysts at Don Carmen's ranch "Nuestro Amo" on the main road to Poneloya. They travelled together in Don Carmen's car, driven by Doctor Castañeda. She had said she was meeting friends but she was lying and Castañeda was waiting to pick her up at the corner of Balladares. He didn't tell her at the time that he was going to poison her sister but he did say that he had had enough and it would be better if there were no obstacles. This was before he killed Matilde; see if I'm wrong. He poisoned Don Carmen so that nobody would find out about the fraudulent accounting that Don Carmen and Doctor Castañeda were up to their necks in. Look for the books in the strong box in the office and there you will discover the whole rotten swindle.

At the time Judge Fiallos did not give this note a second thought, especially when he discovered that it had been written under a false name. This all changed, however, when Oliverio submitted a letter of his own on 15 December 1933. Dropping all pretence of courtesy and respect for the Contreras family, he made a series of revelations which dramatically altered the course of the trial. Among the things he chose to shed light on were a series of clandestine meetings with María del Pilar Contreras at the 'Nuestro Amo' ranch, and details about the fraudulent accounts. Besides this he also included material which had been reported by Rosalío in his infamous exposé and details that Doctor Salmerón had not been able to reveal in his deposition. We shall hear more about this in due course.

It should be said that some of the accusations against the prisoner which emerged in this period of the trial did turn out to be false. For example, on 18 October 1933 Rodemiro Herdocia took advantage of his opportunity to declare:

> On being asked whether he had anything to add to his deposition, the witness replied that he was aware that Doctor Castañeda was in the habit of lunching at Negro Williams canteen in Cinco Esquinas and that while he ate he would call to the dogs that were loitering at the tables in order to feed them little pieces of poisoned meat. He went on to assert that the clientele of that café and its owner were often witness to this behaviour, and to the presence of dead dogs scattered about the place after Doctor Castañeda left the establishment.

The owner of the canteen was Sinclair Williams, originally from the remote Bluefields and a one-time player in the 'Esfinge' baseball team. When Judge Fiallos questioned him concerning this matter on 21 October 1933, he replied that:

> He had no previous knowledge of Oliverio Castañeda and that he never served him at his restaurant. Furthermore, no dogs or other animals had ever been poisoned on his property and indeed he did not permit street dogs to come into the café as they annoyed the customers and that he had no dogs of his own as he did not like them.

On 28 October 1933, *La Prensa* published a story about a young poet from Masaya named Julio Valle Castillo. The article alleged that in January 1930 this youth had died suddenly at the railway station in Managua on his way home to Masaya after spending the day drinking at the Lupone Hotel in the company of Oliverio Castañeda. Prompted by this publication, Doctor Fernando Silva sent a letter to the judge on October thirtieth in which he states:

> I feel obliged to inform you that I knew Julito and that he was in Managua at that time to see me, his doctor. This young man was of impeccable character and good habits, but he was enfeebled by a heart condition from which he had suffered since childhood. The condition prevented him from engaging in all physical activity and indeed from engaging in normal day to day activities. For these reasons he could not smoke and had never even tried alcohol.
>
> This should be enough to disprove the rumours that appear to have linked my ex-patient to the name of Doctor Oliverio Castañeda, with whom he had no acquaintance whatsoever. If he died in the railway station it is because his weak heart gave out on him, something which could have happened at any moment.

On 3 November 1933, the same paper published the following information, which was added to the trial dossier:

> It is a well-known fact that certain legal documents are being sent from Costa Rica on the instruction of Don Fernando Guardia, the brother of the widow Doña Flora Contreras. These documents contain proof that while in the capital of that country as an attaché of the Guatemalan Consulate, Oliverio Castañeda poisoned two gentlemen: Don Juan Aburto of Nicaragua and Don Antonio Yglesias, a native of San José.
>
> Aburto died after spending time with Castañeda in a bout of drinking that took them to many bars across San José. At about one o'clock in the morning, the two of them returned to their shared lodgings. These lodgings were owned by a rich countess from Pomerania, Germany, for whose favours both men were competing. Castañeda it

> seems was determined to eliminate his rival, and the next morning his room-mate was found dead in their room.
>
> The case of Señor Yglesias was similar to that of Señorita Matilde Contreras. It would appear that Yglesias held a party at his home in honour of his first wedding anniversary. As they sat down to dinner, after already having consumed several drinks, Yglesias complained of a stomach ache. Oliverio, who was among the guests and is so well known for his solicitousness and consideration for others, immediately offered help saying: "Look, Yglesias my friend, I have a sure-fire cure for this," adding as he rose from the table: "I'll be back in a moment, I'll bring you some. Ladies and gentlemen, please wait until I return before starting the meal."
>
> Minutes later Castañeda was back with his "sure-fire cure" which he gave to Yglesias. The party got underway, and as the night ended everyone returned to their own homes.
>
> On the following day San José woke to a terrible tragedy: the young and beautiful wife of Don Antonio Yglesias found that she had been sleeping next to his lifeless corpse.

The court in León received no further information concerning the death of Yglesias. However, two days after this story appeared the same paper published this telegram from Managua:

> Dr. Pedro J. Chamorro Zelaya
> Editor of *La Prensa*
> Calle del Triunfo
> León
> Extremely surprised to hear news of own death by poison. Find myself still in land of living enjoying excellent health. When living Costa Rica took care never drink outside home. Never met Castañeda nor courted European countesses. Am man of simple pleasures and married young good lady from Cartago blissfully satisfied in married life. Invite you my business offices toast my health and yours.
> Juan Aburto
> Agent for Murray & Lahmann
> 1 block down from el Arbolito

On the basis of this telegram Judge Fiallos dismissed both allegations as fantasy. Having said this, thanks to Captain Anastasio J. Ortiz we already know that Don Fernando Guardia was in the process of gathering evidence linking Castañeda to another death: that of the young Rafael Ubico. We also know that when Captain Ortiz granted Rosalío the interview with Castañeda in prison, it had been on the condition that the journalist should question the accused about this case.

On 23 November 1933 Judge Fiallos added certain authenticated legal documents from Costa Rica to the case dossier on the request of Don Fernando Guardia. Parts of the three most important of these have been included here and, as the reader will discover, they contain elements of the Aburto story picked up by *La Prensa*:

a) The deposition given by Señorita Sophie Marie Gerlach Diers, forty years of age, single, German national, proprietor of Alemana boarding house who gave evidence on 31 October 1933 before the Public Notary Daniel Camacho:

> The young Rafael Ubico, first secretary of the Guatemalan Consulate, lived at my lodging house over several months. His impeccable behaviour and his charming manner meant that he got on well with all the other guests and indeed myself.
>
> In November 1929, although I cannot remember the precise date, Ubico attended the wedding of Señorita Lily Rohrmoser and returned to his lodgings at three o'clock in the morning. From my room I could hear him talking to another person saying: "I'll get the money." I didn't hear what the other person said but he went off in the car they had arrived in.
>
> I went out early the following morning, I didn't hear anything from his room. While I was out, Ubico called for Victoria, one of the chambermaids, and told her that as he wasn't feeling well he didn't want any breakfast and asked for just some orange juice instead. He also asked her to make a telephone call to his friend, Oliverio Castañeda, the second secretary at the Guatemalan Consulate, as he wanted to see him to go over some business because he didn't feel able to go in to work.

When I came home it was probably around about nine-thirty. While I was in my room I could hear Ubico complaining in his room and calling for the waiter, José Muñoz. I asked the waiter to tell me what was going on, and he said that Ubico had calmed down. However, he was still groaning, and so I went to the young man's room so that I could assess the situation for myself.

What I found gave me cause for concern. He was having terrible convulsions: all the blood seemed to have run from his head and his face was changing colour from blue to white. I tried to get the circulation going by rubbing him all over and while I was doing this he said to me: "Oh, Fräulein Sophie, I am dying, I've been poisoned." I asked him what he had taken and he replied, "I sent Oliverio to get me some magnesium citrate and he has given me poison!"

At that moment Castañeda came in, having just called a Guatemalan doctor whose name I don't recall. While I was within earshot Ubico asked his friend: "What have you given me, Oliverio? You've poisoned me!" I decided to ask the same question for myself and he answered, very calmly: "I brought some Bromo-Seltzer. How could I poison you!" So saying he took a little blue medicine bottle from the bedside table and showed it to me. Speaking very quietly, Ubico added: "And what was in the tablets you gave me?" "Bicarbonate of soda, the pharmacist recommended both," said Castañeda and he laughed, which I found most distasteful.

Minutes later, the Guatemalan doctor Castañeda had called arrived and immediately gave the patient an injection of camphor oil. The convulsions subsided, but as his condition seemed to be worsening I called for Doctor Mariano Figueres, who on examining the patient diagnosed acute poisoning. Ubico was overcome by another even worse convulsion, and Doctor Figueres confided in me that the case was hopeless. The Guatemalan doctor gave him one last injection of camphor but it was not long until he passed away following another brief convulsion. Ubico's last words were: "Oh Fräulein, I am dying. My poor father..." He squeezed my hand. This would have been between eleven and twelve o'clock.

I never forgot Ubico's accusations of poisoning and I decided to call in the police. They sent some detectives to the lodging house and took statements, but then I heard nothing more. Although life went on, every time I recalled that poor youth's suffering I would think of how Castañeda was still walking freely in the streets without anyone investigating this crime. I met him several times and he always gave me a rather provocative look of defiance which I confronted fearlessly, all the time wanting to shout out: "You murderer!"

On the day after Ubico died, the priest Dieter Masur, a compatriot of mine, came to visit and when we talked about what had happened he asked to see the victim's room. We found some of the powders Ubico had been given on the washstand and we collected them carefully on a piece of paper. The priest took these powders to the San Juan de Dios Hospital where he gave them to Anselma, one of the Sisters of Mercy, so that she could test them on one of the many dogs who come to the hospital to be fed. Father Masur later told me that the dog that had taken the powders never came back to the hospital, and so they presumed he had been poisoned and died.

I should tell you also of something that happened two days before the tragedy: a young man came to the door of the lodging house and was seen by the waiter José Muñoz. The latter informed me that the youth had come to see Ubico and finding him not at home left a message to the effect that he should beware of the envy of a close friend. As it was dinner time I didn't bother to come out, but from where I was sitting I could make out that he was a short man about eighteen years old, dressed quite poorly in his shirtsleeves and without shoes or even a hat.

Now that I am told that Castañeda is a prisoner in Nicaragua accused of poisoning an entire family of decent people, I am no longer in any doubt that he was responsible for young Ubico's death. Had the authorities pursued the matter at the time none of this would have happened.

•

b) The deposition given by Samuel Rovinski, a respected pharmacist, married, thirty years of age, to the same Public Notary:

> I was a personal friend of the young Guatemalan diplomat, Don Rafael Ubico Zebadúa and it was he who introduced me to his compatriot, also in the diplomatic service, Oliverio Castañeda. Both these young men led a bohemian lifestyle and they were given to making tasteless jokes at the expense of those in authority.
>
> At the time I was just finishing my studies to qualify as a pharmacist and I had a job in the Francesa Drugstore. I often attended at the counter and had the opportunity to serve both young men when they came in to get their toiletries and the hangover remedies, which they required quite frequently.
>
> On several occasions, Ubico asked me for strychnine. He told me it was to poison the local cats that kept him awake at night, and I supplied him with up to three grams each time. I didn't note these transactions in the pharmacy record book, which we are obliged to keep, because the quantities were so small and I did not charge him. Castañeda joined in with the task of poisoning the cats: he knew their names off by heart and kept an account of how many had been killed and who their owners were.
>
> On the day that Ubico died, Castañeda came in between eight and nine o'clock in the morning, asking to buy some bicarbonate for Ubico, who was once again suffering the effects of a hangover. I recommended that he would do better to take some Bromo-Seltzer instead because it was a newly imported commercial medicine and very effective. He insisted on taking the bicarbonate as well, so I prepared some for him in tablet form (type number 4).
>
> After he had paid, Castañeda said to me: "I'd also like to get a little strychnine to kill the German's parrot." He went on to explain that Ubico found said parrot extremely irritating because it woke in the early hours every morning and made a horrendous noise. To oblige him I gave him four grams of the aforementioned poison for free.

This would have been sufficient to kill two adults but the bigger quantity would be necessary because the parrot would have to be coaxed into taking several pecks as it would find the taste so bitter. I didn't note this transaction either and wrapped the strychnine in a twist of waxed paper. I didn't notice anything untoward in Castañeda's manner; he was as easy-going and talkative as ever.

When I was on my way back to the drugstore after lunch, a friend of mine accosted me on the street and told me that Ubico had died. Concerned, I went straight to the Alemana boarding house. I did not see the body because the police detectives had already begun their investigations and I wasn't allowed into his room. The word was that he had died of poisoning. My thoughts went immediately to the strychnine I had given to Castañeda only hours before, and I was in a quandary: although the matter was serious, I didn't have the guts to tell the detectives who were there.

I was just about to leave when Castañeda came out and, seeing me, he approached, saying: "Well, there we are Samuel, the parrot is saved. It isn't going to bother Ubico anymore, so why should I poison it? You can have the stuff back." I was shocked by his words just as I was shocked by his behaviour over the following days. Indeed, his behaviour was a source of grief and I would even say scandal as far as the other friends of the deceased were concerned; he displayed such a nonchalant attitude during the memorial service that took place at the Merced church and later on the train journey when we accompanied the body to Puntarenas.

During that journey he displayed inordinate calm, such incredible indifference; I would almost say an unimaginable disrespect. All of his friends reprimanded him: he chatted, smoked, joked about and laughed. Worse, he spent most of his time chasing after the daughter of the Guatemalan ambassador, a girl whose pet name was "Coconi"; he offered her cold drinks and sweets as if he were on a pleasure outing rather than the more sombre mission of accompanying his friend's dead body. He didn't even try to hide his flirting, constantly hanging around her seat.

Much later, Castañeda came into the drugstore on several occasions to buy his soap and dental powders, but he never again mentioned returning the poison. Now that I have heard the news from Nicaragua, I am convinced he poisoned Ubico to get him out of the way in order to replace him as first secretary in the Consulate.

c) The autopsy report completed on the corpse by the forensic pathologist Doctor Abel Pacheco on 22 November 1929 in the mortuary at San Juan de Dios Hospital which, in its concluding paragraphs, reads:

> The autopsy has been carried out in accordance with the law and from its findings the following conclusions can be made: blockage of spleen, the liver and the kidney; the blood in the aforementioned organs is liquid, dark in colour and there is bloody foam in the lungs indicating that the cause of death was probably acute intoxication.
>
> Histology of the organs showed a dark growth in the renal tubules and blockages in the spleen's white pulp. The liver was equally congested. I exclude the possibility of acute alcohol poisoning. The presence of poison needs to be verified using the appropriate chemical tests.

These tests were never done, or at least they were not among the documents sent from Costa Rica to the court in León. Nevertheless, the autopsy report and the depositions that had been collected were among the evidence that Judge Fiallos cited when he formally issued the charges against Oliverio Castañeda on 28 November 1933: a count of parricide against his wife, Marta Jerez, and first degree murder against both Matilde Contreras Guardia and Carmen Contreras Reyes.

After the indictment had been read out, a voice in the crowd packed into the corridors of the courthouse shouted: 'He's taken the first step up to the gallows!'

But, as Manolo Cuadra points out, this was a lone voice. The majority of those gathered were rooting enthusiastically in favour of Oliverio Castañeda.

CHAPTER THIRTY-FIVE

Cave Ne Cadas, Doctus Magister!

As evening fell on October twenty-fifth, and once the exhumations had been completed, Captain Anastasio J. Ortiz left the Guadalupe Cemetery bent on teaching Doctor Atanasio Salmerón a lesson. He was determined to lock him in the cells without further delay.

The edition of *La Cronista* containing Rosalío Usulutlán's scandalous exposé had just appeared, and the captain was in no doubt that the man behind this outrage was none other than the ringleader of that band of jokers from the accursed table.

All of his efforts to contact the headquarters of the National Guard in Managua were in vain because the rain had brought the lines down. Events conspired to increase the delay and it wasn't until many days later on November twelfth that the orders finally arrived. On the afternoon of that day, Doctor Salmerón was arrested outside his surgery in a great show of force.

It is best at this point to explore some of the opinions that Captain Ortiz held concerning the character of Doctor Salmerón and which he aired in his deposition of October twenty-seventh, parts of which have already been cited. In this way the reader will be able to better appreciate the direction his thoughts were taking:

> I repeat that I had very little trust in Doctor Salmerón as he is always sticking his nose into whatever gossip he hears, making him the leader of the slanderers, as Canon Oviedo y Reyes rightly termed him from the pulpit recently. He has turned the Casa Prío into a production line for scandalous pamphlets. He is a dangerous individual of shady character and should not be trusted by anyone as a

doctor since he spends most of his time engaged in unsavoury activities, along with his minions.

I know all this because it is my job to know and I have been investigating who it is who has been secretly compiling the Testament of Judas. This appalling pamphlet which appears, stuffed under our doors every Easter Saturday, bears no printer's mark. Within the pages of this malicious document every decent citizen in León is caricatured, given a special nick-name that pokes fun at their physical defects, and insults them with brutal sarcasm. They make light of revealing the most compromising secrets of citizens' private lives, even to the point of driving their victims to the grave. This is what happened in the case of Doña Chepita, the widow of Don Lacayo; she became gravely ill after they used one of their libellous publications to expose a supposed affair that her husband had been having with one of their long-serving domestics.

Equally obscene are the nominations for the crown of King Ugly which are put out around the time of the university carnival week. Overseen by the same people I have mentioned, not even the most virtuous priests nor the pious matrons who work in our sacred orders escape their notice. Often their dangerous allegations alluding to adultery and concubinage have caused terrible rifts between families and even led to gun fights.

For these reasons, I must stress that those amoral gangsters, with Doctor Salmerón foremost among them, have no other interest in this case than to take out their sense of social injustice by attacking the honour of the Contreras family. This family has become their prey as has been demonstrated by the so-called journalism touted in *La Cronista*, which I have already mentioned in the course of this statement. This insult to decency should not go unpunished for any reason; this time Doctor Salmerón has truly overstepped the mark.

As we know, before the scandal broke Captain Ortiz had not had any scruples about using the services of Rosalío Usulutlán, one of the Doctor Salmerón's minions, to undermine Judge Fiallos' investigations. The afternoon of October thirteenth, he went to the offices of *La Cronista* to find Rosalío with the offer of an exclusive interview with Oliverio Castañeda in jail. He knew full well that this offer was, in the final analysis, actually directed at Doctor Salmerón.

That evening, Rosalío was full of excitement when he arrived at Casa Prío bringing news of the surprise visit he had received. Doctor Salmerón listened, not without some surprise. He realised what Captain Ortiz was up to from the questions that he had insisted be part of the interview as one of the conditions for granting it, but he decided not to worry about it any further. He gave his consent for the journalist to go ahead and keep his appointment the following day at the jail; he felt it was a calculated risk.

For Doctor Salmerón, the tests that had been done in the university laboratories had restored his scientific reputation, and left no room for doubt in the matter. He was sure that once the exhumations had taken place, as Judge Fiallos had intimated would happen in the short interview had given to *El Cronista* that afternoon, tests on the internal organs would only add further weight to his theories.

Nothing made him suspect that his old mentor, Doctor Darbishire, would throw a spanner in the works by so emphatically questioning the methods used. He was so sure of himself that if anything he was fully expecting the old man to eventually overcome his ill-temper and pride and, as in the past, come round to his way of thinking. In this spirit of reconciliation he had been preparing himself mentally to let bygones be bygones and forget the insult he had received.

His plan was to put the prisoner on the defensive, and to further this end he went through the full set of questions with Rosalío, adding in a few of his own. He was, however, careful to steer away from topics that he wished to save for when he was called to give his own deposition. The secret letters and the amorous intrigue were also to be revealed later in Rosalío's exposé.

After the prison interview had been published, Doctor Salmerón found himself entirely wrong-footed. On 18 October 1933 he got hold of a copy of *El Centroamericano* containing Doctor Darbishire's article after Cosme Manzo had finished reading it aloud.

He couldn't help feeling offended by the contempt the old man had shown for him.

The strong correlation between Doctor Darbishire's opinions and those expressed by Castañeda endangered the course of the trial, since if the validity of the laboratory tests was called into question then Judge Fiallos might lose courage, and worse still, the Contreras family might be put off pursuing the matter. It had only been a few days ago that, after gentle persuasion by her own doctor, Doña Flora had decided to retract her demand for the prisoner to be set free. It was more than likely that she might change her mind again.

The article suggested that the old man had spent many days deliberating over his course of action; he had researched his material taking data from his own books, and the attacks he made on Doctor Salmerón were so elaborately crafted that they amply demonstrated he was now his sworn enemy. It was not only the younger man's professional reputation that was at stake, but the whole trial process, so there was nothing for it but to reply.

'Your mentor is slamming the door in your face again!' said Cosme Manzo, delicately picking his nose. 'It's like he's kicking you out of the house all over again.'

'It's not the first time it's happened,' said Doctor Salmerón, engrossed in his task of underlining in red certain paragraphs in the article. 'I have had the honour to be run out of the Contreras residence by none other than Oliverio Castañeda.'

'From the love nest,' said Cosme Manzo, extracting something from his nose and wiping it on his trouser leg. 'He was the lord and master in that house and you went and crapped on his dreams. Don't you forget it, Doctor!'

'And Judge Fiallos banished me from the gates of the university,' said Doctor Salmerón, underlining a line with such force that the paper tore. 'You could say that being kicked out of places is my speciality.'

'It's all about the same thing, they have never accepted you because you aren't one of them,' said Cosme Manzo, trembling with emotion. 'The judge is frightened and doesn't know how to contain the flames of the fire he's started. And the old man just wants to bury the whole thing because it's rich people's stuff.'

'And Tacho Ortiz, he's one of them,' said Captain Prío taking out the file where he kept IOU's. 'What's his game risking more scandal taking the case to Managua?'

'There's more to that than meets the eye,' said Cosme Manzo, picking up one of the IOU's to read it. 'You're going to go bust, Captain. It seems nobody wants to pay for their drinks.'

'If he could, Ortiz would take Oliverio Castañeda to Managua. Then they could shoot him and all this palaver would be finished,' said Rosalío as he came back from the toilet buttoning his fly.

'The National Guard can do what they like,' said Doctor Salmerón, glancing up at Rosalío and brandishing his pencil. 'Somoza wants the rich families in León on his side. I think Rosalío is onto something.'

'Because Somoza is still a creole even if he is married to a Debayle,' said Captain Prío, tearing up one of the IOU's. 'This is all I have left to remember Doctor Ayón. He died and left without paying.'

'A creole like me,' said Doctor Salmerón, smiling sadly.

'But you don't have stripes,' said Cosme Manzo, returning his sad smile; 'and you don't have Yankee guns. Don't tear those, Captain. Keep them, you could have a museum: "The IOU's of famous men".'

'You're right, I don't have any stripes. My ammunition is all here though,' said Doctor Salmerón, pursing his lips and looking meaningfully at his Casa Squibb notebook.

'Well, it wouldn't be any skin off our noses if the guards want to have Oliverio Castañeda shot,' said Rosalío, who was now bent over scanning the floor for one of his fly-buttons which had just come off.

'It wasn't me who told him to start poisoning people,' Doctor Salmerón said, peering under the table at Rosalío who was now down there on all fours. 'Captain, do you have any IOU's belonging to Castañeda? You'll need to hurry if you want them paid.'

'If I did, I'd waive them. The way things are for him, he won't be going far,' said Captain Prío, tearing up another IOU. 'Oviedo the Balloon won't be getting credit here any longer. I'm going to have to ask his father to pay me.'

'The way things are for Castañeda,' said Doctor Salmerón, folding his paper and putting it in his pocket, 'he'll soon be carried out of prison shoulder high in a procession led by Doctor Darbishire!'

Rosalío realised that Doctor Salmerón was about to leave. He gave up the search for his button, and still on his knees took a sheaf of papers from inside his shirt.

'Ah, here is the beautifully crafted exposé,' said Cosme Manzo, reaching out his hand. 'Pass it here my good sir. I will read it.'

'Another time. Now I must be off to settle a score with my beloved mentor. That's one person who isn't going to get away from me without paying,' Doctor Salmerón said, already on his feet. He rubbed his hands saying, 'Captain, may I suggest you let Manzo take care of Oviedo the Balloon's IOUs.'

'I've already thought of a title, "True love is a once in a lifetime thing",' said Rosalío, putting the sheaf of papers back inside his shirt. Delighted at his own inventiveness, he looked up at them from the floor, expectantly.

'I don't like it,' said Cosme Manzo, waving his hand dismissively. 'It needs more impact. How much does Oviedo the Balloon owe you, Captain?'

'It adds up to over sixty pesos,' said Captain Prío, taking out the handful of IOU's from the 'O' section of the concertina file.

'We'll think about the title later,' said Doctor Salmerón, patting Rosalío by the shoulder. 'We have time on our hands.'

'Some of us may,' said Cosme Manzo, scraping his chair back as he got up. 'Give me those IOU's, Captain. I'll get Oviedo the Balloon to pay up. I'll take a few drinks on the house as commission.'

Back at home, Doctor Salmerón worked feverishly until the early hours of the morning preparing his riposte to Doctor Darbishire. Over the following days he polished it, making numerous drafts and going to the library at the university to consult the most respected toxicology books and analytical chemistry manuals.

His finished article can be found in the edition of *El Cronista* published on 21 October 1933:

A MEDICAL SCHOLAR'S SCHOOLBOY ERRORS

The opinions recently expressed by my esteemed and wise mentor Doctor Darbishire have caused me the deepest distress. He has abandoned his usual modest stance and sallied forth onto the field of battle lance at the ready to launch a frenzied attack on the windmills which in his confusion he has mistaken for loathsome giants. In the bewilderment of this head-on collision he has perhaps inadvertently destroyed the professional reputations of our own chemical experts, who are serious and dedicated professionals.

The conscientious Absalón Rojas has been battered by his attack. Someone who did not study his science in London or Paris, but only because his humble background did not allow him the privilege of going further afield than the cloisters of our own greatest seat of learning. A privilege that my beloved and under-appreciated mentor fully benefited from; he had the luck to be born with a silver spoon in his mouth.

My beloved but never moderate mentor seems to see himself as Zeus himself. In deigning to descend from Olympus on high to the plains where we mortals dwell, he seems to think that he can sweep in declaring that we ignorant peasants must have undoubtedly confused alkaloids with simple ptomaines. As if no one in Nicaragua was aware that the process of decomposition generates toxins!

Perhaps my heroic mentor requires me to refresh his memory by recalling the case of a certain Doctor Desiderio Rosales, a native of Masaya and educated in the same European universities as yourself, and indeed who also came back with a young French wife who failed to acclimatise to our shores. While conducting an autopsy, he happened to cut himself with the scalpel, and without hesitation he requested that his assistant amputate the digit so contaminated with ptomaines. This happened in 1896 in the operating theatre at San Vicente Hospital in Masaya, which was founded by Doctor Rosales himself. My dear mentor appears to have forgotten this story although he used to repeat it frequently as part of his lectures.

The medical professionals in Nicaragua are scientists, not witch doctors, and the existence of ptomaines has been common knowledge for many years. They are not news to us and we are also entirely capable of distinguishing these chemicals from plant-derived poisons. Has my mentor forgotten that it was he himself who showed me how easy it is to identify ptomaines, and due to their volatility, to eliminate them using ether.

This eminent doctor states that in León we do not have access to the correct reagents to complete the proper toxicological tests. Nothing could be further from the truth. Every doctor and every scientist knows that it is a straightforward process to precipitate both arsenic and strychnine using M. Thatcher's reagent, of which we have more than enough. Moreover, the precipitation of strychnine is so singular that it cannot be confused with any other substance such as a ptomaine or another alkaloid. According to Le Pen, the isolation of strychnine involves hydrolysis followed by a reaction with sodium nitrate. And take note, Doctor Darbishire: it is irrefutable, from here to Cochinchina.

There is also no weight to my one-time mentor's argument that the onset of trismus in a strychnine victim makes it impossible to extract gastric fluid orally using a rubber tube. It is true that it requires great force and skill, as I was required to demonstrate in the case of Señor Contreras. However, if Doctor Darbishire is still doubtful about the skills he himself taught me on the wards at the San Juan de Dios Hospital then I refer him to Fraga who, in his "Treatise on General Applied Toxicology" (and I cite a Spanish author since, unlike my mentor, I am not fluent in foreign languages), speaks of twelve cases of poisoning among the records kept by hospitals in Madrid, where a tube was inserted via the mouth without recourse to any such barbaric procedure as breaking their teeth with a chisel.

As to the veiled mockery my eminent mentor indulges in with regard to the various animal tests carried out at the university, I have only two things to say. Firstly, I am sure that Doctor Darbishire does not wish to imply that these experiments should have taken place on human beings, hence it was necessary to use animals; and secondly that if the animals apparently succumbed to the ravages of strychnine, it was because the toxic substance was present as demonstrated by the specific symptoms of convulsions. Simple ptomaines would not do this, it could only have been an alkaloid, the strychnine which had already been identified through chemical analysis of the internal organs, something that Doctor Darbishire chooses to doubt. Of course, he will say that one of the results was negative; in which case I say, look at the weight of evidence: the application of logic demonstrates on which side the truth lies.

Finally, my mentor's attempts to show off his wisdom can have only one purpose, and that is to discredit the process of exhumation the judge has proposed. He cites a famous example in which a legion of dogs was poisoned, then buried and on examination of the remains no trace of strychnine was found.

My illustrious mentor seems to forget that we are dealing with human beings, and not all of us share his delight in commanding canine legions. He must know that the digestive processes of dogs are not comparable to those of humans; they are able to process poisons rapidly, eliminating them from their systems in their sweat, urine and faeces. The same is true of other animals. The mole is able to eat a snake's head and survive; the goat can eat nightshade berries without being poisoned by the atropine they contain, and finally we have the ostrich which can swallow nux vomica as easily as if it were an avocado.

This is not the case with humans. If either Señora Castañeda or Señorita Contreras died of poisoning, then the chemical responsible will still be present in their tissues, even after a thousand years. In the dog, on the other hand, as with the mole, the goat and the ostrich, the poisonous residue does not persist.

It is not the case that we are backward. León is not trapped in the scientific dark ages. This is a case of professionalism, of being responsible and of making carefully judged statements of opinion so that we do not mislead.

Take my advice as payment for all that you gave me in

better times, because this is the only way to avoid serving the interests of that cunning criminal who must be feeling very secure after reading your words. He could never have hoped that the personal doctor of his victims would be so useful in helping to open the prison gates. My congratulations to him!

I will take my leave now and express my gratitude to you for all your wise teachings which have never been wasted.

Cave ne cadas, Doctus Magister!

CHAPTER THIRTY-SIX

The Bodies are Exhumed After a Day's Delay

THE EXHUMATIONS had been due to begin at eight on the morning of 24 October 1933, but they were delayed by a day because of the intense rain that fell on León throughout that day and only eased as night fell.

The proceedings had been kept a closely guarded secret in order to avoid unwanted observers, but the postponement meant the element of surprise was lost. Judge Fiallos became aware of this the moment he stepped out of his front door early that morning to make his way to the cemetery wrapped in his voluminous oilskin cape. He found all of his neighbours thronging the sidewalk eager to see him off as he got into the hire-car where Alí Vanegas was waiting for him.

All along their route, from the cathedral to the church of Guadalupe, they saw what amounted to a procession heading towards the cemetery. Outside the cathedral, the street-food sellers were already set up with their carts, tents and booths, and when the car arrived it had to hoot its horn loudly to make them get out of the way.

There was a similar atmosphere of excitement in the neighbourhood surrounding the XXI precinct. People were waiting for Oliverio Castañeda to appear, since he had been summoned to identify the bodies. Rosalío Usulutlán chronicles these events in his extensive and final report: 'The Sky Mourns Tragic Exhumation.' The article appeared in *El Cronista* on October twenty-seventh, shortly after his dismissal:

> The crowd seemed to take its cue from the subdued demeanour of the prisoner. They had arrived unbidden and watched in silence under the persistent rain as the prisoner

descended the steps from the prison gate. The silence was almost respectful and not without piety; some men, they may have been simple carters or labourers, even took off their hats as the prisoner went by. The prisoner himself was attired in his usual mourning dress, shirt and tie impeccable, and his black boots also polished to a lustrous shine. His face, however, seemed gaunt and haggard, as if sleepless nights had robbed him of his usual panache. Even more strangely for him, his chin sported a beard of several days' growth which made him seem older than his years. I noticed that he had a linen sheet over one arm, which I managed to ask him about as he passed. The sheet was apparently destined for the body of his wife. In his feverish hands he carried a spray of gardenias, which had wilted long before.

As if by magic, one of the women in the crowd pulled a bunch of fresh dahlias from under a towel and handed them to the prisoner in exchange for his withered tribute. He departed in an official car with Captain Ortiz and two National Guardsmen, their shotguns at the ready. The car drove slowly and the crowd, still in silence, followed it on foot towards the cemetery.

Despite the vigilance of the National Guard sentries, some journalists managed to gain access to the cemetery by climbing over an unguarded section of the wall. Among them were our own Rosalío and the poet Manolo Cuadra. The proceedings took almost ten hours to complete and later we will make use of both of their stories in conjunction with the two judicial reports, the second of which was finished sometime after six o'clock that evening.

Judge Fiallos had named Doctors Alejandro Sequeira Rivas and Segundo Barrera to act as assistants to the forensic pathologist, Doctor Escolástico Lara. They had agreed reluctantly. Two medical students, Sergio Martínez and Hernán Solórzano, were also present to help with the autopsy. Absalón Rojas was on hand as the expert chemist and to be on hand to receive the internal organs in sealed containers. In addition there were the caretaker of the Guadalupe cemetery, Omar Cabezas, the accused and his guards, headed by Captain Ortiz, and a gang of gravediggers and labourers who had all been signed up in advance. Of course, Judge Fiallos and his secretary were also in attendance, to ensure proper judicial process.

It is a matter of official record that no other authorities either from the departments of public health or from the courts wished to be represented, although they had been notified by the Judge. This is stated in the same section of the report relating to the initial part of the day's proceedings:

> The presiding judge swore-in all the medical experts and other assistants, the caretaker of the cemetery, as well as the accused Oliverio Castañeda. He warned them of the penalties for giving false witness in a criminal trial.
>
> He asked the caretaker for the cemetery record books in order to locate firstly, the tomb of Señora Marta Jerez de Castañeda. The burial was annotated in volumes eight and nine of the records, and according to the available information it took place on February fourteenth of this year, the body being interred on a plot owned by General Carlos Castro Wassmer in plot number 15 southeast, in the first grave number 113 north. This was confirmed by the caretaker and Doctor Castañeda himself when they were shown the grave.
>
> The grave was excavated and the coffin removed. The coffin was ovoid, wine-coloured and in a good state of preservation. The lid of the coffin was removed, revealing the body within, wrapped head to toe in a shroud of white linen. The shroud was removed and after cautioning Doctor Castañeda that he was under oath, the judge asked him to identify the body. He confirmed that it was indeed the body of his defunct wife, Marta Jerez de Castañeda.

To see how Rosalío Usulután told the story we must refer back to his article: 'The Sky Mourns Tragic Exhumation':

> Before the coffin containing the mortal remains of Marta Jerez could be opened, cotton masks were distributed to those present; both those involved in the exhumation and those who were merely bystanders. These masks, de-

signed to cover the mouth and nose, were impregnated with antiseptic. When the accused was offered one of these masks he refused it, throwing it to the ground and exclaiming: "Thank you, I don't need it."

The few members of the press who had managed to gain access were also offered masks. I realise that our presence was not sanctioned by him and I thank the judge for his gentlemanly attitude in not opposing this measure. He would have been well within his rights to refuse us access to these masks and even expel us from that sacred ground. I hope that the restrained tone of this article will repay his gesture of goodwill, since sensationalism of any kind is precisely what the judge wished to avoid.

The coffin holding Marta's remains was opened at precisely nine-fifty in the morning. A labourer used a crowbar to prise off the coffin lid; as it penetrated the wood there was a loud creak and the body, wrapped in its shroud, was revealed to all those present. She wore a scapular bearing the emblem of the Holy Third Order along with several devotional medals pinned to her chest.

Oliverio Castañeda had been waiting behind the Debayle family mausoleum. It was only when the body was revealed and Judge Fiallos called for him to be brought over that the prisoner showed any emotion. Accompanied by Captain Ortiz, the prisoner came to stand at the foot of the coffin. In a solemn voice the judge asked: "Do you recognise the body?" Owing to the stench he had had to cover his nose with his handkerchief, placing it over the antiseptic cotton mask. "Yes, I recognise it," responded the prisoner in a bewildered manner after glancing, not without tenderness, at his dead wife's lifeless body. A single tear trickled from his eye and ran down his cheek; he made no effort to wipe it away.

When the body had been formally identified, the corpse was removed from the coffin and placed inside the Debayle family mausoleum; the marble altar within providing the perfect place for the forensic pathologist to conduct the autopsy.

The rain and humidity made the gloomy interior of the

> mausoleum all the more claustrophobic, and the doctors in their white coats looked like priests engaged in some occult ritual. Guarding that hallowed precinct from their lofty pedestals were two marble angels, stern and mute.

The first autopsy results are recorded in the official report as follows:

> The corpse was found in a normal position, and showed an advanced stage of putrefaction in accordance with the length of time since burial. The soft parts of the upper and lower extremities had disappeared. The organs within the abdominal cavity and thorax were still distinct and identifiable. The brain and medulla had been rendered into a semi-solid paste. The skin on the face was coffee-coloured and sunken in appearance. The eye-sockets were empty.
>
> Once the internal organs had been removed, they were placed into six separate glass jars as follows:
>
> Jar 1: Liver and spleen
> Jar 2: Stomach and upper portion of the duodenum
> Jar 3: Uterus and bladder
> Jar 4: Heart
> Jar 5: Right kidney
> Jar 6: Brain and medulla

With the time nearing two o'clock in the afternoon, the little National Guard truck left the cemetery via the main gate, its horn bellowing like a cow. Absalón Rojas was seated next to the driver and in the back, guarded by two soldiers, were the jars. Their destination was the university laboratory where they would be stored in the fridge which was once more on loan from Casa Prío.

When the gates opened to let the truck emerge, Captain Ortiz came out onto the street, having been advised that Don Evenor Contreras was waiting for him. He had come to witness the exhumation of Matilde Contreras, acting as the family representative. Doctor Darbishire was also there. The old man, who had been invited to participate in the proceedings in his capacity as doctor to the two deceased women, had intentionally arrived late.

He had just bought a copy of *El Cronista* and was reading it seated in the driver's seat of his buggy. Rain on the previous day had delayed the sale of that day's edition, and the last few copies were being torn from the hands of the vendors by the crowds around the gates. This was the edition that contained Rosalío Usulutlán's article 'No Smoke Without Fire'.

Captain Ortiz let the two men through, and as they walked up the main avenue Doctor Darbishire handed him the copy of *El Cronista* with a knowing smile.

At two-thirty in the afternoon they began work on Matilde Contreras' tomb. The second report identifies the location as grave number 301 on plot 18 southeast in the western quarter in agreement with the Record of Burials volumes seventy-six and seventy-seven.

Manolo Cuadra offers his impressions in this dispatch from October twenty-seventh , 'The Same Shroud'.

> The blind beggar woman Miserere was not singing here as she had been that day in the law courts, but the tremulous lament of her song seemed to be carried by the cold wind that shook the tall cypresses as the remains of Marta Jerez were returned to the ground. Her body was wrapped in a linen shroud that Oliverio Castañeda had brought with him and which he himself unfolded before handing it to the undertakers.
>
> His feet sinking into the soft ground at the graveside, he cast a bouquet of dahlias into the deep hole as he mumbled a prayer which was carried away by the wind just as that song is lost in my memory. It is impossible to imagine even half of what he must have been thinking at that terrible hour; his head alone hides all the secrets of this case. Again we saw him weep passionate tears that would be difficult to feign. The remembrance of longing? Regret for his dreadful crimes? Nobody but he can know the dark source of those tears.
>
> The casket gradually disappears, this time forever as the gravediggers shovel the damp soil into the grave. We can now follow the accused as he is taken under guard to the other tomb.
>
> Don Evenor Contreras, the deceased's uncle, and

Doctor Juan de Dios Darbishire, the family doctor, make their way to the site of the new exhumation. They are accompanied by Captain Ortiz. Contreras and Castañeda do not greet one another or acknowledge each other, and while Contreras has a relaxed manner, Castañeda appears vague and awkward, although without being impolite in any way. The prisoner receives no recognition from Doctor Darbishire either, nor does Castañeda seek it.

Mariano Fiallos arrives shortly, accompanied by the doctors, the forensic expert and the gravediggers; the latter seem the worse for drink—which they have been imbibing to get them through their thankless task. With the help of the burial records the tomb is identified as before. This grave is marked only by a mound of fresh soil upon which lie wreaths and bouquets of withered flowers left over from the recent funeral. At the request of Mariano Fiallos both Contreras and Castañeda separately confirm the location of the tomb, close to the iron railings surrounding the family plot.

The gravediggers raise their shovels to begin digging in the appropriate place. Little by little, with every muffled thump of their shovels the coffin comes into view, its white surface stained by contact with the soil. When the lid is lifted, the body of the young woman can be seen, a veil of gauze covering her now unrecognisable face.

Contreras steps forward and with a nod of his head confirms his niece's identity. Castañeda is next at the foot of the grave: "It is her," he says, his voice barely audible. Once again the great wings of mystery seem to envelop him, protecting the secrets that no inquest will ever be able to discover. Did the prisoner ever love? Was it a clandestine passion or simply carnal desire? Or in the end was it just to cause harm and deceive? Was she duped into straying from the path of goodness, in love and unaware of her misadventure? And if poison was involved in her death, did her illness prevent her from seeing who was the victor and who the vanquished in this battle of love? My questions, like the quivering branches of the funereal cypresses, are taken by the wind and lost.

The work of the doctors and forensics is nearly done. Mariano Fiallos sits on the raised cement platform of another tomb, lost in his own sense of grief. Earlier I read the inscription on that tomb; it bears the name of another Matilde Contreras (1878-1929). My colleague from *El Cronista*, Rosalío Usulutlán, informs me that she died of tuberculosis in a sanatorium outside the city.

Doctor Escolástico Lara trudges towards us, the details of the autopsy in his hand. He passes them to Alí Vanegas, who is busy writing up the final report, seated upon another of the family tombs. Resting the sheets of paper on his old lizard-skin briefcase, he is trying to finish as quickly as possible so that everyone can sign the document. Although the threat of rain seems to have passed, the sky above León is tinged blood-red, and darkness will soon fall.

They proceed to the re-interment. Followed by his guards, the accused has retired, complaining of a severe headache; he is no longer needed anyway. We must also wend our way lest this article be delayed; it must be dispatched on the morning train.

In the meantime, out in the street on the far side of the cemetery wall, there is no abating the carnival atmosphere created by the rowdy mob gathered there.

As we shall discover, owing to the need to make certain amendments, there was a delay in signing the docket describing the autopsy carried out on Matilde Contreras. Its opening paragraph states:

> The body was found lying on its back with the head turned slightly to the right. The colour of the skin on the face was black and the features were considerably disfigured. The eyes had been pushed out of their sockets and the mouth and eyelids were open, the hair was dry but intact. The degree of putrefaction was consistent with the time since burial; that is, advanced Black Putrefaction. The thorax and abdomen are in a good state of preservation as are the extremities. The hands, folded over the chest, appear to have fused together.

Rosalío Usulutlán was still at the cemetery when the report was about to be signed. At this stage he had more than one reason to worry, but despite this he stayed on, and was therefore able to witness the unexpected petition that Doctor Darbishire made. He later related the episode to the accursed table.

'So the crazy old man made the request...' Doctor Salmerón said with an amused air, 'But it's not possible to tell on a corpse...'

'I think that was the only reason he turned up,' said Rosalío, who was so edgy that he found it impossible to sit down. His notes on the exhumation were clasped firmly in his hand. 'He dictated the paragraph himself: "From an external examination of the genital organs it was confirmed that these were intact, from which it can be concluded that the deceased died in a state of virginity."'

'And the forensic pathologist? What of the other doctors, how did they take it? His old enemy Doctor Barrera kept quiet?' Doctor Salmerón guffawed, slapping the table in his excitement, 'I can hardly believe it!'

'No one said a word. The judge ordered Alí Vanegas to correct the report,' said Rosalío, shuffling his papers. 'He just went along with it. They switched on the car headlamps so that he could write.'

'And Captain Ortiz had already threatened you,' said Cosme Manzo, revealing his gold teeth.

'What did he say?' asked Captain Prío, standing beside Rosalío. He seemed to be the only one to share his concern.

'When he got hold of a copy of the paper he went off to read it,' explained Rosalío sorrowfully. He left his notes on the table and continued: 'When he'd finished, he came over to where I was: "You've gone too far this time," he said, and he warned me: "you just wait."'

'Stands to reason,' said Cosme Manzo, his gold teeth flashing as he threw his head back to laugh in disdain. 'Now that we know the girl was a virgin, everything else in your exposé is obviously lies!'

'Yes, but the paper has already sacked me,' said Rosalío, fiddling incessantly with the copper stud on his shirt and moving his neck like a turkey about to be throttled. 'The boss told me: "The stuff about the exhumation is the last thing you'll publish, and only because it's already written." He was waiting for me at the door.'

'And who else has Captain Ortiz included in his threats?' asked Captain Prío, circling Rosalío cautiously.

'All of us,' said Rosalío, letting go of the stud to make a gesture including all of them. 'As we left the cemetery he shouted: "Those lying sons of bitches at Casa Prío are really in the shit now!" He made sure everyone could hear.'

'Bah, those are the protestations of a drowning man,' said Cosme Manzo, doing a little dance with his feet under the table. 'Captain, if they mess with you, just send for the fridge and see how they like watching all their bits of body rot.'

'They could really screw us,' said Captain Prío. He did not move from Rosalío's side, staring at him intently as if seeing him for the last time. 'That exposé has really touched a nerve with them.'

'But it's just a story, there are no names or anything,' said Cosme Manzo, dismissing all their worries with a shake of his head. 'Escept that this idiot went and put in that photo of Doña Flora. Who told you to do that?'

'So she's a virgin by judicial decree,' mused Doctor Salmerón; he cast a sarcastic look at Cosme Manzo and winked.

'And what are they going to do to us? Shoot us? Arghhhh!' Cosme Manzo said, pretending to cower in fear.

'Well they sacked me from the paper and now I have to live on charity,' replied Rosalío, hanging his head and thrusting his hands into his pockets. 'And although you make a joke of it, we could all end up in jail.'

'More beautiful than both her daughters put together,' said Doctor Salmerón, picking up the paper to take a closer look. 'You were onto something, Rosalío.'

'Who told you to put the picture alongside the story?' asked Cosme Manzo, getting to his feet and looking Rosalío full in the face. 'The names were all false, and then you go and put in that photo.'

'And you, who told you to go blabbing about those letters to anyone who'd listen!' Rosalío retorted. He adjusted his belt, saying: 'Anyway they won't lock us up because of the photo.'

'Well I just hope they put me in the same cell as Castañeda,' said Doctor Salmerón, fanning himself with the paper: 'then I can take his confession in peace and find out all the bits I'm missing. I don't yet know anything about those secret meetings at the "Nuestro Amo" ranch.'

'That's what this gentleman is going to find out for us,' said Cosme Manzo, patting Rosalío on the shoulder, 'and it's about time he got started.'

'Yes, you're late, Chalío,' said Doctor Salmerón, coming over so that Rosalío found himself surrounded. 'When are you off to the ranch? I need the information before I make my deposition.'

'When I've found some work,' said Rosalío, putting his hands on his hips defiantly. 'Perhaps the city council will give me some work sweeping the streets.'

'Don't be an ass, my boy; I've got a job for you!' Cosme Manzo said, pursing his lips and putting his arm round Rosalío.

'What job?' asked Rosalío, glancing at him suspiciously out of the corner of his eye.

'You can do the itty bitty codfish dance, my boy. An hourly rate of one córdoba and a bite to eat,' said Cosme Manzo, pinching his cheeks.

'Your mother can dance it,' said Rosalío, giving him the brush off and equally brusquely straightening his hat.

They broke into laughter which echoed across the now empty Plaza Jerez. From the opposite corner came the distant sounds of the film screening at the González theatre: a plaintive voice, violin music, and then muffled sobbing.

PART IV

Vistos, Resulta

OH! There was a gallant of this town,
OH! He was a gallant of our home,
OH! He came from a distant shore,
OH! And he was tired of travelling,
OH! Tell me what he was looking for,
OH! Tell me what he was a-seeking.

(Asturian Ballad)

CHAPTER THIRTY-SEVEN

Scandalous Revelations Bring Upheaval to City Society

THE TWENTY-FIFTH of October 1933 was not the most glorious day in Rosalío Usulutlán's journalistic career that Cosme Manzo had prophesied. It was in fact one of the darkest of his life. The bad luck that hit him on that day was rivalled only by that of the following days when circumstances forced him into hiding, so afraid of being put behind bars that he resorted to disguising himself in priest's robes whenever he had to venture out on any urgent matter, or even just go to the market.

At first he had been a witness to his own success. That afternoon when he'd been picked up in a car outside the cemetery to return to the *El Cronista* office he had seen the hordes of people on their way home scrambling to buy copies of the paper, which were being hawked by the vendors for one córdoba (not even the coverage of how the Sandinista forces had captured Chichigalpa had been able to command such an exorbitant price). He had also seen a man standing on the back of a cart outside the church of Guadalupe, reading aloud from the paper, while an old woman held a petrol lamp up for him to see by, and a crowd jostled around them, desperate to hear as they tried to contain their laughter.

At the same time, he had felt Captain Ortiz's threat like a stake in his heart. His journalistic ego basked in the glory of success but came to grief on the rocks of a fearful dread.

When he got out of the car he had no idea how quickly he would be subsumed in misfortune. The stench of graves was still in his nostrils and for days afterwards he would find himself sniffing his clothes. He urgently wanted to speak with his co-conspirators at the accursed table, yet despite this knew he had to write the story about the exhumations and deliver it to the typesetters ready for the morning edition. Only then would he be free to go to Casa Prío.

The owner of *El Cronista* was Absalón Barreto Sacasa, a doctor and the first cousin of President Juan Bautista Sacasa. He no longer practised, preferring to dedicate himself to dairy farming, and he never set foot in the office, giving Rosalío complete freedom to manage the news stories and editorials as he saw fit. He had only ever called Rosalío at his home when some conflict required resolution, as had happened when the Metropolitan Water Company had come under attack. When they met on the street or at the cinema he'd remind Rosalío to publish favourable articles about his cousin and the Liberal Party.

Given this precedent, Rosalío was disturbed to see Doctor Barreto come into the office. He arrived at around seven looking flushed from the sun and still wearing his riding boots caked with cow dung.

Rosalío interrupted his assiduous tapping to stand up and wish him a good evening, as affably as possible. The other man hadn't even deigned to answer him, disappearing instead into the shadows of the print-room where he'd begun remonstrating with the typesetters who'd been in the middle of disassembling the galley-proofs and redistributing the pieces of type in their cases. Moments later a group of newspaper sellers had come in demanding more copies of the fateful edition; when none could be found he had sent them packing.

Rosalío had not dared to sit down again; with one paragraph left to write he had continued to type as he stood. He pulled the page out of the typewriter and cautiously approached the chief-typesetter to hand over his copy. Just as he was about to give his instructions to place the article at the top of the front page, Doctor Barreto came up behind him and knocked the pages out of his hands.

Resisting the urge to bend and pick up the pages, Rosalío opted to head for the darkness of the toilet to relieve himself. His discretion did not do him much good. While he'd been in the act of unbuttoning his fly he heard a voice behind him announcing his dismissal: he was to be sacked immediately. The article he had just finished would be his last and only because it was already written, and had probably been paid for in his month's salary. By the time he had given up trying to urinate and returned from the toilet, Doctor Barreto had already left, taking Rosalío's typewriter with him.

The typesetters gathered round him and accompanied him to the door, where each in turn gave him a farewell embrace. This was to be his only source of consolation that day, because as soon as he reached the street his misfortunes multiplied. Walking along the sidewalk the knots of nocturnal revellers dissolved before him; rocking chairs were whisked away behind doors, which were then slammed ostentatiously. To cap it all, one old biddy, instead of fleeing had actually accosted him, and with her arms raised to heaven begun praying fervently as if to ward off the devil. He felt like a rabid dog pursued out of town by a stick-wielding mob, and he made for Casa Prío practically at a run.

As we saw earlier, his warnings were ignored at the accursed table, and so he went home to his place on Calle de la Españolita feeling more distraught than ever. On the way he had to use his hat to hide his face from the hostile gazes directed at him, and when he got there, fearing a night-time raid by the National Guard, he barricaded the front door with some chairs piled on top of a table.

The events which began to unfold the following day confirmed Rosalío's worst fears. These events were chronicled by Manolo Cuadra in a story entitled 'Bloomers and Gun-fire As Unrest Mounts', carried by *La Nueva Prensa* on 27 October 1933:

> León (via telephone). A strange occurrence, the herald of far more serious events, took place very early this morning. Passers-by are used to seeing the shop assistants at La Fama spreading yellow Bayer powders onto the sidewalk to discourage stray dogs. However, this morning they were astounded to see them engaged in the rather more unusual pursuit of using a long pole in an attempt to remove three pairs of lady's undergarments from where they had become stuck on the sign advertising Vichy-Celestins. The three pairs of bloomers, in three different colours, were hooked over the neck of the bottle used to promote the aforementioned medicinal tonic.
>
> News of the hanging bloomers, in shades of aquamarine, fuchsia and mauve according to those who were able to admire them, drew part of the crowd away from the university where they had been eagerly awaiting the start

of the tests on the internal organs taken from the recently exhumed bodies. Once the bloomers had been successfully removed, the crowd did not disperse, but turned on the house, shouting all manner of obscenities at the widow and her daughter; they even tried to entice them to come out, calling to them sweetly, using the pseudonyms given to them in the exposé written by our colleague at *El Cronista*.

The article in *El Cronista* signed by Rosalío Usulutlán is written very much in the style of Don Ricardo Palma, the celebrated author of "Peruvian Traditions". It disguises the true names of its protagonists, but it is obvious that its argument comes directly from the Castañeda drama.

At close to twelve o'clock news broke of the deaths by poisoning of more dogs and cats. This caused the noisy groups who had been coming and going between the family house and the university to become quite uncontrolled. At the same time, calls for the prisoner's release became equally overwhelming.

The rabble became increasingly unruly; stones were thrown at the windows of our Alma Mater and at the Contreras family home, including its adjoining shop, where they had to shut their doors even to their usual clientele. The situation was so tense that it was not long before Captain Anastasio J. Ortiz arrived on the scene with a detail of soldiers. He warned the rioters to leave immediately.

Far from heeding his warnings, the crowd responded with jeers and insults at which the soldiers recklessly made use of their fire-arms, shooting several rounds into the air. With this the streets emptied. From that moment on both the university and the Contreras family home were placed under the protection of the National Guard, whose sentries posted on the street corners barred the way of anyone who tried to pass. According to our sources, the guards at the university will remain in position until the tests are concluded, which is expected to be by midday. With respect to the house, it will remain under guard until further orders.

Although the exposé published by *El Cronista* included nothing that might exonerate the accused, it seems that

> the common people are openly on his side. The strength of feeling displayed on the street shows how unwilling people are to give credit to the charges laid against him. Above all else they seem impressed by the prowess in matters of the heart attributed to him by said exposé.

Captain Ortiz felt it necessary to respond to this report with the following telegram sent to Gabry Rivas, editor-in-chief at *La Nueva Prensa*:

> CONSIDER REPORTING INCIDENTS YESTERDAY LEÓN DISRESPECTFUL AND TOTALLY EXAGGERATED. ALLUSIONS TO INTIMATE GARMENTS HANGING FROM BOTTLE MISGUIDED. JOURNALISTS THIS NEWSPAPER SHOULD CHECK FACTS BEFORE FUEL OBSCENE RUMOURS. TRUE UNDESIRABLES ATTEMPTED PROVOKE UNREST THROWING STONES AT UNIVERSITY AND CONTRERAS HOME. MAJORITY PEACEFUL REFUSING ANY PART IN RIOTS INSPIRED DISGRACEFUL REPORT SHAMES NATIONAL PRESS. AUTHORITIES INTERVENTION LAST RESORT CONTROL DISRUPTIVE ELEMENTS AMONG OTHERWISE LAW ABIDING CITIZENRY. ACCUSATION SHOTS FIRED IN AIR INCORRECT NO SUCH MEASURE NECESSARY. BE ASSURED DECENT PEOPLE HERE NEITHER RESENTFUL NOR MORALLY WARPED AS TO HARBOUR FAVOURABLE OPINIONS MURDERER OR CONSIDER HIM HEROIC AS OUTRAGEOUS REPORT ALLEGES. WE IN LEÓN CIVILISED AND CULTURED.

Tests on the exhumed bodies were finished by two o'clock in the afternoon of 27 October 1933. The animals inoculated with material from the internal organs of the corpses all died violently and the official report made at the time confirms the presence of strychnine in both bodies. A rapid glance at this record shows that, unlike during the previous tests, the number of distinguished citizens interested in witnessing events was scant. Of course these tests lacked scientific novelty since they were repeating the procedures of previous experiments, and the absence of these persons may have been in part due to their understandable distaste for the proximity of rotting bodies, something that they endured at the exhumations.

However, it is more likely attributable to the fact that the great and the good were at the time engaged in more pressing matters.

On that same afternoon, detailed preparations were being made for a meeting at the Bishop's Palace. Monsignor Tijerino y Loáisiga led the well-attended meeting, which concluded in an agreement to begin a 'Crusade for Moral Health'. This crusade was to start immediately and the committee responsible included the following people:

Reverend Canon Isidro Augusto Oviedo y Reyes, representing the Cathedral authorities on behalf of the Bishop of León, Monseigneur Tijerino y Loáisiga

Doctor Onesífero Rizo, Mayor

Don Arturo Gurdián Herdocia, President of the Social Club

Doctor Juan de Dios Darbishire, President of the Brotherhood of the Holy Saint Sepulchre

Doña Rosario de Lacayo, President of the Mothers of León

Doña Matilde de Saravia, President of the Ladies of Charity

Señorita Graciela Deshon, President of the Daughters of Mary

Señorita María Teresa Robelo, Provost of the Tertiary Order of Saint Francis

The first action of this crusade was to collect signatures for a 'statement of penitence and a show of Christian piety'. This document was published in two of León's daily papers, and such was the speed with which the signatures were gathered, it managed to make the evening editions that very day:

> We the undersigned, citizens of León, strongly reject the reports published with such unbelievable audacity and irresponsibility in one of our local papers. These reports are by all accounts false in their attempt to besmirch the honour of the distinguished Contreras Guardia family, which is already suffering under the strain of the unfortunate events currently the subject of official investigation.
>
> No doubt acting out of social resentment, the author or

> authors of this report have forgotten all common decency, resorting to falsehood and derision. These individuals are threatening our cherished traditions of stability, the family and of religious faith.
>
> Their attack has already borne fruit; in fear and disbelief we have seen the mob, its imagination fired by these libels, laying siege at the doors of this respected family, their anger given life by the poisonous breath of demons.
>
> It is for this reason that at this testing time we choose, without hesitation, to close ranks around that irreproachable lady, Doña Flora Guardia, widow of Carmen Contreras, and her daughter. We implore them to have faith in our Saviour, who is the Only Judge of our actions; for good or evil.
>
> We call on all respectable citizens of this city of the faithful to repudiate the atrocious wickedness of the gossip mongers by participating in a High Mass at four p.m. on October twenty-eighth at the cathedral, followed by a procession of the Blessed Sacrament which will culminate in a celebration of the Eucharist at the home of the Contreras Guardia family.
>
> Hail Christ the King!
>
> Hail the Immaculate Virgin!

Alongside the statement, *El Cronista* also published the following explanatory note signed by the owner of the paper, Doctor Absalón Barreto Sacasa:

> It is with great pleasure that we offer space on the pages of this newspaper to the above document, which has been signed by many of the most important representatives of our noble city, both male and female. We have accepted no payment despite the request to place the item in space that we would usually charge for. We feel that it is the least we could do in order to add weight to the general display of righteous anger at the publication, in this paper, of the defamatory libel which was artfully hoisted upon us and whose allegations and statements we do not support in any way.

> Rest assured that *El Cronista* has already taken measures to correct our mistake and ensure that a similar lapse of judgement will not occur in future. It only remains for us to add our voice to those of the distinguished signatories of the above document and cry out with them: Hail Christ the King! Hail the Immaculate Virgin! And to add: Long live the traditions of our elders! Lift up your hearts!

The celebration of High Mass and the Blessed Sacrament procession were the principal actions of the moral crusade. *El Centroamericano* reported on these events on October thirtieth in an article appearing under the byline of its owner, General Gustavo Abaunza:

> At four o'clock in the afternoon a solemn High Mass took place in the Cathedral, the chief celebrant being the Bishop himself, with the assistance of the entire canonry. During the mass, the Reverend Canon Isidro Augusto Oviedo y Reyes was able to demonstrate his well-known, thunderous eloquence as he took to the pulpit to denounce the author of the libels and his supporters. He rightly dubbed them "immoral reprobates" and his heart-felt threat to excommunicate them brought a round of applause: which it must be said is something of a rarity in the nave of our Sacred Basilica.
>
> When the Mass ended, the Bishop headed the Blessed Sacrament procession to the home of the Contreras Guardia family. The doors of this house have been closed for many days, but on this occasion they opened wide to welcome the sacred offering. Many people joined the procession: surrounding the monstrance were the members of the canonry resplendent in their vestments, immediately behind them were the members of the city council followed by the various religious orders and lay associations all with their respective banners and standards born aloft by their presidents, and finally the ladies and gentlemen of the public.
>
> The entire family were present, excepting the young María del Pilar who was indisposed and confined to her room. The family received the Eucharist from the hands

> of the Bishop with humility and placed it on the altar which had been specially prepared for this purpose. The widow voiced her gratitude through her brother Don Fernando Guardia; her words filled with emotion. We were granted permission to include them here: "I would like to thank the Bishop, the priests and the whole Catholic community on behalf of myself and my children for bringing the strength of the Living Christ, present in the bread of the Eucharist, into my home. I greatly appreciate all of the shows of support that we have seen today. Equally, I ask the city of León to remain united and not to give up until the one who is guilty of the barbarous crimes committed against my husband and daughter is brought to justice and is made an example of. He alone is responsible for the tragedy that has befallen this household. Taking full advantage of the hospitality that we offered with open arms, he cruelly betrayed us and destroyed the peace and happiness of our respectable home. I also beg you all to remain united in the Crusade for Moral Health, so aptly christened by the bishop and the other mentors of this project, so that the libels that have attempted to stain us do not spread their filth into more happy homes. My children and I take refuge in the infinite kindness of Our Lord. I am more than certain that we can count on your kindness too. My certainty comes from my sense that, although I am not a native of these shores, the city of León has welcomed me into its great family; as the scriptures tell us, this is how Ruth felt in the land of her husband. Amen."

Despite her appeals, the winds of scandal did return to shake the widow, and in the end she was very much alone. On 29 October 1933, Don Carmen Contreras Largespada revoked the powers granted to Doctor Juan de Dios Vanegas and submitted a statement to the judge in which he withdrew all allegations against Oliverio Castañeda. He did not explain his actions, and this left the widow as the last and only complainant in the case.

In the meantime, the continuing shows of piety at and around the house began to take on a subtly different interpretation: one that was contrary to that intended. Each day, the Canon Oviedo y Reyes anointed the walls of the house with holy water accompanied by a choir of blessed Daughters of Mary who sang prayers of penitence. In the eyes of the observers this began to look very much like some form of exorcism. When even the blessed daughters began to circulate a rumour that her daughter was to take holy orders as the only way to cleanse herself of the stain of guilt, the undercurrents of prejudice forced the widow to close her doors once more. The canon later wrote about this matter in an article we shall refer to in due course.

Worse still, the walls of the house blessed during the day with holy water were at night daubed with lewd messages. This graffiti was written in charcoal, and every morning the shop-assistants of La Fama had to scrub it off. On 12 November 1933, when Judge Fiallos came to interview María del Pilar at the house, he noticed some of this graffiti still visible on the wall near the door. It read: 'This is a hore house!'

Always an outsider despite her best efforts to fit in, the widow had more than enough reason to falter under the barrage of ill-feeling that soon began to come not only from the street but also from her own circle of acquaintances, and even her in-laws. Eventually the widow decided to quit the country, signalling her decision with this classified advertisement that appeared in *El Centroamericano* on 3 November 1933:

FOR SALE

I am offering for sale all of the possessions in my home.

There is a magnificent Marshall & Wendell grand piano and a beautiful Louis XV suite comprising 12 pieces. Also included are several fine items of bedroom and dining room furniture and a Philco radio set.

Viewings will take place every day from 9 to 12 and 4 to 5 p.m.

I will also be holding a sale of all stock at La Fama, the details of which I will announce in due course. The shop fittings will also be sold at a good price.

Flora Contreras (widow)
Tel: 412
Corner opposite the Metropolitan Hotel

Those people who did go to the house at the advertised times, whether out of genuine interest in the furniture or just out of curiosity, found it closed up. The sale at La Fama never took place either.

The widow changed her mind, persuaded by her brother that her place was in Nicaragua. He himself stayed in the country to protect the interests of the widow and her children as the execution of Don Carmen's will was being contested by the family. Don Carmen Contreras Largespada had launched a lawsuit concerning the division of assets of C. Contreras & Co., which reached the civil courts a few months after the conclusion of Oliverio Castañeda's trial.

As a final point, we should recall that 28 October 1933 was the day when Doctor Atanasio Salmerón was due to appear before Judge Fiallos. Unfortunately for him, his appointment took place at the same time that the Blessed Sacrament procession was leaving the Cathedral amidst clouds of incense and the sound of the voices of León's most respected citizenry united in song: 'You will reign forever, forever oh my Saviour'. These voices included the tremulous tones of Doctor Darbishire, who was there bearing aloft the standard of the Brotherhood of Saint Sepulchre.

Doctor Salmerón had lost the jocular insouciance that he'd shown that night at the accursed table when Rosalío Usulutlán had vainly warned him of the dangers about to rain down on them. Moments earlier Judge Fiallos had ordered the court to be cleared, and now Doctor Salmerón sat on the edge of his seat looking uneasily across the desk at the judge. With a severe expression on his face, Judge Fiallos began to order his notes and as he did so he began the interrogation by asking Doctor Salmerón for his name, age, marital status, occupation and address, as if he had never seen him before in his life.

CHAPTER THIRTY-EIGHT

No Smoke Without Fire

(A CHRONICLE IN FIFTEEN PARTS BY ROSALÍO USULUTLÁN)

THE NAMES used in this drama are fictitious; the author has many reasons to disguise them, not least of which is that the action takes place beneath the eaves and bell towers of somewhere not too distant from here. The plot however is entirely based in fact. I will say no more in this introduction because...I don't want to. Are you with me?

I

Laurentina let us call her, was the spoiled younger daughter of Don Honorio Aparicio, a wealthy Spaniard of mature years. She was blossoming into womanhood like a beautifully scented stem of roses, carrying each of her sixteen years like so many spring buds. She had a slightly older sister, by the name of Ernestina...whose fingers could entice the sweetest melodies from the clavichord. Ernestina was not the favourite, but she still had a place in Don Honorio's iron heart, for although the music which brought him most contentment was that of jingling coins, he was not immune to the joys of fatherly love.

This esteemed gentleman had seen some fifty years come and go; his entire world was contained within the walls of his home, from where he conducted his business with prudence and always with a level head. He kept his account books safe in a metal strong box. There were two sets of books: one of these, kept far away from prying eyes, showed exactly how things were, the figures clearly indicating his vast profits; the other set was the one he showed, with a long face, to the tax officials. In this last set of books the profits were meagre, often even showing a loss, and contained no records of certain other secret transactions Don Honorio made. These deals were of the sort that meant he could stock his shop with expensive textiles and trinkets from abroad without troubling to contribute to the public purse in the form of import duties.

Don Honorio had also appropriated all the city's water sources, channelling this natural resource through a network of pipes that he viewed as his own personal heritage. He was like some water god charging the inhabitants of the city to slake their thirst. Not satisfied with the returns he was already making, he sought to raise his prices, and to further his ends he was not above offering gifts and bribes to the Municipal Council. Here indeed was a soul possessed by the insatiable appetites of Mammon!

II

This esteemed gentleman had taken for his wife a lady from foreign lands, by name Doña Ninfa, whose exotic and effortless elegance never managed to win her the acceptance of the town's most powerful old families, stuck as they were in their outmoded customs and pious Catholicism. Don Honorio barely noticed her grace and wit. He was in the autumn of his life and not in the best of physical health, having denied himself for many years the joy of fresh air outside the claustrophobic surroundings of his quarters. Doña Ninfa was more beautiful than her two daughters put together, and could easily have been mistaken for their sister; something that was a source of great envy among the ladies of the town. What a conundrum for the old miser, to have three such beautiful flowers in his close-walled garden!

Doña Ninfa assisted him in his business, taking charge of the drapery-and-trinkets side of the enterprise where she showed herself to be skilled with the measuring tape and an expert saleswoman: recommending perfumes and toiletries to her select and envious female clientele. In the meantime, her daughters Laurentina and Ernestina languished in the ancestral home, their heads filled with dreams of the world outside. Their only distraction was to watch from the doorway where they sat in the evenings, killing time; passing the endless hours of boredom and sloth…until the fateful day arrived when…

III

... a young gentleman, going by the name of Baldomero appeared in that quiet town. Hailing from across the border, he had come to study law. He was gallant and astute; very free with his favours, he had a ready smile and a talent for seduction. In matters of the heart there was no one to better his perseverance and ardour; but once the fortress was captured, he would take his sweet music elsewhere...of this I can assure you. And don't think that he was free and single; not by any means. He had a wife whom he brought with him from his own country; Rosalpina she was called, and owed nothing in beauty to the three roses in Don Honorio's walled garden.

The gallant and his consort took rooms in the best hotel in town which, unfortunately for Don Honorio, was opposite his own abode. Baldomero lost no time in scouting out his surroundings and discovering the three roses; shut away night and day in their solitude, he made ready to pluck them. As we know, walls, moats or battlements were no obstacle to his machinations, and the ill-defended garden of Don Honorio presented little challenge. He entered the garden. He stormed the house, and they surrendered to his will...he won their hearts, wife and all.

How he managed to claim victory with such ease is astonishing, especially when we consider Don Honorio's reputation for being tight-fisted and openly inhospitable. However, we should remember that conquest is best achieved from within: it was none other than Doña Ninfa herself who was first to be ensnared in his subtle web of charm, a butterfly in his net of gauzy enchantment. It was she who offered Baldomero the keys to their home.

IV

It did not take long for poor, helpless Rosalpina to realise what was going on; tired out by his nightly exertions, her husband had little energy left for his legitimate conjugal duties. He betrayed his wife, he betrayed them all, and it must be said, he betrayed himself; although well-versed in the arts of Eros, he found it impossible to keep up his amorous adventures without exhausting himself. Rosalpina was not content to be merely the fourth corner in a love triangle. She quite rightly felt that she alone should be the mistress of Baldomero's body and soul... and indeed his socks, which were always filthy owing to all his tip-toeing about at night.

V

Baldomero was careful not to neglect Don Honorio; using his artful subterfuges, he wove a veil over his activities such that Don Honorio was blind to everything that was going on. This gentleman looked the other way as the treasures of his heart were ransacked, he was so unaware of the cuckoo in his nest that he even showed Baldomero his account books—both the false and the real ones. Baldomero promised him that he would show him more cunning accounting tricks, and that he would devote himself to securing a new contract for the exploitation of his water resources. Indeed, the young upstart became an arbiter of bribes and inducements to finally secure the increase in tariffs that his master desired. Money makes the world go round.

Don Honorio was deeply satisfied by the sound of money clinking in his strong box and the speed with which his young protégée managed to get on top of his business affairs, so he continued to look the other way. The veil before his eyes prevented him from seeing that his home had become an inferno of passions fed by the flames of jealousy; there was jealousy between sisters, jealousy between mother and daughters, jealousy between the wife and the mother and the daughters and vice versa, vice versa...

VI

For a while the poor wronged Rosalpina had her triumph; after much weeping into the pillows of her abandoned marriage bed and after many protests and recriminations she managed to obtain a promise from the gallant that they would leave the garden and go in search of their own love nest. Here she hoped that they would finally be able to enjoy conjugal bliss away from temptation and rivalry.

As the gallant departed, pushed towards the door by his better half (or quarter), Don Honorio's house was filled with sorrow and tears. Only Rosalpina laughed; but her joy was sorely misplaced. As they left, three pairs of eyes followed them, each attempting to pierce Baldomero's heart with its inconsolable gaze. He left them wounded and abandoned, while Rosalpina savoured her pyrrhic victory; this farewell obtained through her stubborn determination to leave was soon to cost her...her life.

VII

Indeed, her life was at stake. Baldomero lost no time in taking it from her, administering a fatal dose of poison to his unhappy consort. It transpired that he was an expert in the poisoner's art, very knowledgeable in 'the Secrets of Nature'. It will no doubt shock the reader to know that while still an adolescent he had decided to help the authoress of his being into the next world: she was by all accounts suffering from the torments of a mortal illness, and he sought to free her from pain.

Baldomero practised his arts by exterminating the city's stray dogs. Unaware of his proclivities, the authorities aided and abetted him by enabling his access to the necessary poisons: handing the keys to death to this thief of life, just as Doña Ninfa had so recently handed him the keys to her home. In this way he procured the dose with which he dispatched his consort. Bitten by the treacherous anopheles mosquito, she had fallen victim to a deadly disease which was then endemic in the city. Disguising the poison in a curative draught, he killed her while pretending to cure her.

Doña Ninfa and her daughters flew to the aid of the hypocrite Baldomero. Together they attended the dying Rosalpina's bedside as, with Christian resignation, she departed the world whose joys had been so cruelly denied her by her inconstant spouse. When she was scarcely cold in her grave, the three of them vied for the privilege of locking the doors on Rosalpina's briefly inhabited home, and on the day of her funeral contrived the return of the gallant to their own home. Don Honorio, who barely had a say in the matter, blessed this arrangement gladly, welcoming his sagacious business advisor.

Anxious to help him forget his dead wife, the three were solicitous to a fault, and the gallant, without appearing too eager but equally without demurring, accepted their hospitality. A bird in the hand, as they say; never mind three! The unfortunate Rosalpina was laid to rest, but the tangled love nest was still intact. Oh what a dangerous tangle! Oh unthinking Doña Ninfa!

VIII

At this point, the reader should be aware that, despite his absence from the house, Baldomero had never actually cut the threads of his amorous entanglement; he had maintained a correspondence with Laurentina, the tenderest flower in Don Honorio's garden. A servant, whom we shall call Celestina, acted as their courier, taking the letters to and from a nearby church. Laurentina went there daily, apparently to pray but in reality awaiting news from her lover (and there were many witnesses in the city to this clandestine correspondence; several of whom are still prepared to testify). The last of these letters, replete with promises, was delivered to Laurentina on the very day that Rosalpina lay languishing on her deathbed! Among his promises, Baldomero vowed to return to the rose garden, which in the absence of his gentle ministrations was in danger of withering. And how promptly he made good on that promise!

And so Baldomero returned to his paradise, or rather, to his inferno, determined to continue stoking the flames of lust that he had continued to feed from afar. We know of only one set of letters, but the reader should not be in any doubt that there were others dispatched by different secret couriers to the two other recipients.

IX

Oh foolish, foolish Doña Ninfa! Oh, so foolish her two daughters! So foolish and so avaricious Don Honorio! The three roses now fnd themsleves competing for the favours of our gallant, the author of their torments. Each of them was equally intent on claiming the greatest privileges, and so all three of them were vulnerable to the pangs of envy. At night, the arpeggios flew once again from Ernestina's fingers as she tried to please the ears of our gallant. Baldomero however was no longer listening to the insistent strains of the clavichord. Since his return, his flattery and flirtatious compliments were intended only for the sweet and gentle Laurentina. Unbeknownst to the elder sister, love had become deaf to her desperate sonatas; these now served only to hasten her own death.

Every evening, Ernestina accompanied Baldomero to place flowers on his wife's grave. As the evening skies were tinged with purple and deep red, the lonely glades of that consecrated ground were the scene of many a feverish and helpless declaration of love. Ernestina wept many a bitter tear over that earth, which within a few short days would receive her own mortal remains.

X

But what of Doña Ninfa? She too found herself thwarted, in a state of limbo. She bided her time, and although deeply troubled continued to keep herself occupied with the business of her shop. She waited and watched, watched and waited. As the saying goes, there's no fool like an old fool.

XI

One day, Baldomero decided to return to his native land. In secret he promised all three ladies that he would be back, even though he proclaimed out loud to them all that he was leaving for good. His motto seemed to be: absence makes the heart grow fonder. Ernestina, the wretched girl, penned him long, passionate letters which she posted herself, going each day to the post office in the hope of finding his replies; which were long in coming. While Ernestina soaked the pages of his letters with her tears, Doña Ninfa decided to go on a trip for business and pleasure, back to her homeland which neighboured that of the hero of this tale. Little Laurentina accompanied her.

Through the imprudent Ernestina's letters, the shameless Baldomero heard of this trip, and so he immediately bought a passage on the first ship he could find that was sailing for the coast of Doña Ninfa's homeland. Baldomero, had you forgotten your motto? You should have retraced your steps, but your ambition far outstripped your caution.

What rejoicing and festivities followed the appearance of Baldomero! He was once again the embodiment of generosity; with open arms he shared his favours between the two women, and if they breathed any complaint it could only have been that it was all too much…

Oh, but what sadness and disappointment for you Ernestina! All too late you realised the train of events that your indiscreet letters had set in motion; the hawk was in the air again, and little did you know how soon he'd come home to roost. In fact, he returned on board the very same ship as your two rivals. Such bitterness, confusion...you felt thwarted and betrayed. However ill-rewarded, your love remained intact, and your jealousy produced a stubborn spark of hope. You still believed you could win him back despite the gains your rivals had made during his long stay abroad, far from your watchful eye. Poor Ernestina, how could you have guessed that you were about to be cast aside?

XII

Oh, perfidious fate, how you conspire! The lovesick Ernestina, bitten by anopheles, began to show symptoms of the same deadly disease. Without delay the treacherous gallant procured poison intending, as before, to hide it in the medicinal concoction supposed to cure her.

One Sunday evening Baldomero invited some friends of his, all of them foreigners, to a dinner at the home of Don Honorio. Such was the respect in which he was now held in that household, he was able to do as he pleased. These foreign guests were wined and dined in a banquet prepared by the three rivals, and while they enjoyed the exquisite wines provided from Doña Ninfa's warehouse, the traitor requested that Ernestina entertain them with her playing. Eager to please, she went to sit at her clavichord, and soon her fingers began to weave their magic on its keys; so full of the pain and longing of unrequited love, it was the song of the dying swan.

Ernestina succumbed the following night. It was as if the skies opened in sympathy for her sad passing, crying torrents of rain in the midst of thunder and lightning. And in the throes of death, allowed a final brief truce by the poison coursing through her, the words that spilled from her lips were pleas for forgiveness from her mother and sister—her rivals!

XIII

The funeral carriage departed for the burial ground, her coffin smothered beneath a tide of flowers. The coffin was white out of respect for her virginal state, but this was a pious deception: our artful young nobleman had already scaled the walls of her virtue, so poorly defended by her father, Don Honorio. The scene was set for a duel between Doña Ninfa and her daughter Laurentina.

With Ernestina's death they sensed that the Fates had unravelled another thread in the tapestry of their rivalry, and their gullible hearts swelled with renewed hope.

Now more than ever Baldomero was the object of great attention, flattery and care. Don Honorio's ancestral home became the scene for the final battle; each contender was decked out in their most resplendent helmets and finest coats of chain mail, their pikes sharpened and their maces at the ready. One and only one of them could win the prize. But who? Foolish women...they did not guess that the next name on the sinister list of victims was none other than Don Honorio himself. Before making his final choice, Baldomero was set on removing the Lord of the Waters. Had he not helped to swell their coffers through his wise counsel? He was entitled to them, he and no one else!

Dressed in strict mourning following the death of her sister, Laurentina distracted herself by attending to Baldomero's wardrobe: starching his collars and cuffs and laundering his shirts. While he worked on the villainous water company contract, she would bring him refreshing drinks. Her eyes blazing with love, she was a slave to his every need, waiting silently as the youth drank so that she remove the empty glass; and if he took his time, she would wait all the same.

One afternoon it is said Doña Ninfa announced: 'Baldomero, gone is the one who used to make your bed and who took such joy in that task. Now it is you, Laurentina, who should take up this duty.' Of course Laurentina was more than happy to take charge of making Baldomero's bed.

But it was not that bed they lay in. Anxious to avoid any nocturnal misdemeanours that might frustrate her own plans, Doña Ninfa sent her own husband to share Baldomero's room, while she slept in Laurentina's. The lovebirds were too clever for this stratagem, however; the hawk and the dove escaped their cage, and of an evening would fly far away to find refuge at a ranch owned by Don Honorio. Here, in perfect solitude, they surrendered to love's baser pleasures; pleasures poisoned by murder...and in what a terrible way! (There are many witnesses still living in the city that recall these illicit meetings and would be willing to testify to them, giving precise dates and times).

XIV

When Don Honorio fell ill with the same endemic disease, Baldomero rushed to his aid, but the familiar pangs of death soon followed. In this case, however, an alert medical man was on hand: the very skilled Teodosio, who had for some time been sworn to investigate the machinations of that artful young gentleman, Baldomero. He had surmised that another death was imminent, and indeed who the next victim would be. He reached Don Honorio's deathbed just in time, and not without some struggle managed to take a sample of his stomach contents using a gastric catheter. Once these fluids had been subjected to chemical tests, the presence of poison was sure to be confirmed, and thus foul play be proven.

Don Honorio was dead, victim of his guilelessness and miserly ambition. The criminal was unmasked. However, when the soldiers arrived, armed with rifles ready to clap the villain in irons, mother and daughter made a hysterical display in an attempt to wrest him from his captors. It was an horrendous and pathetic sight, and the authorities had to make a supreme effort to accomplish their task.

Foolish Doña Ninfa! Did you not realise that the brave action of the doctor Teodosio had saved your ladyship from a similar death by poisoning? On achieving his goal of inheriting the family wealth, our gallant would have married your own Laurentina; but how could he do this if such a formidable rival as you were still living? Your expeditious death by means of poison would have been the unavoidable response.

In spite of everything, you persisted. The prisoner received flowers, perfumes, and all manner of delicacies in his cell. Sometimes these gifts were from you, at others from your daughter; both of you were reluctant to give up the courtship. You unblushingly called for his liberty and in your lack of moderation proclaimed your love for all the world to see. You never could accept the destiny that the Fates dealt you, Doña Ninfa...

XV

The inhabitants of that quiet city, never before the scene of such dreadful events, were rescued from danger by the selfless and skilful actions of the doctor, Teodosio. The attractive and much fought-over gentleman, who arrived on these shores with formulas for mortal venoms concealed in his luggage, has been put on trial. His luck has run out, and we shall leave him in his dungeon where he awaits undoubtedly his turn on the scaffold.

Other medical men have cast doubts on the validity of the proofs put forward for the crimes committed. These men, jealous enemies of the wise Doctor Teodosio, are old,and the light of their scientific judgement has long been extinguished. We can only hope that their outdated opinions will not prevail, and justice takes its rightful course.

This humble piece of journalism, based on true events, will perhaps serve as an opportune lesson. I repeat that the names used here are all false, and the details of the story have been purposely obscured by the author; using light and shadow, some events are highlighted at times, while at others they are hidden in darkness. I do so in order to respectfully spare delicate sensibilities.

Everyone should draw their own conclusion from this story. With this thought I leave you, dear reader, and take my bow.

CHAPTER THIRTY-NINE

A Disastrous Showing by a Key Witness

On the evening of 27 October 1933, the Teatro González changed its billing at the last moment in order to add its support to the 'Crusade for Moral Health' which had begun that day. In place of *The Public Enemy* starring James Cagney and Jean Harlow, it decided to show *The Miracle of St. Bernadette.*

Unaware of this, Oviedo the Balloon arrived punctually as usual. He approached the box office curiously, surprised to see the poster showing the kneeling Bernadette against a pale blue backdrop instead of the expected one with James Cagney as the ruthless gangster emerging from a blood-red background, machine-gun blazing. Before he could get into the building, however, he was intercepted by his brother, the canon. Wearing his surplice and stole as if about to officiate at Mass, he was standing guard on the steps handing out bottles of holy water to the moviegoers. He was accompanied in this task by a cohort of ladies from the Order of the Legion of Mary dressed head to toe in white with pale blue ribbons round their neck and lace mantillas.

'Get thee behind me, Satan!' cried the canon, taking a bottle from the box he carried and brandishing it as if he was about to anoint his brother. 'I trust we can count on your generous support!'

'First I would like you to explain why you put my name on your statement of support for the Contreras family!' said Oviedo the Balloon, fishing inside his jacket pocket. 'Nobody asked me if I wanted to sign it.'

'Your wife signed for you,' said the canon, presenting him with the bottle. 'You should thank her that you weren't left out.'

'This is Satan's money,' said Oviedo the Balloon finally retrieving his wallet and depositing a two córdoba bill into the collection box held at the ready by one of the ladies of the Order. 'I must warn you that I won it playing dice.'

'What you win through Satan, you lose to the Lord,' the canon intoned, making the sign of the cross. 'But He will not be able to release you from behind bars.'

'Behind bars? Why would I be there?' asked Oviedo the Balloon, scrutinizing the blue glass bottle labelled 'Laxol'. He looked at all the other bottles in the box, and saw that there were also some of 'Agua Florida', 'Barry's Hair Tonic' and 'Tiro Seguro': the best remedy for intestinal worms.

'For keeping bad company,' replied the canon, shaking the box so that the bottles jingled. 'The National Guard is keeping tabs on all your cronies. They are all going to jail; for spreading malicious rumours.'

'That's not so bad,' said Oviedo the Balloon, replacing the bottle he had just paid for. 'I thought I was going to be arrested for remaining friends with Oliverio Castañeda. In one of your sermons you said it was a sin to visit him in prison!'

'It is also a sin to poison souls,' said the canon, nodding to the other moviegoers as they went by, and handing each of them a bottle of holy water. 'Don't go back to Casa Prío. Doctor Salmerón and his accomplices are all in the frame.'

'I'm going to give this to Doctor Salmerón,' said Oviedo the Balloon, taking the bottle of 'Laxol' back out of the box, 'to protect him from all evil. Amen.'

'Despite your being such a reprobate you should attend the Blessed Sacrament procession,' said the canon, clutching his sleeve as he made to go up the steps to the box office. 'You've got nothing to lose. Unless of course, you are in favour of scandal!'

'Once I have endured the platitudes of Bernadette I will be sainted enough. I've already seen it three times at the matinée with my children,' said Oviedo the Balloon, his jowls, still raw from their recent encounter with the razor, wobbling as he laughed. 'Put a stop to this circus, you're the ones creating the scandal!'

'Do you realise that this "you" is all respectable society in León?' asked the canon. The lady with the collection box was watching closely, and had just crossed herself on hearing his brother's disrespectful laughter, and so he redoubled his efforts:

'Have you really sunk so low? Rejecting your own kind!'

'All of "you", whoever they are,' said Oviedo the Balloon. With one finger he wiped away the sweat which was running from his brilliantined curls and down his forehead, then went on: 'You with your proclamations and processions. You're not supporting the Contreras family, you're looking out for yourselves. Or do you just want to get even with Doña Flora? Who are you to give María del Pilar a public pardon for her love affairs?'

'Leave that poor, wayward girl out of this!' said the canon, beating his chest with his fist. 'She will purge her own sins. I hear that she is to become a nun in Costa Rica. That surely is a praiseworthy decision!'

'Ha! So you believe she did commit sins?' said Oviedo the Balloon sniffing his finger, which was now covered in hair oil, and wagging it at the canon: 'If you didn't, why would you be absolving her?'

'I hear you, but I do not know you!' said the canon, narrowing his eyes and glaring at his brother. 'Forget the act of contrition and support then, but take note. Distance yourself from those scandal mongers.'

'And I don't know you and don't hear you, because the film is about to start,' said Oviedo the Balloon, hurrying up the steps and waving his ticket at the box-office window.

Although he did not want to admit it to his brother, Oviedo the Balloon was worried by his warnings. Indeed, so great was his disquiet that, breaking all his rules, he left the cinema before the Virgin of Lourdes had appeared to Bernadette for the second time. He went straight to Casa Prío in search of the associates of the accursed table.

He found the place abandoned. Captain Prío told him that Doctor Salmerón was at home preparing his testimony for the following day. The captain also informed him that Doctor Salmerón was aware of Captain Ortiz's threats, but took them as sheer bravado he would never dare to act on, and had even offered chairs to the soldiers stationed opposite his surgery so that they could sit down.

Rosalío Usulutlán, on the other hand, did not share his confidence, and was still in hiding. Cosme Manzo had with great reluctance taken similar precautions, deciding to hide in his office at the back of the store while his assistants told the clientele that he had gone to take care of some business in Managua.

Oviedo the Balloon decided to send Doctor Salmerón a note which he dispatched with one of the bar staff. He sent the bottle of holy water along with it. This note appears in the secret case dossier:

> Dear Doctor Teodosio,
>
> As I'm sure you are well aware, they are coming to place you in captivity due to the situation concerning the three roses in Don Honorio's walled garden. I have been assured of the reality of this threat from unimpeachable sources. Take great care and stop treating it as a joke. The Commander does not make jokes. The bottle of holy water will tell you the identity of my source. The procession tomorrow afternoon will make things even worse.
>
> Yours,
>
> O. O. R

In fact, Captain Ortiz had no intention of arresting either Cosme Manzo or Rosalío Usulutlán, although his spies kept him up to date as to both men's whereabouts. He knew that Cosme Manzo had not left León and was holed up in the back office of El Esfuerzo, and that Rosalío was hiding out in the old oil-pressing mill that his father, the musician Don Narciso Mayorga, had at the rear of their house. He was only interested in the big fish: Doctor Salmerón. He had requested permission to arrest him for public order offences, but it was taking time to get authorisation from the capital because General Somoza was out in Bluefields on the Atlantic coast, and there was no way of contacting him.

Doctor Salmerón in the meantime remained calm and confident as he prepared to go to the courthouse on the afternoon of 28 October 1933. As he polished his boots he hummed his favourite tune, a Maria Grever song called 'In Case I Never See You Again'. He changed his shirt and put on his blue pin-striped cashmere suit, a three-piece outfit he normally reserved for funerals and university medical exams. He put his pocket watch into his waistcoat, looping its gold chain across his chest. He removed all the instruments from his medical bag and replaced them with the Casa Squibb notebook, the pages of his secret dossier and the book, *The Secrets of Nature*.

He had not taken much notice of the warning note from Oviedo the Balloon; he was convinced that his carefully prepared testimony was his best insurance policy. Once he had delivered it in the presence of the journalists and other onlookers who habitually filled the courthouse, he was intending to ask the judge for official protection as a key witness in the case. Then Captain Ortiz could choke on his own bile.

As we know, he got his first shock when Judge Fiallos ordered the court to be cleared. The doleful tolling of the great bell at the cathedral sounded at the very start of the questioning, and tensions were evident from the start. The source of this tension had something to do with the goings-on in the street; the procession of support for the Contreras family had just left the cathedral, and the tumultuous atmosphere induced a profound sense of ill-feeling between the judge and his witness, which ultimately caused the hearing to end in disaster.

The judge had spent most of the morning preparing for the interrogation but, as he later admitted to Alí Vanegas, he made the grave error of straying from his carefully organised notes. As he also admitted to his secretary, he had been aware for some time that he was going to have to hold his nose and wade into the sewers to get to the bottom of the case, and that Doctor Salmerón's testimony was the key to accessing these filthy waters. However, he reacted impulsively, and forgot everything he had prepared, as is clear from the record:

> JUDGE: You are, are you not, aware of the grave situation that has been produced in this city as a consequence of the scandalous libel published under the name of Rosalío Usulutlán in the edition of *El Cronista* of 25 October 1933?
>
> WITNESS: I have read the report, as I have read many other news items in the newspapers published in this city and in Managua concerning the Castañeda case. I have also read the foreign papers and these contain certain information that may be of interest to Your Honour. I

have included these among the documents I shall be giving to you.

JUDGE: Do you agree that the libel in question alludes, albeit in a disguised manner, to deeds now under investigation by this authority?

WITNESS: I have no need to agree since I am not the author of the article to which you refer. As a reader I did note certain similarities, as have other readers less well informed than myself. In the rational and disinterested desire to see justice done, I dedicated myself to collecting evidence related to this case even before the authorities intervened, and it is this information and not any other that I am prepared to talk to you about.

JUDGE: The libel mentions a doctor going under the name of Teodosio. Would you accept that you are the doctor to which the piece refers?

WITNESS: I repeat that I am not, and indeed have no need to be, familiar with all the statements made in that piece. However, as you suggest, I did attend the Contreras home on my own initiative on the morning of 9 October 1933, with the intention of taking a sample of the stomach contents of the victim Señor Carmen Contreras. This is because, according to the deductions stemming from my own investigations, I had good reason to suspect that he had been poisoned; as was his daughter Matilde Contreras and, some time before, Señora Marta Jerez de Castañeda. These suspicions proved correct, as has been demonstrated in the laboratory tests you yourself ordered. Thus there is no need for any fictitious doctor Teodosio to help you by shedding light on these matters. I am appearing before you in person as a witness armed with new and irrefutable evidence.

JUDGE: Are you a friend of this Rosalío Usulutlán?

WITNESS: I am his friend and he is my patient.

JUDGE: The "vox populi" has it that the libel to which I have alluded was prepared by you in conjunction with Rosalío Usulutlán and the merchant Cosme Manzo during certain meetings in Casa Prío. The libel contains many serious allegations designed to sully the reputation of the widow, Señora Flora Contreras, and her daughters. Moreover, it does not appear to concern the authors that one of them, Señorita Matilde Contreras, is already deceased, and therefore unable to defend herself against these slanders.

WITNESS: That is an imputation without any foundation and which I wholly reject! I respectfully inform you that, independent of any statements made in the article, I have at my fingertips proof that will help you clarify the motives behind this crime; these motives are love, if it may so be termed, as well as financial gain. I have brought the relevant documents with me, and once you have them in your hands you can judge for yourself whether we are dealing with unfounded rumour or hard evidence. What's more, I have further proofs which demonstrate that this man was capable of poisoning his own mother!

JUDGE: I must assume that these are the same documents used to concoct the aforementioned libel. I must also assume that, this being the case, their value as evidence is forfeit as a result of your own actions.

WITNESS: With all due respect, Your Honour is incorrect in that assumption. If Your Honour is interested in how the crimes were in fact committed, step by step; how he used the poison, disguising it in medicines innocently prescribed; and how the rogue took advantage of the similarities between the presentation of the final stages of blackwater fever and the symptoms of strychnine poisoning; please proceed to interrogate me about the evidence in my possession. If you also wish to know the criminal's motives, please continue to question me. I have not invented the love letters or the dates of clandestine meetings, the names of those who acted as intermediaries for those letters, or those of witnesses who are prepared to corroborate what I am saying. This will clarify not only the amorous background to the case, but will clarify how certain fraudulent business contracts signed on behalf of Contreras & Co. are also pertinent to the case. For the benefit of true justice, which it is your duty to pursue, I suggest that you stop delaying your interrogation of me and stop trying to implicate me in the authorship of that libel: something which I deny and will continue to deny!

JUDGE: You are not ignorant of the law regarding defamation of character and that it is a crime which may lead to prosecution.

WITNESS: No, I am not ignorant of this, but I am also aware that it is a private matter, which can only be taken up by the party that considers itself defamed. But I now see, because you are warning me in this way, that the Contreras family is being urged to press charges against me as reward for my zeal.

JUDGE: I must assure you that I am not warning you of anything; it is not within my remit to do so.

WITNESS: The fact that you have cleared the courthouse and the direction of your questioning are enough for me. I have already been warned of the National Guard's intention to arrest me for breach of the peace, since they hold me responsible for that article in *El Cronista*. This is, of course, no surprise to me, considering the lack of respect for the law shown by the armed forces, led as they are by a bunch of barbarians. I'm becoming aware of the fact that you require a scapegoat to satisfy those sanctimonious incense burners who have been unleashed on León under the pretext of protecting the Contreras' family honour. I am also beginning to see that you wish to silence me so that the roots of this crime do not become public. As a result, you will never uncover the actual proof of the crime itself. Your Honour is refusing to listen to anything I have to say!

JUDGE: If you feel so threatened, why not make a formal complaint? No one is preventing you.

WITNESS: I don't think a formal complaint on my part would do me any good. Let them arrest me, I am ready. I'm an honourable man and my medical degree was not handed to me as a gift or because I was born with a silver spoon in my mouth. All this serves to demonstrate the state of justice in this country: the one who has the keys to uncovering a crime goes to prison, while the criminal is set free.

JUDGE: For the purposes of this court I would ask you to relate, without omission, all that you know concerning the case.

WITNESS: I have nothing to offer you.

JUDGE: You yourself have previously declared that you possess certain evidence. If this is the case, please proceed to tell the court all you know without further delay.

WITNESS: I repeat: I have nothing to say.

JUDGE: In accordance with the Penal Code, I am obliged to inform you that, in the face of your repeated refusals to speak, I have the power to charge you with perjury, the giving of false statements, and with the crime of withholding evidence pertaining to a case under investigation.

WITNESS: That gives you yet another excuse to arrest me. For the last time I repeat that I have nothing to say on this matter and I want the record to show this.

JUDGE: That is all I have to ask you.

WITNESS: Am I under arrest?

JUDGE: I have said that is all. Once you have signed your statement, you are free to go.

At this point the interview was suspended, and once the witness had read and agreed to the document it was signed: M. Fiallos, A. Salmerón, Alí Vanegas (secretary).

As Doctor Salmerón carefully went through the pages of his statement before signing it, Alí Vanegas fanned his face nervously. Chin in his hands, Judge Fiallos pretended to read some documents he had taken out of his desk drawer. The heat in the office was stifling. The windows were closed and the room was so small that when the public were allowed in to the courthouse, many were left outside, straining to hear the witnesses or relying on others closer to the action to pass the news back to them.

Night was beginning to fall and Doctor Salmerón's purple face was illuminated by an electric bulb surrounded by a cloud of mosquitoes. He looked fit to explode. His cashmere suit was beginning to itch at the crotch and the starched collar of his shirt annoyed him. When he had finished reading, Alí Vanegas handed him a ball-point pen but he refused it and took his own fountain pen from his pocket. He unscrewed the top with great dignity and signed his name with a flamboyant gesture. He picked up his bag, stuffed full of all the evidence he had collected, and left without saying good-bye.

By now the crowds had dispersed. Only the blind singer Miserere was still wandering the deserted corridors in her tunic and bare feet. With her guitar slung across her body she roamed aimlessly as if searching for the way out, although she must have known those passageways like the back of her hand. Doctor Salmerón could hear her hoarse voice as he stood in the doorway: it sounded as if it came from some lonely, far away place. She was singing her favourite song: 'you are so proud, you know you are beautiful, don't stop loving me…you who has the world at her feet, a world I am leaving perhaps, forever…'

On the street he saw a last band of stragglers from the procession: a group of women whose coffee-coloured habits marked them as members of the Tertiary Order. Each had a string of huge rosary beads about her waist, and one of them carried a banner from which hung a collection of pale blue ribbons that fluttered in the sultry evening breeze. He watched them go on their way with a fixed grimace of derision on his face, then hurried off towards his surgery.

He crossed Plaza Jerez. A cripple had tethered his goat to one of the cement lions at the entrance to the cathedral and was selling newspapers from the back of his cart. Doctor Salmerón stopped to buy one. The front page of *El Centroamericano* was adorned by the photograph of a youthful Doctor Darbishire in profile, peering down a microscope. Beneath it was a new article written by the doctor:

> I TAUGHT HIM BUT HE LEARNED NOTHING
>
> In his article carried by *El Cronista* on October twenty-first of this year, the quack doctor Atanasio Salmerón did me the honour of naming me as his mentor. His insistence on so naming me has not persuaded me to support the nonsense that he also insists on peddling: nonsense which goes under the scanty veil of his inadequate science; full of poorly chewed and poorly digested ideas. I beg the

reader to be patient and excuse me of all responsibility for the dreadful indigestion suffered by my one-time disciple. It was not I who fed him these rich dishes despite all the time he spent in my surgery and the six long sterile years he passed in my classes.

Doctor Salmerón claims I do not know the difference between an alkaloid and a ptomaine. Since his own paltry brainpower leaves him in limbo I will answer him myself: subject to the same chemical tests, ptomaines react in the same manner as plant-derived alkaloids; just as the latter, they form precipitates in a solution of potassium iodide, and it is a similar situation in the case of other chemical reactions. They also have the same toxic effects, acting in a similar way; examination under the microscope also leaves them indistinguishable.

As an example, ptomatropine is a cadaveric alkaloid and is a ptomaine that has effects similar to atropine, an alkaloid derived from the plant belladonna. Everyone knows, or should know, that the human body is a living laboratory of natural alkaloids produced by the millions of bacteria that reside within us and that when we die these chemicals become deadly poisons (Théophile Gautier, "Toxines microbiennes et animales", Paris, 1887).

Given the difficulties of identification explained above, it is necessary to employ a spectroscopic centrifuge such as the one designed by Mérimée as the only mode of valid analysis. Such instruments were used in France as early as 1892, and according to my sources one was recently brought to the laboratories of the Ministry of Health in Managua; I doubt this but cannot deny it. This being the case, under no circumstances should any animals have been injected with cadaveric substances without these substances first having been submitted to centrifugal analysis in this modern apparatus. Only this procedure could determine whether we are dealing with an animal-derived ptomaine (naturally present) or a plant-based alkaloid (artificially introduced). The results of injecting either would be lethal, for sure, but without this precaution the results are meaningless. I reiterate: none of this has been done. The supposed presence of an alkaloid (strychnine) in the gastric fluids removed from Don Carmen has not been incontrovertibly proved owing to the inadequacy of the procedures used. To support this, I need only point out that the results were in fact inconclusive: initially coming out negative and only showing a positive result second time around. And where is there any mention of what equipment was used? I could say the same about the tests completed on the recently exhumed bodies.

Science must always be up to date, and my old student does not seem to recognise this at all. Otherwise, he would know that the list of ptomaines grows daily, and he would also know that the ptomaines are bases formed in the living laboratory that is our own bodies by metabolic processes occurring after death: decarboxylation of amino acids (G. Grass, "Zur Kennis der Ptoma", Berlin, 1895). This is how putrescine is formed, and despite being only a simple ptomaine it behaves like a lethal toxin with properties exactly like strychnine, as has been amply demonstrated by Mallarmé ("Documents de Toxicologie Moderne", Paris, 1893). If there is ignorance in these parts about these facts then it is not my fault; but ignorance is no excuse for irresponsibility. I reiterate that the animals which died after being injected with substances from the recently exhumed corpses, a procedure I opposed at the time, did appear to have been poisoned. They were: by ptomaines.

This is why the eminent Doctor Rosales lost his finger in the operating theatre at Masaya Hospital; he was afraid of dying from ptomaine poisoning. I do not need Doctor Salmerón to remind me of this case, although having done so I thank him, as it shows me to be correct. I cannot explain, however, why he chose to bring up the topic of Doctor Rosales' marriage to a French woman, nor his comparison to my own frustrated nuptials. Could it be that in his failure to win the argument with science he descends into backbiting and gossip, as is his wont? I will let the reader be the judge, as I refuse to stoop to such baseness.

I will not try the patience of the reader by discussing

Doctor Salmerón's cowardly incursion into the Contreras' residence. He extracted gastric juices from the victim and these, I insist, did not contain strychnine. Had this been the case he would never have been able to accomplish the action using a tube inserted via the mouth, and as far as I can discern, he made no attempt to do so through the nasal cavity. Let us leave this incident aside and pass on to his ramblings concerning the ins and outs of canine digestion.

My unfortunate disciple thought he was on sure ground in this matter, and took it for granted that the presence of strychnine would be established in the bodies exhumed on October twenty-fifth since the injected animals would certainly die, victims of the very normal processes already outlined. They did die, but this proves nothing and certainly not the concept of century-long persistence of strychnine in human remains.

Very well, Doctor Salmerón; the animals you mention, more like a circus ring-master than a man of science, LIVE thanks to their powerful stomachs, and do not DIE because of it. Perhaps we should call it "refractory idiosyncrasy", following Doctor William Styron of the Society of American Surgeons. Their survival demonstrates that they can not only digest poisons but that they are able to eliminate them from their systems via their lungs, saliva, urine and faeces. But please don't bring dogs into your circus act along with your ostriches, moles and goats. A dog does not have any refractory idiosyncrasy, and if strychnine does not persist in its system after death then it will be for similar reasons that it does not persist in human remains: although ptomaines will be present.

If dogs had refractory idiosyncrasies and were so protected from toxins as are moles, goats and ostriches, please explain to me: why do they die of poisoning? It is a common, if brutal practice in our villages to dispose of dogs in this way. Indeed, are they not being used in this way to decide the contested theories of this case in our laboratories so poorly equipped that in London they would make a preschooler laugh.

I think I have said enough. I am finished with my ex-pupil and ex-colleague. He has lost all credibility, calling me on the one hand naïve, on the other his mentor, and insinuating by the by that I am an apologist for criminals, simply because I have used irrefutable arguments to defend the august majesty of science against the mistreatment and condemnation it has suffered in this case. I will let the accusation of naïveté pass, and put it down to his usual nonsense. And I reject the title of mentor because although I attempted to teach him, it is clear he learned nothing.

I am not debating this matter in order to exonerate Oliverio Castañeda, I am not cut from the same cloth as you, Doctor Salmerón. There are others who seem to like spreading irresponsible rumours, lies, and devious slanders; Señor Oliverio Castañeda is pathologically inclined to do this, as is shown by the testimony of the many honourable persons who have appeared before the judge.

I tried hard to instruct Doctor Salmerón in the arts of medicine, but never in the arts of slander. This he learned of his own account and at his own risk. If he resembles Señor Castañeda in this, it is because they share certain personality traits and not any refractory idiosyncrasy. It is likely that they will someday eat from the same plate. Do not forget this prophecy, dear reader.

Doctor Salmerón read the article by the light of a street lamp and did not resume his journey home until he had re-read it twice.

When he reached the doorway of his surgery he found Rosalío Usulutlán who had been waiting for him for some time, disguised as a priest.

CHAPTER FORTY

The Witness Acknowledges Having Been the Object of Special Attention

NOBODY had seen María del Pilar Contreras since the day her father's coffin had left their house on its way to the cemetery. She had stopped going to classes at La Asunción College, and had never again taken her rocking chair out to the corner door, which was now closed nearly all the time. When the scandal provoked by Rosalío Usulutlán's article exploded, rumour had it she locked herself in her room after reading the article and had not emerged since, not even to eat the meals her mother left for her on a tray at the threshold.

As a result, on the afternoon of 28 October 1933 when Bishop Tijerino Loáisiga arrived at the head of the Blessed Sacrament procession, everyone was eager to see María del Pilar. The Bishop was carrying the casket containing the host in his hands, ready to give communion to all members of the household, and all the participants in the procession followed him jostling for a place as close as possible to the makeshift altar set up on the veranda. They were hoping to see María del Pilar on her knees to receive the host, curious as to whether they would be able to detect any signs of repentance on her face: they had all heard the rumours that she had decided to become a nun. But she did not appear, as General Abaunza records in his article published in *El Centroamericano*. The door to her room, a few metres away from the altar, remained firmly closed throughout the ceremony.

The story that she was about to take holy orders had been encouraged by Canon Oviedo y Reyes (as we heard in the argument he had with his brother, Oviedo the Balloon) and was circulating predominantly among the churchgoers. When Doña Flora announced that she was winding up her business affairs to return to Costa Rica it was assumed that she wished to be near her daughter who, so the gossips said, was to take her final vows to enter the order of Saint Vincent de Paul, which ran a sanatorium for tuberculosis sufferers, located in the foothills of the Irazú volcano.

The canon touched upon the topic, albeit indirectly, in his article 'More People Needed for Vocations', published in the diocesan weekly *Los Hechos* that came out in the first week of November:

> It is easy to see that the female vocations are in crisis. We need legions of pious nuns willing to console those who suffer. The importance of their work cannot be overlooked; with loving care these saintly women who have forsaken all earthly vanities dedicate themselves to relieving the suffering of the sick in our hospitals, leper colonies and sanatoriums.
>
> The path to piety is often beset by hazards, and is often signposted by repentance. Repentance purifies the bodies of lost souls with a revitalizing flame; especially when the fall from grace has occurred in early youth or adolescence. Among the best ways to effect this purification are attending to the sickbed, the deathbed, the cleansing of sores. These are all good in the sight of the Lord.
>
> Some will say that these are not true vocations but simply ways of salving consciences. As the scriptures say: "my sins are always before me"; the mirror of our past life should always be before us so that we can be in constant contemplation of our own guilt so that we might better correct our faults. As pastors, we rejoice when a vocation springs from a calling that is pure and untarnished; but we do not cast aspersions on those that are dictated by the terrible failings of a soul that has been led astray.
>
> María del Pilar's withdrawal from society, combined with the many rumours surrounding her, meant that her testimony was eagerly anticipated. When she did appear before the judge, in her own home on 12 November 1933, there was a crowd of people gathered at the house to see it, including many journalists from both León and Mana-

gua. Manolo Cuadra's dispatch of 14 October 1933 for *La Nueva Prensa*, "Two Plates of Nothing... Or Everything on the Same Plate?", contains her full statement and also the following reflections on the situation:

The press were not granted access when Señorita Contreras gave her deposition. Thanks to judicial discretion, this event took place at her home, and the doors were opened only briefly to allow entry to Judge Mariano Fiallos and his secretary, the poet Alí Vanegas. This city is fed night and day by the vast array of rumours produced by the mysterious workings of the Castañeda case, and from the early hours of this morning the news of her imminent appearance before the judge has been causing quite a stir. The young girl has not left the house in recent times: nobody has seen her. Gossip and supposition are the order of the day.

While we wait, and it promises to be a lengthy wait, we take the opportunity to visit the La Fama shop whose doors have once again been opened to the public on a regular basis. We hope to be able to gather some insights from those who work there; insights that we are certain will be of considerable interest to our avid readers.

The presence of a journalist in the shop sent most of the shopgirls running, simpering bashfully. Only Liliam García, a graceful brunette, clearly from Subtiava, did not hesitate to attend me. I pose the question: the latest word is that the young Contreras is heading for our sister republic, Costa Rica, where she is to take holy orders.

She responds freely: she too has heard this on the street, but she has seen no evidence of any preparations to this end in the house. Doña Flora has decided not to leave the country after all, because she has changed her mind about the sale of her remaining stock, as announced in the local press. This leads the genteel Liliam to doubt the news about her taking holy orders.

Does she know anything about María del Pilar? Can she tell us anything about her current frame of mind, her mood? Has she seen her at all since her self-imposed seclusion began?

> She glances towards the back of the shop; the shop connects with the house via the veranda and she confirms that sometime ago she did see her walking in the garden. She describes her shuffling across the flag-stones dressed in strict mourning, her rebellious curls turned prematurely grey and her lips in constant motion, muttering: aged far beyond her eighteen years. She describes her as being like an old woman: talking to herself, alone with her memories. And since then? No, since then she hasn't seen her.

It was twelve-thirty when Judge Fiallos went into the house. Carmen Contreras Guardia met him at the door and escorted him to the veranda where his mother and uncle, Fernando Guardia, and the prosecuting lawyer Don Juan de Dios Vanegas were waiting. Two of the Viennese chairs had been set out for the judge and his secretary in the corner occupied by the statue of the Infant Jesus of Prague. Opposite them stood four wicker rocking chairs. Between the two sets of chairs was a table ready to be used as a writing desk. When Judge Fiallos and his secretary were seated, Doña Flora went to fetch María del Pilar from her room and led her by the hand to sit in the middle of the four rocking chairs. She sat on one side with her brother on the other, and next to him Doctor Vanegas. Carmen, armed with a revolver, went to the veranda to guard the locked door to the street.

The girl made a respectful nod to Judge Fiallos before she sat down and then remained very still, her knees pressed together and her hands in her lap nervously wringing a little embroidered handkerchief as if she were waiting to start an end of term exam. The only thing that clashed with her schoolgirl air was the severe mourning attire: the high-necked blouse with its matronly cuffs, the hemline below the knees, and black stockings. There was not a single grey hair among her curls, nor did her lips move in the lonely mumblings of senility, as Alí Vanegas later remarked to Manolo Cuadra, accusing him of having fabricated this particularly grotesque image.

Judge Fiallos did not wish to display any hesitancy and had prepared himself mentally before setting out for this appointment. As he revised his notes, anxious not to make any more mistakes, he struggled not to be affected by the charged atmosphere and show of family togetherness. He needed the girl's testimony to fill in the details that he had failed to get from Doctor Salmerón and, although he risked appearing cruel, this would require him to delve into some of the most sordid aspects of the case. The dossier already contained enough evidence to indict Oliverio Castañeda for the crimes which the laboratory tests proved to have been committed. Even so, and despite the scandal that still reverberated across Léon, it was necessary to clarify his motives.

When this thorny interview was finished, however, Judge Fiallos was filled with frustration once more. Just as with Doctor Salmerón, he felt had got nowhere. If in the one instance he had been too insistent, thereby derailing the proceedings, this time he had been too weak; he had allowed the mother to intervene, encouraged by the prosecuting lawyer (in total contravention of judicial procedures), and had even allowed her to call a halt to the questioning.

In the case dossier María del Pilar's deposition is recorded thus:

> JUDGE: What connections do you see between the deaths of your sister Matilde Contreras, of your father Carmen Contreras and that of Marta Jerez de Castañeda?
>
> WITNESS: They are all crimes committed by the same person. And the person who committed them is Oliverio Castañeda. He poisoned my sister Matilde by giving her a piece of chicken laced with strychnine, which he offered to her from his own plate when they were sitting together at the table. She didn't want to take it but he told her: "It is tasty, so tasty." He put poison in my father's medicine which he kept on a table in the room they shared. I went to get the medicine because my father sent me saying: "I need my medicine now," and there was the little box where my father had left it in the night. Oliverio Castañeda could have reached it simply by stretching out his hand. I don't know how he killed his wife Marta, but it must have been with medicine or food poisoned by him.
>
> JUDGE: What leads you to this conclusion?
>
> WITNESS: Because it has been proved that these people died of poisoning when Oliverio Castañeda was there:

he was always close to all three of them. He had the poison because that is what he did; poisoning dogs and people. He'd already poisoned Rafael Ubico in Costa Rica. My mother confiscated a book he had on poisoning which he wanted my sister Matilde to read. I have no idea why.

JUDGE: What do you think Oliverio Castañeda's objectives were in committing these crimes?

WITNESS: He had a plan to get hold of my father's money. In his plan, his wife had to die first and then he needed to kill my sister and my mother so that I would be left alone and he could propose marriage to me so that he could inherit. That's why he was always so keen to find out about the running of my father's businesses and why he offered, without being asked, to arrange the affairs of the Metropolitan Water Company. He said that my father had named him to act on his behalf in business dealings and had asked him to move into his office, but this was a lie.

JUDGE: What makes you believe that marriage to you was part of this plan? Did he at any point make any amorous advances to you?

WITNESS: No he didn't, because I was very proper when I was with him. But I did notice that he showed me special attention that he didn't show towards my sister Matilde, although he never made any obvious moves towards me. There was just this special attention.

JUDGE: This special attention he showed you, did it start before his wife died?

WITNESS: Yes, I remember him paying me attention right in front of his wife. But it's not until now that I realise that there was an ulterior motive to get rid of everyone else to ensnare me. I always behaved properly and was very careful never to accept his attentions.

JUDGE: Do you mean to say that your sister Matilde was never the subject of his special attention?

WITNESS: I don't remember him ever showing her this attention. My sister was very pious and if he'd ever talked to her of falling in love then she would have refused him.

JUDGE: In her statement of 19 October 1933, the domestic servant Leticia Osorio refers to how, before the

Castañeda couple left this house, Marta seemed very upset and tearful. Do you know if Marta felt jealous towards anyone?

WITNESS: I didn't know that Marta felt jealous, nor did I notice her crying. She got along with us just fine, and when she left I remember her being happy about making their new home. We and everyone else helped her arrange things. I think she must have been very grateful to us when she left because my mother found them a house; they were foreigners and didn't know anyone and I don't think she would have been so unappreciative.

JUDGE: So you don't believe that she noticed the special attention shown to you by Oliverio Castañeda?

WITNESS: The special attention was not reciprocated, so she couldn't have noticed and she didn't complain to me about being jealous. She didn't have any reason to feel jealous towards anyone in this house, because she could see that we all behaved very properly with her husband.

JUDGE: Can you tell me what form this special attention to which you refer took?

WITNESS: He was always very polite and considerate: he would always pull back my chair for me when we sat at table; he would also explain my lessons to me when I didn't understand, because he is very intelligent; and he made silly jokes to me that he never made to Matilde; nor did he joke with his wife the way he did with me. I realise now that he was intending to propose, although he never said so to me because I always kept in my place and was very proper.

JUDGE: Were you in the habit of giving gifts to Oliverio Castañeda?

WITNESS: With my mother's permission I gave him a bottle of perfumed lotion. She got it for me from the shop because it was his birthday. If it hadn't been his birthday I wouldn't have given him anything as I had no reason to give him gifts.

JUDGE: Leticia Osorio says in her statement, which I have already mentioned, that on the day that Oliverio Castañeda was taken prisoner, you prepared food and clothing for him which she took to the prison with the driver. She also states that she took a letter for him written by you.

WITNESS: I didn't send him any letters. I wrote a list of the clothing that Leticia was taking so that he would know what had been sent and he could return it when it was dirty. Anyway, it was on my mother's orders that the food and clothing were sent to him that day.

JUDGE: In the days that followed, before it was forbidden by the authorities, these consignments to the prison continued, and the items sent included perfumes, handkerchiefs, flowers. Can you explain what the intentions were behind all these gifts? What was the reason for sending him furniture, including a chest of drawers?

WITNESS: They were things he asked for; he said he needed them. He asked my mother to send these things and we sent them because we didn't know whether he was guilty or not. Now we don't send him anything, because we know he is guilty and had ulterior motives with me: to get me on my own and to rob us of everything.

JUDGE: Do you know if your sister wrote letters to him while he was living in this house?

WITNESS: I don't know if she wrote anything but I don't think it likely. If we were all living in the same house there wouldn't have been any need for them to exchange letters. And there wasn't any reason for them to have any lovers' secrets to tell one another, because he was not in love with my sister.

(At this point the judge proceeded to show the witness a letter, without date or signature, that was requisitioned from Oliverio Castañeda's luggage on 13 October 1933.)

JUDGE: Do you recognise the handwriting on this letter?

(The witness proceeded to examine the letter and then returned it to the judge.)

WITNESS: I don't recognise the handwriting. I have never seen it before, so I can't say who could have written it.

JUDGE: Look at it again and then answer me with the utmost sincerity. Take into consideration that the initials of the third person mentioned in this letter, M. P., belong to yourself.

(The judge proceeded to pass the letter back and the witness returned it after a second examination.)

WITNESS: It could be, but the letter isn't talking about me. It says that the person writing is jealous and my sister had no reason to be jealous of his special attentions towards me since she was not in love with him. It says here that the person M. P. came along and stole him away from her and I didn't steal him away because his special attention towards me started from the beginning when he came to live here and he only gave this attention to me and no one else.

(At this point the witness's mother intervened in order to clarify that the reference "I didn't steal him away" was a figure of speech, and should be recorded as such in the legal report on proceedings. The judge responded to this by saying that any clarification must come from the witness herself. When questioned on this point, the witness confirmed that she had been speaking figuratively so as to emphasise that she had been in receipt of the accused's special attentions from the beginning, as soon as the accused had come to live in their home.)

JUDGE: On 17 October 1933, Señorita Rosario Aguiluz, manager of the post office stated that your sister Matilde sent letters to Oliverio Castañeda when he went to Guatemala; and that she received letters from him. What is your opinion concerning this correspondence?

WITNESS: If he wrote to her perhaps she answered. I expect that they wrote as friends, and that she consoled him because his wife had just died. He was deeply saddened by the death of his wife. My sister is a good Catholic and she would have given him the consolation of religion. I don't see anything wrong with it because he wrote to my mother, too; the envelopes were addressed to La Fama at the address number whatever.

(At this point the mother of the witness asked to clarify that these were business letters since she had asked the accused to investigate some merchandise available in Guatemala at a competitive price. The judge reiterated that the official record could only contain the witness's statement; she then asked in her own words that the record show that these were business letters.)

JUDGE: According to the deposition given by Octavio Oviedo y Reyes on October seventeenth, on one occasion Oliverio Castañeda showed him a letter which the accused assured him was sent by you. When did you write this letter?

WITNESS: I never, ever sent him letters, but it doesn't surprise me that he went around telling his friends that I did because he is a liar and a slanderer who has told many falsehoods about other ladies in this city.

JUDGE: When Oliverio Castañeda arrived in Costa Rica in July of this year, had he contacted you previously to let you know of his arrival?

WITNESS: No, he hadn't contacted me, because we didn't write to each other. My mother and I found out that he was coming to Costa Rica because he sent a telegram to my brother via Tropical Radio. The wire was a surprise to us because we thought we would never see him again; when he left Guatemala he told us: "I will never come back."

JUDGE: When he was in Costa Rica did he visit you?

WITNESS: Yes, he came to visit us in my uncle's house in the Amón district since he was a friend of the family. He sat with me in the living room to chat about this and that: things about my mother and my uncle, if the weather in San José was wet or that it was very cold, about an accident on the trams that happened and things about politics and religion; he was always against religion. He also spent a great deal of time attacking people I didn't know and giving his opinion on issues surrounding the strikes at the banana plantations in Costa Rica; he stood on the side of the strikers. Then there were questions about communism that my uncle always challenged him on.

JUDGE: Did you go out with him while you were both in Costa Rica?

WITNESS: We went out together with friends to take trips and go to parties. We were always accompanied by reliable people. We went to performances at the National Theatre and the cinema; mostly with our friends and sometimes with my uncle and mother, but I never went with him alone because my mother would never have permitted it.

JUDGE: In her deposition given on 19 October 1933 your intimate friend Alicia Duquestrada told us that your sister was very upset when you wrote to her about your constant association with Oliverio Castañeda in Costa Rica, and she made it clear that she did not want him to come back to live in this house. What do have to say in this respect?

WITNESS: I don't think she was upset that I told her about going out on trips and to theatres and the cinema. She had no interest in Oliverio Castañeda, so why would she be jealous? If I told her all those things it was because I had nothing to hide from anybody. If she didn't want him to come back to live in this house it was probably because she thought it would look bad due to the gossip that people were spreading about his special attention to me. Anyway, she may have told her friend that she wouldn't stand for it, but it didn't turn out that way and she welcomed us both when we returned.

JUDGE: This special attention of which you speak. Did it continue when Oliverio Castañeda was with you in Costa Rica?

WITNESS: The attention did continue and it was things like: taking my coat in a very gentlemanly manner when we arrived at places and being the first to ask me to dance at balls and if I was thirsty he'd go and get me a drink with a straw and telling me all the time that I was looking lovely and elegant. He said all these things to my mother too, because he was paying her special attention as well, and I saw nothing wrong in him doing that.

(At this point the mother of the witness requested that the judge suspend the interview to be resumed another day because her daughter was feeling tired and anxious. The judge proceeded to ask the witness if this was indeed the case, and when she confirmed this he agreed to the request, and the legal record remains inconclusive.)

Despite the fact that the record was left open, a second opportunity to interview María del Pilar Contreras never presented itself. Judge Fiallos felt that it had been a disaster, but Alí Vanegas held the opposite view: while her answers had not been explicit, they were sufficient to establish the backdrop of a sentimental attachment. Manolo Cuadra also came close to this opinion in his dispatch for *La Nueva Prensa* 'Two Plates of Nothing...Or Everything on the Same Plate?' which has already been cited:

> The long-awaited deposition of Señorita María del Pilar Contreras leaves many questions still unanswered, but the way in which the interrogation was conducted is even more open to question. The most sordid aspects of the case were treated with too delicate a touch by Mariano Fiallos. He did not even voice many crucial questions. Perhaps this was because the atmosphere was not conducive to the interrogation process; he had to contend with the witness within her own home and protected by her closest family, who were allowed the luxury of intervening on her behalf whenever they felt it necessary.
>
> When questioned on this issue, the legal secretary Alí Vanegas explained that there is provision for this courtesy within the penal code. In one of its articles, The Code of Criminal Proceedings states: "Witnesses whose position, rank or title deserves this treatment, or where the presiding judge feels it is appropriate, can be exempted from the obligation of appearing at the Law Courts, providing that the relevant process can be completed at the home address of the witness." Not every ordinary citizen can enjoy such a privilege, and as has been shown in this case, the prerogative can lead to undue pressure.
>
> This having been said, the attentive reader could still extract sufficient detail from the deposition transcribed here to make definite conclusions. It is an intricate story of love and jealousy, the cause of great scandal in this city so attached to its colonial past, and it may be just the tip of the iceberg: "Look closely at the tip of the iceberg and from this you can calculate the dimensions and bulk of the ice that hides beneath the great ocean waves," as G.K.

> Chesterton's detective priest Father Brown once said to his friend Flambeau.
>
> On encountering your reporters as he left the Contreras family residence, Mariano Fiallos was as taciturn as ever, telling us to refer to the text of the deposition which he would make available to copy. Then with a broad smile he asked us whether it wouldn't be better to report on Jack London, the arctic seal hunter and sailor of the stormy southern seas... or Franklin Roosevelt's "New Deal", on the emergence of the sinister Austrian, Adolf Hitler, risen from meetings held in the rowdy bierkellers of Munich to the chancellorship of Germany, on the fire at the Reichstag...trifles reported on the international cables, or indeed on boxing, a topic that has always been a passion of his. He doesn't give a damn for the upstart Primo Carnera who has just dethroned Sharkey, taking from him the crown as champion of all weights. Like a good referee, he is aware that the final bell has not yet rung for the last round of this case...and we took the opportunity to give him our best wishes, because today is his birthday. Here's to you, Mariano Fiallos!

It was indeed Judge Fiallos's birthday. His wife had organised a surprise get-together for some of their friends and neighbours which awaited him when he got home. When he arrived at his door with Alí Vanegas, an old marimbero who had been dozing on the bench outside struck up a tune, energetically hitting the keys in a rendition of: 'The Last Drunken Chuckle'. On the veranda, the guests were gathered round a table laden with bottles of Campeón rum and great serving dishes of canapés. The music was the signal for them to all come out and greet the guest of honour.

Captain Anastasio J. Ortiz was the first to embrace him; amidst knowing smiles from everyone present, the captain handed him a poster, rolled up and secured with a silk ribbon. It was a reproduction of a print produced by Lahmann & Kemp, originally in pencil. It showed an enormous mosquito with an emaciated victim of malaria imprisoned between its front legs, impotently struggling to free himself from the insect's grip. The inscription written above the picture read: 'Best wishes to Mariano Fiallos, who will rid León of its blackwater fever.'

Judge Fiallos smiled too, although his heart was not in it. Excusing himself, he handed the poster to Alí Vanegas before heading off to his room. Alí Vanegas rolled the poster up again and left it on the table among the bottles and canapés.

'How did the interrogation go?' asked Captain Ortiz, removing his gun holster and clearing a space on the table for it.

'The witness was well coached,' replied Alí Vanegas, brushing away the flies and lifting a corner of the grease-proof paper covering one of the serving dishes containing turtle eggs and baked yucca. He picked out a piece of yucca with a toothpick; 'she had learned all the answers to the questions off by heart.'

'They just want to get all this over with. They're nervous and with good reason,' said Captain Ortiz, grabbing an egg from the same plate and rolling it between his palms. 'Dona Flora was even prepared to leave the country.'

'The delightful young lady was not at all nervous,' said Alí Vanegas, swallowing almost without chewing, and leaving the toothpick dangling from his lips; 'she'd been well taught and performed her lines with aplomb. But when she started ad-libbing, her mother had to correct her and eventually had to shut her up.'

'You have no right to mess them around like this,' said Captain Ortiz, breaking the egg shell with his fingernail and rubbing chilli into the opening. 'Why can't you leave them alone? Someone needs to stand up for them!'

'The streets are still full of the devout and their banners,' said Alí, chewing his toothpick. He watched as Captain Ortiz sucked on the egg with gusto. 'That's a lot of holy water and more than enough prayers!'

'I'm not talking about the holy women and the priests,' Captain Ortiz said, picking up a napkin to wipe his chin. 'I'm talking about Doctor Teodosio and his accomplices.'

'Your Honour should not forget that if it weren't for Doctor Teodosio you'd never have caught Baldomero,' said Alí Vanegas, uncovering another dish and using his toothpick to skewer a piece of pork seasoned and coloured red with annatto.

'Don't tell me you're defending that trouble-maker!' said Captain Ortiz, scrunching up his stained napkin and throwing it under the table.

'I am but the humble scribe of Supreme Justice and I don't dare defend anyone,' said Alí Vanegas, taking the toothpick out of his mouth and depositing it delicately onto the tablecloth. 'You should leave this Honourable System to get on with its job and stop interfering.'

'Some justice. Flora and her daughters have already been judged by hear-say,' said Captain Ortiz, taking his gun belt from the table and feeling the weight of his pistol. 'And now that they've been dragged through the dirt, who is going to compensate them?'

'The wronged party can easily obtain redress by pressing charges of libel against the wise Teodosio,' said Alí Vanegas. The flies were swarming over the table and he grabbed the rolled up poster to swat them.

'What nonsense, they would just get laughed at all over again,' said Captain Ortiz, strapping on his gun belt and brandishing his pistol before sheathing it. 'And Salmerón is laughing loudest. We'll see how long he has to savour his victory.'

'What? So you're outlawing laughter now?' said Alí Vanegas. Hearing applause behind him, he turned to see Judge Fiallos returning from his room showing off his new bow-tie: red with white polka dots, a present from his wife. It was she doing the applauding. 'You wouldn't go that far.'

'Who says I wouldn't. I have just got the authorisation for an arrest from Managua,' said Captain Ortiz as he finished strapping his gun holster against his thigh. 'That bastard has had his day.'

When Judge Fiallos came over the captain had already started making his way out, jauntily slapping his leg with his Marine's cap. The marimbero started up again; after making a few false starts he coaxed his instrument into a version of 'True Love Is a Once-in-a-Lifetime Thing'.

'What fly bit him?' said Judge Fiallos, adjusting his bow tie while he looked for a glass. 'He looks mad!'

'It was no fly, it was the anopheles mosquito,' said Alí Vanegas. He trumpeted down the poster tube: 'The barbarians are coming, fair Lutetia! At last he is going to have the satisfaction of putting the sagacious Teodosio in the stocks. He's off to arrest him now!'

CHAPTER FORTY-ONE

The Black Packard Arrives at the Abandoned Ranch

WHEN DOCTOR Salmerón arrived at his surgery to find Rosalío Usulutlán waiting for him dressed in an elaborately buttoned priest's cassock, he found himself seized by a fit of laughter that brought tears to his eyes despite his dreadful mood. Rosalío's clothes were caked with mud, as were his boots; lumps of dried mud littered the floor, marking out his nervous pacing and showing he had been waiting for some time.

Rosalío bent his neck stiffly and solemnly raised his hand in a blessing, which only added to Doctor Salmerón's mirth. Continuing to make the sign of the cross, Rosalío went over to the little window that gave onto the street. He peered through the bars and making a grimace indicated that Doctor Salmerón should take a look. When the doctor looked through the window, he saw two suspicious-looking men standing beneath the lamp post on the opposite side of the street.

'That's old news,' said Doctor Salmerón, stepping back from the window and wiping his eyes with a finger. 'They've been there for a few days. They're guardsmen in plain clothes. Couldn't you have gone for a different disguise?'

Rosalío gesticulated, signing and mouthing voicelessly as if he were deaf and dumb.

'They are the lackeys who'll cart me off as soon as they're given the order, that's why Tacho Ortiz put them there,' said Doctor Salmerón, making a megaphone of his hands and moving back towards the window.

In fright, Rosalío hurried to stop him.

'Whoa!' Doctor Salmerón started, staring him up and down. 'Why are you frightened? I've already got my pillow and a bundle of clothes ready for when they come to get me.'

Doing a very good impression of a real priest, Rosalío lowered his head and clasped his hands together imploringly.

'You should be marching with those holy ladies in that cassock,' said Doctor Salmerón. He laughed again, but this time he was more subdued. 'It could have been you who gave the angelical María del Pilar her first holy communion.'

'I've discovered that they did fornicate,' Rosalío whispered into his ear, before swiftly withdrawing.

'That's no good to us,' Doctor Salmerón, taking off his jacket. He walked dejectedly to the coat stand, a black pillar-like affair with spidery legs, where he hung it next to his hat. 'That asshole of a judge is more like a priest than you, even without a disguise.'

'And all the evidence? I have more here…' said Rosalío, taking another step backwards, arms akimbo.

'You can wipe your ass with your evidence,' Doctor Salmerón said, taking out an enormous bunch of keys and opening the door to his consulting-room. 'Matilde Contreras has had her virginity officially certified. All that's left now is for Doctor Darbishire to certify the virginity of María del Pilar. And that of Doña Flora.'

'The black Packard did go to the ranch,' said Rosalío, following Doctor Salmerón to the door of his consulting-room. He searched in the deep pockets of his cassock for the sheaf of paper containing his notes. 'The anonymous letter sent to the judge came from the overseer. He's bitter because they made him pay for some banana stems that were stolen from the plantation.'

Doctor Salmerón groped for the light switch on the wall. Turning it, the surgery was filled with a dirty yellow light. The effect was to make everything: the couch, the instrument cabinet, and the hand basin, appear even more ramshackle and battered than ever.

'Pass me the newspaper in my jacket pocket,' said Doctor Salmerón, going over to his desk. 'To top everything off, the pig-headed old fool has decided to insult me yet again in *El Centroamericano*.'

'You should stop taking so much notice of that old cretin,' said Rosalío, bringing the paper over and throwing it onto the desk. A youthful portrait of Doctor Darbishire in profile poring over his microscope came into view as the newspaper unrolled.

'I must answer him, even if it has to be from behind bars,' said Doctor Salmerón as he emptied his medical bag. 'I have to bring him down a peg or two once and for all.'

'You should hear what my informant has to say,' said Rosalío, climbing onto the couch. 'It's stuff we've never heard before.'

'Well then, let's hear it,' said Doctor Salmerón, taking out his Casa Squibb notebook and placing it at the ready.

'But what are we going to do with all our evidence now? Should we publish it as a pamphlet?' enquired Rosalío, arranging his notes across his knees.

'When I get out of jail we'll see,' replied Doctor Salmerón, leafing through his notebook to find a clean page. The little book was nearly full.

The reader should know at this point that early the same morning an urgent message from Doctor Salmerón had reached Rosalío, still hiding in the oil-press at his father's house. The message had charged him with the task of finding the overseer of the ranch 'Nuestro Amo' since he wanted to be able to use whatever information could be obtained there in his forthcoming interview with the judge. Rosalío did try to obey, but had been delayed owing to some difficulties finding a horse for hire. As a result, by the time he returned to the surgery he had been too late to catch Doctor Salmerón.

If the reader will permit, it would be wise to stop here and examine the situation to determine how Doctor Salmerón intended to knit together the many strands of information he had gathered together before his questioning by the judge.

We already know that Luis Felipe Pérez, the codfish-dancer, had seen Oliverio Castañeda give a letter to Dolores Lorente in the porch of the Recolección church on the morning of 13 February 1933. This is according to the story he told Cosme Manzo shortly before he was knifed to death in a bar. Dolores Lorente had confirmed the story to Cosme Manzo later that day, telling him that the intended recipient of letter had been María del Pilar Contreras who would wait every day in the Merced church. Unfortunately, although Cosme Manzo (who was now her employer) had instructed her on several occasions on what to say in her deposition, Dolores Lorente had been too afraid to mention any of this when she came before the judge on 17 October 1933.

Another important piece of information is related to the clandestine meetings between Oliverio Castañeda and María del Pilar Contreras at the 'Nuestro Amo' ranch. Dolores Lorente knew about these meetings be she did not reveal this to Cosme Manzo until after giving her deposition, and so the members of the accursed table had decided to use the information in Rosalío's exposé before having verified it fully.

In February 1933 Dolores Lorente had been working as the cook at the ranch, which as we already know was located on the road out to the Poneloya spa. It was from this outpost that Doña Flora later recalled her to work for the Castañeda couple at their new home, enticing her with the offer of a monthly wage of five córdobas instead of the four she was receiving at the ranch.

At the time, she had been living about half a league away in the tiny hamlet of San Caralampio; she would get to the ranch before daybreak and once lunch had been served hitch a ride back on the cart that took firewood to León, which left her at the edge of the hamlet from where she could walk to her own house. The lovers would arrive in the black Packard towards evening, which meant she was no longer there to see them. However, the overseer Eufrasio Donaire, her common-law spouse, had been there and he witnessed these furtive encounters. She was the only person he told.

The black Packard had first arrived at the ranch close to five o'clock in the afternoon and drove up the avenue of dusty palm trees leading to the house. The overseer was the only person at the otherwise abandoned ranch and he had permission to sleep on the lower floor where they stored the milk churns and farm tools. At night he would unfold his cot by the light of a candle.

The house had two storeys, with a wooden balcony from which the sea was visible in the distance. It was common knowledge that Don Carmen's elder sister, Matilde Contreras Reyes, had died of tuberculosis in one of the upper rooms after a confinement of several years, and that as a result the family had ceased to use the house for pleasure. It was now in a complete state of abandon and this is how Rosalío Usulutlán found it when he arrived there at midday on 28 October 1933.

Eufrasio Donaire was more than happy to tell Rosalío everything he knew, and also confessed that he had been the one to send the anonymous note to the judge on the advice of one of the clerks at C. Contreras & Co., a certain Demetrio Puertas. He had frequent dealings with this clerk since it was his job to collect the wages for the ranch from the company offices every Saturday. This Puertas fellow had also confided in him about the accounting frauds.

As far as Eufrasio Donaire could remember, the liaisons had taken place on several occasions: the first two in December 1931, and then others in January 1933, the end of February, and middle of March, followed by more recent meetings towards the end of September and beginning of October. When Rosalío visited the ranch he was able to see the room used by the couple on these dates; it was the same one where the consumptive had died. The only furniture was a metal bedstead with a rusty frame, two rickety cane chairs and an earthenware pitcher.

What Eufrasio Donaire saw and heard was later transcribed into the Casa Squibb notebook by Doctor Salmerón from Rosalío's notes. A copy is included here:

> The first time was when Donaire was returning from the cattle pens after rounding up a stray cow that the farmhands had left to graze in the pasture. He'd been surprised to hear the sound of a car and thought to himself that although it was unusual, it could only be Don Carmen arriving at such a late hour. Then he saw that the driver was none other than the man dressed in mourning whom he already knew because he'd seen him at the house in León: Oliverio Castañeda. At his side was the younger daughter, María del Pilar. She was dressed in her black-striped school uniform and the man in mourning was trying to persuade her to get out of the car, which she was refusing to do. He thought he heard her crying: quietly, perhaps, but almost certainly crying.
>
> Donaire walked over, oblivious of anything untoward. Castañeda, the man in mourning, saw him and got out of the car asking if he would cut them some sweet lemons because they wanted some for the festival of the Immaculate Conception. Donaire obeyed and went to the house

to look for a basket before going to the lemon tree. When he got back there was nobody there; the car was standing empty with its front doors open wide. He imagined that they'd gone for a walk, although that would have been a strange thing to do as it was already getting dark and the only noise was the racket from the cicadas. He went back to the house with his basket full of lemons to wait for them to return. While he was waiting he became aware of voices coming from the room above him. Then he heard the sound of feet walking across the floor boards followed by the creaking of springs from the bedstead; this noise sounded a little like the cicadas chirping. It couldn't have been cicadas though as these were all outside.

Donaire took his basket of lemons and left the farmhouse again: he didn't want them to think he'd been spying. He placed the basket on the backseat of the car. He sat on the fence of the cattle pen and waited, as far away as possible from whatever was happening in the house. The darkness deepened until it was difficult to see the plumes of the palm trees along the drive. It was some time past six, almost seven o'clock, that the girl María del Pilar emerged and got into the car. The man in mourning followed her at a leisurely pace. Donaire didn't know whether to go over or not, but then Castañeda called to him, just as if nothing had happened. He handed him a two córdoba bill, which was far too much to cover the picking of a few lemons but he took it and thanked him. Castañeda then told him that they might be coming again over the next few evenings to get lemons for the Immaculate Conception.

They came back after a week. Donaire had the lemons ready picked and waiting for them. They didn't bother to take them, probably because the festival of the Immaculate Conception had finished. Castañeda gave him two córdobas anyway.

'Lemons for the festival of Immaculate Conception,' Doctor Salmerón mused, shaking his pen as it seemed to have run out of ink. 'They were in an immaculate whorehouse more like. Is the man prepared to testify?'

'Yes he is,' said Rosalío, lying down on the couch with his hands behind his head and resting his papers on his chest. He was fully illuminated by the lamp light. 'Whether they will want to let him testify is another matter. Now, take note: January, the third visit.'

'Wait!' said Doctor Salmerón. He was trying to open his inkwell but the lid was stuck: 'Did he really believe you were a priest or did he recognise you?'

'He recognised me from somewhere,' said Rosalío, propping himself on his elbows. 'He's a well-read man. First thing he said to me was: "Don Chalío, that story about Laurentina and Baldomero was so good!", before I could even get off my horse.

'"The third time, more crying." Castañeda was leaving their home,' said Doctor Salmerón as he refilled his pen. 'Or was this date later on: once they had already been parted?'

'"They left the Packard hidden behind the wood-shed. This time they had brought a sheet. The bedstead only had a mat to cover the springs." I saw it when I was there,' Rosalío remarked. He gathered up his papers and brought them up to his eyes. 'I think it must have been before then, doctor. How could Castañeda have got hold of Don Carmen's Packard if he was no longer living with them?'

'That's where the letters at the church come in,' said Doctor Salmerón, tearing out a sheet from his prescription book to clean his ink-stained fingers. 'You're right.'

'"They brought their sheet with them. Donaire took on the task of sweeping out the room. He refreshed the water in the pitcher daily, in case they came back. They did return in January and again towards the end of February,"' said Rosalío. He shaded his eyes with his arm to read because the light from the lamp was so bright. 'Marta was already dead. "Donaire learned of her death. He thought about giving his condolences to the widower, but as he didn't seem too upset he decided that it wouldn't be welcomed."'

'I bet he'd have loved that; to be offered condolences!' said Doctor Salmerón, drying the ink on blotting paper provided by Doctor Witt's Pills: *"Lower back pain? The home remedy to make you smile again."* 'Let's get to the next bit. The farewell before he goes off on his travels.'

'"They stayed longer than ever." Donaire remembers that just as they were leaving was the first time she'd ever dared to look him in the eye,' said Rosalío, letting the arm holding his notes drop. '"She smiled at him sadly as she got into the Packard; then she got back out and handed him the sheet." Donaire showed it to me; he keeps it in his trunk. It's embroidered with goldfinches and swallows sipping nectar from flowers.'

'The body of evidence,' said Doctor Salmerón. He stopped writing for a moment to flex his fingers. 'I'd like to see that sheet in the hands of our thick-headed judge. It was probably embroidered by her dead sister, Matilde.'

'I've still got to tell you about the last two visits before the crimes were committed,' said Rosalío as he turned over, tucking up his feet and resting his cheek on his hands. '"They got out of the Packard, and ran hand in hand. They greeted Donaire joyfully," the crying of previous visits was a distant memory, Doctor.'

'The crying can wait for later.' Doctor Salmerón interrupted his writing and gave Rosalío a knowing smile. 'Is that it?'

'That's it. They became quite talkative with Donaire. "After all this time, to what do I owe this miracle?" he greeted him on the first of these final visits,' said Rosalío, still lying on his side. His story was beginning to take on a plaintive tone. '"We've missed you!" was her reply.'

'What they'd missed was that bed!' remarked Doctor Salmerón, shutting his notebook and screwing the cap back on his pen. 'That should be enough for now, Father.'

'Just the kiss left; the one that Demetrio Puertas the clerk saw.' Rosalío curled up a little more and closed his eyes. 'Demetrio Pucrtas spied them kissing from his desk in the office.'

'Don't go to sleep on me, Reverend!' said Doctor Salmerón, tapping his ink pot repeatedly against the wooden desk top. 'Puertas has already testified and he didn't mention it. When did it happen?'

'Just shortly after they returned from Costa Rica,' said Rosalío, sitting up and covering his mouth to yawn. 'He didn't mention the false account books either. But here I have it from what he told Donaire.'

'Kissing in broad daylight!' said Doctor Salmerón, yawning in his turn and trying to stifle it by biting on his knuckles; 'Who kissed whom?'

'She kissed him first, in the doorway to his room. She was collecting dirty laundry,' said Rosalío, clambering down off the couch and brushing down his cassock; traces of mud from his shoes were left on the cover. 'That ride on the nag has shattered me, doctor. I had to trot almost all the way, and even so I didn't arrive in time!'

'Its fine, that's not important now. We have more than enough kisses,' said Doctor Salmerón, slipping the blotter between the pages and closing his notebook. 'You can get off to bed. Leave me your notes so that I can copy out the stuff about the account books.'

'You won't understand my handwriting, I'd better come over tomorrow,' said Rosalío. He crossed to the window onto the street and slid it open very slowly.

'Tomorrow might be too late, give me the papers now,' said Doctor Salmerón, going over and holding out his hand.

'Your two spies are still there,' Rosalío said as he handed over the sheaf of papers without turning from the window. 'What if they grab me as I leave?'

'If they stop you, tell them you were giving me the last rites,' said Doctor Salmerón. He tried to laugh but it died in his throat.

CHAPTER FORTY-TWO

The Secret Dossier Ends Up Down the Latrine

At close to seven on the evening of 12 November 1933, Doctor Atanasio Salmerón was returning to his surgery in a horse-drawn cab. As he came near, the spies posted outside his house surrounded the cab and arrested him at gun-point. They were following orders sent by Captain Ortiz as soon as he had left Judge Fiallos's birthday party. Doctor Salmerón was forced down from the buggy and one of his would-be captors coshed him over the head with his pistol butt, giving him a nasty wound to his temple which, although it may not have needed stitches, certainly bled copiously.

He had with him in the cab several bundles of papers containing his answer to Doctor Darbishire's article in *El Centroamericano* of 29 October 1933. After fruitless attempts to get his reply published in any of the papers based in León (both *El Cronista* and *El Centroamericano* had refused to print his work even in the paid columns), he had finally got it printed at a small firm in the San José district.

Manolo Cuadra commented on the arrest in his dispatch of November fourteenth, which appeared in *La Nueva Prensa* entitled: 'Capture and Public Ridicule'.

> New developments have raised the temperature of the Castañeda case yet again, as on the evening of the twelfth Doctor Atanasio Salmerón was taken prisoner violently. This fellow continues to be a key witness, since despite previous refusals to turn over his evidence to the authorities, it was his enquiries that led them to the first evidence as to the criminal activities now under investigation. Ac-

cording to the cab driver, Santiago Mendoza, who was taking Doctor Salmerón home, during his arrest the well-known doctor was struck and insulted quite unnecessarily. We tracked him down to his customary location at the cab stand outside the railway station to find out more about his impressions of that night.

He is a man of some seventy years, the father of eight children, and he has shown considerable bravery in talking to us. He said: "I saw it all; it was an act of brutality. The doctor had hired me so that he could run some errands and I picked him up at his surgery around five. I took him to El Sol de Occidente, a printer in the San José district: the one with the cute donkey symbol; they were printing some pamphlets for him and we had to wait until they were done. He gave me one. I kept it; here it is," so saying he shows us the pamphlet. "When we got back to the surgery it was already dark and he asked me to help him unload the pamphlets. We were just about to start when we were surrounded by armed men."

We asked him if it was true that Doctor Salmerón had resisted arrest; if he had told him to get the horses going again and flee at full tilt as this reporter heard in the version of the story going round National Guard HQ. He responds: "That's a lie. He asked them, very politely, if they would let him unload the pamphlets. Their reply was for one of them to grab him by the hair and drag him roughly from his seat. He fell, and while he was still on the ground the other one bashed him with his pistol butt, screaming at him to get up. He was wounded and he asked to be allowed to go indoors to dress the cut, but they didn't care and dragged him off at gun point. I picked his hat up off the ground."

Other eye-witnesses, neighbours of Doctor Salmerón, tell of how he had to tear a strip off his shirt tails in order to bandage his head as he was marched off to National Guard HQ. On being advised of his capture, this reporter headed straight to the HQ; I was not permitted to enter, but from the gate I could see the doctor beyond the bars. After a long wait in the guard room he was moved up to the second floor where, without any further process, Captain Anastasio J. Ortiz gave him thirty days' detention with community service. The charges comprised inciting public disorder and corrupting public morals in accordance with article 128 of the Penal Code.

The moviegoers coming out of the Teatro González will have seen Doctor Salmerón as he was taken on foot and under armed guard to the cells of precinct XXI. This reporter was also present to see the spectacle, and I can confirm that his head was bandaged and his suit jacket was badly stained with blood. I tried to get close and called out to him: "Doctor Salmerón! What can you tell us about your arrest?" But he did not dare turn his head, still less answer.

There are many questions to be answered concerning the motives behind his detention. Was he arrested for printing a pamphlet laying out his scientific opinions on the case; opinions which the press refused to publish? This seems extremely doubtful because said pamphlets were not confiscated. In fact, after the prisoner was marched off, the cab-driver Santiago Mendoza tells us that he took it upon himself to unload the bundles, handing them over to the maid. Needless to say, the pamphlet began to circulate in León soon after.

What other motives could there be? What do the military say? Is this about revenge as has been rumoured? They are convinced that Doctor Salmerón is the one behind the exposé written by our colleague Rosalío Usulután. This article is the one mentioned in previous dispatches and in the wake of its publication there had been widely differing reactions. Those who consider themselves respectable feel it is scurrilous, while the ordinary people find it entertaining; Usulután has done a good job of providing them with the ultimate tragicomic romance.

Oviedo the Balloon was on his way out of the cinema and happened to be among the onlookers who saw Doctor Salmerón being escorted to the precinct XXI jail, and he spent the following hours raising the alarm. He informed the Captain, hailing him through one of the windows of Casa Prío and telling him to pass the news on to Cosme Manzo and Rosalío. He then went to the home of Doctor Escolástico Lara, president of the Medical Society in León who called an emergency meeting of its board of directors, but to no avail. He also roused Alí Vanegas at his room in Calle Real and the two of them went to Judge Fiallos's home. The judge's birthday celebrations had come to an end and he'd had a few too many, but they managed to get him out of bed.

Judge Fiallos attempted to get Captain Ortiz on the telephone at National Guard HQ, but the duty officer said that he was not there and that he had no idea of his whereabouts. He was also not at home when the judge went there in person. With all other options exhausted, the judge had no alternative but to send him an official directive. He instructed Alí Vanegas to take it to the HQ and ask for a receipt on handing it over. A transcription of this directive found its way into the case dossier:

> I have been informed that Doctor Atanasio Salmerón was arrested this evening on charges of which I was unaware. As far as I have been able to discover, the order for the arrest did not come from any judge in this municipality, from which I must conclude that it was the National Guard who issued said orders. The aforementioned Doctor Salmerón has appeared as a witness in the case that this Court is currently prosecuting against Oliverio Castañeda and he is under subpoena to give a further statement. For this reason his detention is an unwarranted invasion of my jurisdiction, and he should be released immediately. The repeated interference of the National Guard in this case is inappropriate and indeed, illegal. I demand that the prisoner be brought before me, the presiding judge. In the event that this does not happen I shall be forced to make an official complaint to the Supreme Court of Justice.

Far from heeding this warning, Captain Ortiz took Doctor Salmerón out of his cell early the following morning and set him to work sweeping the streets. Manolo Cuadra described the scene to his readers in the later part of his dispatch:

Could this be an act of revenge? This seems like a trivial question. Doctor Salmerón was taken from his cell on the morning of the thirteenth alongside a gang of common criminals; they were provided with brooms, shovels and mops and set to work cleaning the streets under the watchful eyes of armed soldiers. It is certainly rare to see a respectable doctor, his hair already greying, in a gang cleaning the gutters and sidewalks of Calle Real, the busiest street in León. There can be no doubt that the sentence of "community service" which the National Guard imposed on him was intended to humiliate him.

The Medical Society remains silent in the face of the misfortune that has befallen one of its members. The Faculty of Medicine also remains silent, as does the local press. Tomorrow, so we are told, he will be set to work pruning and weeding in the Guadalupe cemetery with special attention to the grave of Señorita Matilde Contreras. This seems a petty act of revenge. Today they have forced him to clean the street outside the surgery of Doctor Juan de Dios Darbishire on Calle Real. Another act of petty revenge. We are certain that the elderly gentleman has not demanded this, and the vulgar way in which Doctor Salmerón is being made to eat his words must surely astound him.

What does Mariano Fiallos make of these measures? It is in his hands that the Castañeda case now rests. We trust his good judgement and sense of fair play, and must leave the last word to him.

Describing how Doctor Salmerón was forced to eat his words by sweeping the sidewalk outside the surgery on Calle Real, Manolo Cuadra mentions his certainty that Doctor Darbishire would not indulge in such a petty act of revenge. The key to this reference is contained in the bundles of pamphlets that Doctor Salmerón's captors neglected to confiscate and which began to circulate on the night of his capture.

The article printed in the pamphlets put a definitive stop to the battle of words between mentor and disciple. It is included here:

SWIMMING IN THE SAME CESSPOOL

In his article carried by *El Centroamericano* on October twenty-ninth this year, Doctor Darbishire, my one-time mentor, requests that I should never again refer to him with this title. I would like to satisfy him and will not do so. Instead I am tempted to name him "Doctor Ptomaine", due to his insistence on referring to these substances; although I am sure some wisecracker, and there are many around, might prefer to dub him "Doctor Putrescine", which perhaps fits him better.

I can object to nothing that the learned Doctor finds to say about his handy little ptomaines; not even his assertions that they can be precipitated in the same reagents as the alkaloids. Perhaps he would like to tell us how to test for sugared water. However, it is not true that they are all deadly poisons: choline is a ptomaine which has curative properties; when applied in a 5% solution to diphtheria membranes it dissolves the fibrous plug. If the learned doctor does not believe me then he should refer to the work of Professor Emeritus Oswaldo Soriano: "New findings concerning the curative properties of animal- derived alkaloids" (Buenos Aires, 1901).

I am well aware, however, that when people are not disposed to agree it is not worth entering into a lengthy discussion. This is especially so when such people are only seeking to show off their erudition; demonstrating their knowledge of Esperanto and Aramaic by quoting in other languages and when they will only cite those sources that suit their own arguments and proclivities, as Doctor Darbishire has done.

Well, I will speak to you in Spanish, learned Doctor. I will say to you, in plain language: if you confuse ptomaines with one or another of the strychnine-like alkaloids of which there are only four (listen carefully: only four), then you do so because you decide to or because you know no better. The worst thing is to decide not to on account of your own lack of knowledge. This means that you are stuck in a form of ignorance that has no cure: a sickness I would like to call "Refractory Ignorance".

In the case currently occupying the justice system in León, had the poisoner used a toxin such as solanine, delsoline, nicotine, digitalis or myristicine, then very well: then we may have needed instruments with far greater precision and apparatus that cannot be found perhaps in the whole of Central America. In the case of garden-variety strychnine, however: can one doubt the validity of test carried out diligently and in good faith in our own university? No, one can't; unless there are hidden motives for doing so.

Learned Doctor, I challenge you to test me, once and for all. I have three points which I would like to be put before a panel comprising five medical professionals from this city. I realise that you have a low opinion of the scientists in this city, but we could choose them by common consent; that is, if you and I can agree on anything nowadays. If, after hearing us, they decide that you are right I make a solemn promise to come and sweep the sidewalk in front of your surgery on any day of your choosing. The three points that I would like to test against the opinions of this panel are as follows:

1: That there are in existence certain ptomaines formed in the decomposition of human corpses that have physiological effects which are the same as those of the strychnine-like alkaloids. I contend that such substances do not exist.

2: That strychnine disintegrates during the putrefaction processes in humans. I will demonstrate that it does not disintegrate: it has been found in cadavers after twenty years as shown by Bryce, Echenique, Skarmeta, Monsivais etc....

3: That strychnine is soluble in alcohol and ether, as are the majority of ptomaines. I will demonstrate that they are not and never have been since science began.

Demonstrate these three, elementary points to me and I will be satisfied. If not, then cede victory and let us stop arguing; I am not going to request that you sweep the sidewalk in front of my surgery, which is far too humble to receive someone of your illustrious ancestry and fine taste. Please desist in your quest to prove the unprovable and, rather than enter into scientific discussions for which you no longer have the wit or the spirit, dedicate yourself, like any good penitent, to the processions where we have become accustomed to seeing you with such tiresome frequency. If there is one thing that I will concede it is this: your venerable and reverential air allows you to carry your holy banner far better than you know how to carry on this discussion.

Churchgoer you may be, but you are not holy since you have no qualms about using your fossilised arguments to defend a murderer; the killer of your patients. Yes, learned doctor, a murderer though you choose to forget it. You accuse me of being cut from the same cloth as Oliverio Castañeda, when it is you...no one else, who defends him by negating the clear weight of evidence! All that remains is for you to raise Castañeda on an altar as an idol to be worshipped. No doubt you would go and pray to him with the same fervour with which you now march through the streets singing hymns. You would be in good company: the other hypocrites who march alongside you beating their breasts. In the end you are all swimming in the same cesspool.

To conclude: given that the laurels you rest on in this city are getting a little withered, I'll offer you some free advice: you should write a paper on your recent discoveries on how to determine the virginity or otherwise of a corpse. You should then send it to Paris, Rome or even Berlin, where it can receive the same applause it has garnered here. Thus your laurels would be rejuvenated.

And so I will leave you with the confession that although I was your student it is true that I learned nothing and that is all to the good; it is clear that you never had anything to teach me. I must also leave because there are thugs following my every movement, anxious to lock me up in jail. My sources tell me that they accuse me of perjury and slander; crimes which you also accuse me of in your aforementioned article, for which I extend my heartfelt thanks. I must hurry as I do not want to end up in a dungeon before I have finished with you.

So, farewell once and for all...Doctor Putrescine! You can rest assured that your attempts at soothsaying will come to nothing. Foreseeing that I will end up allied to Oliverio Castañeda! What a disgrace! All you need to do now is put on a turban and silk cape, then get yourself to the Big Top with thc clowns...where you can enjoy the agreeable company of goats, monkeys and the rest of the tame beasts.

Post Scriptum: I find myself in a place where the powerful and the wealthy control the lies that are spread, and I have been muzzled as a punishment for seeking to expose the truth. After fruitless attempts to publish my response in any of the city's newspapers I have had to resort to the measure of getting it published as this leaflet. I ask you to frame the page and place it on the wall of your surgery to show that despite everything, I was able to answer you; as I will answer all my detractors and persecutors in good time. Enough.

On the morning of November fifteenth, emboldened by indignation, Captain Prío took it upon himself to visit his godfather, Doctor Darbishire at his surgery. He was hoping that the old man would intervene on Doctor Salmerón's behalf: for the third consecutive day Doctor Salmerón had been among the detail of prisoners sweeping the streets, this time in Plaza Jerez. The captain had seen the group of prisoners arrive while taking a delivery of ice and he had tried to send one of his waiters over with a jug of orange juice for the doctor. The guards had not allowed the waiter to get through, and amidst a torrent of mockery had confiscated the drink and consumed it themselves.

Doctor Darbishire was already back from his daily rounds at the San Vicente Hospital and was in the middle of a meeting with Doctor Escolástico Lara. The latter had come in the hope of getting his signature for the petition he intended to publish requesting an end to the despicable treatment of their incarcerated colleague.

While he waited in the passage the captain could hear heavy hammer blows interspersed between the discussion going on inside the consulting room. When Doctor Escolástico Lara emerged carrying the sheets of his petition in his hand, he looked upset. The dumb boy Teodosio showed him out. Inside the consulting room, Doctor Darbishire was hanging Doctor Salmerón's pamphlet on his wall: he had framed it and had already hammered a nail into the wall.

'Have you come for me to settle my food bill?' asked Doctor Darbishire, noticing Captain Prío when he finally turned to reach for his hammer again. 'It's not yet the end of the month, godson.'

'No, godfather,' said Captain Prío, who had remained standing next to the frosted glass door clasping the door handle, 'I only came to tell you that what they are doing to Doctor Salmerón is unfair.'

'And you think that what he did to me was fair? Come over here and take a look at this insolent rag.'

'I know I'm not in the best position to come here asking you for any favours, godfather,' said Captain Prío, standing on tiptoes to see what was in the frame without moving from his position. 'But a professional like him: how can they make him sweep the streets?'

'A disgraced professional. Only eight out of more than forty doctors practicing in León wanted to sign that petition,' said Doctor Darbishire, thumping the head of the hammer into his palm. 'And I am not signing either. If that person had still been at liberty I would have gone to the courts myself. He was always going to end up in prison.'

'Godfather, these are professional disagreements between doctors,' said Captain Prío, gently pushing the door closed. 'He who forgives is he who wins.'

'Forgive him! Never!' said Doctor Darbishire, hefting the hammer and placing it on his desk. 'That man has offended me. No one has ever offended me the way he has.'

'But how can you allow him to be paraded in the streets with a broom in his hands?' asked Captain Prío, coming across the room with his arms wide open in appeal, 'bandaged and covered in blood!'

'What do you want me to do about it, godson?' Doctor Darbishire said loftily as he adjusted his pince-nez.

'If you called for him to be set free, Somoza would listen,' said

Captain Prío, taking his packet of Esfinge cigarettes from his shirt pocket, 'and the whole city would applaud your nobility.'

'I'm not looking for applause,' retorted Doctor Darbishire, folding his arms and lifting his chin. 'Me, send a petition to General Somoza? Don't even think about it. I won't even sign the one from the Medical Society. And don't smoke in my presence, godson.'

'Pardon me for speaking out of turn, but if you refuse, his life will be in your hands,' said Captain Prío, returning his cigarette to the packet.

'Don't tell me they are going to shoot him for slander!' snorted Doctor Darbishire, his mouth contorting in a derisive smile. He rocked on his heels, his arms crossed.

'They have put him in the same cell as Oliverio Castañeda, that's why he's in danger,' said Captain Prío, putting the packet of cigarettes away. 'They have him in the tiger's den, at the mercy of the beast.'

Doctor Darbishire stopped his rocking and his mouth opened in an expression of surprise.

'Don't think I am inventing this, it's all true,' Captain Prío said, nodding solemnly. 'We still have time to rescue him.'

'They wouldn't let Castañeda have strychnine in his cell,' said Doctor Darbishire, taking off his jacket and walking over to the coat stand. 'Don't worry godson, Castañeda won't be able to poison him.'

'In that case, next time you see him sweeping the street outside your surgery you could at least give him some water, godfather,' said Captain Prío, taking the old man's jacket for him. He hung it up and returned with the doctor's white coat, ready for his appointments.

'I've already told Captain Ortiz not to let that happen again,' said Doctor Darbishire, shaking out his white coat before putting it over his head. 'I don't need anyone to take revenge on my behalf. I am not a vengeful man.'

'Well then forgive, godfather,' said Captain Prío, pausing for a moment at the door as if he was going to add something, but finally deciding not to.

'Godson,' said Doctor Darbishire, calling him with his head

hidden by the white coat and the sleeves still hanging loose above his head, 'don't leave without accepting my blessing.'

'Thank you godfather,' said Captain Prío, coming back and humbly lowering his head.

'May the Lord save you from falling in with bad company, amen,' Doctor Darbishire blessed him. 'As for that ingrate, I forgive him. But I'm damned if I'm signing anything in his support. Tell Teodosio to let the first of my patients through.'

No sooner had Doctor Salmerón been sent to the cells at precinct XXI than Captain Ortiz went to his surgery in San Sebastián to take personal charge of searching the premises. This is where Judge Fiallos finally caught up with him. Captain Ortiz was searching for the pamphlets, forgotten by the men who had detained Doctor Salmerón, realising that they were already circulating around the city. He was also in search of the Casa Squibb notebook and the secret dossier, of whose existence he was already well aware.

Not a single pamphlet could be found. When the maid was interrogated all she could say was that after the arrest they'd been given to some unknown individuals because that was what they were intended for. The guards turned over all the furniture, forced open the drawers of the desk and the doors of the instrument cupboard, but there was no trace of the notebook or the secret dossier. By the time the search was finished the whole house was destroyed. The guards had gone into every room including the bedroom where they had hacked open the wardrobe and ripped open the mattress. They had even gone through the kitchen, turning out the drawers of the sideboard. The slats supporting the mattress and the mattress itself which had been slashed with bayonets, the broken plates and cooking pots, medical texts, surgical instruments, basins and the chairs were then finally thrown out onto the patio.

Captain Ortiz could never have guessed the actual location of the items he'd been seeking so assiduously. A few days earlier, Doctor Salmerón had taken the precaution of placing the book, *The Secrets of Nature*, the secret dossier, and the Casa Squibb notebook into a biscuit tin, which he had then tied to a cord in order to lower it down into his latrine. He had secured it by tying the free end of the cord to a nail located on the inside of the bench where one sat to attend the calls of nature.

When Doctor Salmerón got out of prison on 28 November 1933, the same day that Oliverio Castañeda was formally indicted with parricide and first degree murder, he went immediately to recover his treasure from the depths of the latrine. Although the book, the dossier and the notebook had all been preserved in perfect condition, he never managed to rid them of the stench which impregnated them, no matter how much carbolic soap he used to try to disinfect them.

CHAPTER FORTY-THREE

What Became of that Gallant Young Man?

As we already know, Oliverio Castañeda was formally indicted on charges of parricide and first degree murder on 28 November 1933. At this point the process moved from its initial instruction phase into one in which the case against the accused would be prepared before being presented to a jury composed of thirteen citizens chosen by lottery. However, the case never reached a jury, for reasons which will be explained later.

The accused appeared in court on 1 December 1933 to enter his plea, the first procedure of this plenary phase. The cross-examination started at eight in the morning and concluded at ten that night; the only interruption occurred at midday so that Judge Fiallos could hear the outstanding testimony of Carmen Contreras Guardia. This produced the unfortunate confrontation between the witness and the accused which has been previously mentioned.

Throughout the interrogation, the accused rejected all the accusations and denied all the charges put to him. He further showed himself to be a perfect gentleman at all times, solidly refuting the suggestion that he had any amorous entanglements with any of the Contreras family at any point. This performance reflected the respectful manner that he had always taken towards the women of that household.

His insistence on this point aroused particular attention since at this stage he cannot have expected anything from his former sponsors. The widow for her part seemed bent on taking the case to the bitter end once she had abandoned her plan to leave the country, and in her deposition María del Pilar had not only made it very clear that she had never harboured any tenderness towards the accused but openly held him responsible for the murders.

However, on 6 December 1933, just a few days after the accused had entered his plea, he asked to appear before Judge Fiallos. At this appearance he read out an entirely unexpected and explosive statement in which there was no trace of his prior accommodation and gallantry towards the Contreras ladies.

In this statement, Castañeda gave the most extensive defence of himself of the entire case. It contains many sections that will be of interest to the reader and so it is included here in its entirety:

> I, Oliverio Castañeda Palacios, whose personal details have been duly recorded, respectfully appear before your Honour the Chief District Prosecutor to declare the following:
>
> On 9 October 1933 I was summarily arrested without an official warrant signed by any competent judge. After this illegal act I was then held in custody, and it was not until October fifteenth that I was informed of the case being assembled against me, by which time the case dossier already exceeded one hundred and fifty pages. Only at this point did you take the opportunity to serve me with my arrest warrant; a singular state of affairs when you consider that this interview took place in the jail where I was already being held.
>
> Before then and ever since I have remained incommunicado inside a cell in the precinct XXI jail of this city, without any opportunity to exercise my legitimate right to defend myself. I have not even had access to pen and paper, these being prohibited to me, and it is only now with the aid of certain charitable friends who have not turned their backs on me in this adversity that I have been able to procure them. This is the only reason that I am now able to present this declaration, despite the fact that when I appeared before you on October eighteenth I notified you that I would be representing myself. Against all legal provisions, this has not enabled me to alter my state of defencelessness; so far you have never allowed me an audience on any of the occasions I have requested it.
>
> This case has been conducted in the shadows against all the norms of justice and indeed all humanitarian prin-

ciples. Your Honour, I do not know whether you have also approved my incarceration and muzzling, but as a result of military intervention judgement has taken place behind my back with the clear intention of satisfying the appetites of those who would wish to see me executed in front of a firing squad. There are many reasons for this; personal hatred, animosity, sordid interest, not to mention the possible political motives. It is well-known that Jorge Ubico wants my head as his price for friendship with the Nicaraguan government.

Article 75 of the Criminal Justice Code states that all official business of a criminal case should take place in the presence of the accused and his defence lawyer: I am both of these, and yet have not been permitted to attend the interrogations of key witnesses; nor was I allowed to be present at the experiments that took place. These so-called scientific experiments were nothing of the sort. There are no proper laboratories here, as that eminent medical man, doctor to the Contreras family and person of irreproachable character, Doctor Darbishire, has done well to point out. Everything about this case suggests conspiracy: so much seems to have gone on behind closed doors. All the while I have remained in the seclusion of my cell as if I were a prisoner on Death Row, who has only the inevitable hour of execution to look forward to.

While this conspiracy has been going on I have been forced to behave like a perfect gentleman, enduring the mud-slinging like a stoic. I have bitten my tongue so as not to damage reputations; reputations which no longer deserve such consideration, trusting that feelings would eventually settle and that those who had most to lose would in the end relent. In guarding their own reputations so jealously they have allowed mine to be taken and used to sweep the floors in every salon in León: where hypocrisy keeps its abject court. Your Honour, I am now certain that my silence no longer has any virtue, except for my enemies. Indeed, it is most favourable to those who once felt the greatest need for my favours and are now most relentless in their persecution of me.

The case dossier is replete with depositions poor in imagination but rich in fabrication; painting me in the terrifying guise of a psychopath, a sexual degenerate, a vile slanderer and professional liar. Apparently I am deranged, and anything good that is said about me: complementing my fine manners, my social graces and politeness, my empathy and talents, serves my detractors as proof of my vile and murderous intent. They see poison hiding behind everything good.

The hand of the Costa Rican Fernando Guardia is clearly evident in this conspiracy, in which the widow Doña Flora and her daughter are now conscious participants: whether by the force of violence or of their own volition. Fernando Guardia has thrown his weight around in León and clearly has his sights set on the fortune of his nieces and nephews. He has made reckless accusations against me concerning crimes which if I had in truth committed, I would have been tried and condemned for in Costa Rica. As you can see, I was neither tried nor condemned, rendering it obvious that the testimony presented to yourself by Fernando Guardia comprises evidence that must have been concocted in the offices of some incompetent lawyer to serve his own ambitions. It has never been presented to any competent authority and is invalidated by its late appearance. Such is the case of this supposed documentary evidence on the basis of which they try to implicate me in the death of my close friend Rafael Ubico, whose death I will never be able to mourn sufficiently. This Guardia may well be motivated by his own insatiable ambition, or he may be an undercover agent for the tyrant Ubico, who spends dollars freely to recompense the most despicable lackeys in all Central America.

The damaging intent of those who have signed this "evidence" is clear. These people never paid me the least courtesy when I had the misfortune to know them in Costa Rica; indeed, I could write an entire novel concerning their behaviour. Let me just give you a rapid sketch of the proprietor of the Alemana lodging house: she was a woman of lascivious bent who offered the favours of her bed to Ubico in return for delicious meals and who extended similar favours to the pharmacist Rovinski in exchange for the rheumatism cures and hormonal preparations she took to reinvigorate her lost youth.

Your Honour, you must allow me to laugh at the fact that it is such people who now accuse me so rashly and uncharitably in their "testimony". In so doing they have given me leave to treat them equally uncharitably. Your Honour, can you in all seriousness have any confidence in the word of a woman who, knowing that a crime has taken place under her own roof, says nothing to the authorities? Similarly, the word of an apprentice pharmacist who hands over the poison used to commit this same murder and keeps quiet, only because no one asked him anything? Assuming that Rovinski is still in the habit of making nocturnal visits to Gerlach in her boudoir, it is more than likely that this pathetic plan to sink me is the product of their pillow talk, devised when they found out I was helplessly incarcerated. Why? In her case because I never accepted her invitations to enter that boudoir; and he because, sly and envious as ever, it gave him the opportunity to appear in the press at the expense of an innocent man.

Let me return now to the salient issues of my current predicament. Whichever way you look at it, Doña Flora and her daughter want to, or are content to see me taken to the scaffold. They wish this pantomime to end in the silence of my tomb, thus ensuring that all those secrets which until now I have been guarding so closely follow me to the grave.

Your Honour, this is all well and good, but now I have decided to end my silence. I wish to make use of all the powers at my disposal as defence lawyer in this case and of my sacred rights as the accused. This being so, I the accused, whom you have charged with parricide and first degree murder in your warrant of 28 November 1933, demand that you investigate the deeds which I am about to expose. I demand that you call every one of the witnesses I am going to name here, and that you take charge of the documentary evidence that I will present to you in due course. In the interests of the truth, I also wish to retract in full and in every way all of my previous statements, even though this will open me to charges of perjury:

1. I submit and am disposed to prove that the widow Doña Flora Contreras was in the habit of importuning me with requests of an amorous nature. This began even before I went to live at her home in the company of my deceased wife, a move which I felt forced into as the only way to appease her. Her requests continued throughout the period I stayed in her home and until such time as I moved into my own home. This produced an awkward and embarrassing situation, especially since she was not the only one who had been making advances (as I will explain to Your Honour in later paragraphs).

After I had moved, Doña Flora continued to make requests and inappropriate advances to me. On the death of my wife, she enjoined me to return to her home in order to keep me close by her. When we met later in Costa Rica she persisted in her efforts, just as I persisted in keeping her at arm's length, since she was interfering with my relationship with her daughter María del Pilar, which as I will later confirm began during our time in San José. With her characteristic obstinacy, and knowing that I had plans to return to León, the aforementioned Doña Flora resumed her campaign to persuade me to continue to live with them, giving her the opportunity, or so she hoped, to consummate something that I considered to be an impossibility.

As a testament to the stubbornness of her pursuit of me you only need look at the gifts I received from her while I was incarcerated. These sentimental items are things which only a lover would send to the object of their love, even in the case when this object does not return their feelings. I never once acceded to her requests, although I stopped short of rejecting them outright in order not to provoke her anger or animosity. I maintained this distant attitude not because she displeased me physically—she has adornments and charms aplenty—but because she was married and somewhat older than me, and I had no wish to become involved in a complicated affair. Now it seems that the very situation I once feared has occurred after all, and I find myself the victim of her vengefulness.

Your Honour, concerning this present topic: I have letters written in her hand which are currently in the possession of a third party and which I will present to you. The contents of these letters should demonstrate the truth of what I say. In addition, I request that you order the release of the records which detail the number and nature of the items sent to me in the XXI jail by the aforementioned lady.

2. I submit and am disposed to prove that I maintained an intimate relationship with Matilde Contreras. The relationship began in December 1932 when I moved into her parents' home and it was she who initiated it by means of a letter that unfortunately I did not keep. I do, however, have other letters, also in the possession of the same third party, some of which she sent to me while I resided in León and others that she posted to me in Guatemala between the months of March and June 1933. These are the same letters that the post-office employee Rosaura Aguiluz refers to in her deposition of 23 October 1933. You yourself have in your possession a letter which you confiscated from among my belongings; there is no date nor signature, but a simple handwriting analysis should establish that it was written by Matilde. The letter was sent to me in the last week of February 1933 after my wife had died and when she must have become aware of the fact that I was also engaged in an intimate relationship with her sister María del Pilar.

On this point I demand that you recall the household servants, Salvador Carvajal and Leticia Osorio, who were both witness to many events that clearly demonstrate the existence of these relationships. They must give fresh statements and I must be allowed to put my questions to them; I will submit a list of these to Your Honour in due course.

Your Honour, through the answers given by the witnesses and an examination of the letters it will be clear that a bond existed between us. This will serve to invalidate once and for all the document, so hastily concocted on the exhumation of her body, certifying the intact state of her genital organs.

Your Honour, it will no doubt shock you to know that in common with everything else I am now stating, it is true that the solitude of the cemetery was the scene for our repeated acts of love. Each evening Matilde insisted on accompanying me to visit my wife's grave to disguise her carnal urges. I can show you the mausoleums where we went to hide ourselves from the impertinent gazes of those visitors who came to pray, and where we consummated that which we were prevented from doing in other places. To verify this, you should direct your inquiries to the caretaker of the Guadalupe cemetery, Omar Cabezas Lacayo. He will be able to give you all the details concerning these visits and the days on which they took place; we regularly had to go to the gate house to get the keys and be let out since the cemetery was often closed by the time we were ready to leave.

3. I also submit that María del Pilar is my common-law spouse, since I have had marital relations with her and I am still prepared to take her in marriage if Doña Flora will desist from making her accusations against me. Also in the possession of the same third party are letters written to me by the aforementioned person in which the nature of our relationship is made clear. Once you have these letters you should compare them with the handwriting of their alleged author to confirm that I am not lying. One of these letters was mentioned by Doctor Octavio Oviedo y Reyes in his deposition of 17 October 1933, in which he also states that I showed it to him. This is indeed the case.

On this point I request that you call the maid Dolores Lorente to testify. It was she who acted as courier for our romantic correspondence during the period she was engaged as a servant in my house in the month of February of this year. You should also call the overseer of the Nuestro Amo ranch, Eufrasio Donaire, who was witness to our secret meetings at the farmhouse, which took place between December 1932 and October 1933. It should also be said that we had other rendezvous at various times and in various places including San José, Costa Rica. On several occasions between July and September of this year we rented a room at the Paris lodging house on Paseo de los Estudiantes.

To the same end I beg you to call Demetrio Puertas as a witness. He is one of the clerks at Contreras & Co., and was present when the person to whom I previously alluded kissed me without warning in the doorway to my room in their home. He will confirm the date.

Your Honour, the interrogation of these witnesses here cited (and I would also like to include the household servants, Salvadora Carvajal and Leticia Osorio) should be undertaken according to a list of questions which I will provide for you in due course. As evidence in this instance you should use the register of articles sent to the XXI prison and which I have already requested be obtained in regard to those items that were sent to me by the aforementioned person.

Furthermore I request that a certain article be added to the case dossier: "Casual Witness" by Señor Franco Cerutti, published in *La República* of San José, Costa Rica. By reading this article you will be able to appreciate the truth as regards the rivalry between the two Contreras sisters in respect to my affections, and indeed the preference towards myself shown by Doña Flora.

4. I demand that the books containing details of the business dealings of Contreras & Co. which are kept in the strongbox be examined in detail by expert accountants. This will uncover the existence of two sets of books, one of which has been used to record fraudulent dealings; among these are bribes arranged by myself and which were paid to several city councillors of the municipality of León in order to secure the contract for the Metropoli-

tan Water Company that Don Carmen Contreras Reyes (R.I.P.) so desired.

I had access to these books because Don Carmen consulted me about certain legal matters regarding how to falsify receipts and hide transactions in order to evade import duty. I am ready to admit these crimes and atone for them but they in no way equate to the trumped up murder charges I am faced with. The clerk, Demetrio Puertas, was aware of all of this, but in no way was he an accomplice. I request that he be called to give a statement and answer the questions that I will submit to yourself later.

The strong box also contains other evidence, including copies of several falsified letters of exchange. In particular one bearing the forged signature of Señor José Padilla Paiz, which was presented as payment on a foreign account and of which he was completely unaware. Demetrio Puertas should be questioned on all these matters. Alternatively, you should appeal to the honesty of Mr. Duncan R. Valentine, general manager of P. J. Frawley, of this city, since all these drafts passed through his hands and have probably already been returned by their corresponding banks.

With my head held high, I declare to you that I was coerced into cooperating with these frauds. It was the ignominious price extracted for my shelter beneath the roof of the Contreras family home. I certainly did not instigate this form of doing business, as it was already common practice before I was given access to the secret dealings of the company.

The charges laid against me in accordance with the warrant issued by Your Honour on November twenty-eighth of this year is based on the presumption that since the crimes were all committed using the same poison on several occasions, I must be the common agent because I was close to the deceased persons in all three instances. Well then, based on the same presumption, I put it to you that there is another person who was close to all three victims at the same time as myself.

You will finally have the keys to the case in your hands

once you have collected the depositions I am requesting, and examined the letters that will be turned over to yourself, and once the company account books have been thoroughly inspected. If there was indeed criminal intent and the perpetrator did indeed use poison to commit his, or I suggest, her crimes, then their motives will become evident. It may indeed turn out that I will find myself as the injured party pressing charges for the crime of poisoning my wife against the person whom jealousy induced to eliminate her.

Your Honour will have noticed that Matilde Contreras could also have been the victim of this same jealousy, if someone had desired to remove her from the picture. Don Carmen presented a similar barrier to those same ardent passions and could have been murdered for a similar reason. In addition, to ensure continued profit from the business frauds, his removal would have made it easier to keep them concealed.

I would also draw your attention to the fact that if Don Carmen Contreras Largespada, father and grandfather of the aforementioned deceased persons, has now retracted his accusations against me (so annulling the powers vested in Doctor Juan de Dios Vanegas), it is surely because he knows that the truth is exactly as I am telling it now in this declaration. For this reason, he is also probably aware that the accusations against me lack any solid basis because he knows the sole perpetrator of these crimes is one of his own blood; twisted by an envy born of unrequited love, and driven to murder by her own ambitions.

Your Honour, I would have preferred to keep quiet but I cannot do so at the cost of my own life. My hand does not tremble as I write this, although I know that prison is not the safest place for me; I am certain that my jailers can be persuaded to become my executioners.

Justice is inherently imperfect because it is administered by human beings; despite this it is a superior form of reasoning. It transcends malice and slander, lies and the prurient seeking out of sin, the vices of class and of civilization. Your Honour, it is up to you now. Your youth and good character should serve you well as defence against

> this campaign of hatred. You must make justice serve this higher purpose and ensure that I am heard as it is my right to be heard, and do not dismiss the proofs that I offer since they are at the root of this investigation. Search for the guilty in the direction I have indicated and you will surely find them.
>
> I am making this declaration while there is still time, and I have the right to do so. I await your response in my cell at the XXI precinct.

On 9 December 1933, *El Centroamericano* published a front-page editorial penned by its owner and editor-in-chief, General Gustavo Abaunza, entitled 'Evil's Last Resort'. In his article the general urges the judge to disregard 'the foul and outrageous appeals of a noxious foreigner who on hearing the sound of nails being hammered home to build the scaffold behaves like the leper who in his mortal panic seeks to contaminate everyone else, infecting anyone who happens to stray into his path.'

For his part, Manolo Cuadra made the following comments in his dispatch 'Ticking Time-Bomb', published in *La Nueva Prensa* on December ninth:

> Judge Fiallos has a ticking time-bomb in his hands following Oliverio Castañeda's surprising revelations. León is once again in uproar, and no one can talk about anything else. Feelings are divided and the case is taking on the proportions of a true class war. Dazzled by the intelligence and charm of the accused now turned accuser, the downtrodden lower orders are taking advantage of the situation to vent their ingrained resentment against their lords and masters. In the meantime, those at the top are becoming ever more entrenched in their sense of indignation at the daring assertions of the accused, assertions that have once more seen an aristocratic family pilloried mercilessly. This family, overwhelmed by a tragedy that seems to know no end, seem to be living through a drama straight from the pages of Aeschylus.
>
> That the lower orders feel dazzled by the performance of the accused, and are willing to show their sympathies

quite openly was demonstrated when the accused appeared before Judge Fiallos to read the document he had prepared. They cheered him to the rafters, interrupting him after every paragraph and, conscious of his star turn, he played to his audience, modulating his voice to enhance the drama. At the end of the hearing he was carried from the courthouse shoulder-high, with many in the crowd accompanying him as far as the gates of the prison. The blind girl Miserere has taken to singing a ditty which is now oft repeated in the poor neighbourhoods of León to the accompaniment of guitars. Sung to the tune of "El Zopilote" it begins:

At last Oliverio has won!
And now they must let him live:
They were green with envy for his lovers
But he has more to give…

The question on the lips of the many people who knew Oliverio Castañeda as a gentleman with an easy manner and social grace is: "What became of that gallant young man?" As the ditty suggests, and as the accused himself makes bitter reference to in his letter, he faces a judgement where his life may well be at stake. Persecuted and with little hope of getting out of this situation, he has bared his teeth: the only weapons left to him.

Will Mariano Fiallos call the witnesses? Will he examine the letters that Oliverio Castañeda alleges are in the hands of this mysterious third party? Who is this third party, if they even exist and assuming that the accused is not lying, forced into it by desperation? Will these witnesses dare to support the grave assertions he has made, and of which he is apparently so sure?

What will Mariano Fiallos make of the barely disguised accusations that the prisoner has made against a certain person of the female sex; whom he dares not name but whose identity anyone can guess? Doctor Castañeda has thrown a boomerang by reversing the accusations against him. To some this will seem disingenuous, to others astute; it causes confusion and leaves justice in a quandary…

> These are the questions being posed at every get-together in León, be it a gathering of commoners or a society function.

Within hours of the accused having made his statement, Doctor Juan de Dios Vanegas in his capacity of prosecuting attorney issued a peremptory statement discrediting it on the grounds that it contained unfounded, brazen allegations of no relevance to the case and which were also detrimental to the privacy and public standing of the Contreras family. Paying no heed of this, that very night Judge Fiallos decided to call the witnesses as requested, and to take receipt of the letters and subject them to a handwriting analysis. The only item that he chose to ignore was the issue of the Contreras & Co. account books; he felt that requesting these would not be in the interests of the case.

As Judge Fiallos himself confided to the author of this story many years later, it was not an easy decision to make. We will return to this admission later, but suffice it to say that he had serious reservations and many doubts about Castañeda's petition. In his view it contained far too many insults and inconsistencies. Its brutal and boastful contentions had left a bad taste in his mouth, and he felt it was a cheap tactic aimed at reversing the accusations. He nonetheless felt that the accused had a valid argument, in a strict legal sense, in pointing out the lack of opportunities he had had to defend himself, and thus he felt unable to carry on with the case without addressing his own responsibility for the procedural irregularities that had been exposed. There was also no legal foundation on which to reject the witnesses called by the defence, nor to refuse the receipt of evidence presented by the defence in this plenary stage of the case; certainly not if he had to accept that Castañeda was acting as his own defence lawyer. These factors eventually formed the basis for his writ of resolution.

Years later, he told me that he had known full well what the reaction would be, and indeed it did not take long for the forces opposing him to declare war. From his pulpit, Canon Oviedo y Reyes angrily threatened him with excommunication; there was pressure from his superiors; two of León's papers accused him of inexperience and rash decision-making; and repeated committee meetings at the Social Club debated whether he should be expelled as an undesirable. However, it was a visit from Captain Ortiz that night at the courthouse which determined him to act without further reflection, thus breaking his usual rule of first consulting his best sources of advice: his pillow and his wife.

The captain was on his way to a wedding and appeared at the courthouse in his dress uniform and drenched in cologne. His khaki-uniform was freshly pressed, and his boots and belt buckle shone. As ever, his automatic pistol hung heavily at his waist. His recently shaved chin still bore the nicks from his razor, which he had dabbed with Mercurochrome. Dishevelled and in his shirt sleeves, Judge Fiallos was in the middle of a discussion with his secretary Alí Vanegas about the best decision to take. Alí Vanegas sat half asleep at the typewriter.

'What! Aren't you coming to the wedding?' Captain Ortiz exclaimed. He had substituted his usual Stetson for a kepi which he hurriedly removed and tucked under one arm. 'You should already be dressed for it.'

'You're a sight for sore eyes,' said Judge Fiallos as he leaned over the desk barely looking up from Oliverio's letter. 'Here you are at last!'

'Alright, so I didn't come to see you, but I did release Salmerón. Isn't that what you wanted?' said Captain Ortiz, wetting one of his fingers and rubbing the copper badge on his kepi. He passed his hand over his bald pate and added: 'He got out before his thirty days were up.'

'I sent you an official summons and you didn't reply,' said Judge Fiallos, slowly turning over the pages but still not raising his head. 'It wasn't enough for you to incarcerate one of my witnesses. You had to put him in the same cell as the accused!'

'That was only on the first night, to teach him a lesson,' said Captain Ortiz. He refused the seat that Alí Vanegas offered him; he didn't want to crease his dress uniform. 'Nothing happened. Shame. Castañeda didn't eat him.'

'No, he didn't eat him,' said Judge Fiallos as he carefully inked the edge of a ruler to mark the margin of a document; 'but now he is his ally. It was him leading the applause and the cheers this morning in court.'

'Cut from the same cloth, Darbishire was right,' said Captain Ortiz indifferently as he spun his kepi before replacing it on his head. 'I can put him back behind bars if you like so that he doesn't go around whipping up the crowd.'

'You're going to have to put half of León in jail,' said Judge Fiallos, passing the bundle of files to Alí Vanegas who reached out to take them. 'Today there were at least two hundred people here.'

'And if you allow Castañeda's petition there will be five hundred to hear his witnesses,' Captain Ortiz warned. He drew in his belly, removed his gun belt and laid it on the desk. 'That man is a degenerate, and anyone who listens to him is an even worse degenerate. Of course you are not going to pay him any heed.'

'I am the one who has to decide that,' replied Judge Fiallos, looking Captain Ortiz full in the face for the first time. His Adam's apple trembled as he continued: 'and get that weapon out of my sight.'

'Of course you are the one who has to decide that. But if you listen to him you will land yourself in trouble, and it will be all your own fault,' said Captain Ortiz. He took out a handkerchief soaked in cologne and made a great show of wiping his neck and face. 'Remember that you are in León and this is where your roots are.'

'I was wondering why you had come,' said Judge Fiallos, picking up the gun holster and handing it to Ortiz. 'I didn't have the guts to complain about the business with Doctor Salmerón, but now I am not prepared to put up with any more. I am going to make it public that the National Guard are obstructing the course of justice. You can take me prisoner too!'

'I am not here as a military man but as a citizen of León,' said Captain Ortiz. Forced to take back his weapon, he had to reluctantly put away his handkerchief. 'Don't say I didn't warn you in time. Have they brought you the letters yet?'

'I hadn't officially allowed Castañeda's petition, but I will now. They can bring them to me directly,' announced Judge Fiallos, and in two strides he was behind Alí Vanegas and already feeding a sheet of paper into the typewriter. 'Type this: "Writ of Resolution".'

'Alright then, just listen to this: Castañeda's buddy Oviedo is going to bring you the letters,' said Captain Ortiz, putting his gunbelt over his shoulder so that his gun rested on his chest. 'That bastard has them all.'

'First Criminal Court for the District of León. Sixth of December nineteen thirty-three. At eight-fifteen p.m.'. Judge Fiallos consulted his watch as he dictated, and Alí Vanegas started typing at high speed. 'Considering the petition presented at ten this morning by the accused, Oliverio Castañeda Palacios, who is acting as his own defence in the case now being judged in this court…'

'The more you dig the harder you'll find it to get out of the hole,' remarked Captain Ortiz, raising his Mercurochrome spattered chin and screwing up his piercing blue eyes. 'And I must be an idiot, still here talking to the wall. The happy couple will have left the cathedral by now.'

'As presiding judge, I resolve that: Firstly: the document previously referred to should be admitted in its generality, with the provisos that I shall specify in the following…' Judge Fiallos continued his dictation leaning over Alí Vanegas' shoulder to see what was being written. He did not even look up when he heard the door slam with a resounding crash that dislodged dust and plaster from the wall.

'Caiaphas' centurion came perfumed like a harlot,' said Alí Vanegas, wrinkling his nose and sniffing the air for the scent left in the wake of Captain Ortiz's departure. 'If he wants to cause a sensation, he should use Reuter's luxury lotion.'

'He smells like a tart's boudoir,' laughed Judge Fiallos, rolling up his sleeves without taking his eyes off the sheet of paper in the typewriter.

The reader will no doubt have been surprised to hear of Doctor Salmerón's active presence among the crowd supporting Oliverio Castañeda, but this about-turn in his sympathies will be explained shortly. For now we will leave it to Manolo Cuadra to describe this new twist, again in his dispatch entitled 'Ticking Time-Bomb':

> However, there exist certain other questions which are of no less interest. Doctor Salmerón, released from his imprisonment before his sentence of thirty days was completed, has shown a new and surprising attitude. We now see him heading the band of labourers, porters and

market stall-holders, artisans and others who gather daily at the courthouse to show their support for the accused. During the presentation of the aforementioned document and some days ago at the plea hearing it was Doctor Salmerón who diligently organised the mob. Those involved now constantly seek his advice, seeing him as some kind of leader.

This is a radical and extremely surprising change of heart. Prior to his incarceration, the doctor was among the most entrenched of Doctor Castañeda's enemies; now he is among the most fervent of his admirers. We questioned him about his position when we came upon him in the corridors of the courthouse, but he very politely declined to comment.

What mystery lies behind this transformation? The word on the street is that while he was in jail he was put in the same cell as the accused, but Doctor Salmerón also refused to comment on this point. If the rumour is true, then what could the two of them have talked about in the seclusion of that cell? What, if anything, could have drawn these two adversaries together? We promise our readers that we will not lose track of events; encouraged by the increase in circulation of *La Nueva Prensa* our editor-in-chief Don Gabry Rivas will surely keep us on the case, which is bound to produce yet more surprises.

Oviedo the Balloon, the mysterious third party, was indeed in possession of the letters just as Captain Ortiz had said, and he appeared before Judge Fiallos on 9 December 1933 to hand them over in person. Oliverio Castañeda's supporters greeted him wildly as he stepped out of the car at the courthouse entrance, and he was unable to make any headway through the crowd until Doctor Salmerón opened a path for him. He had placed the letters in a box previously containing Anchor sewing thread; as he walked solemnly into the courthouse he clasped it to him, hugging it against his great belly. With a slight nod he solemnly handed it over to Judge Fiallos.

The letters had been sorted into three different bundles according to their sender; each of these was tied together with a shoelace.

Within each bundle the letters were in date order. The letters were to be held at the courthouse until they could be authenticated by a handwriting expert. Alí Vanegas listed them all and issued Oviedo the Balloon with a receipt.

Only the list remains in the case dossier. At midnight on that same day, persons unknown broke into the courthouse. They opened a hole in the roof above Judge Fiallos' office, forced the locks on the judge's desk, and removed the letters.

CHAPTER FORTY-FOUR

An Unexpected Meeting in Jail

DOCTOR Atanasio Salmerón, his head bandaged and his suit stained with blood, was jailed on the night of 12 November 1933. When his jailers pushed him into the cell he was met by none other than Oliverio Castañeda, who seemed to have been expecting him. The solitary electric lamp, glowing like a dying ember, barely lit the room as he sat immobile by the dark void of the window. For a second he turned and looked at Doctor Salmerón with a hard expression.

The metallic clang of the cell door closing resonated for some time along the passageway. Doctor Salmerón lifted the bandage from over his eyes and started in surprise at the sight of the figure in mourning shrouded in the half-light. Realising his danger, his forehead pulsed with a hammering pain like an alarm call, but Oliverio Castañeda simply turned to contemplate the darkness beyond the barbed wire of the window; there was no trace of menace in his demeanour.

Calm and melancholy in his strict mourning dress, Castañeda looked as if he had just returned from a funeral; it was as though every day of his life had been spent going to funerals. His black tie was done up very fashionably, and the starched cuffs of his shirt were fastened with two blood-red stones set in gold. These were the same cuff-links he had worn when Doctor Salmerón had first seen him close to: at his wife's deathbed on that fateful day back in February.

Oliverio Castañeda turned again for a moment, his myopic eyes avidly searching for Doctor Salmerón through his thick lenses. There was nothing in his gaze that suggested hatred, no mock sarcasm; instead the wry, almost pained smile playing on his lips was one of compassion.

If it came to a fight, Doctor Salmerón knew that he was bound to come off worse; he had been thrown into this trap wounded and exhausted; he also knew he was both older and weaker than his opponent. Nevertheless, he instinctively clenched his fists, ready to defend himself; he would not be taken in by this act of impassivity and pretended indifference only to find himself attacked suddenly. He was prepared to fight back as best he could. He would also be ready for the other man's jibes and insults when they came; he knew Castañeda to be a creature with two faces, a master of duplicity who was quite capable of changing instantly from this picture of melancholic youth to the embodiment of vile insolence. Yes, he knew this man only too well.

When Oliverio Castañeda did eventually speak, however, there was no trace of insult or aggression in his voice. His voice was more like a sorrowful breeze caressing the tombs from which he seemed to have so recently returned; a breeze that carried with it the smell of ancient wreaths and garlands, withered long ago.

'You are the only one who can help me, doctor,' Oliverio Castañeda said, his gaze still directed out of the window, searching for something far beyond the prison walls.

'Help you? Why? You must be joking!' said Doctor Salmerón after a moment's hesitation in which he attempted to summon up some indignation. He failed. The unhealthy odour in the room sapped his strength, and the words stuck in his dry throat like shards of broken glass.

'Because you and I are not enemies. We never have been,' said Oliverio Castañeda. With his finger, he absentmindedly tested the sharpness of one of the barbed wire spikes outside the window.

Doctor Salmerón tightened the knot holding his make-shift bandage round his head; it had come loose and was falling over his eyes. The melancholy voice from the tombs went on:

'Tell me, why should we be enemies? The ones who beat you up and locked you in here with me so that we could destroy one another; they are our common enemies,' Oliverio Castañeda insisted, advancing into the cell on silent feet.

Realising he was coming closer, Doctor Salmerón stepped back and one of his shoes fell off: the guards had removed his shoe laces.

'You have no reason to fear me,' said Oliverio Castañeda, coming to a halt a few steps away from him and holding out his open palms. The scent of withered flowers was on his breath and it seemed to emanate from his clothing.

'And why would I be afraid of you, I wonder?' said Doctor Salmerón squirming as he tried to get his shoe back on without lowering his gaze.

'That's good to hear,' said Oliverio Castañeda, nodding slowly, his hands still outstretched. 'You are not afraid of me, and I'm not afraid of you. Listen to me then without fear.'

'All I know is that it's an injustice that those thugs have left me in here with you,' said Doctor Salmerón, making sure he never lost sight of Castañeda. He finally succeeded in getting his shoe back on.

'You know, you are the only one who can help me,' repeated Oliverio Castañeda, letting his arms fall and hanging his head as if inviting his enemy to choose between delivering his death blow or mercy.

'What are you talking about? Help you, how? We are both in the mire. But at least they haven't split your skull open; you even manage to get your suits pressed!' said Doctor Salmerón. His wound was beginning to throb again, and when he reached up to touch the bandage he could feel the warm blood seeping through.

'They aren't going to murder you; but me they will,' Oliverio Castañeda said, carefully taking off his spectacles and pinching the top of his nose.

Amused and surprised, Doctor Salmerón pursed his lips as if about to spit.

'I suppose you think it's funny that a murderer fears his own assassination?' Oliverio Castañeda asked. Spectacles still in one hand, he closed his eyes.

'I see you're something of a mind reader,' replied Doctor Salmerón. His wound was aching so much that he leaned against the door of the cell to rest his head on the metal.

'One of my virtues is sincerity, doctor,' said Oliverio Castañeda, putting his spectacles back on and delicately looping them over his ears. 'Well, I am no murderer, and it is a travesty of justice that they intend to kill me like a dog.'

'Like Doctor Darbishire's dog?' enquired Doctor Salmerón.

The chill of the metal on his back made his shiver as if running a fever.

'Ah yes,' Oliverio Castañeda said, walking wearily back to the window; 'your mentor Doctor Darbishire. How that old man must hate you. Just like the rest of them hate you. Why is it that society people in León hold you in such contempt, doctor? '

'You should know better than me, you used be so cosy with them,' replied Doctor Salmerón, moving away from the door. He was shivering violently now, and he hugged himself to try to warm up. 'They have never accepted me because I am not one of them. But you…'

'I am a love-child, doctor, and don't you forget it,' whispered Oliverio Castañeda, and once again the cell was filled with the stench of withered flowers. 'A bastard who tried to sneak his way into the fold, just as you say in *El Cronista*. But I have never poisoned anyone.'

'Go tell that to the judge,' retorted Doctor Salmerón, padding slowly across the cell so as not to lose his shoes; 'the evidence is against you.'

'The judge. Well, now that you bring him up: why do you think he didn't want you to hand over your evidence?' Oliverio Castañeda asked. He left the window and went over to the bunk, feeling for it like a blind man: 'because he is a coward; the same as all the other so-called aristocrats. Aristocrats who haven't even graduated to the use of flush toilets. They still shit in cesspits.'

'It would have been worse for you. That new evidence would have sunk you for sure,' said Doctor Salmerón, fixing longing eyes on the jug of water sitting on a table, an upturned glass over its neck. He had noticed it before and now that it was only a few feet away the sight of the crystal clear water made his thirst unbearable. 'The proof that you used strychnine.'

'Don't be so naïve, doctor. Your discoveries on that count don't matter in the slightest,' said Oliverio Castañeda, sitting down heavily on the bunk. 'It was the revelations about my love affairs with the Contrerases and the frauds of Don Carmen that the judge didn't care for. Drink the water; it's not poisoned with strychnine.'

'There is such a bitter taste in my mouth I wouldn't notice if it were,' said Doctor Salmerón, shuffling over to the table and picking up the glass. 'And all that about my proofs being worthless remains to be seen.'

'Neither the proofs you think you have, nor the tests on those defenceless dogs are worth a fig, doctor. Your mentor Doctor Darbishire is correct there,' said Oliverio Castañeda, taking a blanket from under his pillow; it was striped black and orange like a tiger. He began to unfold it. 'But all of that is of no importance now. My enemies and yours are determined to kill me.'

'Your victims no longer matter then?' said Doctor Salmerón, taking a sip of water and swilling it round his mouth. He swallowed it and then after draining the glass went to serve himself another one.

'You and I are the victims now,' said Oliverio Castañeda, coming over with the blanket and draping it around Doctor Salmerón's shoulders.

'Why did you poison your wife?' asked Doctor Salmerón, leaving his glass on the table and wrapping himself up in the blanket. The odour of withered flowers had dispersed and the cell had recovered its accustomed scent of urine, stale faeces and insecticide. 'You could have carried on fucking all the Contreras women without getting rid of her.'

'I didn't poison her, I haven't poisoned anyone,' said Oliverio Castañeda, drinking the water left in the glass. 'You are going to be taken out of this cell in the morning, and it's likely we will never see each other again. Believe me, we don't have much time.'

'And you could have married María del Pilar without poisoning her sister, or Don Carmen,' said Doctor Salmerón as he adjusted his bandage with one hand: 'of all of them he was the one most in your debt.'

'I wasn't looking to get married,' said Oliverio Castañeda, putting an arm round Doctor Salmerón's shoulders; 'but if I had been I'd have chosen Matilde; I always respected her. Come and sit on the bed.'

'You're not going to tell me that she took the poison herself because she found out about you and María del Pilar?' said Doctor Salmerón, allowing himself to be led over and helped to sit on the bunk. 'Because you did definitely sleep with María del Pilar. I have in my possession the testimony of the overseer at the ranch where you went to be together.'

'Don't insult her memory by insinuating that she committed suicide, doctor. I loved her and she loved me,' said Oliverio Castañeda. With an arm still around Doctor Salmerón's shoulders he sat beside him. 'I had many opportunities but I never touched her. The other one yes: she is my mistress.'

'Next you'll tell me you never touched Doña Flora,' said Doctor Salmerón. Hunched up beneath the blanket he stared distractedly at the tongues hanging from his lace-less shoes.

'Least of all, doctor. Her least of all,' said Oliverio Castañeda. He took his arm from round the doctor's shoulders and leaned over to look at the floor, resting his elbows on his knees. 'And yet look how she hounds me.'

'So you only got as far as María del Pilar,' said Doctor Salmerón, turning to look at Castañeda before returning to the contemplation of his shoes. He reached down to pull the tongues of his shoes, saying: 'and Matilde died a virgin. Who are you trying to kid?'

'She was buried in a state of purity, just as I knew her,' said Oliverio Castañeda. With his elbows still on his knees he rested his chin in his hands. 'Why would I lie about it? How would it help me either way?'

'And Rafael Ubico, why did you poison him?' Doctor Salmerón asked, starting to feel hot. He unwrapped himself, opening up the folds around his chest. 'Don't tell me it was an act of love like Matilde.'

'I told you I didn't poison her. And all that about Ubico is the biggest lie of all,' said Oliverio Castañeda, his head sinking between his knees. 'A crime I was never charged with. What sort of a crime is that? General Ubico has asked Somoza for my head because I am his political enemy, not because I killed his nephew. That's why they want to shoot me.'

'Do you have all the letters they wrote to you?' asked Doctor Salmerón. Getting to his feet and leaving the blanket on the bed, he hobbled over to the window to get some fresh air.

'Oviedo the Balloon has them,' said Oliverio Castañeda following him to the window with his gaze. 'But what use are they now? What I need is your help.'

'Are you willing to hand the letters over to me?' asked Doctor

Salmerón, lifting his face to the opening framed with barbed wire. In the distance he could hear the lowing of cattle, the barking of dogs and the yowling of cats fighting in the street.

'They are yours. If you help me, they're yours,' said Oliverio Castañeda, and he slid along the bed to make room for Doctor Salmerón who now returned hurriedly from the window, his shoes flapping.

'Just let me ask you one more thing,' said Doctor Salmerón, pushing the blanket aside before sitting down.

'Ask away,' said Oliverio Castañeda. He stretched his arms and at his wrists the lustrous red stones in his cuff links glittered. In the dimly lit corner they were the colour of dried blood. 'There are no secrets between us now, doctor.'

'Yes, there is one secret,' said Doctor Salmerón, turning to face Oliverio Castañeda and sitting half on and half off the edge of the cot. 'I want to know whether it is true or not that you poisoned your mother.'

Doctor Darbishire had once mentioned that the young man suffered from halitosis and in that moment as he sat with his mouth half open, hesitating to answer, Doctor Salmerón realised this was the source of the unhealthy odour he had identified before.

'Did you poison her so that she wouldn't suffer any more? I want you to tell me whether it's true or not. And don't even think about lying to me!' the diseased smell of the young man's halitosis made the doctor's empty stomach turn.

'I never went to the Chiquimula Hospital until after she died,' said Oliverio Castañeda, his voice breaking into a sob. 'My father didn't want to go to Zacapa to claim her body from the morgue. I went alone. I wrapped her in her shroud and placed her into her coffin. I was barely fourteen years old, doctor.'

'And that book, *The Secrets of Nature*? What was the photo of your sick mother doing inside that book about poisons and euthanasia?' asked Doctor Salmerón, moving closer and holding his breath.

'Doctor Castroviejo, the hospital director, lent it to my mother because she was interested in botany,' said Castañeda sobbing despairingly. 'When I went to collect her body I put it with all her other things in her baggage. Nobody asked me for it. I have kept it with me, with the photograph inside as a keepsake to remind me of her.'

'Is that true? Do you swear it?' insisted Doctor Salmerón, taking Castañeda by the lapels of his jacket and shaking him.

'I swear it,' replied Oliverio Castañeda, making the sign of the cross with his hand and then kissing his forefinger.

'Alright then, I believe you,' said Doctor Salmerón, letting him go, his hands wet with tears. 'I believe you...but woe betide you if you are trying to trick me...!'

'I have no reason to deceive you,' said Oliverio Castañeda, his voice sounding suddenly hard and implacable like a recently sharpened knife.

'Alright then, onto the matter of the letters,' said Doctor Salmerón rubbing his hands.

'I am going to give you these two which crossed in the post,' said Oliverio Castañeda, removing his boots and feeling underneath the insoles. 'This is a copy of one I sent to Matilde from Costa Rica. The other is from her to me sent a few days later. You will see from mine that my intentions were all honourable and full of affection. You will see from hers that she had a passion for me. I have never been parted from these letters because they are proof of the sincere love between us that even death cannot alter. Keep them safe, I don't want to see them sullied in the courthouse.'

'And the others?' asked Doctor Salmerón, taking the letters which were pressed flat and wet with sweat. He put them quickly into his jacket pocket.

'Oviedo the Balloon will give you the rest,' said Oliverio Castañeda, going over to the table. He began to write a note. 'But only afterwards.'

'Only afterwards?' asked Doctor Salmerón. Seated on the edge of the cot he heard the paper being torn off. 'After what?'

'After I have escaped from here,' said Oliverio Castañeda, waving the sheet of paper around to dry the ink. 'It's the escape you have to help me with. That's the deal.'

'Escape?' said Doctor Salmerón leaping to his feet. 'And me, how do I get out?'

'They will have to let you out, however much they hate you,' said Oliverio Castañeda, advancing with the note and handing it to Doctor Salmerón. 'They just want to teach you a lesson for getting above yourself. The Medical College are bound to complain on your behalf. I am the only one here condemned to death.'

'The Medical College...' mused Doctor Salmerón, reading the first lines of the letter. He moved the page away from his eyes: "Dear Montgolfier..." Satisfied, he put it away. 'Those bastards are the worst of the lot.'

'The escape plan must be put in action as soon as you are back on the streets,' said Oliverio Castañeda, spreading the tiger-striped blanket out on the floor. He took off his jacket and went to hang it up on a hook on the wall; he then took off his tie and unbuttoned his shirt. 'First you must understand: don't tell anyone about the plan when you get out of here. It's very dangerous for both of us. Secondly, you must carry on behaving as if you are my worst enemy. Attack me without mercy. No one must suspect that we are working together. Come on, lie down.'

'What else do I have to do?' asked Doctor Salmerón, feeling for the top of the bunk so that he could lie down. 'An escape is no game.'

'You will receive further instructions from me through a woman: Salvadora Carvajal. Only you and she will know of the escape plan,' replied Oliverio Castañeda, now in nothing but his underwear. He tried to make Doctor Salmerón more comfortable, plumping up the hard, greasy pillow.

'I know her,' said Doctor Salmerón. He lay back on the pillow: 'I know where she lives.'

'Magnificent, doctor. Just don't forget: you are my sworn enemy and I will continue to maintain a gentlemanly silence,' Oliverio Castañeda said as he lay down on top of the blanket spread out on the floor. 'You must continue to attack me, and I will continue to deny my love affairs with the Contreras women. This will go some way to putting the hounds off the scent. When I get to Honduras you can have your fun publishing the letters; except the two I have given you. Now, get some sleep.'

'I hope no one is listening to this,' said Doctor Salmerón. Even as the sickly smell of funereal garlands invaded his nostrils once more, he found he had no trouble obeying the order to sleep. He consoled himself with the thought that this sweet perfume was after all the smell of revenge.

'Don't worry, they won't come back except in the morning to see whether we have killed each other,' Oliverio Castañeda reassured him. His voice rose from the floor: a lazy, faraway whisper that recalled the sound of the wind in a graveyard sending fallen petals scurrying before it, rustling the wreaths and shaking the locked gates of the tombs. 'But before they take you out, remember to put the letters somewhere safe: tucked into the knot of your tie or in your socks. Now sleep.'

The order was spoken in a whisper, but it penetrated Doctor Salmerón's dreams like a dagger.

CHAPTER FORTY-FIVE

A Risky Escape Plan is Hatched

OLIVERIO Castañeda never had the opportunity to tell Doctor Salmerón what strange impulse led him to make that daring and unexpected statement of 6 December 1933; the last farewell to his lover's pride, all his deceptions and caprices. Similarly, Doctor Salmerón was never able to explain his own reasons for reneging on his side of the bargain; as the reader will recall, instead of maintaining a steadfast animosity, the day after he was released he placed himself at the head of Castañeda's band of supporters.

Neither of them did as they had promised, but even so the escape plan went ahead. On the same day that he submitted his petition to the judge, December sixth, Oliverio Castañeda contrived to send his first message to his accomplice, through Salvadora Carvajal. Since the beginning of November this long-serving domestic in the Contreras household had had access to the prison. Authorised to take the prisoner's laundry once a week, she also took advantage of that concession to give the prisoner extra rations of food.

The message she conveyed from the prison was very brief. She smuggled it out inside her brassiere, and it is among the papers in Doctor Salmerón's secret dossier:

> On the day that the Christmas cribs are put out in the doorways, the angel of the annunciation who appeared to Mary will beat its wings. It will happen at six in the afternoon when the fireworks explode to celebrate the birth of the Messiah. Saddle a trustworthy horse and tie it to the balustrade on Calle Guadalupe bridge over the river Chiquito. Leave the horse on its own.
>
> The angel will await you at the dwelling of the person

bringing this message. The door of this dwelling will be padlocked from the outside and you must enter via the door to the patio. There we will say our farewells.

You must find a trusted guide who knows the way to the frontier with Honduras; a weapon, preferably a revolver with a supply of ammunition; the sum of one hundred córdobas, as well as fifty Honduran lempiras. When the procession of the Baby Jesus leaves the cathedral (at ten p.m.) the angel will collect the horse. The guide should meet him on the road that goes from the racecourse to Posoltega, San Felipe district.

The angel reminds you: do not tell anyone about the flight—not even to those who share your TABLE, nor our mutual friend (Montgolfier) for whom you took the message. The angel will continue to have faith in you and no one else but you until the day he dies. You however must never confide in ANYONE.

Yours,
THE ANGEL

It appears however that the two allies in the plot then began blindly to violate, point by point, all the terms of the agreement they had reached in the jail. We already know that Oliverio Castañeda decided to place the letters he had promised to Doctor Salmerón in the hands of Judge Fiallos. The doctor, far from being put out by this infringement of their pact, even opened the way for their bearer, Oviedo the Balloon, when he came to deliver them to the courthouse carrying them inside the old box of Anchor sewing thread. Later, despite the warnings contained in the Angel's message, Doctor Salmerón roped in all of his associates at the accursed table to help him with the escape plan, and in so doing not only departed from their agreement but threw all caution to the winds.

In a recorded interview with the author made on 17 October 1986, Captain Prío referred to this disregard for mutual promises as tempting fate. The interview took place in the newest and more modest incarnation of Casa Prío, the old establishment on Plaza Jerez having been burnt to the ground in the revolt against the dictatorship in June 1979. Part of the transcript is included here:

It was December seventh, the day of the gritería for the Immaculate Conception here in León. The Doctor asked us to meet him after six at Salvadora Carvajal's house in the Subtiava district; I'm sure you remember who she was. We'd not got together since they took Doctor Salmerón to jail...well, even before then. The pretext was that we were going to proclaim our devotion to the Virgin at Salvadora's altar and at several other altars in the district; Subtiava is very lively during the festival of the Immaculate Conception, and everyone is out on the streets, so this was a perfect cover. Casa Prío was too well-known, so a meeting there would have been unthinkable; far too dangerous.

Rosalío Usulutlán had come out of hiding. He arrived with a group of revellers from Españolita; he was carrying a star-shaped lantern made of waxed paper. They still have those nowadays during the gritería. Cosme Manzo didn't turn up though, he sent a message saying that he was in bed with a chill and was afraid it might spread to his balls if he got up. I can't say whether this was true or not; the fact is, he didn't turn up. What with his treachery later on I wouldn't be surprised if he had made the whole thing up.

I went along, although it meant leaving the business during a very busy time. It was very noisy inside, where the altar was: thunderous fire-crackers, loud singing to honour the virgin; good stuff. We went out to the patio to talk. I heard what the doctor had to say, but to tell you the truth I wasn't convinced about the plan. It all seemed too risky, and moreover the whole thing was the direct opposite of what we'd been doing until then. Luckily, I didn't have to do anything; he said to me: "Your role is to keep quiet, Captain," and I replied: "OK, I'll keep quiet. Why did you ask me to come then?" Just knowing about it was running a risk. I didn't know what to make of his change of heart, and I told him: "How has this happened, doctor? You didn't have to go to all the trouble of trying to sink Castañeda to do what you're doing now!" But no, I thought: just keep your mouth shut and let him get on with it. In any case, as with all the stuff he talked about, I never really got involved, I was only ever the host: I listened, gave my opinion from time to time, but that was all.

Rosalío was thinking the same as me. He looked at me as we stood out on the patio as if to say: "What's all this about? This isn't the doctor, I don't know this man!" He was a loyal friend though, and so he got on with his part of the plan, which was to obtain the horse: the same one as he had hired to ride out to the ranch that time he'd been sent to speak to the overseer. "You mustn't say where the horse is going, because they wouldn't let us hire it. If it doesn't return, I'll pay for it," explained the doctor, out of breath because he was so anxious for everything to go well.

He sent word to Manzo through Rosalío. Manzo had to get the lempiras: he did business with Hondurans. They were probably black market deals; he had no scruples and got what he needed from wherever. I don't remember about the revolver, I think that was Manzo's job too: I'm not sure. Doctor Salmerón found the guide; I remember he went to look for him in Somotillo, on the Honduran border, with one of his patients who was from those parts.

Manzo! That bastard, I don't know where he ended up: probably back in Honduras. He was from there, from Tela. He sold up here; but don't think he was ashamed of what he had done, nothing of the sort. He kept the grocery business, El Esfuerzo, open for some time. What I do know is that by 1936 when Old Man Somoza gave his uncle Juan Bautista the boot, he wasn't there anymore. He probably ended his days in Honduras, dice tumbler in hand. That's if he's already died.

What a life this is, Sergio my man. Thick as thieves the doctor and Manzo were, but when he most needed him, he betrayed him. He went along with everything, for sure: did what was asked of him: but on the sly he had already been in contact with Captain Ortiz. The doctor only found this out later. Cosme betrayed the whole plan, but I don't think it was for the money; he didn't any incentive. A traitor is a traitor through and through, and fear is the trigger for treachery. If he didn't agree with the plan he could have kept his mouth shut, like I did. There was no

> need to go hotfoot to the Guard HQ and spill everything. I saw him leaving there that same day: would you believe it, he came in here for a Xolotlán beer and told me: "I've just been seeing a man about some permit for the Cod-fish parade. Nowadays you need a permit for everything, just so that they can make money out of you." He lied to me just like that, calm as anything.

As the recording suggests, Rosalío Usulutlán not only collaborated with the escape plan, but also joined the band of protestors led by Doctor Salmerón in the courthouse. His involvement was slightly cautious and fearful, although on a few occasions he dared to accompany the mob following the accused even as far as the gates of the XXI precinct jail.

The letters which were delivered by Oviedo the Balloon were stolen from the courthouse sometime in the night of 9 December 1933, and the following morning Judge Fiallos decided that he had had enough. He sent a telegram of resignation to the Chief Justice of the Supreme Court in Managua. He had gone through the wording of this telegram over and over in his head:

> PREVENTED CONTINUATION LEGAL DUTIES PROPER CARE AND ATTENTION DUE CONSTANT IMPINGEMENT JURISDICTION BY MILITARY AUTHORITIES WHO DELIBERATELY BREAK LAWS IGNORE DUE PROCESS OBLIGED TO FOLLOW. NO OPTION BUT OFFER IMMEDIATE RESIGNATION TO THIS HONOURABLE COURT. WHILE DECIDING SUCCESSOR PLEASE PROVIDE SUBSTITUTE HAND OVER LEGAL RESPONSIBILITIES. ALREADY ENGAGED MAKING INVENTORY FURNITURE, OFFICE SUNDRIES AND REGISTER CASES PENDING.

Doctor Manuel Cordero Reyes, Chief Justice of the Supreme Court, sent his reply, which came from Managua that afternoon and is included in the case dossier:

> SUPREME COURT OF JUSTICE SAT CONSIDER RESIGNATION FROM POST CHIEF CRIMINAL PROSECUTING JUDGE FOR DISTRICT LÉON. GIVEN EXTREME GRAVITY CASE CURRENTLY UNDER INVESTIGATION CONCERNING INDESCRIBABLE CRIMES

AGAINST CONTRERAS FAMILY THAT CITY REFRAIN ABANDONING EXECUTION OF JUDICIAL DUTIES UNTIL THIS COURT NOTIFIES YOU APPOINTMENT SUCCESSOR. REMIND YOU RESPONSIBILITIES BOTH CIVIL AND ADMINISTRATIVE SHOULD YOU DEFY RESOLUTION. ACKNOWLEDGE RECEIPT.

In 1964, when Judge Fiallos was coming towards the end of his tenure as Rector of the University of Nicaragua, and was quite close to his death, I used to accompany him as his secretary during his weekly visits to the faculties based in Managua. We made the journeys there and back aboard an ancient hired Oldsmobile, and while on the road and during our lunches at the El Patio restaurant, the conversation often turned to reminiscences of his younger days: the failures and disappointments of his political career, his world view and what he called belligerent humanism, about art and literature and the life of a writer (he had just written the prologue to my own first collection of short stories at this point). I often used to try to talk about the Castañeda case, which interested me not only because it had been among the case studies we had looked at in class at the Faculty of Law, but most of all because the voluminous case dossier read like a novel, and the judge was one of the protagonists in that novel.

I didn't keep notes of our conversations but, relying on my own memory, I have included some of his considerations about the case in previous chapters. I have to admit, however, that it was never his favourite topic. It evoked a certain nostalgia for him because it was among the outstanding events of his youth, but the memory was always tinged with a bitter aftertaste, above all when he spoke of those final weeks when he had been obliged to continue in post, lacking all motivation and knowing full well that the true outcome of the trial was being decided behind his back.

Once the trial had ended, it was not long before facts emerged showing what should have been obvious from the outset: the National Guard, who were the real power behind the government of President Juan Bautista Sacasa, had been involved in a conspiracy to intimidate those witnesses called by Castañeda, preventing many from giving their testimony and meaning that those who did were deliberately evasive and far from explicit. Years later, as we will let Captain Prío explain, other goings-on came to light concerning the plans concocted by the National Guard to make an assault on the courthouse and steal the letters.

Only the cook Salvadora Carvajal, interrogated on 10 December 1933, responded to the list of questions without hesitation. This was despite her having been pulled in by the National Guard on the previous day and subjected to threats by Captain Ortiz who showed her complaints about the illegal pig slaughter being carried out in her home. Interestingly, they did not give her any warnings concerning her involvement in the escape plan; this would not have served the interests of the National Guard, as we shall learn in due course.

The young Leticia Osorio also appeared to answer the list of questions on December tenth, accompanied by Doctor Juan de Dios Vanegas, the prosecuting attorney. Previously Judge Fiallos had been impressed by the surprising maturity of her answers despite her youth and he remembered her for her lively intelligence. On this occasion there was no sign of her former vivacity:

LIST OF QUESTIONS CONCERNING
MATILDE CONTRERAS:

Question 1: Aware as she is that she is required to tell the whole truth, can the witness confirm that while we were studying on the veranda in the evenings, Matilde Contreras, whom she knew, used to caress my hair and chin. That she observed this when she came to bring us coffee and she also saw that we held hands and that I kissed that of Matilde.

Answer: I didn't notice anything.

Question 2: Aware as she is that she is required to tell the whole truth, can the witness confirm that she saw me leave the aforementioned Matilde's bedroom at the dead of night where she would have been sleeping alone since her sister was away in Chichigalpa visiting Don Enrique Gil's family?

Answer: I didn't see him leave nor do I remember whether Matilde had been sleeping alone or not.

Question 3: Deleted by the judge for attempting to lead the witness.

Question 4: Aware as she is that she is required to tell the whole truth, can the witness confirm that my wife Marta Jerez de Castañeda scolded the aforementioned Matilde in your presence, accusing her of ruining our marriage, accusing her of being a shameless hussy, and using other strong words.

Answer: I didn't hear anything like that. I heard nothing.

Question 5: Deleted by the judge for attempting to lead the witness.

At this point the defence asked for the interview to be terminated since it was obvious that, taking advantage of the witness's youth, she had been bribed, this being clear from her appearance in court dressed in a new outfit including new shoes, all of which were of a fine quality; clothing the like of which had never been provided for her during her time as a servant in the house. In addition, the defence complained that the judge had disallowed certain key questions, rendering the interrogation pointless.

The prosecution then intervened to make a protest against the assertions of the accused concerning the truthfulness of the witness's answers, asking that these be struck from the record as fanciful.

The judge granted the defence's request to suspend the interrogation but also admitted the prosecution's objection, resolving not to allow any statements that questioned the independence of the witness. Concerning the deletion of certain questions, the judge referred the defence to Article 225 of the Code, which empowers a judge to do this without having to explain his reasons.

Eufrasio Donaire, personal details unknown, whom the defence had called as a witness to certain amorous encounters, was summoned by the court bailiff. His place of residence had been given as the Nuestro Amo ranch, but when the official went there to present him with his summons, nobody knew where he was to be found, and he never appeared to give his deposition, despite writs being issued on three consecutive occasions by the court, as required by law.

Dolores Lorente, personal details previously provided, whom the defence had alleged was the courier for the love letters, was questioned on 14 December 1933. She denied all knowledge of the letters and moreover, alleged that she had not been paid for the time she spent working in Castañeda's house, demanding that this debt be settled. For his part, the defence sought to obtain a certificate showing that, days earlier, the witness had been taken on as a cook in the mess of the National Guard HQ, at the same time asking for a summary statement of her pay to be included on the certificate. The Paymaster General of the National Guard delayed the paper work and when finally taken to task on this issue responded that nobody had been entered on the roster under the name in question.

On 15 December 1933, Demetrio Puertas, the accounts clerk at Contreras & Co., wrote a letter formally pressing charges against the accused alleging that he had been falsely incriminated. He went on to claim the right, as injured party, not to appear in court until his accusations had been the subject of further investigation.

On December twenty-first, the defence made a written request for Octavio Oviedo y Reyes, of particulars previously stated, be called as a witness. As the original guardian of the stolen letters, he had had access to them, and it was therefore requested that he give a statement concerning their contents. The request was granted on the same day and he was sent a summons by the court. However, on the day appointed for him to appear, his father Don Isidro Oviedo Mayorga turned up in his place, brandishing official letters showing that the witness had been appointed as the Nicaraguan consul in Santa Ana, Republic of El Salvador. He also confirmed that on receipt of official passport Number 27 from the Nicaraguan Foreign Ministry, he had already left the country on December twentieth aboard the steamer *Acajutla*, a fact confirmed in the records of the harbour master at the port of Corinto.

Because Judge Fiallos never got to hear these witnesses, the assertions made by Oliverio Castañeda in his petition of 6 December 1933 were left in the air. We also know that because of Doctor Salmerón's disastrous appearance before the judge, he never saw the details contained in the Casa Squibb notebook or the sections of the secret dossier which referred to those amorous encounters. These documents only came into my possession in 1981, and consequently did not form part of my talks with the judge back in 1964.

This means it is impossible to tell what role they might have played in the trial or what weight the judge would have given them.

I was, however, able to remind Judge Fiallos that the expert examination he had ordered did authenticate the letter found in Castañeda's trunk: according to the official report, the handwriting was indeed that of Matilde Contreras. I also reminded him that he must have seen the letters handed over by Oviedo the Balloon before they were stolen; did he have the chance to get an impression of their contents? Furthermore, when preparing to question Doctor Salmerón had he really been trying to unravel the tangle of love interests? His line of questioning with María del Pilar certainly suggests this, despite its tentative nature.

I do not have his exact words before me now, but even accepting that the entire case was set against a background of sordid intrigue and jealousy he would not affirm that this would have changed the course of the trial in any way. He said he had never got as far as reading any of the letters handed in by Oviedo the Balloon before they were stolen. It was clear that he did not want to go any further into this aspect of the case. It always seemed strange to me that even for him, a man so modern in his thinking and free of prejudice, it was still a taboo subject, as it remains for the Contreras family, many of whom continue to live in León.

As the author of this story I feel obliged to look on the judge kindly. The details of the Castañeda case inspire strong feelings in today's descendants of its protagonists, and out of regard for them I have, like Rosalío Usulutlán in his exposé, disguised the true identities of the Contreras family by giving them invented first and surnames.

Let us hear again from Captain Río in the recording I made on 17 October 1986, talking about this difficult time for Judge Fiallos and other no less important matters:

> All that was a disaster for Castañeda, but for Judge Fiallos it was even worse. Those in power in León made him feel their bitter contempt for having accepted the petition. And then they went and stole the letters from the courthouse. When Colonel Manuel Gómez turned against Somoza for the electoral fraud in 1947, one of the things he

denounced from exile was that he was the one ordered to carry out the theft: he sent two prisoners jailed for robbery to get in through the courthouse roof. Tacho Ortiz then sent the letters by airplane to Somoza in Managua.

After that, no one came forward to testify, or if they did, they knew nothing about anything. Mariano Fiallos found himself up against not only the National Guard, but President Sacasa, who was from León. Sacasa took it upon himself to defend the honour of the Contreras family. And Somoza himself was determined to bury the whole affair, because he was an adopted son of León and wanted to please the local bigwigs. He had climbed higher than he had ever dreamed possible thanks to marrying a member of the Debayle-Sacasa family, and they were related to the Contrerases, even if when it came to deposing Sacasa, he conveniently forgot he was one of his in-laws.

Fiallos also had Castañeda against him, because he was constantly blaming him for the theft of the letters and the witnesses' refusal to speak, as if it were all his fault. And Oviedo the Balloon, who didn't even say farewell before he took himself off to El Salvador. Sacasa was the one who did that. He arranged it with Canon Oviedo y Reyes, who later became bishop of León and was nicknamed "Madcap" [sound of laughter] because he became crazier and crazier so that his sermons were full of Rubén Dario's fauns and satyrs. "May youths bearing baskets of flowers offer you their laurels!", he used to scream from the pulpit [more laughter].

The entire family got together in conclave after Oviedo the Balloon turned up at the courthouse with the bag containing the incriminating letters. It wasn't a saddle bag? A box? Well then, the box where he kept the letters he had always denied possessing. And in the conclave, his father, mother and "Madcap" accused him of stealing them and made the decision: "You're leaving the country on the spot, you criminal, and taking your wife and children with you." They gave him provisions of sausages and tamales [laughter], but as soon as he boarded the train he was sobbing his heart out. Of course, Oviedo the Balloon eventually came back to Nicaragua, and even became a judge in the western region appeals court, but by then he wasn't a balloon any more, he'd been punctured by too much sugar in his blood; when he died he was nothing more than a bag of wrinkled skin.

So Castañeda's best friend abandoned him, leaving him defenceless in the midst of the storm. Who would have thought it? The only one on his side was Doctor Salmerón, the person who had previously wanted him sentenced to death. Now he was leading the barefoot poor and others to support him. That's how the wheel spins, isn't it?

Doctor Salmerón lost the friendship of Doctor Darbishire forever, as well as many other friends—or rather, people who had never really been close to him: you've been investigating all this, you must have realised he was always looked down on in León. But what happened with my godfather was a blow to him; he admired Doctor Darbishire, and lost a friendship that was a great comfort to him in a stinking place like this, where nobody liked him. And it was over Castañeda that they became bitter enemies. Look at how things turned out: my godfather was right in his prophecy, Doctor Salmerón and Castañeda suffered the same fate.

Doctor Darbishire died in 1960. Were you already studying in León then? Of course, you were already here for July twenty-third, and the massacre of students ordered by Tacho Ortiz when he brought the National Guard onto the streets, outside the big Casa Prío. We buried my godfather the following year. He was very old by then, and couldn't get out of his wheelchair. He didn't even have his dogs any more, the only person still around was that deaf and dumb fellow Teodosio. And just as Bishop Oviedo grew crazier and crazier, so he started talking only in French, with Teodosio waving his arms at him as if he understood.

Doctor Salmerón gave the eulogy for him in the university amphitheatre on behalf of the Medical College; and a splendid funeral oration it was, it even got printed as a pamphlet. They didn't talk to each other in all those

> years, cutting each other whenever they met in the street, almost thirty years as sworn enemies, and yet at the funeral he had nothing but praise for him: a learned man, he called him, a scientific eminence. I call that noble.

(As Captain Prío points out, Tacho Ortiz, by this time a major, was in command of a National Guard detachment that opened fire on a peaceful student demonstration on the evening of 23 July 1959, in the street leading from the university to Casa Prío, the very same street along which the Kelvinator refrigerator was hauled in procession to the Faculty of Pharmacy at dusk on 9 October 1933. That massacre left a toll of four dead and more than sixty wounded.

(As rector of the university, Mariano Fiallos walked at the head of the burial procession, which turned into a noisy demonstration against the Somoza dictatorship, and the bishop of León, Monsignor Isidro Augusto Oviedo y Reyes refused to open the doors of the cathedral for a funeral mass to be said in honour of the fallen. Tacho Ortiz's house, close to the university, was set on fire by an angry crowd the following night.)

In that same street, as Captain Prío recalls because he was an eyewitness from the door of his establishment, and as Judge Fiallos himself told me in 1964, there was an altercation that led to blows between the judge and Captain Ortiz.

Judge Fiallos was heading for the courthouse aboard his Ford 'The Bluebird' to sort out his papers after sending the telegram announcing his decision to quit. Alí Vanegas was sitting beside him in the front of the vehicle. Captain Ortiz had seen him leaving the telegraph office, and jumped into his own vehicle to catch him up, sounding his horn the whole time to make him stop.

'Have you heard about the theft?' asked Captain Ortiz, sticking his head out of the car window as he drew alongside the judge. Alí Vanegas clutched the bundle of papers closer to his chest and shrank back in his seat in order not to be in the way between the two men.

'Yes, I've heard about it,' said the judge, keeping his hands on the wheel, ready to set off again. 'I suppose you've already given the order to burn those letters.'

'I knew you were going to blame me,' laughed Captain Ortiz,

putting his car into neutral and keeping his foot on the brake.

'Yes, it's because I've got an evil mind,' said the judge. Bothered by the sun striking the windscreen, he looked for his hat on the seat. It was trapped beneath Alí Vanegas, who shifted position and handed it to him. 'The poor National Guard, always getting blamed for everything. If you haven't already had them burned, you'd do better to hand them over to my successor.' Although Judge Fiallos had put the hat on, the sun was still blinding him. 'I've resigned.'

'Here you are accusing me of theft, but as you can see, I'm not getting angry. I woke up in a good mood.' Captain Ortiz spits on his hands; his steering wheel is burning like a hot iron. 'If we find the thieves, you'll have the letters back today.' Hearing his engine about to stall, the Captain pressed down on the clutch. 'And that story of yours about resigning is as old as the hills.'

'The resignation has already come into effect,' said Alí Vanegas, taking the telegram out of the bundle on his lap and waving it at the captain.

'Don't be such a baby, and stop this nonsense.' Captain Ortiz switched off the ignition and the engine shook and died. 'Those letters don't add anything to the case. What you are investigating are poisonings, not rape or keeping a bawdy house.'

'Did you hear that? They're the ones who decide what I should be investigating,' said the judge, folding his handkerchief over the back of his neck. 'They decide to carry out exhumations; they kidnap witnesses, and now they steal evidence. This is the new law they are applying in Nicaragua; I'm sure they'll do the same with Sandino.'

'Well, that's your opinion,' said Captain Ortiz, opening his car door. Alí Vanegas saw a boot stepping out. 'So you think we're capable of killing Sandino, do you? He deserves it as a bandit and a murderer, but from saying that to actually doing it…'

'Yes, I think you're capable of it,' said Judge Fiallos, peering across at Alí Vanegas. The secretary nodded, pursing his lips; beads of sweat appeared among the short stems of his hair. 'And I think you're capable of killing Castañeda.'

'You're still insulting me with your accusations.' The Captain's other boot touched the road surface. 'We'll put him before a firing squad, if your jury condemns him to death. When are you going to call the jury anyway? This case is beginning to stink.'

'They're going to kill him because the only justice they recognise comes from the barrel of a gun,' said the judge to Alí Vanegas, who started to fan himself energetically with the pile of papers. 'It's all the same to them whether it's a national hero like Sandino or a prisoner like Castañeda.'

'So this Bolshevik poof of a poet is your advisor, is he? I'm not surprised, he's always praising Sandino in his verses.' Captain Ortiz stuck his head in through their car window. 'But you...'

'Don't talk about verses with them, Alí; the National Guard don't know anything about them.' Judge Fiallos switched off his engine too; the car jumped forward, then halted. 'And I'm not in charge of any case against Sandino. I'm talking about the Castañeda case.'

'I'm not talking to any poet,' said Captain Ortiz, walking round the Bluebird and poking his head in on the driver's side. 'Are you trying to tell me that if you were judging Sandino for banditry, you would have let him go free by now?'

'You mean you have to kill Castañeda before I set him free?' Judge Fiallos puts one hand on the steering wheel, and gives Alí Vanegas a hard stare.

'Don't be so rude, it's you I'm talking to,' said Captain Ortiz, kicking the car door. 'So you want the letters in order to release Castañeda. In that case, you're going to have to wait.'

'Did you hear him? He stole the letters so I can't release Castañeda, and now he's the one who's offended.' Judge Fiallos started to wind up the window on his side. 'Make a note of that, if only for posterity.'

'If you carry on accusing me of theft, you'll suffer,' said Captain Ortiz, putting his hand on the top of the window to stop it rising any further. 'You ought to thank whoever took those letters; they did you a favour.'

'Take that down, too: the thief confesses he is doing me a favour.' The judge struggled to raise the window further, tongue between his teeth.

'I've already told you I'm no thief, so stop bugging me,' said Captain Ortiz, reaching in through the window and knocking off the judge's hat. 'You're the accomplice of that son of a bitch, who is now trying to ridicule his victims.'

'Let's see you fight like a man,' said Judge Fiallos, violently pushing open the door and forcing the captain back. He jumped out and stood in the middle of the street, clenched fists raised. Several billiard players appeared at the doorway to the Lezama billiard parlour, cues in hand.

Captain Ortiz jerked his head back to try to avoid the punch, but the judge's fist caught him square on the nose. Alí Vanegas ran to separate the two men, and dragged the judge away. The billiard players came out into the street and surrounded them, as various passers-by came running up.

'You're the one who followed us to cause trouble,' stammered Alí Vanegas, struggling to keep Judge Fiallos back and horrified to see the blood pouring from the captain's nostrils down his mouth and chin. 'Get out of here, or I won't be responsible. Can't you see that Mariano is a boxer?'

'We'll settle this some other time,' growled Captain Ortiz, taking out his handkerchief and wiping away the blood. He gesticulated furiously at the onlookers for them to disperse. They all obeyed immediately. 'But don't imagine for a minute that your resignation will be accepted. You started the case, and you have to finish it.'

'Are you going to order the Supreme Court to that effect?' said Judge Fiallos, freeing himself from Alí Vanegas and dusting down his jacket. 'Tell me then when the case will be over. When are you planning to kill Castañeda?'

'The day he tries to escape.' Captain Ortiz, clutching the bloody handkerchief to his nose, went to the back of his car in search of the crank. 'He's already planning to escape. And Salmerón is helping him.'

'And how do you know all this?' asked Alí Vanegas. Intrigued, he went up to the captain as he made for the front of his car, crank in hand.'

'If I didn't, I'd be a "poof poet", wouldn't I?' As Captain Ortiz leaned forward to crank the engine, blood dripped from his nose to the ground. 'Tell your boxer friend to ask Cosme Manzo. He knows. And you were right to restrain him, or I would have shot him.'

'It's true, they're going to kill him pretending he is trying to escape,' said Alí Vanegas, scratching his scorching head as he watched Captain Ortiz's car disappearing down the street. 'If Manzo knows about a plan, he could very well have given it away to the National Guard.'

'If there is an escape, my replacement will have to deal with it,' said Judge Fiallos, struggling in turn with the crank to try to start the Bluebird's engine. 'I don't want to hear any more about strychnine, letters, still less escapes. What a good witness that Manzo was.'

'This isn't a game. As soon as Castañeda steps outside that jail, they'll shoot him.' Alí Vanegas continued staring after Captain Ortiz's car, which had already vanished round the corner.

'And who on earth can stop those barbarians if they want to kill him?' Judge Fiallos swung the crank as hard as he could, but the engine refused to start. 'And you, stupid car, are you going to stay here forever?'

CHAPTER FORTY-SIX

Letter Filled with Hope to a Lady. The Lady's Reply

I

YOU ASK how it was, my lady? Well, as these things always are when they are of the soul. The train was travelling along its tracks today when all at once I saw her, a few seats away from me, with her calm, triumphant beauty, the shifting green and grey of her eyes more than a match for any opal or diamond, or the vast flaming tropics.

And I saw her again this evening, in her doorway, just when the mystery of her first apparition was fading. True love is a once-in-a-lifetime thing. I have a song just for you among my records. I crossed the street in search of you, of the unknown sound of your voice. But by then you had already moved from the doorway, and I was left with only the hollow of your body in space. Don't forget though: I have brought with me from afar a music that until now was only for me. When you hear it, it will belong to both of us.

We are separated by no more than a street, the only one my steps have paced since my arrival here. They say you belong to someone else. What does that matter, say I! One day we will meet without anyone to witness it, because I have been blinded by the lightning flash of your eyes. You who enjoy the light, please do not deny me mine; until then my sorrowing heart will live in darkness.

Keep where no one will see it this letter that late in the night your unknown admirer pens with feverish anxiety. Tomorrow is another day, and the night of my intimate, precious joy is bound to come. And while I await that night, I dream that there you will place a garland in which purple roses explode; and while water sings beneath a shady glade, you, in that dream, initiate me in the celestial mystery; and I, resting from my sweet labours, drink the golden amphorae of Epicurus to the dregs.

II

I have thought long and hard before replying by letter to your words, and if I now seek to be polite, you must not see in this response any suggestion of incorrect behaviour on my part. You are very young, as I could see from a distance yesterday afternoon when you were busy with your luggage, accompanied by your equally youthful wife; and it is to your youthfulness that I attribute the audacity of your message, whose allusions and insinuations I prefer to ignore, without fully understanding them.

I am a great reader of poetry: I like Amado Nervo and José Asunción Silva, as well as Rubén Darío, because in the Sión College of Costa Rica I had a very sensitive and responsive literature teacher who awakened in me a love for beautiful, exquisite things; that is why I find your reckless lines so touching.

I hope that since we are neighbours, there will be an opportunity for us to meet socially. A visit by you and your wife to our house would not come amiss, in order to make the necessary introductions in the proper manner.

Do not keep this letter. I am relying on your good sense.

CHAPTER FORTY-SEVEN

The Tragic Events of Christmas Eve in León

OLIVERIO CASTAÑEDA DEAD AT THE HANDS OF THE NATIONAL GUARD • HAD ESCAPED FROM PRISON • OFFICIAL VERSION OF EVENTS • OTHER VERSIONS SPEAK OF HIM 'BEING SHOT WHILE TRYING TO ESCAPE' • PRESIDENT SACASA, IN LEÓN WITH FAMILY AND ENTOURAGE TOOK PART IN CHRISTMAS PROCESSION • WAS GENERAL SOMOZA ALSO IN CITY? • STRONG MILITARY PRESENCE ON STREETS • PRISONER'S MOST FERVENT SUPPORTERS VANISH • LA NUEVA PRENSA WITNESS TO HASTY BURIAL OF FUGITIVE • CLOSE OF SENSATIONAL CASE

(From our special correspondent, Manolo Cuadra)

THE venerable city of León has lived through a bitter Christmas this year, even though the traditional religious celebrations prevented its citizens from being aware of the dramatic events that ended tragically at midnight on Christmas Eve; events that to general astonishment only came to light the following day. Your reporter was equally surprised to hear of them, having gone to bed in ignorance after sharing the Christmas meal at Doctor Juan de Dios Vanegas's house, kindly invited by his son, Alí Vanegas.

Christmas Eve in León. Sweet moments, with the pain of nostalgia. The constellations, shining bright in the depths of the heavenly vault, looked kindly down on us, as they must have done on Oliverio Castañeda in his final hours. The fragrant aroma of the madroño berries, the simple decoration of the cribs wafted from each doorway, and brought with it the intoxication of childhood. The fugitive must have caught a hint of it when he reached the neighbourhood of Subtiava, filled with altars, on the first station in his flight. The sound of flutes, tambourines, and the silvery explosion of festive gunpowder. Would these happy sounds still be echoing in his ears when the shots rang out that were to put such a sudden end to his hazardous life?

The curtain had already been raised on the first act of the fateful drama when in the evening we quit the Chabelita boarding-house to roam the streets with the poet Vanegas. What we wished for above all was to be instilled with the calm joy of the passers-by, to ease the sorrow we felt at being far from our loved ones at such a time, since our journalistic duty has obliged us to remain in this metropolis. Did Oliverio Castañeda, still further from his family than we were from our home in Masaya, feel overwhelmed by nostalgia and longing for his native land as he left his cell at the same moment? He was disguised in a National Guard uniform, the same one that we ourselves wore, in an evil hour, when we fought in the Segovian wastes against the hero of the Indo-Hispanic race...Sandino. But that's another story.

PRESENCE OF DOCTOR SACASA AND HIS FAMILY. THEIR THOUGHTS

We learned that the presidential train carrying Doctor Sacasa, his family and entourage, was about to arrive at the Pacific Railway station, and so that was where we headed, alerted by the locomotive's lengthy whistle. The president descended, accompanied by the First Lady, Doña María, their offspring and brother and sisters, ministers of state and their escort. The President greeted us on the platform, as befits a gentleman willing to forgive insults in order not to seem impolite, even though we have attacked him, and fiercely, for being so docile, in the pages of this newspaper. He even agreed to reply to our questions about the Castañeda case, which was to be so dramatically resolved in a matter of hours: "the executive is closely following the course of justice, an independent and sovereign power, and we are convinced of the probity of the judges charged with the responsibility of dealing with the case. We will on no account interfere in their actions." He went on to declare: "But I don't want to discuss such unpleasant topics. I have come to the city of my birth to spend Christmas Eve with my family, and as is customary, to take part in the procession for the Infant Jesus, a statue offered to the cathedral by my grandfather."

A THRONGED CHRISTMAS PROCESSION

The President brought with him on the train the Band of the Supreme Powers. The musicians, dressed in their blue and scarlet gala uniforms, immediately made for Plaza Jerez, where they gave a joyful concert of carols and Christmas hymns. Doctor Sacasa also brought, at his own expense, the artistic pyrotechnics displays that cast their magical glow over the same square. Accompanied everywhere by his retinue, the president took part in the whole procession through the centuries-old streets, as he had told us he would, and both he and members of his family and entourage took turns to carry the statue of the Infant Jesus.

This is not the most appropriate place to describe the exuberant procession, as it is Oliverio Castañeda's dramatic end that most concerns us, but it is worthwhile quickly noting, by way of a contrast, that from the moment it left the cathedral at ten o'clock, the procession was followed by large numbers of people; that León's most aristocratic families came to accompany Doctor Sacasa and the First Lady; and that the Band of the Supreme Powers distinguished itself yet again with its merry Christmas tunes as it marched along behind the crowds.

The contrast: at the same time as Christmas was being celebrated in this way, uniting all levels of society around the mystery of the Nativity, if only this once, elsewhere, a drama (which as we have already said, went unnoticed) was already being played out in dark, sinister tones that had nothing in common with the explosions of fireworks or the clamour of tambourines: the unnoticed flight and subsequent capture and death of Oliverio Castañeda at the hands of the National Guard.

CAPTAIN ANASTASIO J. ORTIZ'S VIEW: ACCOMPLICES INSIDE THE JAIL

The next morning, we set out to uncover all the necessary information, so as to offer the readers of *La Nueva Prensa* a detailed account of events. In the first place we visited Captain Anastasio J. Ortiz, chief of the local police, who agreed to see us in his office despite the fact that it was [yesterday] a public holiday. That interview provided me with the following essential information:

Oliverio Castañeda succeeded in escaping from the cells of the XXI precinct at six in the evening, a time when skyrockets were shooting into the sky from all the neighbourhoods of León, and exploding firecrackers announced the imminent start of the festivities. None of the sentries noticed his escape because one of his accomplices inside the jail, Sergeant Guadalupe Godínez, had provided him with a military uniform to wear as a disguise.

This enabled him to get out without any difficulty into the gallery containing his cell, the door of which was mysteriously left unlocked: something for which Captain Ortiz also holds Godínez responsible. Castañeda went out into the walled yard, where at that time the other prisoners were lined up waiting to receive the plate of food traditionally offered them by the Sisters of the Tertiary Order each year at this date. And finally he was able to leave through the front gate, after presenting the guard on duty with a fake pass.

NATIONAL GUARD DENIES SECRETLY ALLOWING CASTANEDA TO ESCAPE

"If the prisoner was able to pass through the walls of the jail without difficulty, it was because he had won the confidence of a good number of guards and soldiers who were responsible for surveillance there. We have begun an investigation. Castañeda won over Sergeant Guadalupe

Godínez by means of many tricks and ruses. For example, taking advantage of his lack of education and humble upbringing, he dedicated himself to teaching him to read and write, and had made considerable progress in that," Captain Ortíz said.

When we told him that in León there was a suspicion that the National Guard was well aware that the escape would take place, he replied: "That is false. Some of Castañeda's accomplices are still at liberty in León. They are more than ready to lie in order to conceal their own participation in the plan, because it failed. Castañeda was extraordinarily skilful at planning things, and it seems he did not let a minute go by in carefully organizing his escape, from the first moment he became a forced guest in the XXI precinct jail. He did not overlook a single detail. As I have already told you, he had allies inside. We are investigating how he came to have a counterfeit pass, as well as the origin of a forged memorandum handed to the duty officer in the guard-room shortly after six o'clock, when the prisoner had already left the jail."

THE MYSTERIOUS MEMORANDUM

Captain Ortiz gave me the memorandum to copy. Here it is:

NATIONAL GUARD HEADQUARTERS, LEÓN
León, 24 December 1933.
From: Cpt. Anastasio J. Ortiz, National Guard.
To: Lt. Rafael Parodi, Governor of XXI precinct jail.
Re: Special permit for prisoner.

No alarm is to be raised when absence of prisoner Olivério Castañeda Palacios is noted. He has permission from this authority to leave the jail from 18.00 to 24.00 hours, in other words, midnight. The prisoner is leaving without a guard, with his word as guarantee.

The Governor, or failing that the duty officer, are responsible for the strict application of this order in the greatest secrecy, guaranteeing that nobody becomes aware of the prisoner's absence. If anybody, whether officer, NCO, private or civilian, asks about him, they are to be told that he has been transferred to the "La Chiquita" prison for security reasons.

This National Guard command prohibits any violation of this secret. It should not be talked about, either in person or by telephone, before the prisoner returns to his cell, and not even after that, or face the corresponding sanctions.

A. J. ORTIZ

From the original document that we saw, Captain Ortiz's signature is very convincing, but it is evident it was copied by carbon paper from another document and then, tracing the outline made by the carbon, gone over in ink. As Captain Ortiz demonstrated, if examined under a magnifying glass, tiny grains of carbon are visible.

We pointed out that such a document could be attributed to the same military authorities as part of their plan to facilitate the prisoner's escape, and then kill him. The Captain replied:

"Why, if that had been the intention, would we need documents? A prisoner on the run is an outlaw, and the authorities are permitted to shoot to kill in that case. Whoever faked the document knew that Lieutenant Parodi was on leave in Managua. He would never have been taken in by such a ruse."

A "HUNCH"—THE ALARM IS RAISED

He went on: "Like all the other fathers of families in León, I was getting ready to take part in the Infant Jesus procession with my wife and children. I had no intention of going to inspect the jail that night, but I had a sudden hunch and, already wearing my dress uniform but before heading for the cathedral, I decided to visit the XXI precinct in order to see if the prisoners had been satisfied with the Christmas meal they had been served a few hours earlier.

"Imagine my surprise when I was mysteriously taken to one side by the duty officer and told that my orders were being carried out. When I asked what orders he was referring to, he showed me the fake memorandum. It was at that point that I raised the alarm."

THE FAITHFUL SERVANT SALVADORA CARVAJAL

"As a first measure, I interrogated Sergeant Godínez, the most obvious suspect. Realising it was no use, before long he confessed everything he knew, starting with the complicity of Salvadora Carvajal in the plan of escape. There was no time to lose, and so I formed a squad of fifteen men and we went to the woman's house in Subtiava, using the Departmental truck and two automobiles.

"Carvajal had been a servant in the Contreras family home, and Castañeda got on well with her. Thanks to my kindness, she was given permission to wash and iron the prisoner's clothes. That was how she was able to visit him frequently in jail, acting as the contact with his accomplices outside."

A PADLOCK ON THE DOOR OF HIS HIDING-PLACE. CAPTURED AS HE TRIED TO FLEE

According to Captain Ortiz, it was almost ten o'clock at night by the time they reached the small house. They approached it stealthily, having left the vehicles some distance away. "We found the front door padlocked, as if to demonstrate that no one was at home. This trick made me suspicious: Castañeda could be inside. I posted sentries on each corner, and left several recruits behind an unhitched cart in the street. I chose five men, and we circled round behind the piñuela hedge, until we came to the back of the property. The soldiers received the order to load their guns.

"We crossed the hedge and began to crawl towards the house. At that moment, a shape detached itself from the kitchen shack, running straight for us. I shouted for him to halt, and when he did so, he saw our guns trained on him. It was Castañeda.

"At first he was hard to recognize, because he was disguised as a peasant, with a wide-brimmed palm hat, short cotton trousers and boots. He also had a black false beard made from female hair. Trembling, he begged us not to shoot, and handed me a Smith & Wesson .38 pistol that he was carrying."

At that same hour, the statue of the Infant Jesus was being carried into the cathedral, and the distant peal of bells must have reached the dark yard where this sensational capture was taking place.

HIS AIM WAS TO REACH HONDURAS ON HORSEBACK

The National Guard patrol seized the animal in the yard, already saddled up for the day's ride to the frontier with Honduras. After searching the house, they found the military uniform hidden in a tub. The prisoner was taken back to the XXI precinct. During the transfer in the automobile accompanied by Captain Ortiz, he insisted he had no accomplices, and that no one else should be blamed for his escape. Back at the jail, after a tough interrogation, he revealed that he had intended to leave León by a side road to Chinandega that started from the racecourse on the outskirts of the San Felipe neighbourhood.

"It was almost twelve o'clock at night when I decided that, to complete my investigation of the escape, it was necessary to take the prisoner to the spot he had mentioned, to make sure that there were no accomplices waiting for him there," said Captain Ortiz.

SHOT ESCAPING, OR SHOT IN THE BACK?

Now we come to the most controversial part of Captain Ortiz's story. Was there really any need to take the prisoner to that desolate spot in the middle of the night, considering that his attempted escape and subsequent recapture had not been reported to the examining magistrate, Mariano Fiallos? Could that inspection not have waited until the next day, so that it could be carried out in his presence? We put this to the captain.

"If his accomplices were waiting for him there, as I had reason to believe, they were not going to stay there until the following morning," was his reply. "And he was the one who had to identify them. There was no way I believed that he didn't have accomplices, as he kept on insisting."

And so the operation was carried out. This time there was only one vehicle, with the prisoner, Captain Ortiz and four guards inside. One of them had a Lewis sub-machine gun. In our campaign against Sandino in the Segovias, we knew this weapon brought by the U.S. Marines as "the lewita" or even "la Luisita".

We invite our readers to picture the scene. Silence in the streets. The explosions of gunpowder and the sounds of music have long since died away. Light shone under the doors of some homes where families were still enjoying their Christmas meal. Possibly some stray dog wandered in front of the automobile and came to a halt, dazzled by its headlights.

They passed in front of the already closed cathedral. The prisoner must have looked for the last time at its huge oak doors, its ashen-coloured walls so stubbornly deaf to the agitation of his heart. It was here that he had one day entered carrying his wife's coffin, and a few months later on a rainy afternoon, done the same with Matilde Contreras' white casket. The university, where the controversial experiments with the corpses' viscera helped seal his fate, was completely dark.

The Metropolitan Hotel appeared on their route. Opposite, locked doors confirmed there was no Christmas cheer in the Contreras family home. Was María del Pilar Contreras asleep in her bed at that late hour, or could she not sleep? Did the beams from the headlights of the automobile sweep for a moment under the door of her bedroom, and was that the last bright glow of a departing love? These are questions we leave it open to our readers to consider.

THE FATAL HOUR ARRIVES

They left the asphalted streets. The vehicle bumped over potholes, and Oliverio Castañeda, jolted by the uneven terrain and his own plight, hit his head against the roof as he travelled in silence, hemmed in by his guards. No more street lights. The cold night air of December whirled in through the open windows and clawed at his face. Darkness, the sounds of the countryside...then the automobile suddenly braked...the fatal hour had arrived. Yet again a barbarous law, the law of flight, was about to be enacted.

"We did not kill him in cold blood," Captain Ortiz said emphatically. "The National Guard respects the lives of our prisoners. If you wish, you can consult our military regulations, where it is expressly stated. Besides, we do not need regulations. You were a solider once, and know that the honour of the uniform is far more important than any regulation." We avoided an ironic smile. This was no moment to contradict him.

"Opposite San Felipe cemetery, where the old stables of the racecourse are situated, I gave the order to leave the vehicle to carry out an inspection of the surrounding," the captain continued. "We all got out, except for the prisoner, who lagged behind. I told him to hurry up. All at once, he flung himself from the vehicle and started to run towards the cemetery wall. He had already reached it with the intention of climbing over when the machine-gunner, who by now had recovered from his surprise, brought him down with a well-aimed burst from his Lewis machine-gun. One bullet penetrated his head, another the nape of his neck, and two hit him in the back. He died instantaneously."

Midnight. Cemetery. A prisoner running. We all know the story. Who doesn't in this unhappy Nicaragua of ours? "A Military Court of Investigation has been established on direct orders from General Somoza, to determine responsibilities in this case. Let the official report settle matters, so that the National Guard can silence the gossip that is already circulating. As I have already told you, Castañeda had accomplices in León. These are social misfits, inveterate trouble-makers. We are going to refute their base accusations."

REPORTS THAT GENERAL SOMOZA WAS SIGHTED IN LEÓN

Since Captain Ortiz mentioned General Somoza, we took advantage to ask him if it was true that he had been sighted yesterday in León. Some people affirmed they had seen him leaving the National Guard Headquarters at midnight with his escort, then crossing Plaza Jerez to go to the house of his father-in-law, Doctor Luis H. Debayle, next to the cathedral, where he spent the night.

"What nonsense," was Captain Ortiz's reply. "If that had been the case, he wouldn't have missed the procession for the Infant Jesus. Besides, if the president of the country is travelling, General Somoza cannot leave the capital."

NO SIGN OF MARIANO FIALLOS OR THE PATHOLOGIST

Our final questions: has the judge been informed of these events? Has the pathologist identified the body?

"I notified Judge Fiallos of what had happened first thing this morning. It is now ten o'clock and he has still not been in contact with me. I am not going to force him to do his duty. The pathologist has not appeared either, because it is the judge who has to instruct him to proceed to identify the corpse. If neither of them has turned up by midday, we will bury the body. And to prove that the National Guard has nothing to hide, you can go to the XXI precinct and see the corpse for yourself. You can also attend the burial, if you wish."

This is a full and faithful record of the National Guard's version of events. We went to look for Judge Fiallos at his house, but could not find him; the doors were shut and no one came out to attend to us, however much we knocked.

CALM REIGNS IN THE CITY. OTHER VERSIONS OF THE EVENTS

There was no disorder in the streets of León on December twenty-fifth. Oliverio Castañeda's vociferous supporters were notable by their absence. No billiard halls, canteens or restaurants were open on this sacred holiday. Calm reigned throughout the untroubled city, as though the drama had not yet registered, or was not seen as important. Or was fear at the heart of this indifference? There were more soldiers than usual on the streets of the central area, all of them heavily armed on the pretext of protecting President Sacasa, who was still in León.

And yet a different version of Oliverio Castañeda's death was already being repeated *sotto voce*, a very different version to the one given by Captain Ortiz. Everything is known in León, and quickly. I will copy what sources that we cannot and must not reveal, have told us:

—The National Guard knew about the escape plan in advance, as it had been revealed by one of the plotters. As I promised my source, I cannot reveal the name of this plotter.

—Sergeant Godínez, Castañeda's accomplice in his escape from jail, was acting on instructions from his superiors. The military uniform Castañeda was provided with fitted him exactly, whereas Godínez is much smaller.

—The memorandum calling for silence about the escape, with Captain Ortiz's signature, was deliberately prepared, as was the leave pass.

—The National Guard knew that once he was in the street, Castañeda would go straight to Salvadora Carvajal's house to change clothes, and that the guide helping him cross the frontier would be waiting in the area of the racecourse, where the execution took place. The guide has disappeared.

—The revolver, and some money found in Castañeda's pockets, was given to him by other persons once he was inside the house. The National Guard knew they were there, because the house was already under surveillance. These persons had withdrawn shortly before the arrival of the patrol, but there was no order to arrest them. Nor was Salvadora Carvajal ever caught.

—On leaving the XXI precinct, already well aware of the fate awaiting him, the prisoner begged them not to shoot him in the back. And that if they agreed to execute him facing them, not to disfigure him.

—At his final destination, the prisoner uttered the following words: "This is a political crime. The dictator Ubico has finally succeeded in having me killed."

—He was ordered to start running. At first he tried to

refuse, but eventually did so, unwillingly. He knew he was bound to die. No one runs towards a wall if he wants to escape.

—The body was roped to the front bumper of the automobile to be taken back to the XXI precinct. The head, already destroyed by the bullets, was even further damaged as it hit the ground several times.

Who is telling the truth, and who is lying? In accordance with the laws of journalism, we offer both versions, calmly and fearlessly. It is for the reader to decide.

OLIVERIO CASTAÑEDA'S CORPSE. A LONELY BURIAL

After unsuccessfully going in search of Judge Fiallos, we took advantage of the authorization given by Captain Ortiz and made our way to the XXI precinct jail, where the prisoner's body was still lying on a board in the yard. Bare-foot, face downwards, he lay there in the rough peasant clothes he had donned to make his escape. Nothing glorious about him now, a man who had always been so careful to wear mourning and to take great care over his appearance, with the most refined taste. Pious hands had placed a red handkerchief over his head to protect it from the burning rays of the midday sun.

We were present at the moment when the body was placed in the rough-hewn wooden coffin. As the handkerchief fell, we saw his face, horribly disfigured by the bullet that entered through the back of his neck, which as it exited smashed the jawbone, tearing away all his mouth and part of his nose. The bullet to the head had made a large hole in the skull, from which brain matter dangled.

As soon as the lid of the coffin had been nailed on, four prisoners lifted it. On the way to the cemetery, where a common grave had already been dug, the only escort was the soldiers guarding the prisoners, commanded by Lieutenant Baca, and ourselves. None of the friends who had accompanied him to merry fiestas, none of his student comrades, accompanied him on his final journey.

Nor was there any sign of his fervent supporters, those

who in the last weeks of the trial rewarded his declarations with shouts and applause, and turned him into a kind of screen idol. Back then they carried him shoulder high, and thronged to follow him to the gates of the prison. Today, there was no one to bear his coffin.

No exceptions? There always are. The most striking was that of Doctor Atanasio Salmerón, who silently joined the scant cortege at the cemetery gate, where he had been awaiting his arrival in the punishing sun. He did not leave the graveside until the last shovelful of earth had fallen.

We approached the doctor as the burial was taking place, but he was reluctant to speak, ironically winking in the direction of the soldiers. Once they had withdrawn, all our insistent questions only received the following brief commentary: "This was a murder. Shot trying to escape, my friend. That's all I have to say. Wait to see what I write about it."

We looked at our watch. Scarcely enough time to gather our belongings and reach the railway station, since, now that our mission had come to such an abrupt end, we had to catch the two o'clock train back to the capital. When we were safely installed, we began to order our thoughts for this report.

On the mound of earth beneath which Oliverio Castañeda lies, there is no cross, no bunch of flowers, still less any wreath. That good-looking, enigmatic and gallant young man seems already reduced to oblivion, the excitement surrounding his exploits already fading. Will anyone remember them tomorrow?

Innocent or guilty? We will leave these questions to the wind that suddenly sends ripples through the araucarias lining the silent avenues of the burial ground where he now is laid to rest.

CHAPTER FORTY-EIGHT

We All Will Wear the Same Shroud

I

San José, 23 July 1933

My never forgotten Mati:

As I warned you by airmail letter (which I trust is already in your sweet hands) I was forced to leave for these barren lands. The tyrant's lackeys refused to give me a passport for Nicaragua, thus frustrating my ardent desire to return to your side once and for all, and to enjoy the consolation of your adored presence. Don't be upset, everything is alright now, but those bandits gave me a hard time. They all but escorted me to the port in handcuffs, as though I were a common criminal and not a patriot whose only fault is to refuse to see his native Guatemala humiliated by a tyrant of the likes of Ubico, a cretin who thinks he is Napoleon and goes to the ridiculous extreme of adopting the haircut of the great Corsican, the idiot. But it is not of filthy politics that I wish to talk to you.

I sent an urgent cable to Mito before I boarded ship, and he very kindly had been waiting for me in Puntarenas from the night prior to my arrival. You told me: 'Don't give my brother any alcohol.' As you'll see, he doesn't need me to provide him with any. He offered me several drinks while we were waiting for the train to depart, and we toasted my arrival and our memories of our friendship back in León. He insisted on buying round after round of aniseed liqueur, and on paying for them out of his own pocket. I have to confess that we were quite merry when we boarded the train, so much so that we sang throughout the journey. Do you remember a song which that strange blind woman called Miserere sang one day as she was passing by your house, and who I invited in to sing something for you?:

Better love and affection than being proud
Love and affection mean more than beauty
Remember that in the depths of the grave
We all will wear the same shroud…

That's what I sang on the train, with no guitar to accompany me, and doubtless out of tune, although I did receive unexpected applause from the other passengers in the first-class carriage. A fresh toast. You should have seen how grateful Mito was that I persuaded his father to send him to study in San José. He's a real gentleman now, and has made good use of his time studying… and in other areas, since he told me how in demand he is from the female sector. Don't take this badly, but I'm thinking of introducing him to several old 'friends' I left here a long while ago, and who no longer interest me in the slightest. But I can give Mito a nudge, so that he can take advantage. The customs here are very different from those of León, where even to go to the cinema you must have a chaperone—not that I am against the idea, because I am a believer in morality, and am old-fashioned when it comes to licentiousness.

Do you know, Mati, that in the midst of this warm, friendly atmosphere your brother asked me: 'Tell me, Oli, which of my little sisters do you prefer?' Without a moment's hesitation I answered: 'What a question, Mito. I choose Mati. These months of absence have convinced my heart that she is its only mistress.' What do you make of my reply? If you wish, you can ask him yourself, so that you conquer your silly fears and realize that if I am stuck here, it is only because I was not allowed to rush straight into your arms, my little disbeliever. But I carry the timetable of the steamships in my wallet like a miraculous scapulary, so that I can see which is the first ship leaving for Corinto.

To continue with my news: we reached San José at around six-thirty. A cold drizzle was falling, and the valley was surrounded by mountains as black as my mood. Yes, Mati, I was overwhelmed with grief at knowing this city was not my true destination, for that is the place where you are now reading my letter. I said a sad goodbye to Mito. I went sadly to the boarding-house, my only thought being to go to bed as soon as possible, without eating, in order to indulge in my sadness in the solitude of my room, and to sit to write you a letter at once. But I was still unpacking when I was informed there was a telephone call for me: it was your mother, welcoming me and inviting me to dinner that same night. I excused myself, saying I had a headache, but she insisted so much (you know what she is like) that in the end I could not refuse her. I'm telling you this so that you won't be told something different later on. I want to open your ears to the truth of my words, Mati my love.

I had my clothes pressed and dressed reluctantly to go out. I was still full of sadness when I caught the tram. Why is it that San José makes me feel so out of sorts? Can it be the rain, the cold rooms, the loneliness of its boarding-houses, the dim glow from its lights? Or could it be that I am carrying the sadness inside me? Unanswerable questions, Mati. I would feel just as sad in Berlin or Brussels, if you were not with me. You are the embodiment of my sadness; your absence pierces my breast like a sharp dagger, pitilessly tearing me apart.

Do you remember San José, Mati? I'm staying at the Pensión Barcelona, opposite La Sabana. Now watch me leaving the boarding-house. I'm carrying my umbrella, which is in use all the time here. I walk along the wet sidewalk, slippery with the wax used on the wooden floors of the houses. Dogs are barking behind the stone walls crowned with bougainvillea bushes, dripping from the rain. The tram is waiting at the stop opposite the airport, which is closed at this time of night, its windows lit by a dim yellow glow. There are no other passengers, I am the only one. Later a few more people get on—couples going to the cinema, the theatre, cafés, in search of amusement in places that would be a torment for me, with all their noise and bustle. I am annoyed at the smell of mouldy coats, the over-sweet perfume worn by women chewing gum while they wait from the tram to set off, talking in low voices as if we were in a hospital waiting-room or a mortuary.

Follow me on my journey along the Paseo Colón to Avenida Central. The tram creaks and groans as if in mourning. A small poster in the tram with circus writing announces next Sunday's gala performance at the National Theatre: 'Pagliaci', with the 'celebrated Costa Rican tenor Melico Salazar, the understudy for Enrico Caruso at the Metropolitan Opera in New York.' Next to it, another poster: 'Primavera cough syrup with iodized radish for anemia, rickets, loss of appetite...all of them are avoidable. No need to feel ill. It's national and affordable.' And another one: 'No spitting or throwing cigarette butts on the floor, the Administration'. All this prosaic nonsense deadens me, Mati; dreamy souls like mine are at such a loss in this silly world...second-rate tenors, 'Primavera' syrups, don't spit on the floor, ladies chewing gum. The only thing that stands out against all this is you, and your ideals.

Now I descend from the tram in Barrio Amón. I open my umbrella to protect me from the raindrops dripping from the trees by the roadside. And I think of you: whenever my thoughts fly to you, Mati, they become perfumed, and I am amazed at the thought of the happiness destiny has in store for us the moment I get back to León and talk to your papa to formally arrange our union. Will you allow me to talk to him? I am not planning to say anything about it here to your mama, because I want to present everything as a *fait accompli* to them in León...provided of course that you agree to my proposals. Do I deserve you? Are you keeping that longed-for place for me in your heart? Wet this sheet of paper with tears of joy so that mine will know you are crying—because I am sure it will hear those welcome tears as they fall onto the paper. Laugh if you wish, but I am angry that I cannot be a simple piece of paper to be held between your sweet hands.

Now I am reaching your uncle's villa. The lights of the dining room are visible from the sidewalk, and music can be heard: the gramophone is playing 'Swear to Me', sung by Doctor Ortiz Tirado. What if I don't go in? If I went straight back to my pension? But I hear you whispering in my ear that this would not be proper behaviour from your Oli. 'Please, please, Oli, do it for me, I beg you.' All right, Mati, I will go in, but you should know it is only to please you.

Your Oli rings the bell, and María del Pilar comes to open the door. I see she is not looking at her best: the cold doesn't suit her, she has lost the glow of youth. I say to myself: How can this be the sister of my treasure, when there is such a great difference in their charms? She looks as though she is the elder of you two. I hope to find you exactly the same, Mati, I want to see those same divine eyes of yours, the same heavenly little face, I want your hair to be done the same way, and I want to be able to admire you in the blue dress of yours with the white birds embroidered on the bust. Do you remember that dress you wore on my birthday? And do you remember what I said to you: 'Mati, you look as if you've stepped out of the pages of *Le Chic Parisien*.'

Don't think I am rude, Mati, but you know it is better to reveal your real feelings at all times, and so I held my hand out to your little sister politely but with no great show of affection. Hello, María del Pilar, it's a pleasure to see you. Any news from Mati? Your mother immediately appeared, delighted to see me. Aha, Oli, so you weren't planning to visit us. Have you forgotten your old friends? Not at all, señora, it was just that I was tired from the boat journey. But tell me, has Mati written? That was how I greeted them both, because my intention was for your mother and little sister should know, once and for all, that my thoughts are only for you. So please don't be sad, Mati, and know that over dinner you were my only topic of conversation, I constantly praised your virtues, intelligence, and charms. For example, at a certain moment I was bold enough to declare: Mati would be feted in Guatemalan society if she ever went to live there... Tell me, was it too foolish of me to say that?

You may call me discourteous (because I know your noble soul) but María del Pilar, put out by my sincerity, asked to leave the table with the excuse that she had to get up early the next morning because she had been invited to go and visit the volcano Irazú. Guessing what was going on, your uncle, very much the lord and master in his own home, kept her there; and it did not take him long to find other topics of conversation that were more to your mother and sister's liking. In the end, I was the one who found an excuse to take my leave. Mito, it goes without saying, never raised his eyes from his plate in the whole meal, recalling the very clear reply I had given him on the train.

And period. I want to flee their presence so that you will not be worried. Close your eyes now and think of my prompt return to León. What do you think of marrying before Christmas? That will give us time to make all the preparations, because it has to be a wedding that impresses everyone. You will tell me: it hasn't been a year yet, let's wait for a year to go by, it's only a few months. But my response is: let's forget old-fashioned social conventions and listen to the call of our hearts for us to live together according to the dictates of God and the law. It would be worse for your purity to come under attack from all the viper tongues there are in León if I return to live in your house and we continue in the same situation even if for only a few months longer. Because in a previous letter you told me that my old room is still ready for me, and that you yourself sweep and clean it every day, keeping clean sheets on the bed, and a little vase with fresh-cut garden flowers on the bedside table. What do you think?

I will do whatever you command. Am I not a slave to your wishes? You can send me to wait in the filthiest of León's boarding-houses, Mati, that doesn't matter, because I would be happy with any pigsty if I could be sure you give me your consent. What terrifies me is that, knowing how big-hearted you are, you might say to me: 'I can't take precedence over my sister. If she loves my Oli, I will give him up to her even if it destroys my soul.' But let it be clear once and for all, Mati, that your Oli would never accept any such transaction, and that no such commands can be given to my love, even if they come from you. My compliance becomes arrogance, my kindness turns to pride.

But forgive these ramblings, which are nothing more than the phantoms harassing the mind of a tormented being. Drive away those horrid phantoms by giving me the joy of saying 'Yes, I do'. Anyway, if it is your wish, I am also ready for us to have a quiet wedding followed by an immediate journey to Guatemala, where we would live happily, far from any awkward or unpleasant comments. Think that over in your adorable little head. As for me, all I am doing is revealing my thoughts to you, my beloved. To love you is to touch the hem of glory, Mati. It is to see my soul soar into the firmament, and to die at your feet in adoration. Don't deny me what is mine by right. I beg you on my knees.

A chaste kiss on your brow,
from your
Oli.

P.S: Send my greetings to your father, Doña Yoyita, Leticia and all the maids, as well as to Alicia. Discuss this letter with her, and you'll see she says that I am right.

II

León, 8 August 1933

Oliverio:

Hoping this finds you well, I would merely like to add: whereas you are very happy in that capital—because I know you are having a good time at dances, the theatre, and outings with other women—the one writing these lines after giving it much thought is not at all content. Oli, you still don't understand how much I suffer, and apparently enjoy re-opening a wound which wants to heal if you will only let it. My love: don't tell me it isn't true that you are having a good time with other women, because I have the proof even if you tell me nothing and I don't learn anything through you. Make your mind up once and for all, and allow someone who feels such pain to find rest. Or is it my death you want? If that's the case, then kill me and get it over with, I beg you on bended knee, because I prefer death to this torture. At least send me a greeting in the letters that other women you frequent write me since it appears you don't know how to find the post office in that city.

I miss your kisses, since you first kissed me I've been lost, I am not happy and wish you wouldn't remember anyone because I'm jealous even of any thought that might remind you of a beloved 'person'. What did you go to Costa Rica for? You hadn't lost anything there, I have your treasure here, or have you already forgotten that you did whatever you liked with me, I had never known any cruel people but now I do, if that's how it is better not come back to Nicaragua because no one is waiting for you here and I'm telling you now I don't intend to even glance or exchange a word with you if you turn up here.

Yes, kill me, because this is death in life and all I do is pray to you as if you were a saint and just as in the sacred solitude of the church one feels God's presence without seeing Him I could feel your presence in the world and like God I worshipped you without seeing you, why did you come to me, you devil? It was fine when you were far from me, because I didn't know you and had not burned in the fire of your body or felt the heat of your kisses and if you hadn't appeared you would only have been for me like a fragrance that one smells without knowing what it is or where it comes from.

My love: years ago, when I never even thought I would meet you because fortunately you had not crossed my path, I used to like to go to the Ringling Brothers circus in San Francisco and Krasnodar the Magician used to come into the audience selling chewing gum which had with it a small piece of paper written in invisible ink and if you brought a match up close to it you could read the message, and mine read: you will always be happy in love because you were born under a lucky star.

Well yesterday afternoon Alicia and I went for a stroll in San Juan park and there was a one-armed man who had some lovely parakeets in a wooden cage that's like a castle with turrets and windows, I tried my luck with one of them and it came to its door, rang a little bell with its beak, then took a folded piece of paper from a pigeon-hole where they are lined up like letters—blue, green and yellow. It gave me a yellow one, which you can read here:

TO A SINGLE LADY

> Love knocked on the doors of your heart, and you were right to let it in. Do not change your mind or have any doubts because there is no reason to, persevere with the difficulties. The one to whom you gave the keys of your heart may be absent, but he will return. Do not worry, he is in good health and is in no danger. Do not despair, everything will be fine. The absent gentleman thinks of you always and wishes to lead you to the altar. Remember to say three times before you go to sleep: "Saint Lucia, who lost your eyes for your faith, light up those of my beloved so that he can find his way back. Saint Christopher, patron saint of travellers, make sure he is here soon and does not stray from his path." Close your ears to voices speaking to you in letters from afar, they will only harm you. You are a lucky person. You will have a long life. Buy the lottery ticket No. 2784.

If that parakeet was not lying to me the way that Krasnodar the Magician used to do, my mind would be at rest, but my grandfather prints those bits of paper for the one-armed man, and they do lots in the colour I had, so if I trusted the parakeet I'd be lost, and so I don't trust you either. Come back soon my love, what is there in Costa Rica you can't find here and that I can't give you or tell me the little parakeet is right and can be trusted, perhaps when you come you could bring me three yards of the lace they have in the Feoli store on Avenida Central next to Müller the jeweller's for a dress I've started making that I want to show off to you and there's no lace like that here, I don't want to ask M.P. because I don't like her I hope she doesn't return but stays there getting up to her tricks, I don't like Costa Rica, God forbid you should tell her or mamma that I've written you this letter.

Will you ever come back, Oli? I'd like to travel on the plane inside this envelope. My father says you will be back, and so do the maids, I don't know why they care so much about you because you don't deserve anyone to love you, sometimes I want to fall asleep and never wake up so as not to drive myself crazy imagining what you are doing and tormenting my own poor mind, I swear I've begged God for the night to come soon when I go to bed and never get up again.

Farewell from one who no longer knows what it is she wants, yours faithfully

M.

EPILOGUE

Enter the Documents in the Public Record

Pause a while, good messenger,
Although it may seem late.
God keep you from the importuning
Of a pedantic gentleman.
I am Don Pascual, on my deathbed
In the land of the living
After so many trials and tribulations.
If you wish to know more, pause,
Because far more courteously
The archives can inform you.

GONGORA
(*Letrillas*)

DIVINE PUNISHMENT

AT FIRST light on the morning of 28 December 1933, the day of the Holy Innocents, a distant rumbling could be heard throughout the city of León, and a hot sandy dust began to settle on the rooftops, the ashes of some tremendous fire. As the wind began to blow, this dark rain became more intense, casting a twilight veil over all the streets. The Cerro Negro had erupted.

This natural phenomenon, which was to last for several weeks, greatly alarmed the city's inhabitants. The roofs of several colonial buildings collapsed under the weight of ashes. The apse of San Sebastián church and the main nave of Subtiava church suffered considerable damage. So too did the men's ward and the kitchens at the San Vicente hospital. The accumulation of volcanic ash on the railway line meant that the trains were constantly interrupted.

The Health Department reported numerous cases of respiratory illness. Several of them proved fatal in young children. Other widespread illnesses were: conjunctivitis, due to suppurating inflammation of the eyes; diarrhoea, caused by irritation of the bowel; and severe headaches as a result of breathing in the volcanic particles and their unhealthy effects on food and drinking water. The pollution of rivers in the region led to the death of many head of cattle, which caused a shortage of milk and beef. The same was true of other foodstuffs, such as vegetables and grains, which began to be in short supply in the markets.

Processions of rogation were organized from the second day. The statue of the Virgin of Mercy, patron saint of León, kept in the church of the same name, was paraded through the streets, as was that of San Benito of Palermo, and other venerable images. But since rather than slacken off, the eruption only grew worse, the inhabitants of the central zone soon began a forced exodus to ranches, resorts and nearby villages that were not exposed to the harmful effects of the fateful winds. Due to the frequent interruptions, the available trains could not cope, and the emigrants used any other means of transport they could find. Automobiles with their headlights on in the middle of the day, horse-drawn carriages and carts, ox-carts, and pack mules loaded with possessions, all jostled in the darkened streets to find a way out onto the side roads.

At midday on December thirty-first, Judge Fiallos' house was in turmoil. He was trying to escape the eruption by leaving with his family for their farm in the Valle de las Zapatas. They had to hasten with saddlebags, hammocks, canvas folding beds, kerosene lamps and other necessities if they were to dispatch them on the one o'clock train to El Sauce.

Judge Fiallos, the bottom half of his face covered in the kerchief he used to protect his mouth and nose, was busy doing up the straps on one of the bags where he was carrying the manuscript of his book 'Scorched Horizon' that he was finally going to be able to finish. Alí Vanegas, also with a handkerchief round his face, and with his head covered in a knotted towel, had come to see him off.

'When they forced him out of the automobile, he said calmly

to Captain Ortiz: "I ask only one favour: don't let them disfigure me".' Alí Vanegas was constantly fanning himself. He followed the judge as he took the bag out to the hallway, then came back with him to the dining-room table where there were still a few books to pack. Judge Fiallos' painting easel was propped up against the table, ready for the journey.

The judge peered at his clerk over his handkerchief. He thought about saying something, then changed his mind, and instead went to fetch another saddlebag to put the books in.

'After crossing himself, he said: "It's that dog Ubico who is having me killed. Fortunate Guatemala not to see your earth stained with the executioner's blood… Death to the tyrant! I am ready".' Alí Vanegas took a book from the top of the pile: *The Treasure of the Sierra Madre* by B. Traven, only to put it back again, wiping the dust from his hands.

'You didn't tell any of this to Manolo Cuadra,' said the judge, hastily shaking the books before putting them in the bag. 'Where did you get this nonsense? Only the Guard was there at the time.'

'Rosalío Usulutlán paid me a visit early on the twenty-fifth. He already knew all about it.' Alí Vanegas touched his chest with the fan. 'The guards were talking all about it that same morning. They were going round selling things they had stolen from the dead body. A fob watch, a ring with a red precious stone. I told Manolo the exact words that Castañeda had said before he was shot, but he forgot to put them in his article.'

'What good memories those guardsmen have! I see that the accursed table is still at work: just you be careful.' Judge Fiallos tightened the straps on the bag. 'Are you going to stay on as clerk to Ernesto Barrera?'

'If the forces of nature don't bury the courtroom, I'll stay.' Putting away the fan, Alí Vanegas picked up the easel and followed the judge. 'And as far as the accursed table is concerned, it's been decimated. In the midst of the eruptions, it was decided to expel Cosme Manzo for treason.'

'Well, I have nothing to do with all that soap opera now,' said Judge Fiallos, signalling to the carrier to load up everything still in the doorway. He fumbled in his pocket: 'Give these keys to Barrera for me, would you?'

'And the all-knowing Rosalío also says that Oliverio Castañeda's fake beard was woven from María del Pilar's hair.' Alí Vanegas took the key ring and swung it like a pendulum. 'That Carvajal woman went to ask her, and she was happy to cut it for him. A curly beard. Manolo didn't mention where the hair came from either.'

'Ask María del Pilar Contreras for a further statement to the one she has already given in order to determine whether she did in fact agree to cutting her hair for the purpose you mention,' said Judge Fiallos, undoing the handkerchief and smiling. 'You enjoy that kind of gruesome stuff.'

'If she agreed to cut her hair, that means she still loved him with unbridled passion.' Alí's breathing blew out the handkerchief across his mouth. 'And she loves him still, beyond the grave. She has found his burial place and dares take fresh bunches of lilies to the cemetery.'

'Protected from prying eyes by the veils that the eruption has cast over a city punished by fate.' Judge Fiallos flung his arms open in a theatrical manner, and peered up at the ceiling. 'It is raining fire, and we are all paying the price of sin. Divine punishment.'

'It's a story with a strange perfume,' said Alí Vanegas, closing his eyes. The sand was sweeping in through the porch and filling the yard.

'Perfume?' Judge Fiallos raised his handkerchief again until it covered the bridge of his nose. 'What kind of perfume?'

'The perfume of a branch of magnolia steeped in a chamber-pot.' Alí Vanegas turned to the wall to try to protect himself from the swirling dust.

'A chamber-pot kept for months in a closed bedroom,' said Judge Fiallos, imitating his secretary's action. The cloud of sticky sand whipped at their backs as it swept through the house.

'Some day they're going to want to turn all this into a novel.' The whirlwind died down, and Alí Vanegas headed for the front archway. 'And that perfume will still be there.'

'Whoever writes it has to mention that it all ended with a volcanic eruption,' said the judge, putting his arm round the other man's shoulder and leading him out of the house.

In the middle of the street they spied the light of a lantern coming towards them through the gloom. Rosalío Usulutlán, wrapped in his oilskin cape, was holding it to guide him on his way. Behind him, a boy was carrying an image of Christ the Redeemer in a wooden box. A mule loaded with different possessions and led by another boy brought up the rear.

Rosalío Usulutlán laid the lantern on the ground to raise his hat in greeting, then continued on his way again. He was soon swallowed up by the darkness.

'And that the journalist Rosalío Usulutlán left León for an unknown destination, also fleeing the catastrophe.' Alí Vanegas pulled the towel down over his face and launched himself out into the street. 'The novelist has to make that the ending to his book. If it began with Rosalío, it's only just that it ends with him as well.'

Managua, September 1985/August 1987

An Afterword by the Author

Castigo Divino WAS WRITTEN between 1985 and 1987, during the most critical period of the war that Nicaragua faced between the Sandinistas in power and the Contras financed by the U.S. government, who were seeking the overthrow of the revolutionary government of which I was a member.

The first question I am always asked about the novel is why, when I was living through a time of such great contrasts and contradictions, when there was a struggle to the death between revolution and counter-revolution, I chose a theme that was so far removed from these dramatic events, a theme based around crimes committed several decades earlier in the provincial city of León, by Oliverio Castañeda, an attractive and seductive poisoner whose personal charm drew his victims to him, and who wove a network of intrigue around him by his cunning and lies.

I think I now know the answer. Any novel that took place at the same time as the unfolding events of the revolution would have been bound to deal with it as an overwhelming social and political phenomenon. Since I myself was part of that revolution, I would have run the risk of taking sides and turning the narrative into a discourse tainted by ideological convictions and political propaganda. Not because I would have done this deliberately—even then I knew not to give in to the temptation to write committed literature—but because from a position of power it is impossible to place oneself above events in order to study the characters, whatever their position, and their contradictions, strong points and weaknesses, as a novelist should always do. Nor is it possible to criticise power, and the freedom to criticize is part of the essence of creative writing.

If I say that the novel took me two years to write, I am talking about the actual writing process: the idea for the book itself began to form in my mind in 1960, when I used to attend the lectures on penal procedure in the Law Faculty at León. The lecturer used the Oliverio Castañeda case as an excellent example of judicial procedure that was full of mishaps and inconsistencies, and we students were able to play the roles of defence and prosecution lawyers, state prosecutors, and judges.

In León, the Castañeda case survived in popular memory. Many stories were told about hidden aspects of the crimes, among them the romantic entanglements that were not studied at the faculty. However, the case files containing the documentary evidence, the witness statements, the toxological reports, the legal examinations of the victims' bodies, had all vanished.

That is, until 1980, shortly after the triumph of the revolution. A lawyer in León who had recently been appointed judge in the regional Appeals Court found the more than one thousand pages of the files relating to the case, and gave me a copy. This was an extraordinary gift. It became the basis for all my research, to which I added an intensive reading of the newspapers of the time, and everything I could lay my hands on about criminology, criminal psychology, toxicology, and legal medicine. I often found myself returning to the texts I had studied as a young man in law school.

Those events had shaken Nicaragua in the 1930s. It was a huge scandal that occupied the front pages of the press for months, and was talked about in barber shops, billiard halls, social clubs and private homes. Extensive and exhaustive articles were written about the details of the case, and it was hotly debated in the opinion pages, where religion, morality and the family were discussed. Throngs of people crowded the doors of the León courthouse whenever Castañeda had to appear, and in both city and country opinion soon divided: the better-off were against the defendant, whereas the poorer people were on his side. There was even talk of a class struggle.

Telling the story meant describing Nicaraguan society in those days. January 1, 1933 saw the end of the U.S. military intervention that had followed the war of liberation fought by General Sandino's peasant army. The U.S. marines had left as commander-in-chief of the new National Guard, General Anastasio Somoza, while a civilian president, Juan Bautista Sacasa, had been elected for a period of four years. That same year, the scandal of Castañeda's crimes exploded.

The struggle soon began between on the one hand civil power, respecting the laws and the Constitution, the separation of powers, and an independent judiciary; and on the other hand military power, with an army organized along the lines of an army of occupation, which was trying to invade these civilian areas of authority. When Sandino was assassinated after the peace agreement of 1934, it was a plot by Somoza and the military; two years later he deposed President Sacasa in a coup d'état. Castañeda's murder, carried out on Somoza's orders when he was still being tried by the civilian authorities, was yet another demonstration that military power would win out.

The task I set myself was to write a novel that was as close as possible to reality. I wanted imagination to take the place of events, but to be based on them. I tried to create a parallel atmosphere of the period in which those events took place, to use a language from that time in the journalistic reports, the legal declarations and the dialogues; to create multiple levels of language. I knew that these were the tools I could employ to tell the events of the novel, and to research the passions that Castañeda aroused, the romantic secrets, jealousies, ambitions, the mediocrity of the provincial background, the narrow-mindedness of its bourgeois society, the small daily hardships, the social prejudices. I knew this was the novel's essence, which I had to reach through its language and through the appropriate choice of a narrative structure.

It was to be a historical novel, but also a realist novel, a mannerist novel, a police thriller, a courtroom drama. What I set out to write was all of this, and something more: a close replica of what had occurred, a re-creation, the creation of a parallel world, that would correspond to the world in which the events had taken place, and yet one which by copying it would replace it.

By the time I began to write the novel, I had everything I needed in my head, and so I did without all the files from the trial, my notes, and the books I had consulted. What I now had to use was my memory, channeling its promptings towards my imagination. After that, I let imagination do its job.

Sergio Ramírez 2014

A Note by the Translator

I FIRST VISITED Nicaragua in 1987. I had previously translated two books by Sergio Ramírez: a novel, *Te dio miedo la sangre?* (*To Bury Our Fathers*), and a book of short stories, both published by the enterprising small publisher Readers International in London. I travelled to Nicaragua in July 1987 to take part in the grandly named First International Bookfair of Managua: our British contributors were Readers International, a few small left-wing publishers, and some religious presses. The books for our stall arrived several days late, which gave us time to explore Nicaragua beyond the capital. This was my first glimpse of the society Ramírez was writing about: the traditional colonial cities such as León; the rural heartlands from cattle ranches to banana plantations; the other world of the Atlantic coast with its black Caribbean way of life.

In 1987, the Sandinista revolutionary leaders, including vice-president Sergio Ramírez, were still engaged in fighting the counter-revolutionary Contra rebels financed by Washington. Ramírez, a civilian in the militarised revolutionary junta, was closely involved in such projects as the literacy campaign being carried out across the country, the ubiquitous poetry workshops, and thc Editorial Nueva Nicaragua—an initiative to make Nicaraguan and other literatures available to as many people as possible in cheap, well-produced editions. And at the same time, although I was unaware of it, Ramírez somehow found the hours to write the 500-page novel, *Castigo divino*.

The daring novelty of the Nicaraguan revolution aroused interest far beyond Central America. Sympathisers came pouring in: to help with the coffee harvest, take part in aid projects, or just soak up the atmosphere. So it was that a large U.S. publisher got wind of Ramírez's novel, and decided in 1988 to publish it. I was taken on as the translator. I supplied them with chapter after chapter, and they seemed very pleased with it. Then in 1989, following intense pressure from the United States, the Sandinistas agreed to hold general elections, and vowed to respect the result. They lost, and found themselves handing over power to their old right-wing foe, Violeta Chamorro. A few weeks later I was told that the American publisher had decided to cancel publication of the novel. I was never told why: because they had realised it was not actually a book about the Sandinista revolution? Because an ex-vice president of a revolutionary government no longer in power had lost his selling potential?

Over the next twenty-five years there were several attempts to resuscitate the English version of *Castigo divino*. These always foundered: I could no longer locate the manuscript of the entire translation; the disks I had used had long since become obsolete; Nicaragua was no longer in the headlines. Now, at last, Ramírez's powerful novel is able to find many new readers. As I have gone through the translation again almost thirty years on, my admiration for the author's meticulous reconstruction of an entire society has only grown. The circumstances in which he wrote the novel serve to make it more remarkable still.

Nick Caistor 2014